A LAZY EYE

Life for Dorrie Potter is never going to be easy, beginning with her birth in the blitz shortly after a bomb has destroyed the family home. Dorrie's lazy eye and flights of fancy mark her out as different, and her father is determined to ensure that she fits in. For Dorrie's own sake she must be brought into line – and kept away from her eccentric grandmother, Nora. But Nora Potter knows that what marks Dorrie out as different isn't her lazy eye, but what it enables her to see...

A LAZY EYE

A LAZY EYE

by

Jacqueline Jacques

Magna Large Print Books
Long Preston, North Yorkshire,
BD23 4ND, England.

British Library Cataloguing in Publication Data.

Jacques, Jacqueline
    A lazy eye.

      A catalogue record of this book is
      available from the British Library

      ISBN   0-7505-1630-5

First published in Great Britain by
Judy Piatkus (Publishers) Ltd., 1999

Copyright © 1999 by Jacqueline Jacques

Cover illustration © Richard Jones by arrangement with
Artist Partners & Piatkus Books Ltd.

The moral right of the author has been asserted

Published in Large Print 2001 by arrangement with
Piatkus Books Ltd.

Magna Large Print is an imprint of Library Magna Books Ltd.

Printed and bound in Great Britain by
T.J. (International) Ltd., Cornwall, PL28 8RW

Acknowledgements

I wish to thank Sandra Diamond for casting a critical eye over the hairdressing episodes. Thanks to Anne for being there. Thanks to RGS for memories and inspiration. Thanks to writing groups, past and present, for friendship and constructive comments. Thanks to Elizabeth Wright for her sound advice, Judy Piatkus for saying 'Yes', and, as always, thanks to my lovely family and friends for believing in me. Thanks most of all to Peter, for being himself.

Chapter One

May 1945

They'd been at it for days, scrubbing, sweeping, beating carpets, washing curtains, cooking, wiping her fingermarks off the furniture.

'Look at the child! The state of her!'

'She ain't been in the front room with them 'ands?'

'Hold still, for God's sake. And all round your mouth! Where've you been to get so sticky?'

When they found out she'd been playing in the cellar, they smacked her legs soapy red.

'Little Jack 'Orner, nothing!' Grandma had roared. 'Stay out of there, Dorrie, or it'll be *you* in a pie next, with rhubarb and ginger...'

But the dank spidery cellar was like a magical gloryhole to the little girl. She hadn't meant to open the meatsafe to sniff the cold cuts and savouries, nor to climb up the chopping block to the old wash-stand where cakes and trifles and jellies lay in wait beneath checkered tablecloths, to suck in her fingers.

When she told them she hadn't liked the nasty lemonade and had spitted it back, they'd puzzled: 'Lemonade?' and then 'Oh my Gawd! The beer!' and rushed her down the back steps.

'Which one, Dorrie? Which was the jug you spat in?'

It was important, she could tell. But they all

looked the same, brown and forbidding, with beaded doilies on top to keep out the flies.

'*Dorrie?*'

Misery dragged at her lip, squeezed hot tears from her eyes. Still she couldn't see it. All the jugs had their hands to their throats, playing nervously with their beads. They had no minds to probe, not like people.

'Come on, tell Grandma.'

So she told them one and they tipped it away. But it might not have been. Then they mopped up the puddles, shooed her out and locked the cellar door.

'Oh, Dorrie, Dorrie, Dorrie ... what's your dad gonna say?'

Whoever *that* was.

Now they waited, poised in idleness, and the quiet made everything loud: the clock wheezing to strike the jingle-jangle half-hour, the ceiling creaking as Grandma moved between the clean new beds that weren't for naughty girls to go jumping on with their muddy feet, the women's fingers tapping fidgets on the shiny green arms of the fireside chairs. She could even hear Mummy's thoughts, gnawing and nibbling like hungry mice: about Dorrie, with her tangle of fair curls, and a tall, dark-haired sailor man.

Dorrie was writing. F-F-F. For Flo, Mummy said, though there were too many prongs. Teeth on lips, small explosions: F-F-F, up and down the book. Across the top: F-F-F. But not for Flo. Careful not to crayon over the pictures or the words of the story. About a girl no bigger than your thumb, who slept in a walnut-shell and was scared by frogs. Silly thing. Frogs can't hurt you, Mummy said. Dorrie thought that *she* would like to be a tiny, tiny child asleep in a walnut-shell. She wouldn't be frightened of anything in a walnut-shell, not people shimmering angry red or bad dreams or anything.

F-F-F-F. Grandma had said it was a marvel how she was coming on, but she mustn't write on the mantelpiece. If she did it again she'd get what-for. She was to sit at the table, and write on paper properly. The stiff old fingers had smoothed out paper-bags and envelopes but Dorrie had soon filled them up. Inside and out. She swung her legs against the chair, her heels making a regular tap, tap, tap, her hair-ribbon bouncing, red, white and blue.

Suddenly decisive, her mother took her hat from the sideboard and pinned it to her head, ducking to see the effect in the mirror.

'Nora!' she shouted at the ceiling. 'I'm going over now! It's a bit early but I don't want them arriving and no one there.'

'Right you are, Flo, I'm nearly ready.' The voice was muffled. 'How's the time?'

'Half-past. You coming?'

'No, no,' Nora said quickly, adding, 'I'll put the kettle on,' as a reason for staying, but Dorrie's head came up as she sensed fear in her grandmother's voice.

A question in her eyes, Mummy turned to Auntie Lucy, who nodded, unfolded herself from the deep chair, yawned and stretched her arms almost to the ceiling. 'Yeah, it'd send you barmy, sitting here.'

They were all nervous. So who was coming? Who?

Mummy licked her hanky and scrubbed Dorrie's mouth, tugged a comb through her thorny hair, despite Dorrie's twisting and protesting, straightened the bow, and said, 'Best I can do with that,' as always, and, 'Off we go, then! Off to meet your dad!' in a bright, brave voice.

'Why?' tangled in her breath. Dad? Was that the big, suffocating presence in Mummy's head?

'"Why?"' Mummy mimicked, laughing. 'Silly girl. Because all the men are coming home from the war and we're glad, aren't we?'

Men? In her mind she saw lowering shapes, brown and navy blue, in a fuzz of stale yellows, mouldy greens. It would be horrible. Her face puckered. She didn't want...

'No!' she wailed, slipping off the chair and crawling under the table. 'No-o-o!'

'Dorrie! Oh, for goodness sake!' Her mother bent down. 'Come on, silly. The bus'll be here in a minute.'

'No-o-o! Don't want no Dad. Want to stop with Grandma.'

'Dorrie, come out this minute!' She reached in and Dorrie pumped her legs.

'No-o-o! Go *'way!*' she howled.

'*Ouch!* Stop it, Dorrie.'

Now there were two faces, shadowed by the rim of the table, whites of eyes flashing, knees glaring, hands clutching, and red sizzles of pain where Dorrie's black patent heel had landed.

'She's frightened, Flo.'

12

'I'll give her frightened,' Mummy snapped, rubbing her arm. 'What's she got to be frightened of, anyway? He's her dad, isn't he?' She leaned in again, her face cross and concerned. 'Dorrie, pack it in. He's lovely, your dad.'

But she didn't sound convinced and Dorrie bellowed louder.

'Oh come on, Dor, he'll be wondering where we are. He's been looking forward to seeing his little girl. And all the uncles, they'll think you're a daft ha'porth, hiding under the table.'

She shrank further into her skin.

'She doesn't know what to expect.'

'She can expect a thick ear if she carries on like this.'

'D'you know, Flo,' said Auntie Lucy, in a different voice, 'it wouldn't surprise me a bit if one of them didn't have a present for a good little girl – a silver sixpence maybe, or a sweetie. But, of course, if Dorrie wants to stop under the table...' Her mouth turned down and the shake of her head was one of regret.

Dorrie sensed a trap. Even so, a present sounded quite interesting. Auntie went on talking, but it wasn't *what* she said that persuaded her – about jelly and cake and things she thought a little girl would like – so much as the excitement lighting the green eyes. If Auntie Lucy was looking forward to the visitors it must be all right. She scrambled out on a flood of penitence.

'That's a good girl,' said Mummy. 'Come on, no more tears. Tch! look at you. Here, blow.' She pinched Dorrie's nose in a hanky. 'Now come on, we'll be late. No, Dorrie, don't be difficult! Just two crayons then, no more. *Two*, I said! Oh, go on then ... four. I don't have time to argue.'

With a pitiful, snotty shudder of breath, Dorrie took a handful, just in case there was something to write on.

Grandma called to them out of the window as the front gate squealed. 'What was that hullabaloo?'

'Just Dorrie playing up. She's all right now.'

The lane was scrunchy under their feet and cooler than the rest of the afternoon, with the huge tree on the green shading them from the sun.

She stopped, feeling Grandma's watchful gaze, but realised, when she turned, that the old woman's eyes were following the green bus down the hill from the main road, past woods and fields and farm buildings. She was pinning a brooch to her bodice and the pin wouldn't fasten. 'Come on!' she urged and, surprisingly, sobbed. 'Come on!' But she wasn't talking to the brooch.

'Come *on*, Dorrie! What have you lost? Your crayon? Leave it, love, it's only a little broken bit. We'll get you some new ones. Look, there it is. There, by your foot.'

'Just there, sweetheart,' said Lucy pointing. 'Look. Can't you see it?'

'Dorrie?' Mummy's voice was sharp. 'I don't think it's anything, that squint. The doctor says she'll grow out of it, when she gets her glasses. She's just not with us. In a world of your own, aren't you, Dor? Look, here you are, Mummy's

14

got it. Now come on, do!'

The bus was coming. You heard it before you saw it, that noise like blowing lemonade with a straw. Over the bridge, up the lane, past the big house where the robber lived, the man Grandma paid her rent to. He wasn't really a robber, Mummy said. That was just Grandma's little joke.

Mummy and Lucy were bobbing about in the bus queue, waggling their heads and uttering little cries like birds, and everyone was smiling and waving as the bus growled to a stop outside Fitzell's, which was hung with flags, all criss-crossed red, white and blue, big ones, like the one fluttering from Grandma's bedroom window and little ones, like they had hanging on strings across the front of the pub. Dorrie was going to have a flag to wave. Tomorrow. Grandma had promised.

Behind her the shop door went 'ping' as Mrs Fitzell came out onto the step, puffing a cigarette. She wanted to look at her friend, Nora's, 'comp'ny'. The bus stood patiently, shudders rattling its metal sides. Dorrie patted comfort into the warm mudguard.

Flo pulled her away, 'Ugh, dirty!' and wiped her hand.

Dark shapes inside, tugging bags and cases from the luggage racks, shuffling slowly down the aisle, becoming grinning faces and big waving palms as they passed open windows and then back into the blur again.

Dorrie's heart beat faster. Flo, on tiptoe, held her hand so tight it hurt. Then the sky darkened. Dorrie, among the legs, clung to her mother's

15

skirt until she was hoisted into the light, into a bank of eyes and mouths all wanting to gobble her up.

Cigarette breath and peppermints. Pink powdery ladies, dark-chinned men. Lots of laughing, loud voices. Too loud, too fast for her to catch the thoughts behind them, as the bus went away without her.

'Who's this, then? This big girl can't be our little Dorothy, can it? Well, I never.'

''Course, she must be ... how old? Three? Gaw Bli, don't time fly?'

'Ain't you gonna say hello to your Auntie Joan?'

'She been crying, has she?'

'Where'd she get that hair from, Flo? You sure the birds'd done with it?'

'Oh *don't!* I've tried everything. I'll have to let it grow and put it in plaits.'

'Poor little love. Oh, don't suck your thumb, treasure. You don't want your teeth sticking out and all.'

'She'll be all right. Little smasher, ain't yer, duck?'

'Wish I had eyelashes like that. Who's she take after then?'

'Not Arthur, for a fact, eh, Flo? More like the milkman, if you ask me!'

'Oh Mick, don't be 'orrible. Like your mum, ain't you, darling?'

'Got a kiss for Auntie, then? Oh, love 'er, she's shy.'

'Proper little 'eart-breaker, she's gonna be.'

What they said and what they thought didn't always match. As her head spun from one face to

16

another she caught a sour whiff of envy.

'That Flo ... all got up like a dog's dinner and only a blooming hairdresser when all's said and done.'

And a disdainful, *'That's never the colour she was born with. Talk about bottle blonde.'*

Critical barbs were tangling in her own hair, bouncing off her bony elbows and knees, snicking her pale skin, salting her wonky eye.

'Oh dear, what a face! Ain't gonna cry, are you, duck? Ah, poor kid, she don't like all this...'

But as Dorrie took a breath to yell she was thrown into the air so fast, so high, she left her breath behind. Dropped another crayon. Strong arms caught her and squeezed her. Who was he, this man with liquid brown eyes and a sailor suit?

And where was that crayon? She wanted to look for it but down there was a forest of trousers and big black shoes.

The man whisked her higher onto his shoulders, out of their reach. She didn't like the scratchy material rubbing her bare legs and her arms yearned towards her mother who was smiling up, her eyes very bright. 'It's all right, love. Dad's got you.

This was Dad?

He said, 'Let's go and find your granny,' and her heart jumped, but he meant Grandma, not the ghost. He was another one, like Mummy, who couldn't see for looking, Grandma said.

They began to move and, because he held her legs tight, she found she could sit up straight, looking down at the white disc of the sailor's hat.

Neighbours smiled and waved to see her riding high, holding on tight round his forehead. She

17

was the highest of them all and bouncing to a stride ten times her own. Higher than the front hedges, higher than the neighbours' kids who swung on the gates, goggling to see her at the head of the procession trooping in at the garden gate.

Grandma was at the door, wet around the eyes because she was so lucky to have them home – her boys – safe and sound. She was thinking of the missing ones: Jack, up in Newcastle, and Siddy, still at war, fighting the Japs with one hand tied behind his back, or so his letters would have her believe. She looked so small as they hugged her, lifting her off the ground, making her squeal. Strange to think that all these big men were her children. Just as Dorrie was Mummy's child. Mummy's.

Granny Farthing sat in her corner, knitting, and watching the people come in. Nobody hugged her because she was a ghost. Dorrie ran to tell her about the flags decorating the village. The old woman put her finger to her lips.

Auntie Lucy whispered in her ear. 'Granny knows, love. Leave her be.' Took her hand and led her to the table.

'A little bird told me you like to draw.' He spoke softly, the man called Dad. He pulled out a chair, piled up some cushions and sat her on top. She watched closely as the big, hairy hands moved cups and plates aside, making room for her surprise – a colouring book and a brand new pack of crayons, two reds, two purples, two of everything. She tried drawing black hairs on the backs of *her* fingers, but the crayon wouldn't

18

work on skin. Looking up, she caught him winking at Mummy. Winks meant secrets between grown-ups and were impossible to ignore. Like jelly they sucked her in. Dad was signalling to Mummy that he thought Dorrie was a funny little thing, trying to draw hairs like his. But there was more to it than that. Thoughts were quite complicated. Mummy would have caught the happy part of it, the joy that the war was over; that he was home again with the people he loved. She might not have caught the sorrow – that his black-haired hands had never cradled the baby, caught her as she'd taken her first tottering steps, spooned gravy and mash from his big plate into her tiny mouth, had never comforted her, tickled her, tucked her into bed. And right at the back of the wink was a teensy-weensy something else that he hardly dared acknowledge. Which was regret. That she hadn't inherited his film-star looks and curly black hair.

As the tea flowed, as the ginger cake disappeared and the jam tarts dwindled, as the cottage loosened its belt to make room for them all, Dorrie kept her mind on colouring – safe blue skies, comforting red roofs, grass that was always, reliably, green – shutting out the roar of their flaring thoughts and the crackle of their words. They'd loom out of the smoky confusion, aunts and uncles and cousins, with names like Charlie and Joe and Barbara and Brian and forgettable faces, demanding that she charm them, like little girls were supposed to. But she just turned her face away until they'd gone.

A man with hot eyes wanted to give her a sweetie. 'No, thank you,' she said politely, jumping off her perch, ready to run as she'd been taught, but Mummy gave her a poke. 'Go on, silly, it's all right. Uncle Mick's not a stranger.'

Wasn't he? The sweet was very big and hard and made the roof of her mouth sore and Mummy had to mop the green dribble off her chin and off her new frock and off her shoes. Auntie Joan seemed to belong to Uncle Mick. She had to take his jacket when he handed it to her, and hang it on the door; she had to find his glasses in the pocket, fetch him beer and cake and matches off the mantelpiece so he could smoke. She smelled of kippers and wet wool and when she said she'd always wanted a little girl to cuddle and tried to lift Dorrie onto her spongy lap, Dorrie ducked and quickly resumed her seat at the table.

Peter was her cousin. He was five, bigger than Dorrie, with black hair done in a gleaming quiff. He sat beside her, reeking of hair-oil and melting her crayons with his dad's glowing cigarette. She yelled and was immediately sorry when Uncle Mick leapt up and gave the boy such a clip round the ear his quiff fell into his eyes. He'd teach him to behave, he said, his hot eyes all small and piggy. Joan had spoiled him rotten but now his dad was home they'd soon have him knocked into shape.

'That's right, innit, son?' And Peter had to nod agreement.

Dad came and sat between them. He drew a DORRIE bird for her, inside the cover where it

20

was white. A big R was the body and tail, O was its head and the other R was its eye and open beak; D was its wing, I its leg and E a sort of crown on its head. She wanted to laugh but Peter was there, all red and hurting. Dad did a funny man for him with ees for eyes and, when nobody was looking, Peter poked his tongue out at Uncle Mick and crossed his eyes.

After a while Dad said it was too nice to sit indoors all day. He and Flo were going to stretch their legs. Grandma said good idea, why didn't they all go for a nice walk? She'd put the kettle on for them coming back. The children could stop with her.

When Dad took his hat off the peg, he said, 'Oh that's nice, innit? She's only been and written all over it.'

'Oh Dorrie! For goodness sake...'

'It'll wash off,' said Grandma. 'It's only crayon.'

'No, it's very nice. But me name's Arthur not Frank.'

'*What!* Let me see.' Mummy snatched the hat away, her face pink. 'No, that's her Fs. She's been practising all day.'

Dorrie took a breath to put her right, but thought better of it. The old ghost, over in the corner, had her finger on her lips again.

Like the Pied Piper, Lucy led the crowd across the green. She wanted to show them the beans coming up in Hooper's field, the ones she'd planted. Dorrie followed them in her thoughts, sucking her thumb wistfully. She wouldn't have minded going up that footpath to the farm. Mrs

Hooper made lovely cream from the skin of boiled milk. But Grandma was going to turn the jellies out any minute.

The aunts and uncles began to loiter and lag. Mick and Joan went into the church. He sat down at the organ and played 'Abide with me' while she beat time, badly, from the front pew. Mummy and Dad continued past the shop, towards the bluebell woods. Mummy's head was on his chest; his hand, over her shoulder, reached down inside her dress. Her hand stroked his bottom.

'Dorrie, what you doing?'

She jumped. She was colouring, that's what she was doing. That's all. Lying on her arm at the table, one eye nearly shut, colouring a pig. But she knew where her mind had been. And Granny Farthing knew. Her mouth screwed up like a twist of toffee-paper.

'Dorrie, you're a naughty little gel!'

'What?' Grandma came bustling in, red in the face, water dripping from her fingers. 'What's she done now? Not drawn on me tablecloth? Gawd, Dorrie, can't I take me eyes off you for a minute?'

'They gone off to do a bit o' courting and she's sending to 'em.'

'Oh, *Dorrie!* How many times do I have to tell you? You keep your second sight to yourself. You got a gift there, a precious gift. You use it prop'ly! Spying on your mum and dad – I never heard the like! Well, don't you go asking me for no jelly, teatime, 'cos you ain't getting none.'

'Nora...'

'I know she's only a baby, Mum, but she's gotta

learn and there's only me to tell her. Lucy's far too soft. If she gets away with it, gets into bad habits... I'll have to answer for it. I mean, people are entitled to a bit of privacy, when all's said and done. Bli, comes to something, don't it, when they can't go off by themselves without Miss Nosey Parker stringing along? Oh no, I ain't having it.'

'*Nora*,' Granny jerked her head at the kitchen door. Peter stood there, eyes black with interest, gaping like a codfish.

'Oh Peter. You finished hulling them strawberries, son? Good boy. I'm just coming. Now Dorrie, like I told you. That's a pig, that is, and one thing a pig ain't is thick orange and purple. Use your gift nicely, there's a good girl, and *stay inside the lines!*' Each word was tapped home by a bony finger on her skull. Dorrie was left in no doubt as to what Grandma really meant.

The lamps were lit. Auntie Lucy wound up the gramophone and people began tapping their feet, nodding their heads to the music, singing: 'If you were the only girl in the world...'

Grandma held Dorrie's hands and they stepped to the music. This way, that way – she was dancing! Everyone watched and smiled, jiggling in their seats until they could bear it no longer. They piled up the chairs against the walls and rolled back the worn old carpet.

The record changed. 'First you put your two knees close up tight...' Sudden madness. People laughing. Finding room to walk round the table, squeezing past the sideboard, out of the front door into the summer night, crunching gravel, crushing grass, whirling around in sudden showers of petals, the scent of lilac at odds with the smells of beer and sweat, children tearing madly in and out of doors, between legs, their yells drowning the music.

'Where the blue of the night meets the gold of the day, someone waits for me.' Dad and Mummy sweeping her up and dancing with her between them, singing the words.

Then Uncle Mick, with a hanky to his eyes, being Al Jolson, down on his knees making Grandma giggle: 'Ma-a-ammy...' and the moths fluttering sadly up to the window and in at the door and sticking to the dangling fly-paper.

The rhythm was seductive. Her head grew muzzy, her eyes heavy. She remembered being carried up to bed, arms and legs being threaded into pyjamas, having a night-time nappy pinned in place, her mother pulling the blanket up to her chin, Dad kissing her forehead.

Overnight the bedroom had filled up. She took herself downstairs, leaving aunts and cousins asleep. The kitchen was empty but the stove was alight and the kettle beginning to snuffle and spit. Grandma wouldn't be far away. In the front room two uncles were snoring in the armchairs and a third was on the sofa. Dad lay on the floor in a blanket. Dorrie knelt beside him and peeled his eyelid back.

'Wake up,' she demanded.

'Shit!' said Dad.

'Dorrie,' said Grandma from the doorway,

trying not to laugh, 'Dorrie, come 'ere, duck. Leave your dad alone.'

In the kitchen she sorted out Dorrie's soggy underwear, washed and dressed her in clothes that had been airing on the fireguard round the range, sat her in the big carver until Dad stumbled out, yawning and scratching his chest.

'Fine thing when a bloke can't have a lie-in on V-Day. D'you know what she did?'

'That's what being a dad's all about, Arthur.'

He groaned. 'Any tea in the pot?'

Afterwards, when he'd recovered from his dreams, he took Dorrie on his back to gather mushrooms. Grandma insisted she put on her cardigan and Wellington boots because of the dew.

'Lovely day for it,' Dad said. For what? For mushrooming?

He and Mum had found a clearing in the woods, he said, where the mushrooms grew, sprinkled like blobs of whitewash on the grass. And so they were, their skin bloodless and human, their gills so delicate they bruised at a touch, giving off a clammy smell.

Dorrie was worried. If they picked them, the fairies would be homeless.

'Who's been telling you stories?' said Dad, amused.

No one. It was true. It was in the Thumbelina book.

'Tch!' Dad tossed his head. Well, mushrooms grew in no time flat. The fairies would soon have nice new homes. Now, how many had they picked? Dorrie tried to count but she lost track after five. Numbers jiggled around in her head like bubbles in a stewpot. They rose to the top and burst before you could be sure they'd been there at all.

'It'll come,' said Dad. 'Can't expect to do it all at once. Barely three and reading already – and writing. That's a good enough start, I'd say.'

They left a mushroom in the ground in case it rained and the fairies had no shelter.

Back at Grandma's, people were up and porridge was plopping in the pot. The mushrooms were greeted with joy and fried with eggs and bacon and the last of the bottled tomatoes. Grandma asked where they'd found them and Dad told her about the clearing where the fairies lived. And winked. But Mummy didn't smile back. Instead she told him off with raised eyebrows and her mouth pursed, all prissy and tight.

'...*as a cat's arse!*' was behind Dad's sudden scowl. Dorrie sucked her thumb as his thoughts mustered to justify his action. '*All that fairy nonsense! Stuffing her head with romantic twaddle! I won't have it. Far better to teach her something useful, like numbers.*'

Dorrie frowned. '*Curiosity killed the cat!*' was what Granny Farthing would say. She didn't like Dorrie mindreading. '*Eavesdroppers never hear anything good about themselves!*' Not that she'd meant to pry; she never did. But sometimes, just as her fingers touched things they shouldn't, and her eyes stared at people for too long, so did her mind. She tried to be good, to be polite, but it was very hard.

It was too early in the day for granny ghosts to be abroad but Auntie Lucy's eyebrow was an arch of reproof over her fried bread. Dorrie hid her face in her mother's blouse. The satin slid cool beneath her cheek as she stole another guilty glance at her aunt. The green eyes were stern. Don't, they said.

While the women washed up the breakfast things and fed the chickens and emptied the slops and put fresh Jeyes in the lavvy out the back and boiled water for the men to shave and the children to wash, while they made the beds and took out their curlers and dodged for room in the upstairs mirror, putting on lipstick and best dresses, the men took the children out for a game of rounders on the green.

They played with Peter's junior-sized cricket bat and Peter's ball that he'd had for his birthday in March and had hardly used. Others soon joined in – PC Stone from next door, the Turners from the other side, even grumpy old Horace Batts from a few houses along. The vicar stood to watch for a while and they took pity on him and invited him to join them. Mr Wilson came over from the schoolhouse, bringing Derek, his little boy. In the end there were lots of men 'showing the kids how it should be done', and only one bat. You had to hit the ball and throw down the bat before you ran, so the next man in could bat, too.

After a lot of argument about whether you had to run even if you missed the ball, Mrs Wilson was roped in to umpire because, although she was a woman, she was a teacher, too, and she knew the rules.

There were cries of, 'Oh well hit, sir!' from the vicar and 'Tough luck, squire!' and polite applause. But the Potters and the village men used words that Dorrie had never heard before.

'Wallop it, then, Arthur. Give it the old one, two.'

'Gercha, silly bugger, can't 'ee go no faster'n that?'

'Wake up, you dozy git! Look out!'

'Catch it! *Catch* it! Oh my sainted aunt!'

'You ... *twerp!*'

'Butterfingers! You want your ruddy eyes testing, you thick sod.'

'Go, go, go, ye silly arse. Don't 'ee stop! R-u-u-u-n!'

Granny Farthing turned up to watch and Dorrie, picking daisies and dandelions, tried to explain to the old woman the aim of the game. They were both thoroughly baffled.

'Mark my words, it'll end in tears,' the ghost predicted. It did.

Peter, like all the other children, had been made a fielder and wasn't at all happy. He wanted to bat. It was his cricket set, after all. He sulked at the edge of the green, amusing himself by calling Dorrie 'wet-the-bed' and stamping on her flowers. When the ball came their way he wasn't ready for it and the men all shouted at him.

'To me! Over 'ere! Gawd, what the 'ell you playing at, son?'

'Do as you're told, you little perisher. Throw

the ball to Uncle Arthur. Now!'

But Peter picked up the ball and put it up his jumper. Uncle Mick went redder than ever, slapped the boy's legs and took the ball away. Peter had a paddy, running on the spot and screaming that it was his ball and his bat and he wanted to *play!* And so his dad took him by the ear and marched him indoors for a good talking to. Auntie Lucy came out with a tray of lemonade and glasses and play stopped for a spell.

'I hear Ma's doing all right these days,' said Dad, lying on the grass with his hands under his head. There were dark wet patches on his navy sailor's shirt.

'Packs 'em in,' agreed Uncle Mick, mopping his face. 'Course, that's what happens when the cat's away. The mice go effing barmy.'

'Mick,' said Auntie Joan weakly. She'd come out to tell everyone that Peter was sorry and they could play with his ball if they wanted. But most of the batting team had gone home for their dinners.

'No, you're right,' said another uncle. 'That's the war for you. All these women missing their men, they get bored, don't they? Do daft things. I mean, you wouldn't see a man getting mixed up in all that spiritualist mumbo-jumbo, would you? A man's got more sense.'

'Wouldn't let my Joan mess around talking to the dead, would I, duck? It's unhealthy.'

'There are blokes at Ma's meetings,' said Dad.

'Oh yeah, your yokels.' Uncle Mick's grimace was meant to show what little regard he had for the judgement of country folk.

'Still, if they keep her in shoe leather...'

'There's lots of nice things to eat,' said Auntie Joan. 'Blancmange and jelly and cakes. You want some of Grandma's cake, don't you? And fizzy lemonade, with bubbles that make your nose tickle.'

They were trying to get her to stop drawing and let them have the table. The sun was out, the war was over, the King had been on the wireless, Peter was happy again and they needed the table for the party. Dorrie hung on with all her might and squealed.

Mummy tried. 'They said to Grandma, "Nora, would you lend us your table so we can put all the lovely food out for people to eat?" And Grandma said, "Oh yes, I don't think Dorrie will mind, just this once, but you must promise to bring it back again when the party's over".'

Dad told her not to be so silly. He was going to count to three...

'Each child gets a flag to wave, Dorrie,' said Lucy, her green eyes twinkling, her eyebrows waggling.

After the Tots' race, which she'd have won if Peter hadn't tripped her, after the Punch and Judy, during which she'd wept and wailed when Punch hit Judy with his stick, and she'd had to be carried back indoors, sobbing, then she and Peter had their faces washed and their clothes changed for the fancy dress. Peter was an Indian brave in a hat made of chicken feathers, with lipstick in

30

zigzags on his face, and she was a hula girl with a grass skirt and a necklace of felt flowers. They were attempting to fix more flowers in her hair when she realised Peter was missing.

'Dorrie, don't twist, there's a good girl.'

'Do hold still, duck.'

'Good heavens, you're a right little wriggle-bottom. Just one more flower. Quick, Flo. Whoops! Come back, I've not finished!'

But Dorrie slid through their fingers into the front room, where Peter was scrawling black crayon, round and round, as though stirring paint, defacing one page of *Thumbelina* after another and another. Aware that she was coming for him, growling as only a three-year-old hula girl can, he simply worked faster, flipping pages and scribbling, flipping and scribbling, even as Dorrie snatched the book from him and bit his hand, hard. He howled as the women came running.

You don't bite people, they said. No. No argument, you don't – *(smack)* – bite – *(smack)* – people! *(Smack, smack!)* What were you, an animal?

Poor Peter, he was only looking at the book, trying to be good. Spiteful little girl! He'd have a nasty place there, with his colouring. Always marked easy, that sort of skin.

While they were soothing the sobbing victim with witch hazel and sweeties, the monster slunk away. Up the front path, onto the green where the fancy dress contestants were being herded by their parents. Trident-wielding Britannias goading boiler-suited Winston Churchills into

31

retaliatory offences. The Queen of Hearts having to have her ringlets prised from A Little Bear *(sic)* Behind's fist and being made to promise never, never to do such a disgusting thing again.

No one noticed a tiny girl with difficult hair and a squint, clutching some crayons to her chest, running away for ever.

The sun leaned in through a crack in the bark and prodded her awake. Tiny motes, lighter than light, danced slowly for her amusement. New leaves uncurled in the heat, catkins grew long and swollen. Time was passing. Her nest was as cosy as a walnut-shell, lined with last year's leaves that scrunched as she yawned and stretched, and were as fragrant as currant buns. It must be nearly teatime.

She crawled out of the hollow as had other small creatures before her and gasped at the size of everything. The trees had become surly old giants whose sinewy arms held up the sky, and the bushes loomed, dark as ogres. Even the bluebells had a colder gleam as they stretched away into a purple gloom. She plodded through them and their perfume palled as more trees appeared, more flowers, more bushes. More shadows.

A bird twittered sleepily. But there had been something else, hadn't there? A noiseless noise that a mushroom might make as it grew big enough for a fairy to sit on. Or a frog that was bigger than she was. Fear drained her legs and she sat down in a heap. 'Mum-my!' she whimpered. Then 'Oh,' when she saw who it was.

'*Nice here, innit? Quiet. But it'll be getting dark presently. Might be as well to call it a day. Cut along home.*'

Dorrie gave it some thought. 'My knickers is wet,' she confessed.

'*Best get you home then.*'

It was a slow trek back, dawdling behind her ghostly grandmother, being pulled this way and that by distractions, flowers to pick, squirrels to watch, spider webs to touch.

'*Well*' said the old woman, waiting for a ladybird to launch itself from Dorrie's finger, '*It's been a day to remember and no mistake.*' There was no mistaking, either, the irony in the flat, Cockney tones and Dorrie's scalp prickled with guilt.

The Victory party had been a washout. No one had the heart for any tea after she'd gone missing. They'd all joined in the hunt. And the police. It was when they started talking about dragging the lake that Granny Farthing had decided it was time to fetch her home. It was a wonder, she said, that Dorrie hadn't heard them calling. They must have passed her hidey-hole a dozen times. Running round like blue-arsed flies they was. One good thing – they'd found the book, seen what a dog's breakfast Peter had made of it. Mick had given the boy a hiding and packed him off to bed. Good job, thought Dorrie nastily.

'*Be nice to put everyone's mind at rest though, so they can enjoy what's left of the day. I expect they'll have a bit of a do out on the green later, dancing and that, and a big bonfire and fireworks. Be a shame if*

33

young Peter was to miss it.'

Dorrie tried to slip her hand into the ghost's for comfort, but there was none to be had.

'What will they say? Will they be cross?'

She shook her grey head firmly. *'They'll be too busy being happy. Over the moon to have you back – droopy wet drawers and all.'* She laughed her wheezy, pear-drop laugh. *'Tell you what, though, Dor, if I was you I wouldn't say nothing about me finding you. Not everyone's partial to ghosts and there ain't no point upsetting people. Best just say you found your own way home, eh?'*

Stories? Her teeth dug doubtfully into her lower lip.

'Do as Granny tells you, duck, or it'll be "Who'd've thought it".' But there was a warmth that took any sting out of the words, like an arm squeezing her fondly. It would be all right, just this once.

She nodded. They had come to the gate.

'Go on, then, give 'em a shout.'

When she hesitated again, her guardian angel suggested that if she was quick she might find that Nora had saved her a dish of jelly and some sticky cake. And a balloon, maybe. And a flag.

Chapter Two

'What is it, Dorrie? What's the matter? Tell Mummy.'

You told yourself that this would be one of the times she would laugh and give you a hug and say, 'Silly old thing,' and to Dad over tea, 'You'll never guess what Dorrie said today...'

But these days it was never anything to laugh about. These days, when you heard her tongue suck the roof of her mouth – Tch! – when you saw the blue eyes widen, then harden to enamel and the lips press tight together, you knew you were for it.

Afterwards, when you'd cried yourself hot and hopeless, she'd gather you onto what was left of her lap, say she was sorry, she hadn't meant to shout, to smack you ... it was just that it frightened her to hear you talk that way.

It wasn't your fault. It had to be the war, didn't it? All the bombing and that. And what had happened to Mummy before... It must have left its mark. Made you dream up those awful stories.

Because that's what they were: stories. There was no such thing as a mushroom that grew so big and so hot and fiery it sucked people and trees and houses and pigs and chickens into it and swallowed them down. All that stuff about burning winds and screaming children, it wasn't true. You had made it all up. It was called

35

imagination. Not real at all. Though it was hard to believe that her little girl would come out with such vile... Well, never mind, they wouldn't talk about it any more. God, old Hitler had a lot to answer for, may he roast in hell.

She'd stroke the sticky hair from your forehead in a silence thick with roaring planes, crumbling buildings, and fearsome, stifling dark.

Then she'd go on. It wasn't as if she didn't have enough to worry about, what with Arthur wearing himself out looking for a decent job and no money coming in and everyone getting under everyone else's feet. It was good of Aunt Polly to have taken them in but the strain was beginning to show. How they were going to manage when the baby came God only knew, what with your Nan being three sheets to the wind half the time and her and Aunt Polly rowing night and day.

Best thing all round if Dad took you down to Great Bisset for a little holiday. She must be feeling lonely, poor old Grandma. And she seemed to have a soft spot for you. Maybe she could make you out. And when you came home there'd be a new little baby brother or sister for you to play with. That'd take your mind off your heebie-jeebies.

Grandma's soft spot was like a bird flying, like a fish swimming. Smooth and easy. No slaps or stinging words that swelled in your chest into hard lumps of tears.

When, one night, she woke whimpering from the dream about the people with stars on their coats, Grandma took her into her creaky old bed and told her about the third eye.

'Lucy's got one and all. And me. That's what makes us different.'

'Can you see it?'

'Oh, yeah ... great big hazel eye, right in the middle of your forehead, and them lovely long lashes, just like the other two.'

There was a little girl who had a little curl right in the very same place. A nursery rhyme. Gingerly, she felt between her eyebrows, and above. There was a curl all right, two or five, but the skin beneath was smooth and whole. She rubbed Grandma's forehead and it was warm and slightly damp, with lumpy lines across, like Dad's corduroy trousers. But there was no extra eye. No curls neither. Grandma's hair was scraped back inside a net, only let out on holidays.

And then, there it was: Grandma's third eye, bright and beady, not needing glasses like the other two.

'There y'are,' said Grandma, giving her a squeeze, when she told her. 'Easy-peasy, eh? That's your third eye seeing that – "I spy with my little eye..." your secret, psychic one, that is, the one that can see them on the Other Side and what's going on in people's heads. Most people can't and you got to remember that. Not that they ain't got a third eye, just they've forgot how to use it. Don't know what they're missing, do they? All right, sometimes it shows you things you'd rather it didn't, like them poor souls with the stars on their coats.' Her mouth twisted in the candlelight and she muttered. 'What the hell they think they're doing sending stuff like that to a baby I don't know. Every kid has nightmares but...' She shook her head. 'I'll get Mum to have a word. Ain't as if you can do anything about it, is it? Or anyone, come to that. Can't have our little Dorrie worried, can we, eh? Any old how, what I'm getting round to, lovey, is this: that old third eye of yours opens up like any other eye. *And shuts, and all.* If you don't want to see something, don't look. You don't have to.'

After that, the dreams were kinder and mostly she forgot them, though there was one she remembered, about aeroplanes flying over a city a long way away and filling the sky with parachutes. Happy people were running and jumping up to catch what was coming down to them: parcels of food and medicine and Christmas trees and tins of petrol. When she woke her hand was reaching to catch one of the little handkerchief parachutes that was tied to a big bar of chocolate.

Apparently, the Other Side had got their wires crossed, their Potters confused and they were very sorry. They'd done this kind of thing before, said Grandma crossly, and sent the poor little psychics doo-lally-dippy, else they'd shut their third eyes so tight they'd lost the gift altogether. Good job Dorrie had a guardian angel to act as go-between. And Dorrie was to remember that. Grandma wouldn't always be around to tell her what was what, but Granny Farthing would be. Always.

When Dorrie told her grandmother that

Mummy was sweeping the yard back at Aunt Polly's, or scrubbing the step on all fours with her big baby-tummy, or that the morning bus was coming along the Sowness road, or that a princess was getting married in a white dress, the old woman would look up from raking out the ashes or from doing the *Daily Mirror* crossword, down in her big shiny green armchair, and say, 'Go on!' or, 'Well, I never,' and she'd want to know which princess, Margaret or Elizabeth, or where the bus was exactly. Had it passed the Blue Lion? Then Dorrie'd better finish her toast and jam and get her shoes on and perhaps they wouldn't have that second cup of tea or they'd be wanting to spend a penny before they got there. They'd treat themselves to a toasted bun in Doddingworth; how about that?

And if her great-grandmother's ghost was there, she'd nod, too, and say, *'She's a gel, ain't she?'* They both had soft spots for her.

Peter didn't. He was horrible. Up for a few days to keep her company, while Auntie Joan and Uncle Mick moved house, he insisted on playing 'War' on the green. His Messerschmitt had just flattened Dorrie's hide-out (the hollow tree), with its cap on back-to-front and its raincoat flapping between outstretched wings, from a button round its neck, when Grandma called them in for dinner.

Dorrie was about to run inside when she heard a bomp, bomp, bomp, bomp of music, a heavy, demanding beat, like a marching band. What was it? Where was it? She scrambled to her knees. No glimpses of scarlet and gold coming down the lane, no flashes of sun on brass. But there were voices. Behind her. And a wonderful smell of ... chips? Her head whirled.

That was quick, what they'd done to the Rose and Crown. She hadn't even noticed any workmen. The crouching brown toad was now gleaming under a fresh coat of white paint, and sporting new gold lettering. And all those flowers! Loads of them. All along the sills, hanging from baskets, bursting from tubs. It looked as though they'd cleaned the windows too, but you still couldn't see in: the glass was all sort of squirly, like bottle ends. The grass patch in front, where the old men had bent over their dominoes, had been quietly cobbled and there was a new stripy blind over the doorway. If Dorrie tipped her head she could just make out a thick patterned carpet inside and winking metal and glass and polished wood and coloured lights.

That was where the bomping beat was coming from. In there. And the chips. And a voice on a loudhailer.

'Number twenty-four!'

Some people had come outside to sit and eat their dinner, at tables with umbrellas up. Scrubbed and shiny people – in what looked like their *underwear!* Brightest pink singlets, yellow yolky liberty bodices, purple underpants, dragonfly-blue winter combs, mummies and children, too.

How funny! Perhaps it was a circus. She giggled and turned to nudge Peter.

But his thin face had vanished. So had the

hollow tree. Dorrie found she was now standing beside a weathered wooden bench. Where had that sprung from? A brass plate was screwed to its back. She couldn't read it all:

This seat was don … donn-ated by the pe-ople of Great Bisset to com … something the Silver Jub … Jubblee of the Cor … no, that was too long, that word, but the rest was easy – *Her Maj-esty Queen Eliz … Eliza-beth eleven. June two* and then a big number with a one and a nine and a seven and an eight. They weren't up to big numbers yet at school.

She pulled the spectacles down her nose so the good eye could see past the covered lens. Swung round. Things had definitely changed.

Even with the glasses on properly, with just the lazy eye working, colours were brighter, edges sharper. And she realised that she was seeing with her third eye. It wasn't really now. She only had to shut it, like Grandma said. But look – even the schoolhouse was changed. There were curtains at the windows and cars in the playground. Big, shiny cars, all different shapes and colours. There were more in the lane. The grassy banks of the village green had been shifted, pushed back to make room for them.

And, Dorrie gasped, realising for the first time the enormity of what 'they'd' done to the village, at its core, where the oak tree should have raised its massive branches to the sky, ducks swam on a rushy pond! She swung round. Behind the seat, up on the knoll, crowded among leaning, lichen-spotted gravestones, the church was drawing into itself, like an old grey snail. Over at Fitzell's there

41

were more changes: a new long window was full of light and posters and shelves of bright packages. When would all this happen?

She must tell Grandma. But she stopped in her tracks.

Something was wrong with the terrace. It took her a second or two to work out what. They'd taken down one house in three. Mrs Nextdoor's one way, but not the other. All along the row. One, two, gap, one, two, gap, like Peter's teeth. And the cottages that were left, like Grandma's and Mrs Turner's, Next-door-with-the-ferrets, they'd been made into one house, with one front door in the middle with a white-pillared porch. All the houses were standing up straight, with their shoulders back, smart and clean, like it was Sunday. There were fresh-painted shutters at the windows and flowers at the sills.

A strange man was in the front garden where the pear-tree used to be. He was washing a shiny red car, a car like you'd never seen, all pulled out in front and behind, with lots of glass and chrome.

Grandma didn't live there any more. Nor did Mrs Next-door-with-the-ferrets. Oh. She caught her breath, feeling hot and fluttery and wanting to cry. What would she do without Grandma? Who would look after her?

'Dorr-*eee!*'

There she was, standing at the front door looking for her, wiping her hands on her pinny, her glasses flashing as she turned her head one way and then the other.

Dorrie ran down the path that wasn't a

driveway after all, under the spreading pear-tree, ran at her, fast, burrowing into the broad safety of her, making her stagger.

'Dorrie, what's the matter?' She hugged and stroked her, trying to read the beating wings of her shoulders. Her pinny smelled of soap and potatoes and cheese and woodsmoke. Peter was sitting at the table, stuffing down dinner as fast as he could.

'Weren't me,' he mumbled, spitting bits of cheese pie. 'I never touched her.'

Dorrie confirmed his innocence with a shake of her head.

'Hmm,' said Grandma.

'I thought you were ... you were...' She gasped out her story of loss, watching, with intense satisfaction, the shades of emotion passing across her grandmother's soft, wrinkled face, some that she couldn't interpret. Peter poked out his tongue behind Grandma's back, pushed up his nose and pulled down his eyes. He thought she was telling fibs.

'Let's have a look, then, Dorrie.' Together they went and leaned on the gate and, as Dorrie pointed, Grandma marvelled at the things she had seen. For now there were no bright tables at the pub, just old men snoozing away their pints in the sun, and Hettie Fitzell's window was cramped and dark, reflecting a majestic oak tree and filled with faded packets of Oxydol. Back to normal.

'There's a turn up,' said Grandma, her eyes narrowing, her mouth twitching into tight lines. 'You reckon they're gonna tart up the cottages, do you?' she growled. 'Get some fat geezer in my house, will they, with his car and all? Like to see 'em try! Don't you worry, my pet, only way they'll get me out is feet first. I like it here. Never thought I would, not after Walthamstow. But once I got me chickens in and me sticks of furniture, I was home. Bit thin on mod cons but you get used to it.' She raised her voice a notch. 'I say it suits us all right, don't it, Mum?' and lowered it again. 'No, Dorrie, if they want us out they'll have a fight on their 'ands. Be ready for 'em now, won't we? No idea when we can expect our marching orders, I suppose?'

Granny Farthing observed, *'Poor kid, she can't 'ardly make sense of the world as it is, Nora, leave alone fifty years' time.'*

'Fifty? Blimey, we'll all be dead and buried by then. They can do what they like. Come on, your dinner's getting cold. And cheer up, mate. It's meant to be a gift, this psychic.'

Afterwards, when she went to find her cousin, he was playing with Derek Wilson from the school. Cops and robbers. A dangerous game.

'Can I play?'

Peter gave her a funny look from behind his machine gun; shot an enquiry at Derek, a big boy of nine, who said, 'What, her? Thought you said she was dippy. Don't wanna play with no dippy girl.'

Dippy?

'She could be a Doll,' suggested Peter, generously.

'What, her?' Derek repeated. 'With they

44

glasses? Robbers don't have four-eyed Dolls. They have to be lookers.'

'She could take them off.'

'I'm not allowed.'

'We could kidnap her, lock her in a dark secret room until they hand over a hundred pounds to have her back safe.'

Derek looked thoughtful. 'They wouldn't give us 'undred pounds for her.'

'They might.'

'They wouldn't. Not if she's dippy. They wouldn't give you tuppence for her.'

She pushed up the pink wire frames to wipe away a tear.

'They would,' she affirmed, without conviction. 'Any case, I don't want to play no more,' she muttered. 'Not with rotten boys.' She turned away, began the long lonely trek back to Grandma's.

But they were upon her. Dragging her across the green to the school where Derek lived.

'No!' But she could hardly get the word out. She wanted to cry, was inclined to giggle. 'Kiss Chase', that's all it was, she told herself firmly. Like they played at school. The boys running after the girls and making them squeal, catching them, kissing them and letting them go. If she went quietly...

'In the lav!' yelled Derek, grabbing Dorrie's arm with glee.

'Get off! Get–' But he hung on, his nails digging to the bone. No 'Kiss Chase' this. Why was Peter just standing there like a dollop of lard?

Dorrie struggled, kicked Derek's skinny leg

45

with the toe of her sandal. He punched her, hard, in the stomach.

She doubled over, winded more by shock than pain, sick and speechless. Only her sliding lazy eye told this boy how hurt she was. But he had gone back to the wild, his face contorted with savagery. Now she was frightened. He had hurt her once, he'd do it again. She struggled, and could probably have twisted out of Derek's grasp if Peter hadn't then grabbed her other arm.

She found her voice. 'Let go of me, you ... you ... nasty boy!' she yelled. Swearing didn't yet come naturally. 'Peter?' feeling tears dribbling down her nose. 'You mustn't,' she begged, 'you're my cousin! I'll tell Grandma!'

Peter scowled; his face went red and his eyes glittered beneath black eyebrows. 'Don't care if I am. You're daft, Dorrie Potter. Like Gran. You see things, you do.'

They took her into the tiny schoolyard and shoved her, weeping and sweating with fear, into an evil-smelling lavvy, crowded with shameful taboos, with poo on the seat and puddles on the floor. They tied up the latch with Derek's green and yellow striped elastic belt, and after yelling 'Dafty!' and 'Loony!' and 'Dippy Dorrie!' for a while, went indoors in search of high-jump canes and cricket bats to begin her 'torture'.

Dorrie wasn't waiting around to see whether their actions matched their thoughts. Thoughts that had to do with willies and bums. She hurled herself at the door. It wouldn't budge. So she climbed onto the pooey seat, stepped over to the cross-beam and pushed, squeezed and sobbed through the gap at the top of the door. Hanging over the top, like a rag doll, her toes on the narrow beam, she just managed to reach down to the belt. The stench from the urinal wall opposite was overpowering. It made her eyes water and she couldn't see. One-eyed glasses didn't help. Stupidly she picked at the belt, hearing herself whimper. She hadn't yet learned how to unpick knots and her tormentors were on their way back. She could sense them, almost smell them.

Flinging off the wretched glasses, she tried again, but there was no sense to be made of it. The S of the buckle was too tightly knotted into the elastic.

Now what?

'Climb through the gap.'

Granny Farthing was there.

'Think, Dorrie, think,' the granny ghost urged. 'Head first ain't the answer. You don't want to end up a dollop on the floor.'

One leg at a time, then. She walked her toes as far to the right as they would go, pressed her shoulder into the jamb, and brought up the left knee, leaving the right hanging free. The door jiggled and rocked beneath her, digging into her bones.

'Mind you don't fall! You'll smash your head open on that concrete.'

She steadied herself.

Almost astride the door now, holding tight to the raw wood, she just had to twist a bit, bring the left foot through and the right leg would follow. Probably. Then she could swing down to the ground.

47

Come on.

'*Come on!*'

But her foot wedged in the gap. Her sandal. The crêpe sole. She tugged. The door bucked. The free foot found a purchase on a wall or a ceiling and blindly pushed.

Suddenly, in rattling, grazing pain, she found herself through, like a fat parcel posted, hanging on by one hand ... one foot ... and then hands clawing at dull, blistered paint, as she fell, smack in a heap, her chin slamming last of all into the slime-green concrete.

She was outside. That much registered through the threatening blackness.

'*Upsy daisy! Get up, Dorrie!*'

Staggering against the lavvy door, fighting sleep.

'*Deep breath, duck!*'

The smell of boys' pee somehow saved her, gave her the wit to pick up her glasses and run. It all happened so quickly she was out of the school gate before the boys swung through the door.

She didn't tell Grandma about it. Didn't need to. In compressed silence, as the old woman removed the stinking dress and underclothes, washed her with warm water and a soapy flannel, and bathed her wounds with milky Dettol, Dorrie saw that she knew everything. Granny Farthing had told her. She flushed.

'Right,' she said, when Dorrie was dressed and bandaged. 'Stop 'ere.' Then she went out.

She looked very stern when she came back some time later. Mrs Wilson had found the boys still trying to undo the belt. They said they'd been playing cowboys and this was where their horse was stabled. They'd run away when Grandma had appeared at the door, a tidal wave about to break.

Mrs Wilson had been horrified.

'The poor child! She could have broken her neck!'

'Or worse. No knowing what them little loves was gonna dish out.'

'Oh, I'm sure Derek would never...' But even so, she'd given him six of the best, on each hand, with the very cane they'd been going to use on Dorrie.

Peter went missing for hours. Grandma found him eventually, curled up in the coal cellar. His dad, when he came at teatime, gave him a thick ear and he was still sobbing and saying how much he hated Dorrie when they boarded the bus that would take them to the station.

Little devil, said Grandma. There had been talk of Dorrie attending the village school until it was time to go back to Walthamstow, but now the idea was dropped. And still she was miserable, crying into her pillow at night. It took Granny Farthing to plumb to the source of it.

'Dippy?' she squawked. 'My Gawd, girl, you ain't dippy. You got more sense than them two boys put together. You got six senses. They only got five. Can they see ghosts? Can they read minds? Next time you see Peter, you tell him you're gonna tell everyone in Walthamstow what he does in bed of a night. See him jump. You're an extraordinary little girl and don't let no one tell you different.'

'But I want Peter to like me, Granny. I don't

want him to hate me.'

'I dunno – little girls – they do love a melodrama. He don't hate you, duck. He's had a fright.'

'A fright?'

'He could really've hurt you, that's what's upset him. Only he can't tell you how sorry he is – boys have to look big, don't they? He'll make it up to you though, mark my words.'

Chapter Three

Grandma wasn't dippy, either. She might have been old and slow and baggy but she was wise and good. She taught Dorrie all sorts. About the Other Side, about making cakes, about feeding hens, about scattering a handful of seed at one end of the run so that while they were peck, pecking, their eyes beading on the next grain, their wattles waggling, she could lift the wooden shutter at the other end and scrape the steaming bran-and-potato-peel mash into their trough without becoming part of their dinner. She learned to check that no bird was sitting on the nest when she opened the door to collect the eggs. And then to pick them up, one at a time, only not the china one, which was just to encourage them, and to put them in the basin. Smooth and warm and white with downy feathers clinging, each egg fitted so perfectly, so tenderly into her palm, she couldn't have hurt it, squeezed it or dropped it if she'd tried. She'd bend and put her cheek to it. Grandma didn't ever tell her to be careful. She didn't need to.

Once, when all the eggs were piled in the basin, Grandma told her to hush. Listen.

What?

At first all she heard was the contented chirring of the chickens. Then, further off, Mrs Wilson ringing the handbell that brought the children in from the playground. She heard their shouts and calls dwindle to silence. Two women at the far end of the terrace were chatting on their high back steps, their country voices rising and falling on gossip. A blackbird was singing in the peach tree.

'Listen harder.' Grandma was watching her, secrets bubbling behind her glasses.

What else, then?

A horse clip-clopping in the lane, the rumble of wheels as the cart was drawn over the bridge. A cow mooing to its calf. A distant cockerel. An aeroplane.

And then, close to her ear, she heard a faint piping noise. Someone very small, very young.

Grandma was bursting. 'Sit down, sit down,' she ordered.

Dorrie sank onto the worn grass beside the chicken run, her heart beating fast.

'Shut your eyes. *All* of them.'

She shut them tight, hearing a wooden squeak. The door of the broody box. A rustle of straw, a smell of ... what? Not quite egg...

Cheep, cheep, cheep. Louder now, more insistent.

'Don't look yet.'

Something was placed in her cross-legged lap, a small lightness in her skirt that forced her eyes to look.

A handful of yellow fluff wobbled there on spindly legs, a fragile little person with a creamy beak and wings that made you want to cry. It winked at her with a tiny black eye.

'Oh,' she breathed, entranced, stroking its back

with her finger.

'*Next year's Christmas dinner,*' said a voice.

'Gaw blimey, mate, leave the child some illusions, won't you? Take no notice, Dorrie,' Grandma continued, trying to ignore the beefy ghost, beetling at them under black brows. He was preceded by a wheelbarrow heaped with weeds. The path by the chicken run was one that everyone used. It was wider than the others and led to the compost heap. They would have been in his way if he had been on their plane.

'This little chick's gonna live to a ripe old age. My next broody hen. I can see her winning prizes.' But the spell was broken. And anyway, Grandma was only saying that for the ghost's benefit. *She* couldn't see into the future, not without Granny Farthing's help, everyone knew that.

When he had trundled past, hardly missing their toes and stomping through Grandma's strawberry patch, they put the little chick back with her brothers and sisters.

'Blooming old men,' she muttered, clearing out the eggshells and filling the trough with a special bran mash to help Molly Hen regain her strength. 'Don't know why I put up with them.'

There were two of them and they came with the house. What she'd done to deserve them she didn't know – always hanging round with their toothless country saws about skinning rabbits or making bread poultices for boils, usually when Grandma was up to her neck in cake mixture or trying to sneak a crafty forty winks. That's what old men do, she told Dorrie. Get under your feet

53

so you have to take some notice of them. But they weren't hers and she didn't see why she should.

Dorrie could see why they didn't want to leave. It was a nice house. Nicer than Aunt Polly's. Though Aunt Polly had a lav with a chain that pulled and taps over the sink and a geyser that clanked and banged but spurted hot water into the bath when you wanted. All Grandma had was a standpipe in the backyard that dripped a mossy slipway through the cobbles to the drain, and a tin bath that hung on the back wall.

Aunt Polly had a tiny garden with fences either side. There was no fence between Grandma's and Mrs Next-door-with-the-ferrets, whose name was Mrs Turner. They shared the yard and the peach tree and the lavvy, across the yard, which was a brick back-to-back: one side for Potters, one side for Turners. Inside theirs was just a board, scoured and bleached, with a hole through to a black bucket of Elsan, and when you sat there you could watch beetles and caterpillars and you could hear the chickens on the other side and the twigs scritch-scratching over your head, from the peach tree's lowest branches. Sometimes you could hear one of the Turners. It was interesting. Last summer she had been sitting there with the nightlight, minding her own business, when BANG! a peach had dropped on the roof and Dorrie had knocked over the nightlight and Mummy had had to come and get her because she howled so. But she'd only been a baby then, not even at school.

Between Grandma's back steps and Mrs Next-door's, called Stone, there *was* a bit of fence, but you could go round it and you'd be in their yard. It was just to stop you looking into their kitchen, or them into Grandma's. Beside the fence was a narrow bit of scrub where old flowerpots and rusty buckets and bedsprings and wires from Grandma's stays were laid to rest, and low down, hidden behind sticky willie and cranesbill, where you'd least expect to find one, was a mossy window. The cellar. Its door lay on the other side of the steps, on the ground, like a trap door. It had a bolt and a rope handle. When you slid the bolt and tugged on the rope the door flapped back and there – ta-rah! – was a flight of secret steps leading down to a dimness that smelled of firewood and paraffin and soap. A heady perfume.

(It wasn't secret really because Grandma left the door open most of the time except if it rained or snowed or if she went away somewhere, like Clacton or Newcastle.)

Built against the wall down there was Grandma's pride and joy, the huge brick copper, where she poked and prodded in the billows, with a long stick, for sheets and towels and nighties which she levered out, 'Oof!' into the sink, and doused with cold water from a big enamel jug, and scrubbed and pummelled and squeezed and wrung, before letting the water run through to the bucket. She was up and down the steps all morning, with clean water, dirty water, hot water, cold. And the tin bath would heap higher with blue-white washing ready to be mangled and hung out in the yard. Dorrie grated soap for her and fetched sticks to fuel the flames behind the little iron door, but mostly she kept out of her way. Grandma's brawny arms ran with water, her fingers crinkled, her jaws knotted and sweat boiled in her face.

You'd have thought the ghosts would have known better than to crowd Grandma on wash day.

'You don't wanna bother wi' all that scrubbin' and wearin' yourself out.'

'S'only gonna get dirty again, arter all.'

The beefy one was propped in the doorway sucking an ancient pipe and the other, thinner version, was sitting half in and half out of the copper, scratching. Grandma rolled her eyes and swatted at them with the copper stick as though they were flies. 'Hop it!' she said. 'Go on, sling your hook! I'm busy.'

They didn't move.

'Waste o' time, washin' they clothes, missus,' the scrawny one repeated.

Grandma drew herself as tall as she could which wasn't very, her cheeks flaming. 'Look, mate, if you don't mind stinking like a dead dog, that's down to you. Me, I like to be a bit sweeter. So if you don't mind, I'll get on with me washing and you can sod off. Down wind, preferably. Gawd,' she said when they were gone, 'I thought them poltergeists was bad enough when I first moved in, chucking me stuff around, breaking mirrors and that. Your Auntie Lucy helped me clear them lot out, along with the spiders. She said we shoulda seen them two off while we was

56

at it. But I thought, Ah, poor old souls ... so what if they do pong a bit? They don't mean no harm and they got a right to haunt their own home, when all's said and done. But they're just taking liberties, Dorrie, interfering in me washing. That takes the blooming biscuit that does. I bet their own wives didn't stand for it. Well, I tell you, Dorrie, I ain't putting up with it, neither. I think the time's come for a bit of friendly persuasion.'

'What's a fenly-parsation?'

'Getting rid of pests.'

'Like flies?'

'Just like.'

Dorrie stared hard at the brown fly-papers fluttering above the meatsafe, stuck with tiny black corpses, like an onion with cloves.

There were two rooms under the house: the coal-hole, where Peter had hidden, through a dark, forbidding doorway, and the cellar proper, for chopping wood and hammering things, for potting plants and cooling milk. It was laundry, larder, toolshed, workshop and glory-hole. Dark shelves winked with jars and bottles – black-currant jam and preserved peaches and pickled onions and homemade wine. A wash-stand, dusty with rust, was hung with old jackets and cobwebs, and cluttered with tins of all shapes and sizes which yielded untold treasures: gas-mantles, candle-ends, nuts and nails and washers and screws, buttons and hairpins, old gramo-phone needles.

Things you never saw at home hung on Grandma's wall: three or four amputated legs, knobbly as Nanna Hubbard's, which, when you looked close, were only lisle stockings stuffed with onions. A brace of rabbits, shot and paid for that morning, their eyes filmed blue with death, their soft paws stretched down the flaking distemper for a mad dash to an astral burrow.

And bicycle wheels and hurricane lamps and Mickey Mouse gas-masks left over from the war, that had to be tried on and adjusted to fit.

'And what's this, Grandma?' in a holding-your-nose sort of voice that the old lady didn't hear over the slapping and scrubbing. It was hard to see through the dusty eye-pieces of the mask and Dorrie was forced to resort to second sight.

It was a razor strop, one that the brothers had used when they all lived in Walthamstow.

She saw a hand take the padded grip, saw a thin blade, swish-swashing up and down the leather, saw a shaving mug full of soap and the lather worked into long downy cheeks, chin and neck. Her father's younger face. Centred and careful, his eyes reflected his own image to infinity. Though she smiled and waved, took off the mask, he didn't smile back. The razor, delicately held between finger and thumb, cleared a wide path through the snow. And the pink skin was as smooth as her own. He wiped the razor off on a piece of newspaper and went back to scraping off the blue-black whiskers.

She watched as each of her uncles came of age and took his place before the mirror, Perce and Mick and Charlie. Two she didn't know. One, the youngest, lifted his chin to the razor and caught Dorrie watching. Muscles above the foam flickered in spasm. Lips parted, almost came together in a 'Wh–?' He spun round, thinking to catch her behind him. Turned back to face his puzzled reflection. She said shyly, 'Hello, I'm Dorrie.' But he couldn't hear, and when he returned to his task his mind was closed, the moment of contact denied.

There was someone else watching the mirror, behind her. A man with a heavy moustache and a severe centre parting in his curly brown hair. A man whose long-sleeved underwear buttoned to the neck and whose braces dangled at his sides. But the youngest son kept his third eye tightly closed. He didn't even want to see his dead father.

Dorrie's skin prickled.

She trailed up the steps to the heavy rumble of rollers, the squeezy splash of water into a bucket.

'What are your boys called, Grandma?'

A sheet rested on its journey, dripping heavy on one side of the mangle, stiffly folding into the big enamel bowl on the ground, blue, the colour of her mother's eyes. Grandma let go of the handle and straightened with a grunt.

'What?' she demanded, her wet palms pushing a hollow in her back, her face pale and tired.

'There's my dad, and Uncle Perce and Uncle Mick and who else?'

'Eh?'

'Your boys. I can't remember them,'

'Blimey, Dorrie, I thought it was something...'

Nevertheless she reeled them off. She never minded talking about her boys. Arthur, Siddy, Perce, Mick, Charlie and Jack, in Newcastle.

Jack was the one. He was psychic, too. He was the one who'd been meant to get the dream about the poor star people.

'Is that all you wanted?'

'Auntie Lucy's coming down the lane.' They both cocked an ear for the roar of her motorbike.

'Oh Gawd, ain't there no peace for the wicked? What's she want, I wonder?'

'She's got the sack.'

Lucy had been expecting it, she told them, but not so soon. She thought he'd wait, at least until the harvest was in. But that was Hooper for you. He'd got what he wanted out of her – the peas picked and the new barn up and ready. The men, those that had survived the war, were back in their old jobs, and with her sharp tongue and inferior muscle power she was dispensable. In vain, Mabel had pleaded for her friend. But, he wasn't a charity, he said. Lucy had her uses but he'd rather have men about him.

So now she was home, if Ma would have her. She wouldn't say she was sorry, but the money had come in handy. She'd miss Mabel's cooking, of course, she winked, and dirty old men spying on her having a bath in front of the fire. 'Don't worry, love,' she said, reading Dorrie's mind, 'I'm not turning you out of your bedroom. I'll kip in with Ma for the time being. Needs must and we've done it before, eh, Ma? Remember the honeymoon?'

People usually had honeymoons after their weddings, but Lucy had had hers instead of, and Grandma had gone, too. That was long ago, apparently, before she'd married Uncle Joe.

In the wardrobe, hanging beside Dorrie's mac and the spotty dress Mummy had made for her and a lot of Lucy's dresses and coats, there was an airman's blue-grey uniform with a wing over the pocket and a line of coloured ribbons representing the medals he'd won. Next to that was a posh suit, still with a sickly carnation in the buttonhole and confetti in the pockets. He'd taken most of his other clothes over to Cambridge, Lucy told her, unpinning the bloom with a funny smile on her lips. 'The day after the wedding,' she said. 'Not the ideal way for newly-weds to spend their honeymoon.'

'Why?'

'Why what?'

'Why does Uncle Joe have to live in Cambridge?'

'You may well ask, Dorrie.' Auntie Lucy sighed and shook her head, explaining that Uncle Joe was studying at the university, which was a bit like school, only for grown-ups.

'Why?'

Because if he stayed there and passed all his exams he would be able to get a good job at the end of it.

'Better than yours?'

'Better than the one at Hooper's,' she smiled. Because Auntie Lucy had a sideline. On Sundays and days off she would put on Uncle Joe's old flying jacket and helmet and tear along the tar and gravel roads of East Anglia on her motorbike, to churches and meeting halls where she would lay on hands, conduct meetings, give private and public readings, with or without Grandma.

She could even do 'absent healing' from the armchair in Grandma's front room. Dorrie would look up as the clock wheezed to strike the hour, to find her aunt staring into the fire with a letter open on her lap, or a photograph of the person needing healing, or fingering some small object someone had sent her to help with the visualisation. By the sixth or seventh chime her eyes would have closed and her breathing become so slow and deep you might have thought she was asleep but for her long fingers fanning out in her lap, like the fronds of some sea anemone. Gently her hands would rise, and wait, perfectly still above the spirit of her subject, as it took shape before her. A stroking motion then, along its length and breadth, moulding the head, the torso, the limbs, moving slowly along, over, around, returning, checking, examining for imbalance and energy blocks. Her wrists would rotate, her hands dance, her brown, workworn fingers become graceful, tapering instruments of healing as, with infinite patience and care, she drew out rods and needles of spiritual discomfort – *dis*-ease – and handed them to a spiritual 'helper' who would appear to dissolve the affliction between its palms. White healing light would then pour into the breach, redressing balances, making good.

And then, leaving the subject slumbering in a bubble of sweet healing light, and Grandma snoring over her knitting, Lucy would cart Dorrie off to bed and read her a story before heading off back to the farm.

But if she was home to stay ... Grandma's library books were due back on the 31st. Tomorrow. With the young woman home to keep a weather eye out for the washing she could get to Boots and back before tea. And a new Ethel M. Dell to read with her cocoa. It was all working out for the best.

Out in the yard, Lucy took over the mangling, cranking the heavy wheel round with sinewy gusto. Grandma hung out the clothes, Dorrie handed her the pegs, and the wind filled the sheets and frocks and promised to dry them before teatime.

'Teamwork,' said Auntie Lucy, grinning. Grandma rolled her eyes.

That afternoon while Grandma and Dorrie were in Doddingworth changing their library books, Lucy made herself useful, doing all the heavy gardening jobs that Grandma had been putting off, trimming the hedge, weeding, that sort of thing. She had it all done by the time they arrived home.

'Oh my Gawd!' said Grandma, as they came in the front gate to find the garden littered with petals. 'What's she done? My poor roses! They only wanted dead-heading!' She swallowed, 'Well, I suppose it'll save me pruning them in the autumn. And the weigela *was* getting straggly,' she said, bravely regarding the two naked stumps sticking out of the ground. She wasn't quite so reasonable about the jasmine. 'O-oh!' she wailed, surveying the bare trellis by the front door. What had promised to be a brave splash of yellow on a frosty morning, a beacon glowing in the dark depths of winter, now wouldn't. 'Oh, Luce! What have you done?'

She'd got chatting to two old ghosts who had happened along and who, on discovering that she knew a lot about agriculture and virtually nothing about horticulture, had proceeded to instruct her. Hard pruning was the thing. It might look a bit drastic now, she assured her mother, but there'd be a lovely show next year, or in the jasmine's case, the year after.

Grandma's mouth was dangerously tight, her fingers flexing for a neck to squeeze. And then she froze, sniffing the air. 'Someone's lit a bonfire,' she breathed.

'Yes, come and see. I didn't know what else to do with all the rubbish. We've had a lovely blaze, the old fellers and me. You like a bonfire, don't you, Dorrie?'

'Lucy ... you did get the washing in before you lit it, didn't you?'

But one look at her face told the story and one look at the washing sealed the fate of the two old ghosts. Soiled with smuts from the bonfire, smelling of smoke, it would all have to be done again.

The 'persuasion' took place the next afternoon, half-day closing, after the shop shut, so that Hetty Fitzell could join Grandma and Auntie Lucy and Granny Batts from down the road, round the parlour table. Dorrie was allowed to sit next to Granny Farthing and watch, provided she kept very quiet.

It wasn't Granny Batts' fault that her hair hung down in silvery wisps over her widow's weeds. She'd done her best but her arthritic fingers couldn't quite manage to poke it all into a bun these days. It wasn't Hetty's fault that she had deepset smoker's eyes and aquiline features, or that her chin sprouted a hairy wen. It was nobody's fault that anyone looking in at the window might have supposed they'd happened on a witches' coven.

The two brothers were finally persuaded to leave the home they had known for over a hundred years, for a 'well-earned rest' on the Other Side – which was the ruse that Grandma resorted to – but no one could have foreseen that, at the moment of their crossing, when the temperature dropped, as it did on these occasions, and the resulting draught made the windows rattle and the overhead light swing wildly on its cord and newspapers fly about and the door blow open, that Dad, and Mummy with their precious new bundle in her arms, would be standing, open-mouthed and aghast, on the front step.

Chapter Four

'You can't blame her for trying, I suppose.'

They were there behind the curtain, watching her drag herself up the street, all blotch and snivel, her legs still wearing her father's hand-print. She *hadn't* been trying it on. She *wouldn't*. She'd've given the world to have been able to fetch him a loaf of crusty white bread to mop up his fried egg and tomatoes. Just that she knew there wouldn't be any when she got there. The baker had sold out early. With bread coming off the ration people had gone mad.

In her mind, she heard what they said.

'Third eyes! Whatever next? It's *her,* ain't it, my barmy mother, filling her head with rubbish.'

'Oh, don't say that, Arthur. She's not barmy, she's psychic.'

'Psychic! Don't talk rot, Flo. It's a cop out, fairy stories.'

'She really believes in it, Arthur.'

'Don't stop it being a load of codswallop. That's what religion is, Flo, the opium of the masses, like Marx says, dulling her to the real issues of life.'

'The class struggle,' said Mummy wearily.

'That's right.' He nodded his approval, and then shivered with distaste. 'What Dorrie made of it all I dread to think. She's so bleeding fanciful, thanks to you. Poor little scrap, sitting there, eyes on stalks, while those old crones sat round their ouijee board.'

'And Lucy,' she reminded him.

'...Who was so blooming cool about it. That's what I can't get over.' He put on a funny voice, supposed to be his sister, '"Caught us on the hop, Arthur!" On the *hop!* With her hand in the cauldron more like.' He was shaking his head in despair. 'I'd've thought she had more sense. Gawd help her kids if she has any.'

Flo laughed. Began to sing, 'The bells of hell go ting-a-ling-ling...' taking Stephen's little hand in hers to conduct.

'I'm glad you think it's funny! Did you *see* the state she was in, poor kid – talk about in the wars! What was Ma doing of, I'd like to know, while our little girl was falling off doors? Talking to bloody ghosts, that's what! Criminal neglect, that is, Flo.'

'Arthur, she hasn't got eyes in her backside. You know what Dorrie's like, into everything. And she's bound to fall over in those soppy glasses. Poor child can't see a hand in front of her face. And they give her headaches.'

'They're free, aren't they?' he challenged. 'And they'll sort out her squint, given time. That's what the doctor said and I've no reason to doubt him. No, what's giving her headaches is all that claptrap Ma's filled her up with. I tell you, Flo, I'm really worried about the girl – talking to herself, gazing into space.'

'They all do that, children her age.'

'Nah, this ain't normal – making out she's seeing things, like that baker's shop window. That

67

can't be right.'

'She is wrapped up in herself, I'll give you that, and little Stephen could be a bag of beans, all the notice she takes of him.' She gazed down at the baby adoringly. 'Couldn't you, my ickle sweetie-pops? You could be a mouldy old bag of beans.'

'If we ain't careful, Flo, she's going to finish up just like Ma – round the blooming twist.'

The gnawing yeasty smell of early baking was almost gone, gobbled up by the morning. As she crossed the street, as the shop window cleared of reflections, her heart sank: there were the empty shelves as she'd seen them in her head – a few flakes of golden crust, a sprinkling of poppy seeds and a handwritten notice – SOLD OUT. Hopeless tears rolled under her pink wire frames as she pinged open the door, stood on tiptoe and pushed her pennies across the counter.

When she'd trailed back home with the baker's message scrawled at the bottom of her mother's note, when they bombarded her with questions...

'Who told you, Dorrie?'

'How did you know Pritchard's had sold out? And don't say you saw in it in your head.'

...she decided, wearily, to take Granny Farthing's advice and tell them what they wanted to hear. She said she'd heard Mrs Prowse, next door, talking to Mrs Edwards outside, in the street. Mrs Prowse had said that there wasn't any point in going to the baker's because she'd bought the last loaf. But she would lend Mrs

Edwards a slice or two till Monday.

'Damn,' said Dad.

'Why didn't you say that in the first place, Dorrie?' Mum reproved.

'Dunno.'

'Nor do I. You're a naughty girl, telling fibs!'

'So what are we gonna do till Monday, with no bread?'

'Let them eat cake,' said Mummy, smiling suddenly, 'and pie-crust. Good job I've plenty of flour.' Dad was still looking fed-up. 'Oh, cheer up, Arthur, there's a bit of stale bread left in the bin, if Mum hasn't had it. If I fry it in the bacon fat, it'll be lovely.'

And because that day the postman brought them a letter about the new prefab in Haroldson Road, they forgot all about the morning's upset and began making plans.

Nanna Hubbard said it was made of aspidistras, and Mummy laughed and told Dad. Asbestos sheeting is what she should have said. It was a house made for quickness, Mummy said, for all the people living with aunties whose own houses had been knocked down in the war.

Neat and white and square, it was better than Aunt Polly's. You had your own bedroom, if you didn't count Stephen, and cupboards for clothes and one for toys and one for dressing up. And you didn't need a po under the bed because there was a lavatory by the bedroom door. And if Stephen woke up and cried or you were frightened by cats fighting you only had to bang on the wall and one of them would get up. There was a bathroom and a front room, with a fire that heated the water, and a kitchen, and a smell of paint and putty and sawn wood and new lino.

Mummy had never been so happy. She kept stroking things – the fitted cupboards and drawers and all the electric things that came with the house, the fridge, the cooker, the kettle and the wash-boiler that fitted under the draining board and was going to make wash day a doddle.

She made curtains and frills for every room, covers for the armchairs and sofa (so you couldn't tell they were second-hand), bedspreads and rag rugs and cushions.

There was a sideboard and a lamp-stand and a table, Dorrie discovered, that had been salvaged from their old house, after the bombing. They'd been stored in Aunt Polly's attic, all chipped and scratched and mucky. Out in the back garden Dad sanded and stained and varnished them and, come Christmas, the sideboard was crammed with winking bottles and shiny boxes, bowls of fruit and dishes of sweets, the lamp-stand was smart with a parchment shade, trimmed with holly, and the table was dressed for dinner.

Dorrie had laid places for five, a serviette by each fork, a bon-bon by each knife, a water glass by each spoon; she'd arranged the twinkly-holly-candle thing in the middle with the cruet on one side and the water jug on the other. Then, when they'd stopped finding jobs for her to do, when she was almost faint with the smells of food coming from the kitchen, she sat down to wait.

Nanna and Aunt Polly were coming. You

couldn't not invite them, poor old things. But that wasn't why you were eating in the front room at the gleaming new-old table. Christmas dinner was special. You had glasses beside the plates at Christmas and you didn't eat in the kitchen.

She swung her legs, weaving her fingers in and out of the lacy tablecloth. Mummy had made it when she was first married, and rescued it from the rubble when they'd pulled her out. It had mended as good as new.

Tea for two. The table spread with her best crocheted cloth, jam sandwiches cut into triangles, the best tea service and twenty tons of rubble.

Flo dared not move again. Just pulling her foot free had started a landslide. Appalled, she had listened to the rumble and shift, the thunk of brick against brick, things crunching and creaking as they pressed down tighter and tighter onto the table-top above her.

Adding to the weight on her shoulders.

'This is it,' she'd whispered, hearing a rushing like water finding a bed to flow along, spilling over and around obstacles, filling hollows. Like under tables. She cowered, limbs curled around her swollen belly like a bean's first shoots, eyes squeezed shut, bracing herself and the baby, for the end.

Gritty bits pattered onto paper beside her, the first raindrops in a storm. Or the last.

She waited ... but the slippage had stopped. Short. She drew a shuddering breath. Things

71

must be rammed solid out there, she thought. She'd never shift them. Never get out.

Her foot was coming back to life. Prickling and aching.

'Pins and needles,' she explained. The thing to do was to bang your foot on the floor to get the blood flowing. Ordinarily. Instead she wriggled her toes. Leaned forward and rubbed them, wondering whether she'd ever find her shoe again.

Still nothing moved.

Bolder, she crawled her hand over the oilcloth, hearing her hard, buffed nails encountering lumps of plaster, sticky bits of bread, broken china...

Whose delicate, fluted edges brought her to the edge of tears. Damn. It had to be the best set, didn't it? With the orange and blue flowers and gold trim. The set Nora had given them when they'd got married. She sighed. Whatever had possessed her to get the best set out? Swanking, that's what. That'd teach her.

But, thinking about it, *all* the china would be smashed, wouldn't it? Every last bit, in or out of the cupboards. The Woolworth's white, the hand-me-downs, all her pretty ornaments, the 'gazunders', the glass Mum kept her teeth in, everything. All gone. Oh bugger Hitler! Bugger the war!

Unclenching her fist she came upon a tea-spoon. An apostle spoon. Clutching it like a talisman, she stroked the teeny-tiny head with her thumb. For luck? The hands were clasped in a teeny-tiny prayer, the silver robes flowing down the stem.

'Wedding present,' she said.

Hark at her, talking to herself. First sign of madness, talking to yourself. But she'd go mad if she didn't. Down here, buried alive, all by herself.

So she went on. 'Jack and Charlie gave us the set. And your Auntie Lucy,' she added grudgingly.

Auntie? Mum was talking to *her*, Dorrie. Not Dorrie aged five and three-quarters, sitting waiting for her Christmas dinner, but baby Dorrie, in her tummy who, if she'd heard, hadn't understood. Not then. Dorrie wriggled rounder into her chair, not minding the brass studs round the new seat cover making red dents in her legs.

'Well,' Flo had gone on, 'Lucy's name was on the card but I doubt she gave much towards it. Still at school in those days, "trying to better herself",' she mimicked. 'Stuck-up little madam. Poor old Nora, not two ha'pennies to rub together and Miss Lucy sitting on her backside not lifting a finger to help. Not even a Saturday job. I'd be ashamed, having them all running round after me like I was the Queen of rotten Sheba.'

Her bile surprised her. 'Stop it, Flo,' she reproached herself. 'What's the matter with you? Lucy's all right. Just young and... And unkind remarks about your sister-in-law are not going to go down well with God, Who's going to get you out of this. Somehow.'

She put the spoon in her pocket and reached out further. Found loose threads that wound themselves like peas' tendrils, about her fingers. Oh, it was her tablecloth, its lacy border ripped and snaggled to the floor by something heavy and very smooth to the touch, like polished metal. She traced its familiar grid pattern and frowned. What was it? She should know.

Dorrie knew. Flicked a glance towards the fire, its funny doors with the windows glowing red, the fire-irons, twinkling with Brasso, and the... Come on, Mummy. I spy with my little eye something beginning with F. But Mummy couldn't guess, not in the dark, not by touch, not when her mind was all higgledy-piggle with being bombed out.

It had ruined the cloth, whatever it was. Made wasted effort of all that stitching, all those dreams, all those evenings working all those loops of cotton into chains that divided and divided again like the cells of her embryo, growing into perfect, precise rings and scallops and whorls, thousands upon thousands to make the whole. A beautiful thing and she its creator.
    'Don't know how you have the patience, Flo,' they all said.
    Known for it, she was, her patience. Her ability to see things through, no matter what. In spite of the wedding distractions and the war starting and Arthur going to sea and the Blitz, she had finished it, washed and starched it and put it away in the sideboard cupboard, with the best china and the apostle spoons. A cloth for special

occasions: Christmases and birthdays.

And intimate tea-parties...

The brass fender! She was there at last. And it had caught in the *tablecloth?* Blimey! Imagine the force that could make a heavy fender leap across the room like that. And finish up... God, another couple of inches and it would have smashed her head open and that would've been her lot! *Their* lot!

Her hand dropped to the floor, strength gone. Onto paper. All covered in grit. That'd be the *Daily Mirror,* knocked down in the rush.

'Pity we haven't got a light down here,' she remarked to her child. 'Could've done the crossword between us. If we'd had a pencil.' She twisted her fingers for her knitting, or sewing. She hated being idle, wasting time.

But there'd been no time to think about lights and pencils or knitting. Just the siren and wallop! Down had come that bomb, up the street somewhere. All she could do was dive under the table. She'd never even *heard* the explosion.

You had to smile – or weep; when she'd come to in the dark, she'd thought she was in bed. Hadn't been able to think, for the life of her, why it was so close, so difficult to breathe. Had she forgotten to open the window? Only caught on when she tried to get out and found that her foot wouldn't go over the side. Of course – she wasn't *in* her bed.

She'd come over all woozy then – all hot and cold – blood rushing in her ears, but when the baby jumped, catching her panic, she'd had to get a grip for its sake.

At least she was in one piece. Everything seemed to be working. The blast hadn't deafened her. That happened – people being deafened by the bang or losing their memory. And she hadn't lost her memory, more's the pity. She kept having to shove thoughts to the back of her mind.

What if he...? What if...? Don't think about it. Don't.

Dorrie frowned, catching rags of images. *A man in a long coat, hurrying along a street. Rooftops silhouetted against the sky, now light, flash, flash, dark again. The air trembling with a roar of engines. A screaming, a whistling of missiles, a crackling of ack-ack. A hand raising a door-knocker. Crummpppp. A blinding brightness.*

Flo clenched her teeth, screwed her eyes tight to drive out the horror of what might have happened. Blinked. Hard.

She didn't think she was blind, though how could you tell? Black as Newker's Knocker, down here, eyes open or shut. It was so dark she was beginning to see with her mind's eye. Feeling the smooth barley-sugar twist of the table leg and seeing the polished sheen she had put there yesterday. Going to all that trouble.

A sob welled up, a terrible grief.

'Oh Frank! Oh what am I going to *do?*'

But the wail dredged up from her womb had nothing to do with her present predicament. She sniffed and wiped it away. The back of her hand was coated with dust. She felt it against her lip.

76

She stroked her lump. 'Take no notice,' she said. 'Just getting a bit fed up with myself. We'll get you out of here, I promise. Just a matter of when. I'd shut my eyes if I were you, get a bit of kip. When you wake up they might have dug us out.'

The air was beginning to smell bad, what with one thing and another. She'd disgraced herself, hadn't she? Couldn't help it. Didn't seem to be able to hold it these days. The baby must be lying against her bladder. Only had to cough or sneeze, and all this dust...

And it was so blooming hot! You'd never have thought it was November and the house like an ice well. Just that miserable fire in the back room. She'd taken off her woolly but she was still sweltering, trickles running down the back of her neck, under her arms. When she moved she caught again the sour whiff of the senior girls' changing rooms after netball. All too much for the perfume she'd dabbed behind her ears, the minute Mum had gone out. More like *Night in the Rue Morgue* than *Evening in Paris!* And, on top of everything else, this burning smell. There always was after an air raid, but she'd never been this close to it before.

She listened. Heard the blood pumping in her ears, her own heart beating, and the baby's, tiny and fast.

Remembering, Dorrie put her hand on her own chest. Under her new Christmas cardigan, under her dress, under the rubber buttons of her liberty bodice, her heart was measuring the seconds, slower than her baby self, faster than Flo's. Still beating. Somehow they had got out from under that table.

'Hey!'

Dorrie jumped. The baby jumped. Her mother was yelling with all her might. 'Down here! Get us out, for God's sake! In the back, we're in the back room!'

Had she heard something? They both listened again, as Flo's words ricocheted off the underside of the table, fell back warm and weak and stinking of fear. Nothing. They hadn't carried. She'd been a fool to think they would. No one would hear her down here.

'They'll never find us. Not until it's too late.'

'Do it again,' urged Dorrie from the future. 'Shout louder!' And the baby gave an almighty kick.

'All right, all right,' said Flo. 'I didn't mean it. Keep your hair on. Just getting my breath back, aren't I?'

'Dorrie? What are you doing? Playing hide and seek? Come on, sit up, love, Nanna's here, and Aunt Polly.'

She managed a mouthful or two of chicken, but she wasn't really hungry.

'All the excitement,' said Nanna Hubbard, so Mummy stopped trying to coax her. She looked so pretty today, you'd never believe she'd once had a house blow down on her. Flushed from cooking, her eyes bright and blue, blonde wisps

78

curling over the edges of her paper hat, she was up and down, spooning mush into Stephen's eager lips, helping Dad and the two old sisters to more potatoes and gravy, pulling bon-bons with Dorrie, exclaiming, shrieking, laughing over the corny jokes. Glasses clinked, cutlery clattered and scraped against plates.

Voices rose and fell and were soon muffled by a weight of debris. Now there were other sounds, a scraping of bare hands clearing clinker, heaving away rafters and floorboards spilled like match-sticks, picking out shards of glass, silvered and plain, lifting out splintered wardrobe doors, bedsprings, bricks, lumps of plaster, carefully so as not to pull out a human arm instead of a chair-leg, so as not to cause sudden falls of debris, so as not to smother her.

The men's voices came nearer, nearer, shouting encouragement. Giving her hope. Flo shouted back at them to 'mind the blessed tablecloth'.

Cold light flooded in through a gap at the table's edge, and Dorrie saw her mother powdered grey as a statue, except where tears had washed white runnels down to her chin. Grey lashes beat at red-rimmed eyes, that changed from black to enamel blue as the pupils shrank to pin-pricks. Grey lips parted to a pink tongue. Grey fingers fastened tight around the grey table-leg. She saw the raw struts supporting the rough underside of the table-top and the mark-down price in chalk –19/6d – and a spider getting on with the job of building a web in the corner. She saw the bentwood chairback poking through the bricks and broken pieces of the ceiling rose. The gap widened and a man's face appeared.

Her father raised his voice. 'Dorrie! Ahoy there, sweetheart! Is there anyone on board?'

Her thumb plopped out of her mouth and she gave him her winning smile.

'*There* you are!' he said. 'Jelly or Christmas pudding? What's it to be?'

No contest. Jelly was wonderful and required her undivided attention, to suck it like a backwards kiss through her lips, to slide it, gloop, gloop, along her tongue, to roll it slippery against the roof of her mouth, to force it through her teeth, squish, into a delicious mess and finally to swallow it.

After dinner, when the washing up was done and Stephen was having a nap and everyone else had just closed their eyes for a minute, Dorrie sat up at the table, the wonderful table, the lifesaving table, and sorted out her new toy soldiers, little men in skirts and busbies, marching along in ranks with their bagpipes and drums.

'Oi, gel, what you doing of?'

Someone shouting at her mother. They'd given her soup and bread and hot, sweet tea for shock and wanted her to go to hospital until they were sure the baby was all right, but she wouldn't leave the site.

'You want blooming seeing to, a woman in your condition. This 'ere's a blooming death trap. One slip and you're a goner!'

Dorrie could see Flo teetering on the rubble that had been a house, her borrowed coat flapping in the bitter wind, weeping to see all the broken things, the mains pipe bubbling water, the back door banging skew-whiff against its frame and the kitchen sink sliced through. Nanna Hubbard had been roused from her bed at Aunt Polly's and was now hopping from one foot to the other on the icy pavement, as cold truth penetrated her morning-after headache. Neighbours were patting thin comfort into her shoulders. A cup of something hot steamed between her gloved hands.

'Bleeding Hitler,' and other words steamed between the sips.

'Just keeping an eye on things,' Flo told the man. 'Turn your back for a minute round here and they'll pick the place clean.'

Necks stiffened across the road, feet shuffled. She couldn't mean them. They turned up their coat collars against the cold.

'Don't you worry, gel, we won't let nothing go astray. We saved a bit, see – that sofa, that fender? That's all yours.'

Her lips were a grim line as she climbed down and looked in the sacks they'd already filled: books, photos, Dad's shirts, Nanna's woollies, pots and pans, her frocks.

Nanna Hubbard turned things over, too. 'You got the things out the wardrobe? The drawer at the bottom?' There was an edge to her voice, almost panic. 'There was some things wrapped up in a... Oh, me clock ... still ticking, Flo, still bloody ticking.' For a moment she was diverted,

81

and 'Oh, Flo, your dad's picture.' Then she saw what she'd been looking for – an orange headscarf knotted around small bulky shapes. As she snatched it to her skinny chest it rattled. Something in a tin – curlers or make-up or coins, maybe. 'S'pose my old joanna's a write-off, is it?' she asked her daughter as though she could bear the truth from her. 'And me wireless?'

'There were some apostle spoons,' said Flo to the salvage man.

'We'll find them, love. You go and 'ave a sit down in the warm.'

'I want to help.'

'Be a long job.'

'I've nothing else to do.'

He looked at her hard. 'Everyone *is* accounted for, are they? No one else in the 'ouse? Cats or dogs?'

She shook her head, quickly. 'No, no pets. And my husband's at sea.' She sniffed and pressed her lips together. He waited. She took a breath. 'Th- that crater, that's where the bomb landed, is it?'

He shut his eyes, jerked his chin up, meaning yes. 'You was lucky being in the back. You'd been in the front, you'da been coming down in chops and briskets, table or no table.'

Nanna Hubbard was telling people how lucky *she'd* been – Tuesday night being her whist night, she'd been round her sister's. If that bomb had fallen half an hour earlier, she wouldn't be here now to tell the tale. Poor Flo, though. When she thought how close she'd come to losing her and that dear little baby... She lowered her lip over the cup.

Her daughter ignored her. Swallowed. 'I was ... I was actually expecting someone. You couldn't, um ... where the front door was?'

Necks craned to see what the salvage men turned up. But as far as anyone could tell there'd been no callers when the bomb went off, though how could you be sure? The front door was halfway up the street, and the knocker had flown through the window across the road!

She found the cloth, scraped off the bread and jam, shook out the dust and took the rips and ruins and her mother round to Aunt Polly's. And eleven apostle spoons.

'What about '*im*, Flo?' The chink of a bottle on glass. Nanna Hubbard's gritty voice. 'Ain't still down there, is he?'

Flo sipped her tea before replying. 'No, he never turned up, Mum. I had the table laid, my best face on and he never showed.'

'Pity. Best thing all round if a bomb dropped on the bugger.'

'Ah, don't be like that. He's been good to us.'

'Good? I don't think so, Flo, and I don't think Arthur'll think so neither. All very nice, all them frillies and tins of ham but they was just on account of his guilty conscience.'

'He could have buggered off and left me to it.'

'Looks like he *has* now, don't it?'

'Oh, he'll turn up sooner or later. Bad pennies always do.'

Nanna Hubbard turned down her mouth and shrugged, unconvinced even about shibboleths. Looking for certainties she picked up her glass and drank deeply.

Mummy carefully unpicked the worst of the damage, slid the stitches onto a safety pin and, like a spider, filled in holes and tidied drawn and broken threads until her handiwork was whole once again.

There was something on the Christmas tree for everyone – hankies sewn with an M for Mick, C for Charlie and A for Arthur, knitted scarves for the two younger aunties, a tea-cosy for Aunt Polly, bed socks for Nanna, gloves for the two big girls, a balaclava for Peter. Mummy had made them all, knitting and stitching into the night, except for Dorrie's present, a little brown teddy bear, which came from a shop, and which Dorrie loved because it had been given with love. She whispered its name into its little brown ear.

The grown-ups were saying, 'Oh you shouldn't have,' and 'You have been busy, Flo,' and Dad was cross because he hadn't noticed there were presents on the tree and he hadn't put one on for her.

Don't be daft, she said, he'd given her enough. That new coat from Selfridges was the nicest she'd ever had. Bang up to date. The 'swagger' look. She had to go and put it on then, so that the uncles could whistle and the aunts could say how clever Dad was to choose the coat all by himself. Mummy smiled wanly. She and Dorrie knew that Dad hated shopping and had given her some money to go and buy it herself. Even so it had cost more than she told him and she'd had to take the difference out of her rainy day tin at the bottom of her wardrobe. But it fitted her perfectly and looked wonderful.

It wouldn't suit everyone, said short and dumpy Auntie Joan. She sipped her sherry thoughtfully. 'Tell you who would look nice in it,' as though she had only just thought of it and wasn't trying to steer the conversation at all, 'Mick's sister, Lucy. She's tall like you.'

'Oh, *wouldn't* she just,' gushed Auntie Liz, unmindful of the smile stiffening on her hostess's face. 'She could really make something of herself, could Lucy, if she wanted.'

'She could be in films.' Her daughter, Barbara, looked up from a card game, soggy with adulation. Dorrie guessed Lucy was a favourite topic in their family.

'She'd hate that,' said her sister Jean, her pubescent spots glowing in the heat of her conviction, and Peter, who was losing, used the diversion to swap a few cards around, change a few numbers on the scorecard. 'She's a country girl, only happy in the open air, making things grow, talking to the animals.'

'Well, that's her choice,' said Uncle Charlie, shuddering slightly at the awfulness of women. 'And it means she can keep an eye on Ma.'

'They both want watching if you ask me,' said Uncle Mick, taking three more bottles from the crate. 'Chip off the old block, our Luce. Poor old Joe's got his work cut out, if you ask me – a medium *and* a quack doctor.'

'And you wonder why he spends so much time away, poor sod?' Dad chuckled, draining his glass for the refill.

'Whoever would've thought Lucy would turn

out to be as daft as Ma?' Uncle Charlie shook his head sadly as he worked at his bottle top. There was a clatter as the wire clasp fell back, a fizz of bubbles. Peter almost dropped his winning hand. Nanna, nodding off at the table, reached for the comfort of her glass. Polly twitched in the armchair.

'Daft?' snorted Dad. 'That's not what I'd call it.'

'No,' said Auntie Liz, getting the wrong end of the stick, 'they ain't daft or wicked. Good luck to them, I say. If people are stupid enough to believe all that guff, that's their look out.'

'Arthur thinks they're a bad influence,' said Mummy, returning coatless from the bedroom across the passage. The draught flickered the candles on the tree, caught the paper chains, raised the hairs on Dorrie's neck.

Auntie Joan nodded. 'I know what you mean, Arthur. I don't know *what* got into my Peter that weekend he was up there. Wouldn't surprise me if there were bad spirits knocking about.'

'Dorrie, have you shown Peter the new tricycle that you got for Christmas?' Dad asked.

She pouted, feeling thoroughly miserable. Why didn't Dad like Grandma any more? Perhaps she should probe his mind but her head ached and she felt hot and cross. 'He says it's not new; it's old, off a bombsite and Dad fixed it and painted it blue round their house. He just put a new bell on it.'

'Little swine!'

'Oh Peter,' Auntie Joan reproached him, 'that's naughty, dear. It was a secret, I told you.'

Uncle Mick's face was red. 'Right!' he barked, lips flopping. Aunt Polly's eyes flew open. Nanna slopped her drink. 'You know what you're getting, my lad, a taste of Mister Stick!'

'Not at Christmas, Mick,' pleaded Auntie Joan.

'Flo, any more of those delicious mince-pies?' said Uncle Charlie. 'Light as a flipping feather. You must tell Liz your secret.'

Secrets. Some you tell and some you don't. Some concern flour and lard, some are about bikes, and some, never to be told, are about a man in a raincoat coming to tea when Dad was away in the war.

Soon Uncle Mick was strumming his banjo and Uncle Charlie and Dad were singing songs about cleaning windows, which made Peter roar with laughter and slap his scabby knees. The women made pussy faces and drowned their embarrassment in egg-flip and port-and-lemon. But they couldn't keep it up. Rosy-nosed and bleary-eyed, they surfaced, to warble their way around 'Mother Kelly's Doorstep' and 'The Ruins that Cromwell Knocked About a Bit', and after Aunt Polly's monologue about people with twisty mouths trying to blow out a candle, Dad did his party-piece and everyone joined in with the actions.

First they shaded their eyes as he sang, 'I saw the old homestead and faces I loved,' and made the shapes of houses with their hands, and hugged themselves tight. The next bit was about 'England's valleys and dells' which they drew in the air. Then they listened (hand over ear) to the 'sound of the old village bells', which was jumping up and down, pulling on a rope. When 'the fire was burning brightly' they all had to rub their hands in its warmth and 'banish all sin' which Dorrie didn't understand. It ended up with the bells 'ringing the Old Year out', and everyone pretending to have backache, and 'the New Year in,' which was about dancing.

And that, for some reason, made Mummy cry.

Chapter Five

Sunday was supposed to be a day of rest, wasn't it? But who for, Flo would like to know? For *whom?*

Not for women, that much was certain. Women didn't get a sit down all day, not even after the slog of Christmas. Come the very next Sunday after dinner, in every kitchen in the land there was a woman in a pinny, up to her armpits in Vim and grease while, in the front room, with the paper over his nose and the wireless tuned to *Down Your Way*, the Guv'nor was so stuffed with good old English beef he couldn't move, except to lift his behind to fart.

Flo, on her knees before the oven, gritted her teeth at the burnt-on black, and still it wouldn't shift, not even with wire-wool. Her fingers were soggy and ingrained, a nail broken to the quick. Last resort – a knife. But the ghastly scrape and squeak of steel and scouring powder shot through her teeth and dragged her nerves out by their roots.

Greasy brown scum spattered the wall over the sink as the heavy utensil flat-bladed into the washing-up water.

She knew she was working herself up. Banging doors and drawers, rattling tins, hurling saucepans into the cupboard so hard they slid straight onto the floor again, with a clattering and shattering of ear-drums, falling out as fast as she chucked them back in, so that she found herself kicking the door, and growling with a rage that rose like a warning siren into a scream.

A cry for help. To get him to notice. To get him off his backside and notice. Knowing that when he did, whatever he said, he couldn't make it any better.

Sleep gummed his eyes as he wrapped her in his big, clumsy arms, patting her, as though she were Dorrie, yawning, ''Ere, 'ere, we can't have this.' Shocked at the depth of her misery. 'Getting you down, innit, poor old girl, having her ill in bed. All these broken nights. She'll be all right, give her a few days. It's only tonsillitis, after all. Come on, come and have a sit down while she's asleep. The oven can wait. I'll put the kettle on, shall I? Make a pot of tea?'

She swallowed and shook her head, seeing the pointlessness of it all. Tea couldn't change anything, couldn't give her back her freedom. She didn't love him any more. Not properly. If ever she had. *Now* she knew. Now that a word, a touch, a look could make her go limp, she knew that Arthur had never made her heart beat faster, her pulses race, her knees go weak. She'd never lost her appetite over him or a minute's sleep.

She'd been seventeen when war broke out, and agog with the drama of it all – boys she'd known all her life becoming fighting men overnight, off to join this battalion, that unit, to give Jerry a bloody nose. There were parties and dances and last minute booze-ups to give the boys a good send-off.

It had been the uniform she'd fallen for. All the nice girls love a sailor, they ribbed her in the salon, and she was so nice she squeaked. Navy-blue made him seem even taller, set off his dark curls and made his brown eyes smoulder. He looked brave and Italian and romantic, like Rudolph Valentino they assured her as they patted their new perms. How deceptive looks can be.

He was to be posted overseas and everyone knew what sailors were ... nudge, nudge. She was jealous already of the dusky maidens on distant shores. So when he asked she accepted. And, without a moment's hesitation, would you believe, she was married. Oh joy! To a sailor! Mrs Arthur Potter. The new gold ring looked so right on her finger as she cut their hair, pinned their curls.

His long absences made her heart fonder. (*'You must be missing him, Flo. How long is it now?'*) Lonelier, anyway, with just her mother for company in the evenings, whiling away the war with knitting and seams. And on the few occasions he did get shore-leave, the poor man was so desperate it was hardly surprising he went at it hammer and tongs and left her feeling sore and ... used.

They were so new to it they were bound to make mistakes. And having Mum in the next room didn't help. You couldn't expect the soft words and caresses, what there were of them, to hit the right note when you knew her ear was glued to the wall.

And a weekend pass hardly gave you any time at all to, well, experiment. She couldn't help comparing him to...

Perhaps it would be better next time. Or the next.

And it was so romantic and sad waving him out of sight at the station. (She didn't go down to Dover.) People said they were the picture of wedded bliss, she and Arthur, and she believed them.

The war lumbered on – 1940, 1941 ... and she found that secretly, she was quite enjoying it. There were good times as well as bad and even the fear, the sorrow, the hardship were things you shared. You were never bored. People dropped in, neighbours and friends, and one in particular, to keep you company, take your mind off your troubles, take you dancing and have a laugh.

More and more she found parting from Arthur a relief rather than a sadness. She began to look forward to his leave ending, to having time to herself again, for the things she wanted to do, the people she wanted to see.

She even found herself praying for Arthur's ship to go down. 'Please, please, please, let him *die*,' she would whisper into her pillow.

'No, we won't do that,' said the gods, 'that's not in our brief. We'll send you a baby, instead. Lover-boy will vanish in a puff of fond regrets and you'll welcome Arthur home with a big, smoochy kiss.'

But the gods don't know everything.

Lover-boy hung around. So the gods sent a

bomb and dispatched him.

It could have been worse – just about: she could have lost the baby, too. Somehow she got over it and, come the end of the war, there was Arthur in his demob suit looking very different. Very ordinary really.

Everyone was saying that nothing could be as bad again and we must all pull together to make the best of it. She did, and eventually fell for a second child.

With motherhood and then the prefab to think about she was busy, busy, busy, setting up home, feathering her nest with the nice things she made. With her nice husband bringing in a regular wage these days, and nice kids, she reckoned she was as happy as she had any right to be.

But now that the dust was settling, now she had a moment to get her breath and take stock, she found that the picture of bliss wasn't hanging straight any more. Not quite. Strangely Arthur didn't seem to notice.

He did them proud, did Arthur: his job at Cunningham-Bayliss was rock steady and paid well. He was a bit too involved in the union for her liking, too much paperwork and too many meetings, but he was a good father and the kids adored him. Just that she didn't.

Little things irritated the hell out of her, like when he crunched a child's toy underfoot and blamed everyone else for leaving it around, like when he blew his nose and examined the contents of his hanky, like when he cut his toenails in the fireplace, like … like…

Like when he mended his bike on the kitchen table and wiped his greasy hands on the towel, like when he fixed a clock and had her running round looking for minute missing screws, like when he dunked a biscuit and slopped it down his newly knitted Fair Isle pullover.

And his collars and cuffs were always grubby, and no matter how she darned his socks there were always holes in the toes, and he had dandruff, and boils, and black grease in his nails.

And he whistled through his teeth to tell them he was home, setting her nerves on edge.

As for romance – it never crossed his mind. Nor surprise. Arthur was predictable. In bed and out.

But he meant well and was kindness itself.

She'd heard Dorrie's cry in the night, had got up to find Arthur already there beside the child, stroking the sweat-darkened curls. He'd cleaned up the sick and changed the sheets without bothering Flo, put her into clean pyjamas and, when she seemed to be sleeping peacefully, had been about to come back to bed when she'd held up her arms.

'Dad, Dad.'

He'd told Flo to go back to bed.

He was still there at six, asleep in the chair, as Flo crept in. Birds were stirring, cocks crowing and the bedclothes were kicked off onto the floor, the thin body rigid on the damp sheet, pyjamas all twisted. Flo began to straighten the bed.

'Mu-mmy!' The voice was dragged painfully over the gravel of her swollen throat. 'Shout, Mummy! Shout!' The small fists clenched, the head was thrown back but only croaked, 'Here! We're down here! In the back, under the table!'

Flo gasped. She knew! How did she know? They'd all agreed – *not yet*. It was too much for the child; it would bring on the nightmares again. She murmured helpless comfort as hot tears squeezed onto her daughter's cheeks.

'They can't find us, can't hear. The table's too heavy, too heavy.' Suddenly she reared up and pulled Flo to her. She whimpered, 'It's dark, Mummy. Don't like the dark. Take it away.'

'Ssshh, ssshh!' Who'd done this? Mum? Aunt Polly? She'd kill them. She rocked the child in her arms. 'There, there, it's all right. We're here, we're safe.'

Arthur was awake. His eyes found hers and he shook his head, mystified. He wasn't the one. He switched on the bedside lamp. Dorrie blinked and looked around.

'Where's,' she paused to swallow broken glass and her eyes were dull with pain, found a rasp of a voice, 'Where's Frank?' and her mother froze.

What, how, did Dorrie know about *that?*

'He's here, somewhere. Lost...' her voice sounding so unlike a child's. She was hallucinating, of course, but that name, that voice. She was beating blindly at the eiderdown. 'Where are you, Frank?' she sobbed.

Flo grasped the frail shoulders, trying to see beyond eyes that were focused in another time, another place. She wanted to shake her. How

95

did she know? *How?* She listened with double despair to her daughter reliving her own suffering.

'*You can't be. No-o-o! Don't be. Please, Fra-a-ank…*' she wailed and broke Flo's heart all over again.

She flicked a glance at her husband. What on earth was he making of all this?

Arthur's brow was furrowed as though he were trying to remember something important. He began scrabbling under the bed, under the chair, behind cushions, under the pillow. 'Where is the damn…?' and then gave a little crow of triumph, holding the brown teddy bear aloft. 'Found it!' he cried, and tucked the toy in beside his daughter. Who sighed, smiled and snuggled down.

Flo was open-mouthed. The teddy bear?

'Frank,' Arthur explained.

Still, it was weird she'd chosen to call it that. Her husband explained how it had come about.

Bedtime, Christmas Night. They'd been considering names. Why not Teddy? he'd suggested. Typical, thought Flo.

Why Teddy? Dorrie had wanted to know. She had a little more imagination.

He explained that Theodore Roosevelt had had bears named after him.

Weren't there any other Roosevelts?

Eleanor, he'd told her. She could have a little girl bear called Eleanor, or Nelly. Or there was Franklin D. Good name, Franklin.

Frank, she'd decided. Frankincense. That was a Christmas gift, too.

'She's a bright kid,' said Arthur.

'Too blooming bright,' said Flo.

She'd gone back to bed but hadn't been able to sleep, of course.

Perhaps Arthur's explanation covered it – the Franklin D. Roosevelt thing. But her face against the pillow twisted with doubt. Just who was kidding who?

It had to be more than coincidence. *He'd* bought that bear for Dorrie. Flo couldn't refuse when he'd begged her to put the parcel on the tree for the child, anonymously. But Dorrie couldn't have known.

Flo could hardly have failed to notice him. Head and shoulders above the press of women in the Lingerie department, in his white shirt and well-cut suit, she'd known him immediately, from two or three aisles away and had had to grab the counter to stop herself sliding to the floor. The rough edges were smooth, nipped with a gold tie-pin, tucked smartly into a top pocket with the right amount of hanky showing, but it was Frank all right. With all the old charm. The women behind the counter were falling over themselves to serve him. He was still as good-looking – more so, his light-brown hair, cut short and neat, subtly altering the planes of his face, from a boy's to a man's. Light-brown laughter crinkled light-brown eyes and made her heart flip. If you didn't know him you'd think 'class'. What was he doing, *alive*, in *Selfridges*?

And then, as though he'd somehow sensed her

there, he turned towards her.

Oh God, don't let him see me, she prayed, hiding her burning face in a rack of corsets. Not like this. No make-up, hair all anyhow, a ladder just starting in her stocking.

'Flo? My God, girl, you're a sight for sore eyes! How are you?'

What? What was the question? Oh God, how was she? Dizzy with his slow, brown voice, melting under his gaze.

'Fine,' she said.

And ... um, Arthur, wasn't it? How was Arthur? What was he up to these days? Still living in Walthamstow, were they? *He'd* moved to Ilford. Big four-bedroomed place near the park. Though why they needed *four* bedrooms... He'd come up to Town to get a present for the wife. Marion. He didn't think Flo knew her. Her dad was big in the import-export trade. Thurley's? She might have heard of them. He'd given Frank the leg-up he'd needed, out of the docks into the business world and doing nicely. So he'd had to marry the girl, hadn't he? To show his gratitude. A few years ago now. No kids, not yet. Thought he'd get her a nightie or something. Silly, he didn't even know what size she was. About Flo's height but smaller tits.

His cheek took her breath away. She straightened instinctively, pulling in slack muscles. Her hiccup was half-giggle, half-sob. He was a devil, standing there grinning at the blushing, fluttering fool he'd made of her, his long fingers flexing about an image of warm naked flesh, knowing that memory served them both right.

He had lovely teeth, Frank. A lovely smile, his eyes brimming with her. He still found her attractive, for heaven's sake! Six years, two babies, and the chemistry was still there.

Somehow she found herself round at the lingerie counter helping him sort through a pile of Utility nighties.

'This all you got?' he complained, holding out to the assistant a pink satin passion killer, identical to the one under Flo's pillow at home. 'I was looking for something with a bit more oomph. So I could make out the wife was Rita Hayworth. Or someone.' And the way he looked down at Flo sent her heart racing.

He blinked under her steady gaze and cleared his throat, drawing her eyes down to his mouth, his full lower lip, which he licked, nervously. 'Yeah, well ... perhaps I better get her something else. They do scarves, do they?'

His hand burned through her coat as they moved to the scarf counter. She heard his intake of breath.

'Oh sod it, girl, you've put me right off me stroke. What say we go and have a cup of tea?'

They were shown to a table for two beside a huge mirror. She didn't dare look at her reflection, at the red spots of guilt on her cheeks, the eyes bright with illicit happiness. As the waitress, in black and frilly white, brought them tea in a silver pot and a selection of fancy cakes on a stand, Flo tried to act as though she was an old hand at it. At whatever this was.

She told him about the bomb that had buried

her and groaning, he reached across for her hand. But she picked up her trembling cup, instead, steadying it with her lips. He hadn't been there. And she was a respectable woman with children, her hands red with drudgery.

He told her that the same air raid had put him in hospital for two months. He'd been on the bus, on his way to her. Got as far as Hoe Street and Stoffers Fish Shop. They'd all had to get off when the siren sounded and he'd spent the next fifteen, twenty minutes in the shelter at the corner of the High Street. They'd discussed the weather and cracked a few jokes, as you do, while the bombs boomed and jarred their bones. One landed so close the ground shook and the people on the bench opposite shimmered like a mirage; there was a shower of mortar and brick-dust and half a dozen spiders abseiled off.

When they got the All Clear they all trooped out to get back on the bus and found it with its nose stuffed down a crater in the middle of the road. And fish all over the shop from where Stoffers had taken a direct hit. Well, they were going mad, pocketing bloaters and crabs. He'd just picked her out a couple of nice plaice and some for his mum, and was looking round for a bit of newspaper to wrap them in when there was another explosion – delayed action or something – and he was out like a light. He'd woken up in hospital with a couple of busted ribs and a broken arm. He rolled up his shirt-sleeve to show her the livid scar that clung there like some vile parasitic insect.

'But I checked the hospitals,' she said, her eyes hovering over the horrible thing. She wanted to touch it. Kiss it better.

'Landed on me head, darlin'. Didn't know who the hell I was for a fortnight.'

She nodded but she didn't believe him for a minute. He could have broken his arm anywhere, at work on the docks or in a bar-room fight. As for the fishy story, it was just that. He was always making up stories. Ducking and diving was what Frank Leary was best at. Ten to one the reason he'd not come round on that dreadful night was because he'd been carrying on with one of his other girlfriends, probably this Marion. Lucky for him. Not that Flo cared one way or the other.

'Did the, um, did your baby survive?'

'Dorrie? Yes, she's doing well.'

'A little girl.' His eyes were soft.

'A fat lot you care!' She hadn't meant to say that. The bubble of bitterness burst and surprised them both. Her lip trembled. Now she was started she might as well get it off her chest. 'First chance you get you disappear without trace. I thought Jerry had got you.'

'Oh God...'

'Not a single word in over six years, Frank!'

'Six? Oh Flo, I'm sorry.' He pressed his fingers into his temples. 'You don't know,' he mumbled. He looked up. 'Honest, Flo, when I come out of hospital and saw the state of your house... Christ! I thought you were dead.'

'I suppose it didn't occur to you to ask.'

'I *did*. And they said you'd gone round Polly's

101

to live. It just seemed like... Flo, I thought, what if you had been ... dead? I'd have had to've got on without you then, wouldn't I? So it seemed like it was, well, fate – like it was a good time to call it off. I had no claim, nothing to offer you. You were married to a good man, having a kiddie. I just thought...' Then, more firmly, 'I thought you'd be better off without me.'

He was right, of course. She was. Much better.

When he'd gone she dragged herself to the coat department but her heart had gone out of it. She wanted to be home. To sit very still.

It was almost the first coat she saw. Far more stylish than was practical for bus rides in Walthamstow, costing far more than they could afford. Arthur would have a fit. Nevertheless she tried it on, and imagined *his* warmth cosying her round, his chin on her shoulder, laughing at her blushes in the mirror. She hugged the cloth to her and stroked its softness.

After that she seemed to be bumping into him all over the place – in the park with Stephen, walking down to the school to pick up Dorrie, waiting at the bus-stop. Just a chance meeting, a brief word. Very brief. She always cut him short, was always in a hurry. He mustn't get the idea ... it could easily get out of hand.

So easily.

She was married, she kept telling herself. So was he. *Happily* married. Well, anyway, there were the children to worry about.

A week before Christmas she was buying birdseed from a stall in the High Street, when she found him making faces at her from the other side of a birdcage.

'Who's a pretty boy then?'

She nearly died. She'd left Mum across the road, queuing for potatoes. Aunt Polly was in Woolworths, buying toys for the kids. Thank God. The last thing she needed was for those two to learn of the prodigal's return. They'd have it broadcast round Walthamstow in next to no time and Arthur would be bound to find out. Not that she'd done anything to be ashamed of, this time, but what he didn't know wouldn't hurt him.

Luckily the crowd, surging up and down the road like the Red Sea, had come to a push and shove standstill, with small children and Christmas trees being carried at shoulder-level to avoid the crush. Mum's growth was stunted – she wouldn't be able to see over the heads. But who was to say someone else hadn't spotted them and put two and two together? Everyone and her old man was out shopping – last chance before the kids packed up school. The vendors were shouting themselves stupid.

''Ere y'are, lady, 'ave a feel of me sprouts!'

'Get your bird here, gels! Fresh off the farm this morning!'

'Hot chestnuts, piping hot chestnuts!'

'Once in Royal David's City' started up down the street. The Sally Army were cashing in on the seasonal goodwill. The blind man with the violin – *War veteran. Wife and three children to feed* – didn't stand a chance.

Flo bit her lips to keep from laughing as Frank

ducked under the cage, a millet spray behind his ear.

Po-faced she paid the man and took her bag of seed.

'And this, and this,' And there was this crazy loon, pushing in front, buying the millet, and a mirror, a seed bell, a plastic budgie on a spring, a ladder...

'Frank, no, stop. That's enough, Frank!' Nevertheless she allowed him to poke the things into her shopping bag.

'What else? A bird-bath? Cuttlefish?'

'Frank! Stop it. Arthur'll think I've gone barmy. Frank, get lost!'

'Anything else for you, love?' said the man on the stall. There was a queue of curious, indulgently smiling people. She shook her head, still laughing. Looked for him and he'd gone.

She fussed around Stephen to hide her confusion, tucking the blanket more securely into the sides of the pram and discovering that his little glove had come off. She concentrated on the task, chattering baby nonsense, and noticed that his eyes were focused over her shoulder. Slowly she turned.

'I think he dropped this.'

'Oh.' His face was inches from hers, his mouth so close. He was holding out Stephen's dummy.

Down there, at baby level, she took it from him, and because she couldn't take her eyes from his, sucked it clean and found Stephen's mouth by touch. She saw Frank's nostrils flare. They stood up and her ears rang with silence.

Only gradually did it dawn on her that

Stephen was screaming blue murder and turning crimson with it.

'He's hungry,' she explained over the racket. 'It's past his dinnertime.'

'Mine and all,' said Frank. 'Fancy a plate of jellied eels?'

Jellied eels or stronger meat?

'Frank, I...'

'Oh my Gawd, he's got some lungs on him, ain't he?' Mum burst through the crush, all elbows and shopping bags and a determined gleam in her eye. 'What's up with my baby boy? 'Ere, look what Nanna's got for you...' By the time she'd rummaged in her bag and found the bottle, Frank had melted into the crowd.

The next day he came to the door.

'Frank! How did you find us? Oh God, you mustn't do this. Suppose Arthur had been at home.'

He'd brought mistletoe. He closed the door behind him and kissed her. That was the day he gave her the teddy bear for Dorrie. He'd also brought a rattle for Stephen which Arthur trod on when he came home. She wrapped the teddy up and put it on the tree.

Chapter Six

'Nice day for it,' said Dad, and Mum sniffed. It wasn't a nice day – it was raining. Drops sashayed across the windows and the drains snickered nastily. The Coronation was likely to be a washout, but that wasn't why she sniffed. She sniffed because she might have known he would say that.

'We're in the best place,' he went on, 'aren't we, Barney-boy?' offering his lips for a tiny kiss. The budgie ignored him and continued his perambulations along the narrow sill, stopping every now and again to tap-tap, like a blind man, at his green and yellow reflection and to murmur his sweet budgie nothings. He wasn't a talker, Barney, but he was the tamest and trickiest they'd ever had. He'd fly round the room and land on your shoulder, tweak your ear, crawl up the inside of your jumper and emerge under your chin. He'd pull at Dad's nose hairs and flutter out of harm's way when he sneezed. Dorrie had even got him to turn over a page while she was reading. You had to be careful, of course, to keep all the doors and windows shut, which wasn't always convenient in the summer. Today was okay. 'Foul outside and fowl out inside' as Dad joked. Repeatedly.

'Wouldn't like to be that lot standing in the Mall, getting soaked,' he said, for the second or third time, 'that lot' being Uncle Mick and Uncle Charlie and their combined families who had gone up on the special train that morning, loaded with flags and Thermos flasks and red, white and blue windmills and funny hats, streamers and cardboard periscopes, like the one Dorrie had made in school.

It had been a good one, almost as good as the red fold-up ones they were selling at the paper-shop. If she knelt on the floor with the top mirror to the window she could see the Town Hall clock. Back to front, of course, but since each of its four faces showed a different time anyway, each one wrong, what was the difference? Only now she couldn't because Stephen had taken it apart to see how it worked and had ruined it.

He took everything apart. Sometimes they went back together okay; sometimes they didn't, like her headless doll, and her snowless storm in a glass paperweight and her empty kaleido-scope. You didn't let Stephen get his hands on anything you valued. Mum hadn't been quick enough this morning when the wireless went wrong. Now it stood silent, waiting for Dad to take it to the menders. A new valve was all it needed, Stephen assured them. His eyes had sparked and fizzed when the television arrived, but Mum had said, 'Don't even think about it!' and had given him a clip round the ear to defuse his enthusiasm. He was only six, Stephen, but you could see the inventor he was going to be. Well, you could if you were Dorrie. As a matter of fact he would use the periscope idea in his best-selling solar-powered mole deterrent, which was why she hadn't actually throttled the little pest. Naturally, she didn't tell him he was going to be famous – she wouldn't dream of it. Somewhere, at the back of her brain, her great-grandmother's voice was saying, 'Keep Ireland green! Tell 'em nothing,' and she was learning, at last, to listen to it.

It had been a hard lesson. It was so tempting to give out warnings when you could see trouble looming. She told herself not to but they just slipped out:

'It's no use waiting for the bus: it's broken down at the depot.'

'Don't bother learning that: we won't get it in the test.'

'Don't explore that old house: the stairs'll give way and you'll break your leg.'

They weren't grateful. When things turned out the way she'd predicted they began looking at her sideways, edging away from her, muttering about spells. As though she'd *caused* it! Her friend, Fiona, had an older sister, Margaret, a plump and jolly fourteen-year-old. When she began buying Energen rolls and eating raw carrots Dorrie had a vision of a skeletal figure, scarcely recognisable as Margaret, lying helpless on a hospital bed. So she told Fiona what she'd seen. Fiona curled her lip in scorn. Curling her lip was her speciality. So Dorrie told Margaret, and Margaret laughed. Margaret could wiggle her ears. Six months later, her parents were warning her, doctors were warning her. She laughed at them. Two months later she was beyond laughter and ear-wiggling. Fiona dropped Dorrie. Somehow she thought that Dorrie had caused her sister's death, sown some sort of self-fulfilling seed in her mind. Dorrie was bad news.

When she found her circle of friends dwindling, when she'd had too many pinches and hair pullings and her glasses had been snapped, smashed, and twisted this way and that, when she'd had enough of sticking them together with Elastoplast, of being called names, of being shoved into puddles, down manholes, and into coal-cupboards, she decided that THAT WAS IT! They were on their own, these so-called 'friends' of hers. If she saw them walking into the path of a runaway train she wouldn't try and stop them.

Well, maybe she'd just tell Jenny about the swing in the park.

But when the chain broke and Jenny fell sideways and swung into the upright, banging her head as Dorrie had foreseen, she and her brother had tied Dorrie to the slide with her own skipping rope. And left her there. If that nice man hadn't come along and untied her she might have been there all night.

Dorrie's own future was a mystery but she guessed that if she could only hold her tongue she might, at least, stand a chance of having one.

The television meant that they would see the procession in comfort, *and* the service in the Abbey *and,* Dad said, they wouldn't get wet. Though what Dad didn't know was that the weather was going to improve before the Queen left for the Abbey. On the way back the golden coach would glitter in radiant sunshine.

Never mind. Dorrie had seen the entire thing, already, in glorious Technicolor, from the sprung comfort of her new divan bed. Second sight wasn't like going to the pictures, though – you couldn't determine what you were going to see in advance. Otherwise she wouldn't have needed to spend her pocket money, a whole shilling, on a seat in the Granada to see *Robin Hood* for a fifth time. Milly, Next-door-but-one, wouldn't have seen her in there and told Mum, and Dorrie wouldn't have got a hiding for telling her she'd spent the afternoon round Jenny's house. How was she to know Milly had taken a job as an usherette? That was another thing she hadn't predicted. Still, it was worth it. Richard Todd was lovely in Lincoln green and she now knew all the words to 'Whistle a Song'.

They were of an age, all the women in the prefabs. When they'd moved in they'd all had two children, one in nappies. That was how you'd qualified, Mum said, your kids and your points: so many for being bombed out, so many for overcrowding, a few more for no inside lavvy, or bathroom or hot water, or for having to share, like them, with Aunt Polly and Nanna Hubbard. It all totted up and got them rehoused.

As soon as Stephen and all the other 'bulge' babies started school, their mothers started thinking about getting jobs. Doll, Next-door, worked in her husband's butcher's shop, Barbs, Next-door-the-other-way was a typist at the

Town Hall over the road and, since Mum had gone back to hairdressing at Bettina's round the corner, three days a week, they'd had the new divan beds, a new magazine rack with balls for feet, like they'd had in the Festival of Britain, new coconut matting in the kitchen, a garden swing, a new lightweight mangle, a holiday booked for August in Weymouth and the television set, two and six a week from Radio Rentals.

Dad switched on and they waited for it to warm up. Richard Dimbleby was speaking, with a voice thick and sweet as condensed milk: *'In the streets of the capital, the crowds wait patiently with their banners and their flags. Some have been here all night, despite the rain, to greet their young monarch on her way to be crowned.'*

Dorrie had had to take the note round at school, being a prefect and having finished her morning's work.

The King died early this morning, it announced. Some teachers said, 'Oh dear. Righto, Dorothy, thanks,' and got on with their spelling test or their painting. Some rapped the desk with a ruler and called for silence so they could read out the message like Laurence Olivier doing that Shakespeare film. The class then had to stand up, in a racket of banging desklids and seats, hands together, eyes closed, as the teacher led them in prayer. Miss Hurst, 2D's teacher, burst into tears and most of her little dunces did the same, fisting their eyes and smearing their smelly faces with snot. Outside 4A, Richard

111

Brown, on his way to the headmaster for the cane, kicked Dorrie on the shin, pulled her hair, called her 'a four-eyed cow', just when things had seemed to be going better for her, so that was why she was sniffing a bit when she went in. Mr Fox, their teacher, used this as an excuse to put his arm round her. Yuk! His breath smelled of bad eggs and the other kids had made fun of her in the playground afterwards, and called her 'teacher's shag-bag'. And she *hadn't* been crying for the King. She'd got that over with months ago. Anyway when a king dies you're not supposed to cry. You're supposed to say 'The King is dead, long live the King,' or Queen in this case, and be glad that a new reign has begun.

And so she was. Fairly glad. She watched Elizabeth lift her heavy skirts over the threshold of the Abbey. She was young and slim and pretty, prettier than Dorrie would ever be. *She'd* never had to wear brown National Health glasses and a brace on her teeth. *She* didn't have crinkly hair that wouldn't perm, plait or stay in any sort of style whatsoever. *She* didn't have chalk-white skin and freckles on her nose, or stubby bitten fingers or flat feet that made it impossible to walk or run or jump with any sort of style or grace. (Though let the Queen try climbing trees or swimming against Dorrie Potter and she'd be left standing!)

Elizabeth was swept along on the people's adulation, even though she wasn't clever or brave. Dorrie was, and would never be adored, not by her peers. In fact they groaned when she scored top marks again, calling her 'cheat' and 'swot'. She couldn't help it. She just seemed to know what the teachers wanted. It had crossed her mind, during the eleven-plus, to give the wrong answers. But when it came to it, she couldn't. Couldn't think of a wrong answer that would look convincing.

A drawer contains forty separate socks, twenty blue socks and twenty yellow socks. How many socks would a blind man have to take out before he knew he had a pair?

What a daft question. He could still put on one of each while holding the matching one in his hand. Unless he had second sight.

How anyone ever failed she didn't know.

As the Queen turned from the altar, loaded with the trappings of monarchy, the orb and the sceptre, the crown and the ermine-trimmed robe, as paeans soared, rapturous, from choir to vaulted ceiling, as the organ thundered, as bells rang, as pictures flickered in the darkened front room and Dad and Mum and Aunt Polly and Nanna Hubbard and Stephen sat glowing in the reflected glory, Dorrie saw what age would do to an English rose, saw her colour fade, her skin wrinkle and sag, her mouth become thin and stitched with bitterness, saw her body thicken, her eyes grow dim, her hands stiffen and swell, her steps become slow. Saw the people turn from her in dismay. Knew that in the cruelty of time, her loyal subjects would look for someone younger and prettier to love.

Dorrie closed her eyes, hearing Dimbleby's cloying reverence, *'And now, Her Majesty, Queen*

113

Elizabeth II, returns through the main chancel, bearing the full weight of the Crown of England,' become a whistle of bite-clean air.

And now the cold makes Dorrie's face ache. She blinks at the dazzle, at the wink of sun on dark glasses. Smells the cold, the sweat of men, their hungry breath. Hears the creak of boots compacting snow, the rumble of voices, muffled in fur-trimmed hoods, quieter now after the victory, bent on descent.

'Dor? Dor? She all right, is she?' Nanna Hubbard was patting her hand. Dorrie was shivering. Her eyes brimmed and her nose had a drip on the end.

'Blimey, she's freezing!' said Dad. 'She's gone all goose-pimples. Quick, Flo, get a blanket to put round her. Polly, put the kettle on. No, it ain't a joke. Oh Dorrie, you can't be ill for the Coronation. You got a street party this afternoon.'

She wasn't ill – it was cold in the mountains. A cup of tea and she was as right as ninepence. And now she knew exactly what to wear for the fancy dress, later on.

They argued. It was silly. Why didn't she go as the Rose of England as they'd planned? And Stephen had his heart set on being Stanley Matthews, didn't he? He didn't want to wear all those hot clothes now the sun had come out. And Mum had gone to all that trouble of making Dorrie a lovely crêpe paper frock, all pink and frilly.

Dorrie didn't care. She and Stephen were a topical twosome. Trousers, windcheaters, mittens, scarves, bobble hats and satchels. She looped the washing line over her shoulder and made them both ice-axes out of cardboard. Then she squeezed her five-and-a-halves into David-next-door's size four football boots. Stephen got to wear his new ones, which was all he was worried about. They tucked their trousers into their socks, stuck a Union Jack on a pole, put on Mum's and Dad's sunglasses and went out to join the parade.

'What are you, dear?' asked the judge, Mr Blackledge from number 46.

'Edmund Hillary and Sherpa Tensing,' she said.

'Eh?'

'Who?'

'Never 'eard of 'em. Singers, are they?'

'Conquest of Everest!' a man shouted from the pavement. 'It's just been on the wireless.'

'Everest?'

'Highest mountain in the world, mate, and England've done it. John Hunt's lot. Ain't that something? Yeah, there's a Union Jack on top of old Everest now and them two, Edmund Hillary and Sherpa Tensing, put it there.'

'Fancy!' said Aunt Polly. '*I* never heard that. When did *she* hear that?'

'Search me,' said Dad, puzzled. 'Our wireless is on the blink.'

'Quick off the mark, your two,' said Mr Blackledge, all the same. 'I'm giving them the prize for topicality.'

Yessss! A postal order for seven and six. Brilliant! Three and nine each. She would buy that magazine with all the pictures of Richard Todd as Robin Hood and put the one she'd 'borrowed' from Jenny back in her desk. She had a bad conscience about that now they were friends again.

'That bloke,' said Nanna Hubbard, nudging Mum and squinting over the top of her glasses, when the applause died down. 'Isn't he...?'

'No,' said Mum.

'Funny, I could've sworn it was him.'

'*No,*' said Mum.

'Hmmm!' said Nanna, making a tight suspicious little mouth.

Dorrie knew who he was, the man who'd shouted, who'd made the difference, who had now disappeared. He was the man who had helped her that day in the park. She remembered what he'd said, now, after she'd thanked him for setting her free.

'It's *me* should be thanking *you.*'

'Why?'

'Don't often get the chance to rescue a damsel in distress.'

The rest of the afternoon was spent mostly eating. There were some running races in between, and a man who made swans and reindeer out of balloons, and a band marched through on its way to the Town Hall, and some Morris Dancers came and did 'Picking up Peascods' and there was a play about Saint George and the Dragon and another dance

116

which involved a lot of banging sticks and stamping.

At five o'clock the two children went in to watch *Muffin the Mule* while the men took the benches and tables back to the church hall. Muffin whispering in Annette Mills's ear was all a bit silly, but Dorrie thought Stephen would probably like the programme and she owed him a favour.

And then Dad burst in.

'Look who's here!' he cried. 'Flo! You'll never guess who's come to see us?'

Mum came bustling in from the kitchen.

'Good Lord!' she said, on seeing the hall bulky with people – three uncles at least, and an auntie Dorrie had never seen before. Down from Newcastle for the Coronation. Then that must be Uncle Jack, carrying the little girl, who was a bit big to be carried: three or four. Uncle Jack, though! There was something about this man that was important, that she should remember. He was taller than Dad and looser-boned, though the set of the eyes was pure Potter, and the broad forehead. But it wasn't likeness that made him seem utterly familiar; there was something *in* the eyes, an intensity when he looked at her – and the muscles of the mouth, bunching into that thoughtful pout, the slow release into a smile.

'Dorrie, hello. I've heard a lot about you.'

Who from? Who'd been talking to him about her? Not Mum. Not Dad.

'This is Vivien. Just seen the Queen, haven't we, Viv?'

117

The little girl's mouth hung open and her eyes hung open, too; her blonde head twisted awkwardly on a thin white neck and she looked up at her dad without focusing. Now Dorrie noticed her hands, curled softly into dead baby-bird claws. Long-nailed long fingers that didn't move or twitch and long, wasted legs dangling uselessly. There was something wrong with her.

'Dorrie, Cousin Dorrie, hello from Viv.'

A strange squeaky little voice. A voice that had never spoken except mind to mind.

Dorrie's heart leapt. Another. Like her. She smiled with lips that wanted to cry. 'Hello, Viv,' she said.

'Dorrie-cousin, you're the first child I've conversed with in this world. Hello, Dorrie. Friend and play? Other side are spirit and they don't want to be children and play. They outgrow me. Robbie is nice and tries to play but he only knows cricket and even in spirit I cannot bowl over straight.'

'What would you like to play, Viv?'

'Game for you to guess a word.'

And while her dad was telling them about the awful journey from Liverpool Street, Dorrie played a surreal sort of game with her little cousin, a sort of shared dream. Viv was picturing something in her head, a tin of soup, an *empty* tin of soup. Then a comb was standing in it, a comb with few teeth missing and blonde hairs attached. Now there was Dorrie at the optician's, staring at the letters on the card with her lazy eye. 'What letter is the clearest for you to see, Dorrie?' The O, of course. Down it bounced like a ball, and bumped into the tin with the

118

comb inside. That was it – now Dorrie had to guess. Comb in a tin, plus O? Got it – combination! *'Yes, oh yes, Dorrie-cousin. Your turn.'*

Stephen was staring at his poor, drooling cousin, his head on one side as he would consider a broken clock. He didn't know that her brain was ticking away inside the shell, sixty seconds to the minute. Spit-spot accurate.

Uncle Jack was shaking his head. Standing room only, he was saying. Bloody rugby scrum – and that was just Mick's place when they got back! They'd dropped the others off and thought they'd look in on Arthur and Flo while the women rustled up some food. My God it must be... Far too long. They were staying at Mick's tonight and popping in on Ma and Lucy on the way home tomorrow. That was the beauty of a car. You could go where you liked, when you liked.

It wasn't new, of course, he assured them. Who could afford a new one? But it did them all right – got them from A to B – and had come 300 miles without a hiccup.

Apart from the windscreen wipers, his wife, Susan, told them, laughing. They'd fought long and hard against the rain all the way down and then this morning, on a simple trip to the railway station, they'd started on each other. The wipers, that was. Both knocked flat in the first round. It had better not rain any more. She had a lovely lilt to her voice, Auntie Susan, as though she were asking questions all the time. She took Viv from Uncle Jack while they all trooped out to admire the gawky little Ford Ten waiting self-consciously for their admiration. Shiny black with red leather seats, it smelled gorgeous. Petrol and polish.

'Fancy a spin?' asked Uncle Jack, brushing Next-door's cat off the bonnet. Stephen didn't need asking twice. He was in the front seat, opening flaps and flicking switches, while Mum was still umm-ing and ah-ing. In the end she said she'd be more use putting the kettle on – she was sure Mick and Charlie were gasping and the two old ladies never said no to a cuppa. Dad said, 'Right you are,' and hoicked Stephen onto his lap. He cracked his usual joke – how he liked any colour car so long as it was black – and started fiddling with the wiper switch.

'What about you, Dorrie? Want a ride round the block?' So she slid into the back seat, while Uncle Jack cranked the engine. It started cough-cough-coughing and he got in and they were off.

'Through a glass darkly,' he murmured, regarding her in his driving mirror. Smiling as though they shared a secret.

Now she was remembering. Seeing him in another mirror. One that had straddled a mantelpiece. He'd been doing something to his face and had caught her eye. There'd been no friendly smile then. Fear, rather. *He* had been afraid of *her*. When was that? What was that? A dream?

'Don't look so worried, Dorrie,' he said. 'It'll come to you.'

She gasped. It was as though he'd read her

thoughts. But Dad turned to reassure her with a smile over his shoulder. It was only his brother's gentle 'penny for them' dig at her deep frown. Signifying nothing.

Uncle Jack turned his attention to his other passenger. 'And how about you, young Stephen? Want to drive? Does a fish swim?' He drew to a halt, leaving the engine running, lifted her brother onto his lap and allowed him to steer the car neatly round the corner, up the avenue, along the main road and down to the prefab again.

'Wow!' breathed Stephen, his eyes big. 'Oh ... wow!'

Dad laughed. 'Runs like a dream, mate.' Dorrie knew, with sudden insight, that they were strangers, these two, one the oldest, one the youngest of six brothers. There was a gulf, of more than years, between them.

Uncle Mick and Uncle Charlie were sitting at the table waiting for the News.

Barney began screeching. The opening music seemed to set him off. *The Billy Cotton Band Show* had the other tune that jarred his tiny nerves. Every Sunday you'd hear the 'Wakey, wa-a-a-key!' yell from the wireless, and click! as Mum hit the OFF switch, forestalling the budgie protest. She didn't know which was the worse racket, him or Billy Cotton, though the bird clearly had good taste, she said. Dad liked Billy Cotton and would switch him back on after a few minutes, quietly, if Mum was still busy in the kitchen. She would sigh and tut and roll her eyes. Dad, presumably, had *no* taste.

121

They couldn't switch the *News* off – it was IMPORTANT. Besides, it would take forever to warm the set up again, so Mum slung the cover over the birdcage.

'Poor little cock,' said Dad. 'Too early for beddy-byes, innit, mate?' As soon as the music stopped he whipped off the cover and brought Barney out into the room and Mum had to rush around shutting the doors and windows in case the bird escaped. Vivien's mouth was an O of wonder as Dad transferred Barney to her finger and it began pulling at her thin curls. He looked around for approval but he wasn't the centre of attention.

'This all they got? Just the carnation again?' grumbled Nanna Hubbard. 'I want to see about them putting the flag on that mountain like Dorrie said.'

'Coronation, Mum,' said her daughter, amused.

'That's what I said, carnation. We seen it once. We don't wanna keep on seeing it. Where's that Sherbert Tensing and that other one? That Hillary Edmunds?'

They had a long wait. Barney fluttered from head to head as the Queen was crowned again, as she rode again in her golden coach...

'That's us!' said Uncle Charlie. 'On that corner – see, that's where we was! Behind that horse's bum... See, there's Jack holding Viv up to see. There's me. There's the girls, Babs and Jean. And look, there's old Peter right up the front – trust him.'

But his finger stabbed at blurred faces – apart, that is, from Peter's. Taller now, Dorrie's horrible cousin had evidently spotted the camera over the heads of his female relations and was grinning and waving madly, thumbs up to all his mates – and other, more offensive, gestures.

Uncle Mick muttered something about disrespectful little swine.

'Get a good view, did you?' Aunt Polly was wistful.

'Smashing,' said Uncle Charlie. 'All the bands come right by us...'

'And the Queen? What was she like?'

'Pretty as a picture. A real treat. Give us a wave, didn't she, Mick? And all the rest – all the royals. Oh, it was well worth it.'

'A day to remember,' agreed Mick, still smouldering.

It was a fitting end to a triumphant day – the conquest of Everest on 29 May, 1953, such a hot item they could only produce pictures of John Hunt and Edmund Hillary and a photo of the Himalayas from the BBC archives, none of Sherpa Tensing.

'What was he, one of these bearer-wallahs?' asked Uncle Mick.

'A guide,' said Dorrie.

'Oh, a *guide*,' said Uncle Mick heavily, sarcastically. 'So how come you know so much about this then, Dorrie? Been doing it at school, have you?'

There was a frowning silence. Even Barney stopped wittering to help Dorrie beat off Uncle Mick.

'The wireless,' Aunt Polly began.

'No,' said Nanna, with her mind on liquid refreshment, 'their wireless is busted, innit?'

'Saw it in the paper, didn't you, Dorrie?'

It was nice of Uncle Jack but even Dorrie knew it hadn't been in the *Daily Mirror*.

'Weren't you telling me? Your Dad sent you over to the paper-shop this morning, to get the special Coronation issue? You had to queue in the rain, you said.'

Nor was he fazed by her blank expression.

'Yes, that's right, you said that while you were waiting you saw it in somebody's *Times* – that article by James Morris. What a scoop for the guy, eh, being at Camp IV when the party came down?'

She smiled and nodded.

How did he know she'd been over to get the paper? She hadn't seen it in any *Times,* of course. Dorrie had had prescience of the event, and somehow, he knew it. He was lying to protect her. He must know she was psychic. *He* must be psychic.

'Daddy and Mammy speak telepathy. I read them, and they read me,' Viv piped up.

'Well, that's a stroke of luck,' Dorrie told her.

'Not any luck, Dorrie-cousin. It was planned that way, from my birth. They were prepared. I am ordained to be good at psychic and no distractions. Daddy told me. He told me, too, that you also are ordained, but with *distractions. It will be harder for you.'*

'Joan'll have a spread waiting for us, if I know my Joan,' said Uncle Mick, pushing back his chair – the signal for everyone to say their goodbyes and to promise not to leave it so long next time, as they always did.

How had Uncle Jack known about her? She was so careful these days. Had Grandma told him, or Auntie Lucy? She couldn't ask him, in front of everybody. Perhaps just this once.

She reached out to his mind. And he blinked.

It was like a mirror – he was looking at her looking at him. She was much younger, five or six, a cross-eyed kid with her thumb in her mouth, yellow cobwebby hair before it started looking like a gorse-bush. He was younger, too, shaving for the first time. Somehow she had bridged the years to appear in his mirror and frighten the shit out of him!

She jumped. He'd spoken, surely? Their eyes met. He smiled and apologised for his language. Without opening his mouth.

So now she knew. They were a tribe, the psychic Potters. Dorrie, Viv, Jack, Lucy, Nora. Even Susan had a smattering. So she wasn't alone, he assured her. If she needed help, ever, she just had to whistle.

'You'd think they'd have said, on the telly, about the mountain,' Nanna was saying.

''Spect they was told to save it till after she'd been done.'

'S'right. Didn't want to steal her thunder, Poll, not on her big day.'

'Bet they got their knuckles rapped, on the wireless. 'Cause that bloke said he heard it, didn't he?'

'Oh?' said Uncle Jack, the last to shuffle through the door into the hallway. 'What bloke was that?'

125

'At the fancy dress. I know 'im from some-where, just can't think...'

Uncle Jack looked at her hard and Aunt Polly blinked, just missing a small, unforeseen flutter of yellow and green through the open front door and up, up into a welcoming sky.

That was the day Dorrie began to realise that her father had feet of clay.

Chapter Seven

Dorrie did her best not to pry into her parents' private thoughts, having learned, long ago, that trying to remember what she'd been told, what she'd overheard and what she'd read in their minds was a juggling act that she wasn't particularly good at.

'*Please* let's go and see Grandma,' she nagged Flo one day. 'I haven't seen her for years and years! And you *said* we could go up and see her when the summer holidays came round.'

'Dorrie!' Flo's glare told her immediately that she hadn't and, even if she had, Dorrie shouldn't have said anything, not in her father's hearing.

'Oh, *I* see.' The words were larded with sarcasm, and Mum closed her eyes in despair. 'And just when were you planning to inform *me* about all this?'

'I wasn't going to, Arthur – I mean, I never said anything of the sort. It may have crossed my mind but–'

'We agreed, Flo. You know how I feel – she's a bad influence.'

'But it's been so long. She is their grandmother, and they're that much older.'

His eyes narrowed. 'It's enough they have to put up with your mother – falling down drunk in the street.'

'She wasn't drunk. She's not well.'

'She was paralytic! And not for the first time.'

'She's prone to dizzy spells.'

'She's prone to gin!'

'Arthur!'

That was before Nanna took to her bed. Doctor's orders.

Or, over tea, Dad might put down his knife and fork, deliberately, to create a dramatic beat. Then:

'*More* money? Blimey, Flo, I gave you four quid at the beginning of the week. What've you done with it?'

'What do you mean, what have I done with it? The usual things – food, rent, the electric. We have to live. It's just gone.'

'*Just gone?* You should be able to account for every penny. Write it down.'

'I don't need to write it down – I can remember. I haven't frittered it away if that's what you think.'

'Write it down, Flo,' the master of the house repeated, heavily, 'then you'll know for sure. Here...' he ripped a sheet off the pad on the wall.

'What, now? I'm having my tea, Arthur.'

'Now.' He wasn't often so insistent. 'I want to know where my money's gone.'

'Things are expensive – you don't realise.' She was earnest and worried. As though she'd done something wrong.

'Show me then.'

There was a long list of bills – the grocer's, the

butcher's, the baker's and the milkman's. The insurance man, two bob a month. Coal, bought cheap in the summer months and counted, by the sackful, into the shed. The television rental. The shoemender.

'How much? Half a nicker to sole and heel four pairs of shoes? Daylight robbery! I've told you before – a simple job like that, I'll do it.'

'But you don't, you're always too busy with union business.'

'I'll do it if you remind me.'

'Remind you? I'm always reminding you.'

'You're always nagging. Come on, come on, you've got thirty bob to account for. Where's that gone?'

Four cod cutlets, greengrocer's, bus fares, newspapers, a pair of stockings, two and eleven, a couple of remnants off a stall in the High Street to let into Dorrie's last year's summer dresses, so they could do another turn, four bob. A reel of cotton, sixpence. A card and a florin for Stephen to take to Eddie Flynn's birthday party. New socks.

'New socks?'

'His old ones were more darn than sock.'

He clicked his tongue. 'So, is that it? That's all the shopping for the week?'

'Yes.'

'And now you want some more?'

'Dorrie still needs some things for starting her new school – a swimsuit and plimsolls and a couple more blouses.'

'And what's that gonna set me back?'

'Three pounds, four to be on the safe side.'

'Four quid!' he bellowed. 'What are they, flipping fur-lined! Oh no – me name's Billy, not Silly. Anyhow, I thought we said all her school stuff was coming out of *your* earnings. You must have a fair bit stashed away by now.'

Which was when Dorrie shook her head so firmly that they both stared at her in horrible fascination.

'What!' said her father, his mouth agape, his ragged teeth laced with bits of sausage. He rounded on his wife. 'You ain't got *nothing* left? I was counting on that for the holiday.'

''Course I have,' her mother lied, frightened now. 'Dorrie, keep your nose out.'

'Mum, you said, in the shop...' she began. Whoops. As Flo's eyelids beat rapidly, trying to recall exactly what she *had* said in the schools' outfitters, Dorrie had an awful feeling that it had only been a mother's anxiety that had fed into her brain, her worry that the money was all gone. Of course, she wouldn't have said it. She wouldn't have told an eleven-year-old girl all that about the secret Post Office account where her hair-dressing tips were drops in a 'rainy day' bucket. Her running away money.

'You gonna have enough or what?' he demanded now, his eyes dark with premonition.

'It's not a bottomless purse, Arthur. It was all perms and colourings last week. They take ages and the customers only tip the same. And she takes the lion's share, old Betsy.'

'Have you got enough?' he flashed and his hands worked themselves into fists beside his plate.

'I wouldn't have asked if I'd had enough,' she said, trying to be reasonable. 'Can't you just let me have thirty bob?'

The trouble with living in a house made of asbestos was that the walls were whisper-thin and, though she and Stephen were sent to their room, out of harm's way, the harsh sounds of un-contained emotion ripped through them. And hurt. The sniping hurt, the raking up of old resentments, the rubbing of noses in home truths that no one should hear, least of all the children. Hurt. And the tears.

When the back door slammed, when the front gate clattered, when the last angry footstep died away the street, you crept out to see. Sometimes it was Mum in the kitchen, pale and trembling, with a wild lost look in her eyes. Sometimes it was Dad. And that was worse.

After about an hour, the gate would click properly shut, and the exile would be back, treading softly. Not that they could unsay anything, but life had to be returned to normal, as nearly as possible. There was simply no alternative. If Mum had been round to Aunt Polly's she'd have had a cuppa or maybe a nip of something stronger, and a cry on a shoulder or two and have sorted out on which side her bread was buttered. If Dad had called in on one of his brothers, or the pub, he'd have defended the ref's decision on Saturday and argued about the foul that wasn't; he'd have urged everyone to stop carping about pay and conditions and to join the bloody union; he'd have raged about 'that madman McArthy' and his paranoid hounding of thinking men, and have alerted them all to the coming crisis in the Middle East, but he wouldn't have breathed a word about the row. And have people think he was soft? Good God! So he'd be just as churned up inside at the end of his visit as at the start, and his upper lip would be ever so stiff.

In March 1956, when Dorrie had just turned fourteen, she finally put aside her art homework – a pencil drawing of a daffodil in a jam-jar, pleased with the flower's delicacy and the jam-jar's highlights, and turned with some reluctance to algebra. She could see the answers right away but her period pain was fuzzing the formula. If you didn't show the right working out you lost marks. As a last resort she turned to her father for help. An engineer should know something about third-year algebra.

'Not now, Dorrie.' He was working at some papers in his armchair, scratching his head bald with anxious fingers.

'It won't take long.'

'For God's sake, girl, I've got my own figures to work out. They're a bit more bloody important than your piddling homework.'

Tears stung her eyes. 'Charming!' she muttered. And because she hurt, she probed his mind. And found that Cunningham-Bayliss were making changes on the shopfloor, introducing a wonderful new toolmaking machine that would do the work of four men and save the company thousands of pounds. Unfortunately

those four men were now surplus to require-
ments and one of them – last in, first out – was
Cousin Peter. Dad had pulled strings to get him
on the payroll and took it personally that the boy
was being treated so badly. In his capacity as
shop steward, he had called an emergency union
meeting for the morning. The 'brothers' would
be behind him. Unless the men were reinstated
they'd all be out by dinnertime, apart, that is,
from the usual bloody wimps and scabs.

'You're wasting your time,' Dorrie told him.

Not that she was lacking in sympathy. It was
true there was no love lost between Dorrie and
her cousin, but Dad said he was a grafter and
had the makings of a decent tool-cutter. She
wouldn't wish him ill, even if he did wear stupid
Teddy Boy drapes and crêpes and had a mouth
like a sewer. Apprenticeships were hard to come
by. But she could see, with the benefit of
foresight, that no matter how many strikes there
were, technology would continue to take over
the work of craftsmen, until the only manpower
at Cunningham-Bayliss would be a few key
workers on a central control panel. But if she'd
said that, Dad wouldn't have believed her.
There'd be a revolution before the 'toiling
masses' let it get so far, and how had she known
what he was thinking anyway?

So 'You're wasting your time,' was all she said.
Maybe it *was* ill-judged, that curl of the lip and
that toss of the head; maybe the long-suffering
sigh *was* disrespectful...

His eyes narrowed and his thoughts were
jumping. He said, 'Cheeky little cow. I've a good

mind to–' And then he did. Hard.

Her face stung and her teeth ached and her heart was broken. A scrunch broke the shocked silence as though someone had stepped on a boiled sweet. Only it wasn't a boiled sweet – it was her glasses that had been knocked off by the blow. Her mother peered round the kitchen door, took in the situation at a glance, and Dorrie fled the room as they squared up for another shouting match. Poor Stephen, sitting cross-legged in front of the television, was forced to turn up the volume.

She sobbed, she fumed, she stared at the window and cracked it.

Stared at the picture of the crinoline lady, a clever crafting of embroidery and quilting, and it slipped its string and smashed onto the floor. She stared at the books on her shelf and they flew out like bats from rafters, butting blindly into the wall. Stared at Stephen's puzzle on its tray and a thousand cardboard pieces jumped about like popcorn in a pan. Stared at the cupboard and the door fell off its hinges.

'Dorrie – for God's sake!' Her mother came upon her picking up books. 'Look, look what you've done!' She gazed round the room in disbelief. 'Look at my picture! No – don't touch it,' pushing her away from the wreckage, the long splinters of glass, 'you'll cut yourself.' She tutted as she picked out the needlework with her fingertips and shook it, tinkling, over the waste-basket. 'And that window's going to cost a fortune. Well, it'll have to come out of your savings, that's all. Whatever got into you?

Showing off, that's what. God, do we have to have this every month? We all have periods, love. You just have to cope with them.'

All night she lay awake, going over and over it. He had hit her. Unbelievably. Her wonderful dad, who'd been her sanctuary, wasn't man enough for her now.

He was sorry, she'd known that, read it in his eyes, before the slap came, as he snatched his hand back, too late. Too late. The mask had slipped and what was he?

And what was *she?*

She stared dry-eyed into the blackness of night, hearing remembered sounds of destruction. Mum thought she'd gone round smashing things in temper but it was mind-power, not muscle-power. She was a freak, another species, and that was too terrifying for tears.

Next morning, everyone was pale and prickly, huddled over their grief, protecting their own soft underbelly, and it was all her fault. At breakfast, the radio doctor was burbling on about 'growing pains', in his reassuring, warm porridge voice. He had no idea. No idea. Offered no cure for the ache in your throat that had no name, that couldn't be put into words.

She dressed for school, squeezed a pimple in the dressing-table mirror and met Uncle Jack's anxious eyes, peering over his toast into the gloom of her bedroom! Behind him, Susan was spooning groats into Viv's gaping mouth and massaging her throat to make her swallow.

Dorrie's protestations were met with – sorry, he had a mouthful of toast, which he swallowed and choked on and had to wash down with tea, and then – sorry, he was just the messenger-boy and it would be all right, he was sure. She ought to go. There were some things only she could deal with and – sorry, he had to dash – football practice before school. Viv sent her best and Susan suggested Germolene. For the spot.

'By the way, Uncle Jack, while you're here, you don't happen to know anything about simultaneous equations, do you?'

But he'd gone and it was her own reflection that was frowning at her.

Gosh. Her heart was going like the clappers. She put up hands to cool her cheeks, then rubbed at the breathy mist forming on the glass. She hadn't dreamt it, had she? She really had to do this?

Her mother's voice. 'Dorrie, you're going to be late!'

Suddenly decisive, she stuffed some sanitary towels and spare knickers into her satchel, grabbed an orange, a packet of biscuits and a strip of Aspro while her mother's back was turned, and set off for the station, cashing in her savings stamps at the Post Office on the way.

One pound seventeen and six might have paid for a new window but it only took you as far as Ipswich on the railway, half-fare. A shilling, a couple of sixpences, a threepenny bit, a few coppers and a farthing, chinked pathetically in her purse as she wandered up the platform. She always kept a farthing in her purse, for luck or something.

She needed a penny. Her insides dragged as if

they were falling out; she was tired, sick of Marie biscuits and thoroughly miserable. She sat in the Ladies for a long time, waiting for a miracle, but none happened. Nor inspiration neither. She drank deeply from the water fountain to help her Aspro go down and, since there was nothing else to do, trudged out of the city, buying a threepenny Mars bar from a sweet-shop on the way, to cheer herself up. Why on earth the Other Side had chosen her for this venture, heaven and maybe Uncle Jack, knew. She followed the signs to the edge of town, where she could see the A12 threading north through open country, beaded with hamlets, towards Doddingworth. She had thirty miles to go.

A light shower turned into a squally one. And no doorways to shelter in. She'd forgotten how uncomfortable the countryside could be. How exposed. How long between shops. For once she was grateful for her gabardine and its button-on hood and she had to admit that the sensible, size-too-big brown lace-ups her mother had insisted on buying when she started at the High School, kept her feet dry enough. Though by Woodbridge she was sure she had a blister. She sat down on a rickety bench by a telephone box and thought perhaps she would phone someone to let them know she was coming. Perhaps they would come and fetch her.

Rain tracked down her legs into her socks as she remembered that Grandma wasn't on the phone – she didn't hold with them. So how had

Uncle Jack let them know, last year, that he and Susan were paying Grandma a visit?

Lucy was on the phone! Dorrie could ask Directory Enquiries for the number. No, she couldn't. She had no idea of Lucy's married name. They hadn't even gone to the wedding.

The shop in the village where Grandma lived – they had a phone. What was it called, that shop? She could see it in her mind, she could even see the woman who owned the shop, Hettie, a smoke-dried husk of a woman, but she couldn't see the name over the shop, try as she might. Hardly surprising: it had been a long time ago, seven or eight years, more than half her lifetime. Oh, why could she never do this second-sight thing to order? It wasn't fair. Perhaps if she kept on walking it would come to her.

An hour later, two plodding miles on, her crotch was chafed and sore where the Dr White's was rubbing. It had stopped raining, though clouds rolled about the sky, uncertain what to do, and her coat flapped in the wind. She went behind a hedge to sort herself out, rinsed her hands in the wet grass and sat on a stile to eat her orange. She'd never get there before dark. It must be about three o'clock already. The kids would be coming out of school soon, and Mum would start to worry when she didn't appear for her tea. She'd search the back bedroom and find the note. Then what? Dad would be sorry. Would he call out the police? It was a bit of a blur, that bit.

Never mind, she'd remembered the name – Fitzell's – but now there was no phone box. Just repeated patterns of cows and sheep on a green backdrop, with the occasional field of early crops: wheat, rippling and changing in the strange light like shot silk, or young cabbages or beans.

At the next village, then – Ufford – she'd phone Fitzell's. If she had enough money. Perhaps they'd let her reverse the charges if she said it was an emergency. Another half-mile or so. She could see the church spire poking up through a fuzz of trees.

A car pulled up just ahead. A man leaned across the passenger seat and opened the door.

Was this all part of some Grand Scheme? Were her guardian angels aware that this was happening? He called to her, as she'd known he would, and she moved towards him, propelled by inevitability, as though she were acting out a forgotten dream. Half a dozen voices yammered in her head, 'Run away!' But she didn't want to appear rude.

He didn't look like the nasty old man her mother had warned her about. He wasn't really what you'd call old, at all. Probably the same age as her parents. Nor was his wickedness etched on his face, like a Walt Disney witch. In fact, if he'd been offering her a rosy red apple rather than a lift she'd have taken it. Her mind-probe bounced away like spit off an iron, but it wouldn't have told her much, in any case, not if he was deceiving himself. Her friend Jenny, whose brother knew all about it, told her that sex-maniacs had the best of intentions until a person was in their power.

Nor was there anything in his voice to make you think that he wasn't on his way to Sowness, as he said, and that he wouldn't be happy to drop her off along the way. His concern was take-it-or-leave-it, matter-of-fact. Her tired and aching body cried, Oh yes, please yes.

No, she heard herself saying, firmly. Thank you. Right, he said, he quite understood. You had to be careful of strangers. Just that it was such filthy weather and she'd looked such a drowned little rat, such a long way from home, he'd felt he had to ask. He shut the door and the car pulled away. Damn.

Ufford seemed to consist of three ancient cottages and no telephone kiosk. An old woman, planting a row of seeds in her front garden, informed Dorrie that there was one, in the village proper, a mile down the lane, past the bridge, though it had been out of order when she'd tried to phone her son in Chelmsford at Christmas time. Or... She called her back. Or she thought they might have a phone in the transport caff, just along the road. It was worth a try.

Smoke billowed around her, trapped by the closing door. Ancient ghosts of fried eggs and bacon-fat, woodsmoke and roll-ups, formed swirling layers under the ceiling, thick enough to slice. Lorry-drivers crouched under the cloud, furiously refuelling with greasy food. Dorrie's stomach turned. If she had been hungry when she walked in she wasn't any more.

She went to the counter and asked to use the

phone. Without looking up from the bed of thick white cups that she was hosing down with tea, the fat woman sniffed, 'Customers only.'

'Sorry?'

She raised her chins and the tea-pot, though not her eyes, and repeated: 'Paying customers only.'

A spidery man, with tattooed arms, stopped licking his pencil over the day's runners at Kempton to translate.

'You have to buy something, love – beans on toast or something. Then she'll let you use the phone.'

'What about a cup of tea? Would that do?'

'Three ha-pence,' said the woman, wiping a drip off her nose and down the front of a once-flowery apron. Dorrie took that as a yes and rummaged through her satchel for her purse. Handed over the money.

'Sugar's on the table.'

She walked with the brimming cup to an empty seat, trying not to limp. The blister had come to life and her leg muscles seemed to be in spasm. She sat down, awkward under the scrutiny of a dozen pairs of eyes. They had clearly never seen a schoolgirl in green uniform before. Everywhere she looked she met scowling resentment – she was probably breaking some ancient male taboo by coming in here at all – or frank appraisal. God, they must be hard up. So she stared at the wall where drops of con-densation ran down like Camp coffee, or out of the window, when she'd cleaned a hole in the dirty mist. It was a dismal view, of trucks and lorries mostly. Finally she settled on the man opposite's newspaper – a pink one. It was so much easier to read without the patch over her good eye; the words didn't jump about, and she was deep into the likely effects of the end of food rationing on the market when she realised that the man had moved the paper to one side and was now regarding her with some amusement.

She turned away, embarrassed, her eyes stinging. It was the same man – the one in the car. The tea was too hot to drink quickly. She wouldn't resort to tipping it into the saucer as some of the diners were doing. Not here. Not with *him* looking. He looked posh, with his hanky showing discreetly over his top pocket, his good cloth overcoat, his clean, well-cut hair. She took her purse from her satchel, left the tea steaming on the table and went to make her phone-call.

'Sorry, caller, there's no reply.'

'There must be, it's a shop.'

She heard the ringing tone as the girl tried again.

'Sorry, caller, there's no one answering that number.'

'It's half-day closing,' the man at the table reminded her when she went to finish her tea.

Wednesday. Of course.

The warmth, the sweet tea, the disappointment, made her careless. She told him where she'd come from and, when he asked, that her name was Dorrie.

He grinned suddenly. She liked his grin. It

made him look mischievous, almost good-looking if he hadn't been so old. He said an amazing thing. That there couldn't be many Dorries who came from Walthamstow. He thought he knew her mother.

'Potter, isn't it, your surname?'

'Gosh,' she said. 'Fancy your knowing that.' But she'd thought he looked vaguely familiar.

He said they'd grown up together, he and her mother. Went to the same school. Bumped into each other from time to time. He knew she'd married a bloke called Potter and that they had a little girl called Dorrie.

'Gosh,' said Dorrie again.

'Now she did tell me what Dorrie was short for. It's not Doris or Dora, is it? Or Dorinda? It's Dorothy, isn't it? Pleased to meet you, Dorothy Potter!'

She told him how she hated the name. People expected you to be a drippy wide-eyed Judy Garland. He said there was Dorothy Parker, the wittiest woman in America, and Dorothy L. Sayers who wrote the Lord Peter Wimsey books. Lots of decent Dorothys. Mostly they were called Dot for short, or Dolly. Dorrie was unusual.

She told him she was paying a surprise visit to her grandmother and had run out of money so was having to walk. This time, when he repeated his offer of a lift, she accepted. If he knew Mum he must be all right. Anyway, if he were a predator he'd have tried harder to get her into the car back at Ufford. He wasn't to know that she'd turn up here, was he?

She was sure she'd made the right decision when she climbed in beside him. It was a brilliant car. A Rover something or other, big and roomy and the seats were real leather and you sank down and felt safe, protected from the gusting wind. It started without a handle and flowed like oil over the bumps. He was very quiet as he went through the gears, and he kept turning to her as though there were something he wanted to say. Probably trying to gauge her reaction as they reached sixty miles an hour. Show off.

She awoke with a jolt. They'd stopped at a road junction and he was looking at his map.

'Nearly there,' he said.

She sat up straight and pulled her skirt down. Dear oh dear, she'd been well away. Anything could have happened. It hadn't though, so that showed he was a decent sort of bloke, didn't it?

'You say your Grandma lives in Great Bisset. Looks as though we can take this road to the left and it'll bring us right there.'

'But you said...' She stifled a yawn and the map blurred. She knew her eye was wandering. It did that when she was tired. 'You said you were going to Sowness. Great Bisset is miles out of your way.'

'Doesn't matter. I don't have to be there till seven.'

She argued that he could just drop her here, by the bus-stop – she probably had enough for the fare. She rummaged through her satchel for her purse and he averted his gaze to avoid the embarrassment of seeing her underwear and

144

toiletries. There – two and tuppence farthing. That was plenty.

Suppose the bus didn't come? he said. Country buses were few and far between.

She said she'd wait ten minutes and then start walking. It'd only be a mile or two. He made a sour face. More like five, he said. It'd take her two hours at least and it would soon be getting dark. The wind butted the side of the car. Okay, she shrugged.

The major road became a minor road, became a narrow country lane, winding between dark, blustering trees and high untended hedges. The car went slower and slower as the ruts became deeper, the bumps bumpier.

She was uneasy. This wasn't the way. She remembered the road down to Grandma's – it was wider than this and laid with gravel. And cottage gardens spilled violets and periwinkles onto the grass verges.

'This isn't right,' she said.

'It's a short cut,' he said.

'I think we'd better go back.'

'Just a bit further,' he said.

She bit her lip as she swung her mind back to the café, where he'd established his credentials. He knew her mother. Knew *her* name was Potter. Dorothy Potter. How could he have known that if he hadn't...? When it struck her she groaned aloud. What a fool, what a twerp! *He had known when to turn his head away. Known about the Doctor White's and the knickers.* He had seen inside her satchel, seen her books, her maths exercise books with *Dorothy Potter* written on the front. Had had a good old rummage while she was on the phone! He had conned her in order to get her into his car. He might have known she'd call in at the 'greasy spoon' for a cup of tea. And if she hadn't he'd have caught her up on the road soon enough. Her heart began to bang insistently against her ribs. She had to get out of this somehow.

They appeared to be following muddy cart-tracks into a wood, with primroses dotting the banks under the trees and an untrodden path of grass down the middle. Standing water riffled in the wind. Very pretty, very romantic, if it weren't so sinister. With a sudden lurch, the car pitched her forward and he flung out an arm to save her. He swore and apologised. Whether for swearing or for touching her breast she couldn't tell. It might have been an accident. He might not have been aware that there *was* a breast, just there, just beginning, rather lumpy and sensitive to touch. But *she* was. Her fingers shook as she buttoned up her coat and reached for the door handle.

'Don't Dorrie, don't be silly, dear.'

It was the 'dear' that did it. The familiarity. Who did he think he was? Her boyfriend? He was a pervert. He was going to force himself on her. He was going to stop the car out here in the absolute sticks, where no one would hear her if she screamed, and force her to do something horrible and then he was going to murder her.

'What's my mother's name?' she demanded.

'What's that? Hold on a minute.' He was negotiating some obstacle, pretending he hadn't heard.

'Let me out! I want to get out!'

'Not now, Dorrie.' he braked and the wheels spat mud. Oh God, they'd stopped. He twisted towards her, slid his arm along the back of her seat and there was a wild look in his eye. 'Just let's–'

'No!' she squealed, backing away. 'Don't touch me!'

That got him rattled, dulled the twinkle in his eyes. 'For God's sake, girl – I wouldn't hurt you.'

But the door was open now and she flung herself out, rolling and twisting away, through puddles and over stones and horse droppings and young nettles. She caught up her satchel and glanced around for a bolt-hole, a place to run. But first, she had to slow him down. She stared at the front tyre and burst it. Scrambled to her feet and that was when she saw that a tree had fallen across the track, its twigs twitching with buds, its roots clodded with earth that separated into last year's leaves and blew away. *Could he have been about to put the car into reverse?* Could she take the chance? While he was cursing and kicking the damaged tyre she made a dash for the trees, looked back to see him with his head in the boot. The spare! Bother. She'd forgotten motorists carried spare tyres and things. As soon as he'd taken off the damaged one and screwed on the new one he'd be after her. So she burst another tyre, for good measure. And his radiator. She'd gone too far by then to hear what he was bawling after her. It might have been curses or it might have been, 'Flo! Her name is Flo!' More trickery.

Chapter Eight

Flo was run off her feet. The dryers were going full-blast, Mrs Daley was waiting to be combed out and Mrs Fanshaw's timer had gone off five minutes ago. If she wasn't taken out of the perming machine straight away she'd fry. Valerie had her hands full with those two at the basins and the Ascot playing up, and Dulcie Greenbaum couldn't decide whether to have an Ava Gardner or a Deborah Kerr.

Carol had no business being off. Wednesday was always busy, with the half-price perm offer. Flo had done Inecto colourings and all sorts with a poisoned finger. You just slapped on a finger-stall and got on with it. Carol was just a lazy cow with no consideration. And Betsy wasn't much help. She was a great stylist but she couldn't cope in a crisis. Like an ostrich she was burying her head in shade cards. Oh Lord, she wasn't planning on doing a dye job? Not today? Her lady had only booked for a cut and set.

'Oh Flo,' Dulcie wanted to talk. 'Did you see that bit in *King Solomon's Mines* when she cut her hair off? Lovely long hair she had – must've taken her ages to grow. And the colour! Wouldn't you love to have red hair like that? Though yours is nice. What do they call yours? It's not platinum, is it? Honey-blonde? Ooh, I wouldn't have said that was honey-blonde.

Nice, though. And she just chopped it off, didn't she? 'Cause she was so hot. Hundred and ten degrees in Africa, can you imagine? Can't stand the heat, me. Brings me up in blotches. Itch? I nearly tore me legs to pieces last summer. And she just washed it in the river, didn't she? No mirror. And it looked lovely, like she'd just come out the hairdresser's.'

The eleven-ten appointment was frowning at her watch.

'Valerie, could you wash my lady's hair for me?'

Mrs Fanshaw's test-curl was looking decidedly singed. Flo re-wound it and unclamped the rest of the curls, quickly, deftly so as not to burn her fingers. Two dozen grizzled sausage curls lay on their insulating pads, cooked. As Flo wheeled the stand away, the clamps clashing, the rubberised wires dancing around the pole, she caught Mrs Fanshaw's anxious glance in the mirror and bunched her mouth in sympathy. They weren't quite out of the woods. Gently, she poked out the metal perming rod from the core of each cocoon. Not until the last rod slid free did she dare to hope that all might be well. It was not unknown for the odd ringlet to find its way onto the receiving tray. They were lethal, those electric permers. She knew of salons where the siren had sounded in the war, they'd all gone scampering down the road to the shelter, the customers with pincurls and hairnets, the staff with their pockets full of wave grips, scissors and pins, to carry on cutting and setting before the hair dried out; they'd all be sitting there listening to Hitler destroying their homes and then somebody would remember Mrs So-and-so, left behind in the salon, wired up to the Eugene perming machine. Sometimes she'd have had the presence of mind to pull the plug and trundle the whole apparatus out of the salon. Sometimes not. If she wasn't bombed to bits when they'd got back her hair would be a write-off.

She pulled off the rubber pads and threaded them onto their hook. Good. No damage apart from a couple of minor burns. She left Valerie to apply the neutraliser, combed out Mrs Daley and persuaded Dulcie to have the Ava Gardner. It was all the rage at the holiday camps, she'd heard, and went well with tartan trews and a sweater and a small scarf tied round your neck. That set Dulcie off again. Another film. Joan Collins, this time. Flo began to snip.

He was a bully, let's face it. Slapping Dorrie's face like that. Like a big sulky kid. And he still didn't get it, afterwards, when she'd told him. All right, so maybe the girl had been rude but she was too old to slap. And sensitive. She'd never forget.

Flo had actually got her coat on – she'd come *that* close to walking out. But you can't, not when you've got kids. And where would she go? Not to Mum and Aunt Polly. They were both getting on. If she went to live with them she'd be no more than an unpaid nurse in time, a skivvy. And what about the children? He'd never agree to part with them. Or to a divorce.

They'd dreamed about running away together,

150

she and Frank, but that's all it was – a dream. He'd never leave Marion. Poor delicate Marion. Poor pathetic, manipulating Marion, with her big brown eyes and her suicide threats. And her doting daddy, Harry Thurley, who was able to command total, unquestioning loyalty from Frank, despite being an out-and-out snake. What he had on his son-in-law she couldn't imagine and Frank wasn't telling. It must be something bad...

'Eh, Flo? Would you?' It was a whisper.

She looked up. Dulcie's reflected image was tilted in enquiry. The cut was almost finished.

'Sorry, dear?' She feigned deafness over the dryers. Her head ached. Lack of sleep and worry were fighting it out with the chemical mix of perm solution and singed hair. But customers don't want to hear your troubles. She tried to concentrate. Was Dulcie really asking her to perm her boyfriend's hair? Apparently he'd had a Tony Curtis at the barber's but it lost its curl in this damp weather.

'Some of us frizz and some of us just go limp!' Hoots of laughter. Flo smiled wanly. It was supposed to be a joke. She booked him in for a quiet night and pinned Dulcie's hair in the new style. She'd look good in spite of the pancake make-up, but Flo wasn't responsible for that. She settled her under the dryer with a *Woman's Own* and tamed Mrs Fanshaw's corkscrews into the neat distortion favoured by our own dear Queen and the twinset and pearls brigade at the Conservative Club. She apologised to the eleven-ten appointment, twenty-five minutes

151

late and fuming and determined to hate everything Flo did. It was gone one before she was
able to take her turn at the front desk with a
corned-beef sandwich and a cup of coffee. But
the apprentice had learned at last to make it the
way she liked it – milk and a dash of Camp,
sweetened with condensed milk, and she sipped
it gratefully, watching the sky darken over the
High Street shops. There'd be rain before long.
Good job the kids had their raincoats.

Then Doll blew in, the butcher's wife. 'What
was it you wanted, Flo? Four sheeps' hearts and
what? Oh, rib of beef. What, about three
pounds? I'll tell Bill to pop 'em in tonight, shall
I? You can give me the money then.'

She lived next door in the prefabs. Blowsy and
peroxide blonde, she needed her roots doing
and a bit of a trim. She still dressed her hair in
rolls and bangs, fancying they made her look
like Betty Grable. 'Legs apart,' she would
wheeze with a wink. 'Get it? Legs *apart*.'

''Ere, Flo.' She leaned across the desk now
with chinwobbling conspiracy and tobacco
breath. 'What was your Dorrie doing, down the
station first thing? I said hello but she never
heard us.'

Flo's heart jumped. 'The station?' She tried to
be casual. 'What time was this, Doll?'

Her twisting fingers must have given her away.
Doll never missed a trick. 'Oh bli,' she said, 'you
didn't know, did you? Oh Flo, sorry, mate.' She
pulled a face denoting sympathy, then scratched
her porous nose with a long red fingernail. 'Let's
see now. I know we'd opened up 'cause I was

152

outside doing the blinds. We live in hope even if we do die in despair.' This, a reference to the 'iffy' weather. 'I suppose it must've been quarter past, twenty past nine. I thought at the time, "You should be in school, young lady." She looked a bit down in the mouth, now I come to think of it. Not hopping the wag, was she?'

'What, Dorrie? She wouldn't – she loves school. No, she was probably on an errand for the teacher, getting a railway timetable, or something.' She ran her finger down the columns. And again. Oh God, what? What was she looking for? Dorrie, of course. No, a twenty-minute slot. 'How about ten o'clock Monday? For your roots?'

What should she do? Go round the school and make sure she was there? She didn't want to get Dorrie into trouble if it was nothing. But after last night – she'd taken it so badly and she'd hardly said a word over breakfast. The station though. She had no reason to go to the station unless... Oh God, suppose she'd been running away when Doll saw her? You heard such awful stories about young girls who...

'You all right, Flo?'

'Mmm.' She'd made up her mind. 'Betsy, all right if I pop home for a bit? Something I've got to sort out.'

She found the note pinned to the pillow – *Dear Mum, Gone to Grandma's. Back soon* – and stood wringing her hands as her brain whirled beyond reason.

Oh God. Oh, the silly kid. She'd get on the wrong ... finish up in the back of be ... get picked up by some awful... And there was a child killer loose. It had been on the News, just after Dorrie had left for ... just after Dorrie...

She sat down heavily on the bed, sniffing and cuffing her tears. Her hands smelled of perm lotion; her nails were soft. She should have worn rubber gloves but had left them off for quickness. She closed her eyes to think. That poor little boy on the news, the murder victim, had only been six. Patrick something. Younger than Dorrie, much younger. And a child molester wouldn't kill twice in one week... would he?

Why Nora's, though? They hadn't seen Arthur's mother in years. Perhaps that was it – absence making the heart grow sentimental. Or was it some hold Nora had over the girl? Had she lured her there somehow?

Flo gave herself a shake. To believe someone has occult powers you have first to believe in the occult. And she didn't – of course, she didn't! Nora just had a screw or two loose, that's all that was wrong with her. No, Dorrie was a calculating little cow. She'd worked it all out. What would really get Arthur going? What was really taboo? Going round the corner to Nanna Hubbard's didn't pack the same punch at all.

But she'd left a note to take the sting out of it. Flo chewed her lip. *Back soon,* she'd said. As though she'd just popped out to the shops. How soon? A day? A week? *Back,* anyway – there was that. She intended to come home after she'd visited Nora.

Providing she made it there in the first place!

She was only a child, tall for her age but only just fourteen. Flo wasn't really worried that she'd lose her way. She'd been coping with buses and trains for years. Dorrie was a capable girl. Clever. But ...

Should she report her missing? Or telephone Lucy to let her know to expect her? Ask her to put the girl on the next train back? Flo could meet her at Liverpool Street. Except there was Stephen to think about. She was halfway up the road to the police station before she thought of phoning Arthur. He'd be devastated. His little girl running away, and all his fault.

Instead, when she reached the phone box, something prompted her to phone Thurley's. It had been a long time but the number was engraved on her memory. He had a car. He could, he *should* help. It was an emergency.

Her heart thudded. Her ear burned against the receiver. Her fingers left sweaty prints on the black Bakelite. Come on, come on.

Mr Leary didn't work there any more, they said.

And Aunt Polly was out. Flo had already let herself in and shouted, 'It's only me!' up the passage when she remembered that Wednesday afternoon was when her aunt did the cleaning up at the Lord Clyde.

Damn.

There was a slipper-shod shuffle on the landing above.

'Mum, it's me!'

'Flo? Shouldn't you be at work?' Her mother

sounded drunk. She wasn't; her teeth were loose. She must have just put them in.

Damn, damn, damn.

She sighed. 'Go back to bed. It's all right.'

'Poll's out, you know.'

'Yes, I forgot. Sorry if I woke you. It's not important.' Just a matter of a child's life or death, that's all.

The slow scuff and drag arrived at the top of the stairs. There were the invalid's worn pom-pom slippers, her blotchy ankles, her pyjama bottoms. 'What's the matter, Flo? Ain't your half-day, is it?'

'Don't come down, Mum.' She ran up the stairs. 'Let's get you back to bed.' But her mother was already on the second tread. She helped her down, noting the sour smell of her. She could do with a bath – Polly should have said if it was too much for her. She settled her mother in the armchair by the hearth. Fetched a shovel of coal to liven the fire. Put the kettle on.

'I can't stop long, Mum, I've got to ... em, I only came to... Oh Mu-um!' And the stupidest thing – she began to cry. To blub like a kid in her mother's lap, while the sick old woman stroked her head.

It all came out about the row the night before, and Dorrie's disappearance, and how she hadn't been able to get through to Lucy or the shop and how the police seemed to think she was making a fuss about nothing. The time to worry, they said, was when Dorrie *didn't* get there, but they'd inform Doddingworth to keep an eye out for a schoolgirl in a green gabardine and they'd

156

send someone to check she'd arrived safely at her grandmother's around teatime. It would probably be sensible to let her stay the night and bring her back in the morning.

But Flo wanted Dorrie home *now*, she sobbed. She'd wanted Aunt Polly to meet Stephen from school and give him his tea while she went up to Great Bisset to fetch the girl, and she'd forgotten that Auntie Poll wouldn't be home until gone four.

'I can do that. Give us ten minutes to have a wash and put some clothes on.'

'Mum, you can't. Look at you!' It was even funny in a way, the thought of her attempting to get down to the school. She was so thin and weak; she was hardly eating a thing, just pappy mush and liquids. There wasn't a drop of alcohol in the house – Polly's orders – hadn't been since she was sent home from hospital before Christmas, but the old woman's eyes were still jaundiced and her hands still trembled. It couldn't be DTs after all this time.

'I'll be all right. Do me good to get out.'

'Don't be so stupid. I'll pop in the school on my way to the station and tell the headmaster to send him up here. And I'll call in at the Clyde and tell Polly he's coming. With a bit of luck she'll get home before him, so you won't have to get up again. I'll phone Arthur when I get up there and tell him what's happening.'

'Ain't you told him?'

'Mum, I'm in such a state I don't know if I'm coming or going. What could Arthur do, anyway? He's on overtime this week. He won't

157

get off till seven.'

'They'll let him off early for a thing like this. He could fetch her. Save you going.'

'I'm *going* – that's all there is to it. I'll have to call in the salon and tell Betsy – might not be in in the morning, either. God, I hope Carol's back. Mum, do you want to stop down here or shall I help you upstairs?'

She waited while the old woman used the lavatory. 'Might as well improve the shining hour!' But the shining hour stretched into five minutes, ten.

'She's just like you was,' said her mother conversationally. 'Headstrong. Like getting mixed up with that Frank. I said he wasn't no good, but you would go your own way, wouldn't you? You knew best.'

'Mum, don't start. That's all over now, and it's got nothing at all to do with Dorrie.'

'Oh, ain't it, though?' She sounded mysterious but Flo knew what she was implying. 'Good job she takes after you in looks.'

Flo said nothing. This was an old hobby-horse of her mother's.

'Yeah, she's the dead spit of you at her age. Though you never made the most of your looks, did you? Marrying *him*. Cutting hair for a living. You could've made something of yourself. Missed your chance, you did.'

And that was another old refrain. Over and over, on and on. Worse now that someone had told her Frank was rolling in money and living in a big house. In the old days, when he was working down the docks she hadn't had a good word to say for him.

'Bet you ain't got no money, neither.' Flo's problems seemed to invigorate the old woman, give her something to think about. She was waiting for a reply. When Flo continued to make none she said, 'On the ear'ole, are you?'

'We-ell.' She made a wry face at the closed door. 'Could you lend us a bit?'

'How much?'

'I don't know ... Ten?'

'*Ten!*'

'Return ticket for me, single for Dorrie. B and B if it's too late to start back tonight.'

'Get Arthur to fetch her. It's his fault she's gone, innit? He can make his peace.'

On that Flo was adamant. 'No,' she said.

Arthur had shown how sensitive *he* could be. She didn't expect him and his size tens to make things any better at all.

She caught the three-forty from Liverpool Street by the skin of her teeth, and spent the first part of the journey staring at the rain-lashed window, wondering whether she should have left it to the police. Would Dorrie thank her for chasing after her? Was she making a mistake, *another* mistake, in a lifetime shot full of wrong decisions? Her mother was right. *If only I hadn't, if only I had.* The wheels on the track beat out the rhythm of her regrets. If she'd tried harder at school ... if she'd gone into some other line of work ... if she hadn't met Arthur ... if she hadn't met Frank ... if she hadn't fallen for Dorrie. She bit her lip. *Oh, Dorrie, be all right.* She'd pray if there was anyone

159

to hear. If she wasn't so wicked. Maybe the biggest mistake was diving under that table in the war. Maybe she should have let the bomb finish her off.

'Excuse me, madam. Are you all right?'

'What? Oh.' She sniffed. Discovered there were tears seeping down her face. Where had he sprung from, this man offering her a neatly pressed handkerchief? They were quite alone. The carriage had been full when she'd boarded it.

She shrank into her corner, smiled weakly and refused. She had her own hanky in her bag, she insisted. And a hat-pin to stick in him should the occasion demand.

Stranger on the train. Every bad B movie included the scene. Predator and prey. Where was the emergency cord? Above the window. If he attacked her would she be able to reach it in time?

Oh Lord, why hadn't she been paying attention as the compartment had emptied? Gone to look for the Ladies Only at the last stop?

It never blooming rained but it poured.

He had removed his hat to speak to her, revealing the receding hairline of middle-age. He looked like a gent, with amused blue eyes and a sensitive mouth, but you never could tell.

He didn't insist, didn't press her and when he asked kindly if she was all right now, somehow she found the story of the runaway unfolding without her help. Hairdressers will talk to anybody.

He couldn't understand why she was so upset.

She knew where her daughter had gone and she sounded a sensible young lady – she'd be all right, he was sure. Flo sensed he'd be embarrassed if she told him that she was sick of her husband, so she told him about her mother-in-law.

'And you think she's intending some harm to your daughter?' He spoke well, not plummy but he sounded his tees and aitches. Like Frank when he remembered.

'She wouldn't mean to. She's very fond of the child – well, she was years ago. But she's a crazy old woman and it rubs off. She looked after Dorrie when I was in hospital with our youngest and she was a different child when we fetched her home.'

'In what way?'

'Oh, talking to herself, moony, imagining things. You know. In another world. She was always a bit of a dreamer but after that visit to Great Bisset she was hopeless.'

'Great Bisset?' he repeated softly. 'Good Lord, they say it's a small world. I live at Beeding.'

'Oh?' She'd never heard of it.

'On the other side of Doddingworth. I know Great Bisset well. Wonderful old oak tree in the middle of the green.'

She nodded. 'That's right. Though I haven't seen it in ages, eight years or more.'

'You've kept your daughter away from her grandmother for eight years?'

It did sound a long time. And mean. 'She's supposed to be a medium,' she explained.

'A medium?'

161

'Yes, you know, she talks to ghosts.'

'I know what a medium is.'

'Oh. Anyway I'm not having Dorrie mixed up in all that. When I think...' She took a breath, decided to tell him. 'The last time we were there we caught the old girl sitting round a table with her cronies, summoning up goodness knows what fiends from hell.' It was an exaggeration but you do when it's a story for strangers.

'Ghosts,' he said calmly. 'That's what mediums usually do. They raise ghosts. Not fiends,' he added and smiled gently.

She frowned. Whose side was he on? 'But the table was rocking and there were things flying about – ornaments and things.'

He shrugged. '*Reluctant* ghosts. Did you notice a drop in temperature, strange smells?'

'It was a hot June day,' she said, 'but it wasn't warm in Nora's, now you come to mention it.' His eyes seemed to widen momentarily. Pale blue eyes. Shrewd. A businessman's eyes. 'I remember because I thought twice about taking the baby's little matinée coat off. And there was a terrible smell, a sort of mixture of dirty old men and pipe smoke. Vile, it was. I thought she was burning rubbish on the fire.'

He nodded, pushing his lips together. 'Par for the course,' he said, 'if the medium's worth her salt.'

'And my little girl was sitting there taking it all in.'

'*Was* she? Mmm. Don't know if I'd go along with that entirely. Though it depends on the little girl, I suppose.'

162

'What do you mean?'

He frowned. 'I don't know what I mean, exactly. It's just a thought.' He paused. 'Maybe your daughter... No, forget it.'

'What?'

'It's just that, well, the medium sounds a genuine psychic and these things sometimes run in families.'

'Oh, don't say that!'

The question of Dorrie's genetic inheritance was one she would chew over constantly, until her inside lip bled, in fact, as she worked at her stitchery beside the fire. Dorrie, sitting opposite, a book or a sketchpad open on her knee, would be staring, lost in some bottomless imagining. You could talk to her, pass a hand in front of her eyes and she wouldn't even blink. Not that Flo considered the possibility of psychic powers at all. Inherited madness, maybe. Or badness.

'Arthur's not in the slightest bit, you know, psychic,' she told her companion. 'He has no imagination at all.'

'It could have skipped a generation.'

'I don't *think* so!' she said, affronted.

Bruised silence. She hadn't meant to sound so rude.

'I don't think so,' she repeated, with a smile this time.

The lights came on in the carriage and she glanced at her watch. Twenty past five. She'd probably have done better to get a through train to Ipswich and change. It'd be ages before they reached Doddingworth. They seemed to be stopping at every other station. Her fellow passenger brought out a Thermos from his briefcase and offered her tea.

The wind was up. You could feel it buffeting the carriage and seeping in draughts through cracks and jambs. Stray bits of twig and straw were plastered by the rain to the window. Smoke from chimneys streamed flat and trees strained at their roots. A bolt of lightning lit up a field of cows before the train hurried on. Thunder rolled around the blackening sky. She hoped, with all her heart, that Dorrie was safely indoors. If she'd set off from Hoe Street at half-past nine she should be there now, talking about whatever it was she was so anxious to see Nora about.

She remembered Dorrie as a small child, sitting at the table, drawing in Nora's front room, with its log fire and winking ornaments. The man was right. There was no wickedness there. Perhaps Arthur had been a bit hasty. Jealous, even. Perhaps now that Dorrie was older he'd see things differently.

And then that other image came into her mind, of mayhem and whirling things and three old crones bent over the table, and Lucy, too, and the startled looks on their faces as she and Arthur had burst through the door. Guilt. They'd known that what they were doing was wrong. Well, they weren't getting their bony mitts on Dorrie. Dorrie was going to concentrate on her lessons and make something of herself. And if that meant Flo stopping with Arthur to the bitter end then that was how it would have to be.

The tea was strong but hot and sweet and welcome. They talked about him now. Walter Barrington. He had been up to London on business, tying up the loose ends of his mother's estate. She had died just before Christmas. He thanked Flo for her sympathy, but the end had come as a blessed release. Mother had been in failing health for some time and they'd both been quite prepared for it. As a matter of fact, he'd been attending services at Sowness Spiritualist Church since. Found them a great comfort.

He paused and sipped his tea thoughtfully, looking up at her and down again as though considering whether to tell her something more. But when next he spoke it was about music or books or something. Before they reached Doddingworth she'd learned that he read *The Listener* and preferred the Third Programme to the Light, that he didn't have a telly, that he loved the cinema, which he regarded as a great art form.

'Go and see *Blithe Spirit*,' he suggested. 'It's frothy nonsense but it might help you to see your mother-in-law in a new light.'

Squally rain bowled them along the platform at Doddingworth. The backs of Flo's legs were soaked and her hair was stuck to her face as she handed in her ticket.

'Look,' he shouted above the howl of the wind, holding onto his hat, 'my car's round the corner. Let me give you a lift to Great Bisset. I'd really like to know that your daughter arrived safely.'

Thank God for gentlemen, thought Flo.

165

Chapter Nine

Dorrie hadn't the slightest idea where she was. There was thick mud filling her shoes, she knew that, and brambles scratching her legs, twigs whipping her face and catching her hair. She broke from the woods, panting and desperate, to find herself in someone's garden. More than a garden. These well-tended and sprawling lawns had to be part of some estate, and the 'someone' had to be a little more than just any old body if they owned that ancient pile up there on the knoll.

Perhaps if she presented herself at a tradesmen's entrance some kind menial would direct her to Great Bisset or let her use the phone or something. Such was her intent as she hurried over the grass.

And that she might have achieved if the grounds had not been suddenly cluttered with a vision of the future – an aggressively bustling building site. Ladders and scaffolding and half-built walls rose up before her and there were piles of bricks to be dodged, deep dug foundations to be skirted, pipes and planks and window frames to be negotiated. Knowing that it was an illusion she could have walked straight through the lot, ignoring the din of drills and diggers, the clatter of concrete mixers, the ribaldry of builders, but her presence of mind was already shot to pieces and her knees were beginning to tremble.

'Hey! You there, girl! What the hell are you doing!'

Now she saw that her wanderings along ghostly duckboard and half-paved streets had brought her to within shouting distance of the house, a mansion three storeys tall. An angry man had the window open, halfway up.

'I'm being chased! He wants to kill me!' she yelled back, over the racket of building work, but her voice was lost in the wind.

'What? What's that? Are you mad? Get off the grass, for God's sake – it's just been spiked and treated.'

She tried again. 'Great Bisset – is it near here?'

'Listen to me, young lady – you're trespassing. Now either you get off my land or I call the police.'

'Which *way?*' she pleaded. There were other people in the room, whose expressions ranged from frank curiosity to offended disdain. Hard and haughty faces, but perhaps one of them would answer her question.

He made a ticking gesture of dismissal. 'Back the way you came.'

She looked. Saw her footprints making a crazy, black-negative snail track in the silver of rainsoaked grass, back, back to the wood. She couldn't, of course. She'd be bound to run into the ... what? Maniac? Whatever else he was, he was clever. He'd learned everything about her and she didn't even know his name. And if he hadn't been mad before, he would be now, after

167

she'd burst his tyres. Best not to take any chances. She glanced around quickly. Now that the building work had returned to the future she could see a tentative fuzz of pink and a boundary fence running behind. The road lay beyond. It seemed a long way off. She hesitated.

'Get off my ruddy property! *Jenkins, fetch my gun!*'

'But–'

'Did you hear me!' he screeched, side-whiskers bristling, eyes popping in an unhealthily red face.

She broke into a sprint, suddenly finding muscles that responded. She ran defiantly *across* the hill, hearing the owner's sensibilities exploding in little yelps at her back, and fading as she ran down some steps, past a rose garden and a lily pond, across more grass, into the budding orchard. As she pulled herself up into the gnarled old tree that would help her over the fence she thought she heard gunshots. But she was over and brushing herself down before they got her range. Her heart was still pounding as she paused briefly to get her breath and take stock. There was blood trickling down her leg from a scratch. The scramble down to the verge hadn't been clean. Rusty nails or ragged wood had ripped her school tunic and buried splinters under her skin. But she was in one piece.

And now, which way? The road looked utterly unfamiliar but then she'd hardly have known her own backyard in the strange reflective light cast by the sun squeezing between dark clouds. She turned left with the wind, her heart almost stopping whenever she heard a car. There was a crossroads up ahead and what looked like a signpost. It wasn't. Someone had substituted a gibbet with a decomposing felon attached to it. What mischief was this? If it was a message from the Other Side she did not understand it.

Two hundred years before, naughty children would have been taken to see that poor corpse, as a terrible warning to quit their wicked ways. For most, like Dorrie, the smell would have been enough. Flies buzzed around the rotting lips, around the milky eyes, as the man's grin of horror stretched wider and wider. One look and she was heaving and a hundred yards down the road to Brand End before she even realised she'd broken into a run. She dashed the tears from her eyes. She had to get on. But she had never seen anything so horrible. It wasn't fair. Why her? Just because she was psychic. It was either a diversion or an omen that something worse was to happen, though how much worse things could get than this, she couldn't imagine.

Winds were roaring through the treetops, bending branches to snapping point. A wriggle of lightning caught everything offguard, the hawthorn hedge with its spikes unsheathed, the ditch a dark trickle, decked with pallid prim-roses, a vole frozen in its dash for cover, and then it had gone, and everything was drained and bloodless. Thunder cracked, ripping a seam in the clouds, releasing the rain in a whoosh, the sort of rain her mother would have called her to the window to witness, the sort that came down in stair-rods and ladders, hitting the ground so hard the splashes made soldiers that marched smartly down the road. You wouldn't put a dog out in such a downpour, let alone a fourteen-year-old girl. It hissed and stung as it hit her face. In seconds she was soaked, every fibre, every pore, and the wind rushed in after and chilled her bones. She ran on down the lane, not daring to stop as branches were torn from trees and flung into the road like bones from a giant's table, and wires snaked down, sparking, from telegraph poles.

A tarpaulin flap-flapped over the hedge then flew off into the darkness, bellying and curling like the sail of a wave-tossed yacht, with ropes dangling and wisps of hay sticking to its under-side. A primal need for shelter alerted her to possibilities. She found the gate, slithered over it, and sought the sadly depleted haystack, only a few feet high, in the corner of the field across squelching troughs of mud. It was now only partially protected from the elements but there were some remaining covers, and like an animal she squirmed underneath. At least it was dry. At least it was warm. Surprisingly warm. Steamy warm. She supposed the dried grass must be compacted lower down and fermenting, like Dad's compost heap. Though it still smelled sweet, as she burrowed down, leaving the tarpaulin a roof over her nest, pounding and pouching with rain, lifting from time to time with the roaring of the wind.

She may have dozed a little. She may only have dreamed it, but suddenly she was wide awake, nerves twitching. There it was again. Close to

170

her ear, drowning out the storm. A scratchy sound like a pencil scribbling ... or tiny paws doing things with dried grass. Probably only a mouse, a dear little harvest mouse, woken from sleep. Though even mice and voles were not so sweet close to your ear, or beetles. Or snakes. They also hibernated in nice, warm haystacks, didn't they? Or *rats*.

She froze. Something was pricking her ankle but she didn't dare move – until she heard the squeaking. And then she was out of the haystack with a squeal and a yelp and blown through the rain and the mud back to the road. She was shivering again, more with fear than cold.

When she saw the lights of an approaching car, she was almost beyond caring. She made herself step off the verge and watched, with interest, as rushing water made eddies round her shoes, washing away the mud. She didn't mind that the braking wheels drenched her with spray; she didn't mind that the driver of the Land Rover, a young man, looked somewhat askance as she threw herself, dripping wet and stuck with hayseeds, into the passenger seat. It was a hayseed, stuck in her sock, that was itching her ankle. Puddles were forming round her feet on his nicely hoovered floor.

'I know it's out of your way, but could you *please* take me to Great Bisset?'

'Not out of my way at all,' said the youth, over the rattle of rain on the roof and the swish of the windscreen wipers. He could only have been sixteen or seventeen, almost too young to be driving. 'That's where I'm making for, actually.'

He had an accent plummier than any she'd heard in Walthamstow, except on the television. Perhaps Sylvia Peters came close.

'R-really?' She was too cold to feel intimidated or indeed, surprised. She couldn't feel her fingers or toes.

'You were headed in the wrong direction. Great Bisset is down this way.'

When they reached the crossroads, she breathed a thankful sigh that the gibbet had gone. She asked him whose orchard lay behind the wooden fence to their right, and wondered why he looked at her strangely.

'That's the Doubleday place,' he said. The name meant nothing.

The warmth of terrible realisation stole into her cheeks as familiar landmarks loomed out of the rain, darker, more solid than she remembered – Fitzell's shop, a sign on the wall swinging madly in the wind, clattering, the oak tree, thrashing its enormous branches in gigantic rage, the green. *Only a step from where she'd scaled the fence.* If she'd turned right instead of left...

But that meant the maniac had been telling the truth. It *was* a short-cut he'd taken. He probably wasn't even a maniac. He'd brought her to within a hundred yards of her grandmother's house and, for thanks, he'd got two flat tyres and a busted radiator!

'Which way?' He'd stopped.

'Oh thanks, this'll do. I can walk from here.' Somehow it was so imprinted on her own mind she'd expected *him* to have known.

'What number?'

'Five.'

He dropped her at the gate. She thanked him. He'd saved her life, she said. It sounded gushing, but she was so grateful. And then, out of politeness, she asked, 'Do you have far to go?'

He jerked his thumb over his shoulder. 'Just up the road. The Doubleday place.' And then, with a small *moue* of apology: 'He's my father, actually.'

Grandma had shrunk, shockingly – she had to tilt her chin to see the visitor's face under its sopping hood.

'Who is it?' she said, squinting against the wind, battling with caution and the heaving door.

'It's Dorrie, Grandma.'

'*Dorrie?!* Come in, come in for Gawd's sake, gel, and let's shut the blooming door.'

Together they leaned against it and the squall outside. Dorrie closed her eyes and breathed in the blessed warmth and quiet.

Her grandmother was regarding her in some alarm, and for the first time since leaving home Dorrie had doubts. Her grandmother's hair was silver, prettily permed but almost white; her eyes were fading, her apple cheeks shrivelling. As they embraced, as she put her arms around her, Dorrie's heart sank. Saggy flesh, protruding bird bones that would break, would crush to dust if you hugged her too tight: her grandmother had grown frail. *She* was the strong one, weary though she was. Their roles had reversed.

173

Grandma must be over sixty. Perhaps harbouring a runaway was too much to ask of her.

Not a bit of it.

'Just look at the state of you, blue with cold! Now you just get them wet things off and we'll see about a nice cup of tea.'

She put the kettle on to boil and fetched towels, scrubbing Dorrie's dead fingers like dirty linen, back to life, and grunting with the effort.

'You was lucky to find me in, Dor. Wednesdays I'm at Sowness, as a rule. But I thought I'd stop home, seeing we was in for a storm. They don't mind, long as I tell 'em in time – they can usually find someone else.' Her voice, her jowls, the muscles in her arms wobbled with her efforts. She took the other hand.

'Ain't you *grown*, though Dor! Too big to sit on me lap now, eh? Funny, I wasn't expecting you to be so big! Course, you must be thirteen, fourteen?' She caught Dorrie's puzzled frown and explained: 'They said you was coming in the spring. But this ain't 'ardly the weather... My Gawd, they don't half choose their moments, the Other Side.'

Then she went out to make the tea, leaving Dorrie to dry herself in front of the fire. When she was comfortable, in clean, if baggy underwear and a woolly dressing gown, with a blanket round her shoulders, she let Grandma tuck her into the armchair, with a hot-water bottle for her tummy, and massage her poor numb feet until they could bear to be placed gently in a steaming mustard bath. There was hot sweet tea

174

to drink and a wodge of apple cake 'to be going on with'.

In return she had to tell the old woman the ins and outs, the whys and wherefores.

'Tch! That Arthur. He don't learn. Bull in a blooming china shop. He never meant to hurt you, duck. Soft as they come, he is. But kids can drive you to distraction. I should know, with seven of the buggers. Little monkeys. And they ain't none of 'em too big for a clip round the ear even now. Except Lucy.' She gave a short laugh. 'She'd hit me back, knowing her!' But there was no amusement in her eyes as she compressed her lips and made a kissing sound of disapproval. 'Nah, you don't hit girls – it goes too deep.' She sniffed. 'Still, we all do things in temper, don't we? Things we're sorry for after.'

Which was Dorrie's cue to tell her about the breakages in the bedroom.

'Dorrie! Now that's just showing off! No, I don't hold with that. Windows cost a lot of money.'

'Grandma, I didn't know it would happen. I just sort of looked and it broke!'

'What if your Mum had seen you? Eh, what then? That'd really've put the cat among the pigeons, that would.' And, as she calmed down, 'You must be more careful, duck. See, that's your tele-whatsits, your kinetics, that is. All that spare energy you're channelling. Lucky I never suffered from them as a girl, nor with spots neither, nor them things on me teeth.' Dorrie closed her mouth, reminded of the ugly brace she wore. 'I ain't no telepath, not like you, but

175

I'll tell you this for nothing, Dor – you want to keep it to yourself. Gaw bli, the wrong people get wind of that, you could finish up over the Iron Curtain playing I Spy!' Her eyes grew big with the enormity of what she'd said. 'No, duck, best you go off by yourself next time, somewhere quiet, and let off steam. Up the forest or somewhere.'

Dorrie thought about the Rover's tyres and bit her lip. Better not say.

'Oh, don't look so worried, lovey, it won't last for ever, only till you get your energy levels sorted out. Like your teeth. They'll straighten up in the end. Lucy'll help you. She can do it long distance.'

'Did Auntie Lucy break things too?'

'Oh no. She didn't come into it, the psychic, till late on. It must have been there but she wouldn't let it out. I always say, it don't never do to bottle things up. A right little cow she was! Gawd, what a temper! I mean, she can still come the old acid when she wants, but as a girl...' she made her mouth into a tight O through which to suck her breath '...there wasn't no talking to her! Now your Uncle Jack was different again. Lovely nature he had, easygoing...'

'And he's just come to it, too – second sight?'

'And your Auntie Susan. Well, she's coming along. She ain't a natural, of course. He's having to teach her everything, him and Viv. You know about Viv, don't you? Poor little scrap. Don't hardly seem fair that her gift is all locked away like that.'

'So am I the only one, the only Potter to, you

know, have had the telekiny thing?'

'Telekinesis. Far as I know you are, duck. Only one in the family. Very special you are. 'Cause we thought it was going to be one of Lucy's lot. Just goes to show, don't it? You never can tell.'

She left Dorrie picking over her last remark while she popped next door to where there was a phone. There must be some way of letting Flo and Arthur know that Dorrie was safe, she said. Dorrie sat back in the chair and listened to the wind in the chimney, watched it making the logs glow and spark.

She was woken by the smell of stew simmering in the kitchen. Another old woman, in a long black dress and shawl was sitting opposite, knitting something striped – a sock? A fat ginger cat was draped over the arm of the chair, watching the needles fly, with narrow eyes.

'Granny?' The mustard bath was gone. Her feet were fluffy in pink bedsocks. She tried to get up and found that everything ached.

'Thought you'd forgotten us, duck.' She had, somehow she had, as you'd forget a dream, but it all came flooding back as the needles clicked.

'I thought you'd forgotten *me!*' Suddenly she felt very sorry for herself. 'I can't remember the last time I saw you.'

"Ere, 'ere, 'ere, no tears. It has to be like that, sometimes. You gotta be left to get on with things on your own. Else you get soft. Can't 'ave guardian angels there at your beck and call, you know. But I always kept an eye out for you, course I did.'

'Gran-nee!' She could have done with a little guardianship today, and yesterday, the start of it.

'*No, Dor, it's been brewing a long time, this.*' She'd forgotten that Granny didn't need to hear her speak. '*It had to happen. You had to find out things about yourself and you couldn't whilst you was Daddy's little gel. That's why you're 'ere, see. Why you come to us. So's we can tell you what's to do and what's what. That's right, innit, Luce?*'

Auntie Lucy's curly brown head popped round the door, followed by the rest of her and a red-haired baby balanced on her hip. 'Oh you're awake,' she smiled. 'Feeling a bit better, are you? Ma says you were in a right state when you arrived. According to her you looked like you'd been pulled through a hedge backwards.' She came across and kissed her and Dorrie breathed in a sweet softness of baby talc.

'Excuse me a minute. Hold this.' She plonked the baby on Dorrie's lap while she worked a hayseed loose from the young girl's bird's-nest hair. 'Nice to see you again, Dorrie. Eh, little Jack?' She was talking to the baby who turned solemn brown eyes on his cousin and reached up to touch the wires on her teeth. She caught the soft little fingers between her lips, thinking how vulnerable he was.

'Isn't it nice to see Dorrie? And we haven't seen her for so-o-o long.' She managed to time the 'so' to coincide with a baby yawn. 'Oh dear, so that's what you think about it all. Come on, Mister...' picking him up '...let's get you fed and off to bed. Back later, Dorrie. Oh, I'd better tell you, we're not having much luck, phonewise. I thought we might get Uncle Mick to pass on the message to your mum and dad but it looks like the lines are down. They'll be going barmy, poor things. But don't worry, Joe'll ride over to Doddingworth on his way to work. The police can get messages through.'

'But if the phone lines are down?'

Her aunt cocked her head and made her free hand into a microphone. *"Calling all cars! Calling all cars!"'*

It was a famous line, one with which every child in the country was familiar, uttered by Snowy or Jock or even Dick Barton, himself, at least once during every episode of 'Dick Barton – Special Agent'. It meant, of course, that the police contacted each other by radio, not telephone.

Dorrie grinned as Lucy whisked the baby into the kitchen. She wasn't worried. Mum would know where she was – she'd left that note.

'Auntie Lucy lives quite close, does she?' she asked her ghostly gran.

'Next door.' Both their heads lifted to the smell of stew and dumplings as Grandma put the steaming plates on the table. *'I was saying, Nora, they don't have far to go, eh?'*

Her grandmother finished the story. 'The minute the Turners was out, she was in there, having babies. Come and sit up, Dorrie.'

'Not before time,' said the ghost. *'Yous two would've come to blows if she'd stopped here much longer. Some right old ding-dongs you had.'*

Grandma ignored the old woman. 'Your Uncle Joe wanted to knock a door through, to make it more like one big house.' She put up a finger for Dorrie to listen and over the wailing of the wind

179

she heard a child crying. 'Don't like his nappy changed, he don't, our little Jack.' And then, competing with the rattling of the window and the gusts in the chimney, came the roar of a motorbike engine. 'That's Joe now, off to the police station.'

'Does he work at night, then?'

'He's a weather-man, a metro-lologist.' She had difficulty with the word. 'Over the RAF station. He works all hours – days, nights, Christmas. He tells 'em if it's all right for them to go up in their planes and that. He's the one told me it was going to be rough tonight, why I never went to Sowness.'

Dorrie wondered fleetingly whether she should have said something about the sex-maniac. Uncle Joe could have warned the police to be on the look out. But there would have to be questions and reports about burst tyres. Perhaps not.

Grandma lowered her voice to a mutter. 'I'm glad he didn't knock a hole in the wall, to be truthful. I love them little uns but you can have too much of a good thing. Live wires they are, all three of them. That red hair...' she added darkly, shaking her head. 'Any case, *he* wouldn't hear of it, old Doubleday.'

Dorrie's ears pricked up. 'Doubleday?'

He owned most of the land round about, she was informed – Great Bisset, Little Bisset. Brand End, Stanbury Woods; most of the village paid rent to Doubleday. Horrible man, in Grandma's opinion.

Why? What had he done?

Blooming parasite, sitting on his ... *privilege* ... up there in that great big house, with his servants and his guns, sending his kids to boarding school, giving his dinner parties, having his foreign holidays and his floozies, living off the fat of the bleeding land.

'*Language, Nora.*'

'O-o-oh,' she growled helplessly. 'It just gets my goat. Some have it all and some ain't got nothing.' She jabbed a carrot with her fork. 'It ain't right.'

'*An accident of birth,*' said Granny calmly.

'You're telling me! That's just about what he is – a flaming, rotten accident.' The apple cheeks had colour in them now, Cox's Orange, grainy. She turned to Dorrie. 'When old man Turner got his foot caught in that rabbit snare, Doubleday made out it wasn't nothing to do with him. Poor old git was off work for weeks, no wages coming in, except what young Eric was making on Hooper's Farm, and Gawd knows *he* pays a pittance, so o'course they fall behind with the rent. Old Doubleday's round like a shot wanting his money or else. I'd hear 'em of a night working out how much they'd get for the silver cup the village give 'im for war service. Oh, it broke your heart. I went in there once, said I'd lend it 'em. Well, they'd never've taken it as a gift. But they said No, Bert was going back to work. He was sure he could manage. But he couldn't – his leg went poisonous, didn't it? He'd've lost it if I hadn't got Lucy to give it the once-over. Right as rain he was, in the end, but he'd had enough working for Doubleday. Moved out, they did, lock, stock and barrel, over the other side of Doddingworth. Got a council house and a job in the car works, ten bob a week more'n Doubleday was paying. And Lord Muck lost a blooming good stockman.'

'*Serves the bugger right,*' said Granny Farthing, her four needles sparking but not with firelight. The sock wasn't a sock at all. It had grown a thumb and three fingers and turned round and round as the little finger grew longer. The cat tapped it, from time to time, with an enquiring paw.

'Could you manage another dumpling, Dorrie? The thought of him's took my appetite clear away. A right chiseller, he is – a weasel. D'you know, when I first moved in with me chickens, he tried to make out I was selling the eggs and he was entitled to a cut, seeing he owned the premises. You'd hardly credit it, would you? I could've been some poor old widder-woman for all he knew, taking in washing and selling eggs to keep the wolf from the door. Sorry to disappoint, I said, but I gave away any I couldn't use meself, and he could go and whistle.'

'*That told 'im.*'

'Yeah, and he didn't like it neither. He couldn't hardly bear to be civil for a long, long time. Then he finds out I'm good for a bob or two. Turns out he's seen me picture outside the Assembly Rooms, on the same bill as Wilfred Pickles. Oh and then,' she screwed up her nose and shook her head, 'you wouldn't believe the change in the man. It's "Mrs P this" and "Mrs P that" and "next time you're passing, Mrs P, do call in and it'll be my pleasure to show you round the manor house". Talk about slimy. Ugh!' she shuddered.

'Did you go?' Dorrie said, through a mouthful of beef and parsnips and wonderful herbs.

'No. Don't like the look of the place. There's *vibrations*.'

Dorrie knew what she meant. 'I was there today,' she admitted. 'I was ... having a bit of trouble finding you and I sort of wandered into the grounds. I didn't know it was his place till he started shouting at me. He went mad!'

Granny Farthing was fastening off. *'He wouldn't be best pleased,'* she said, her strong teeth severing the glove from the ball of wool. The cat opened his ginger eyes wide to see the five-fingered corpse lying in the skinny lap.

'Very twitchy about people trespassing on his land,' Grandma nodded.

'The thing was, I had a vision about it.'

'Did you, dear?' She put down the plates to listen. That was the difference. You could be yourself with Grandma.

'There was building going on. Streets and houses. A new estate. Sometime soon he's going to have to sell up.'

'I never knew that,' said Grandma indignantly.

'Don't look at me,' said the ghost. *'I ain't no prophet, Nora. I'm just a go-between. It's news to me, and all.'*

'Well, there's a turn up. I thought he was sitting pretty. Fancy!' Her eyes blinked with

183

possibilities as she bustled through to the kitchen. There was a rattle of cutlery and then she shouted through, 'If he's hard up, he could be thinking of selling the cottages, and all. 'Cause these are due to be knocked through sometime, ain't they, and modernised. You said, didn't you, years ago?' She came to the door and addressed the girl. 'Remember? You said they'd knock two into one? Well, I reckon this new vision means things are on the move. What do you think, Mum? Think we ought to put in for one of them new houses?' Back to Dorrie. 'You didn't notice if they was council or private, did you, duck? Any lorries or workman's huts or anything with Doddingworth District Council on?'

But Dorrie couldn't help. She'd been too bewildered to pick up any clues.

'Well, it couldn't happen to a nicer bloke, could it?'

'*Nora!*'

'His son's all right,' said Dorrie unwisely, because then she had not only to explain how he had given her a lift down the road in the rain, but also sit through a tirade through the kitchen wall against accepting lifts from strangers.

Coming in with peaches and custard, her grandmother enquired. 'So how did you get here from the station, then? I thought you come on the bus?'

And Granny Farthing said, *'You must have come all round the houses to finish up on Doubleday's place.'*

So, against her better judgement, she told

them that, too. About the long trek from Ipswich, the café, the lift, the predatory driver…

'Oh, my Gawd, Dorrie – it was that murderer, I'll bet. The one that killed that poor little boy. Oh, you silly gel – don't you know no better than to take lifts from strangers?'

Near to crying Dorrie told them about the burst tyres, her narrow escape.

Granny Farthing put down her knitting, horror making a crêpey mask of her face.

'Oh, you poor little gel. I never knew you was in danger. And just round the corner, too – I could've been there in a jiff. Oh, that ain't good enough. What do they think they're playing at, eh? A guardian angel's s'posed to be the first to know!' And with a determined shake of her old shoulders, muttering about management inefficiency and things not being what they used to be, she faded from view. The cat patted a trailing ball of wool behind her.

Chapter Ten

At ten to seven Flo attempted to catch Arthur at work, from a call-box in the station yard. The line was dead. When she confronted the station-master with the problem, demanding to know where she might possibly find a telephone that worked, he pointed out, equally irritably, that the storm had brought down the lines, madam, and a lot more besides; there was at least one tree across the track and a derailment just outside Woodbridge, and trains banked up from here to Timbuctoo and he couldn't get through to the engineers to find out what was going on and she thought *she* had problems!

Her new friend, Walter Barrington, suggested she drop into the police station and get them to put through an emergency call on the radio.

They greeted Walter as an old friend. He seemed to be quite something in the town. When they heard who Flo was they became even more animated. Nora Potter's daughter-in-law? Ah yes, they knew Nora. Very well. Quite a character. As a matter of fact, Joe Torrance had just been in to inform them of the arrival of a young visitor, his wife's niece, a Dorothy Potter – would that be the young lady in question? Ah. Well now. The family had guessed that the young lady's parents might be concerned as to her whereabouts. They had tried to get through

186

on the telephone and, finding the line dead, had sent Joe. Yes, very thoughtful. So. Mrs Potter could put her mind at rest, couldn't she? Her daughter had arrived safely at, em... Through tears of relief Flo helped the desk sergeant decipher his notes ... 5, The Green, Great Bisset, and would remain in her grandmother's care until such time as the young lady's parents or, em, parent, em...

The message had already been passed on to the police at Forest Road, Walthamstow (*'No, we don't hang about, Mr Barrington'*), who were sending a car round to number 10, Haroldson Road.

'Oh, thank you, thank you! No, there'll be no one in because I'm here and he's been working overtime. He shouldn't be long. But thank you!' said Flo, making full use of her friend's handkerchief again. 'She's all right, Walter! She's all right!' and she blew her nose hard. Between gulps of hot tea which the police seemed to have on tap, she managed to give them her mother's address, which they passed on to Walthamstow, together with the information that Mrs Potter intended to take her daughter home the following day.

'Oh no – tonight,' she insisted. 'I've got work in the morning. I'm not hanging about here. I want to sleep in my own bed tonight.'

'But Mrs Potter...' the desk sergeant began.

'Dear lady...' said Walter.

Between them they persuaded her that she couldn't possibly. Joe had reported trees down and mud-slides on the road from Great Bisset.

He'd had to make detours through fields and farms and villages, easier with a motorbike than a car. If you didn't know the area in the dark you'd be stuck. Even if, by some miracle, Flo were to make it to her mother-in-law's, Dorrie would be in no fit state to travel tonight. According to Joe Torrance she was exhausted. What was more, there were no trains running between Woodbridge and Ipswich. It would be far more sensible to book into a guesthouse, have a good night's rest and set off in the morning.

It just seemed a waste, the afternoon off work, the urgency, the rush to get there.

'How will Dorrie know I'm here?'

'She doesn't need to know, not tonight,' said Walter reasonably. 'You've satisfied yourself that she's in safe hands. Why not give her some time alone with her grandmother?' He over-rode Flo's sharp intake of breath. 'There's no knowing how long it'll take to reach her in these conditions. The weather's appalling. And you haven't eaten. You'll be dead on your feet, woman. What good are you going to be to Dorrie or anyone? The morning's soon enough.'

There was no arguing with him.

As they left the police station, the desk sergeant asked to be remembered to Mrs Torrance and to let her know that there had been no recurrence of the tinnitus since she'd fixed it that time.

At ten to eight, Flo was emerging from a deep bath of hot scented water, prior to dinner, and wrapping herself in the biggest fluffy white towel she had ever seen.

When Walter had put it to her that he would have a hot meal waiting at home, of which there was bound to be plenty, that there was a comfortable guest room, and that he would be happy to drive her down to Great Bisset in the morning, she had said, 'Your wife'll have a fit, me turning up on the doorstep!'

He didn't have a wife, he said. He shared the house with a friend.

Heavens, she thought. She couldn't see him with a paramour, somehow, neither a slinky siren nor a dizzy blonde floozie. It just showed how deceptive appearances could be.

She said, 'Well, *she* won't be very pleased to have an uninvited guest.'

He. And Eric would be as delighted as Walter to have her stay.

Her mind did a couple of backflips. Two *men!* She wondered, fleetingly, whether she was supposed to be the hot meal. Of course, they could be ... but he didn't seem the type. He was nothing like the hand-flapping old queens who came into the shop. She looked more carefully. Oh dear, *was* he? In any case, a married woman just didn't go and stay the night with a man she'd met on the train.

To hell with it. She was too tired to argue. And hungry.

At a quarter past eight, while Flo was settling down to a tantalisingly aromatic *coq au vin,* in the company of two delightful men who were clearly devoted to each other, but who fussed around

189

her like royalty and made her laugh, Dorrie was helping her grandmother to make up the bed in the back bedroom.

They were working by the light of a hurricane lamp, the upstairs of the cottage not having been wired for electricity. Grandma flicked a sheet across the mattress with an expertise acquired during her years as a hospital orderly-cum-cleaner. She had already demonstrated the art of folding in the ends to make mitred corners, and was showing Dorrie how to hold the pillow under your chin as you slid on the slip, when they both cringed, hearing something slithering down the roof over their heads and crashing onto the cobbled yard.

'Slate,' Grandma diagnosed. 'That's all we need, rain pouring in. Joe'll see to it when he comes off shift. You could wait forever for Doubleday to send someone round. Gaw, listen to it.'

The wind was ramming the cottage, jiggling the doors and windows and wailing in blind frustration. Trees were creaking, dustbin lids were clattering and dogs were barking.

'Hope me chickens are all right. I battened them down with sacking and bricks on top. It should hold.' As she went to the window to check, her shadow lurched across the ceiling. 'Look at that!' she said, her jaw dropping. 'One of Lucy's nappies! It's gone flying over Battses' roof like a flipping seagull. She won't never get that back.' She pulled the curtains closed, shivering. 'I'll fetch you another couple of blankets,' she decided, 'it's cold up here,' and hurried after her leaping shadow into the next room. Dorrie, left alone in the dark, heard her gasp 'Oh my Gawd!' and was already feeling her way across the room when the call came. 'Dorrie, come 'ere, quick!'

Her grandmother was at the window now. 'Look at the tree!' The mighty tree was an old wet dog, violently shaking branches that were so long they whipped and cracked against the wild sky. Broken bits were flung off in the twisting, and a sound like rapid gunshots reached the two spectators as the taproot was wrenched across. There was a moment of resistance, of holding on, while the hooligan tempest shrieked, beside itself. Slowly, slowly, the earth released its grip with a snapping of cords and bonds. It seemed to Dorrie that the great tree took a step out of the ground, tottered forward and...

'*Grandma!*' she screamed, dragging her back.

...came crashing down across the green, across the lane, across the garden hedges, crushing the daffodils. It fell unbelievably short of the houses but smashed into the telegraph pole by Grandma's front gate.

'Standing there like two penn'orth of eels, I was,' said Grandma, for the second or third time, sipping tea while Lucy checked her over for injury and Dorrie envisioned that sad plateful of jellied eels. 'Bleedin' mesmerised. If Dorrie hadn't pulled me away I'd've had me chips. That's why she was sent, you see. They knew I was a bit slow off the mark. Ooh blimey, Luce,' she winced, 'take it easy!' Lucy's long fingers continued their hunt for harm. 'That's it,

191

ooh, just there, duck.'

'More glass,' said Lucy. 'In deep but I can probably get it with the tweezers.'

'Can't you do the business?' the old woman asked, her brow creased in pain.

'Healing? I will. But we must get the splinters and glass out first. They won't just disappear – it's not magic. Hold still. JoJo, you'll need to hold the lamp up a bit so Mummy can see.' Four-year-old Joanna had been woken by the commotion and been given an important job to do. Her little brothers were sleeping soundly, their dreams milky sweet and far removed from storms and destruction.

'Been on the cards a long time, ain't it, Dor, the old tree going?' As Lucy worked her mother talked stoically on. 'Remember that vision you had. I said to you, didn't I? "Wouldn't be surprised if tonight's the night".' She hadn't actually spoken aloud but Dorrie didn't contradict her and they both fell silent as the healer probed deeper into the thread-veined thigh.

'Come on, you wretch ... don't slip.' They held their breath, wincing. 'Gotcha!' The small splinter of glass she held up to the light did not glitter. 'Swab, please, nurse.' Dorrie dunked a wisp of cotton wool into her tin cup of Dettol and water that was pinker now than when they'd started, and handed it to the young woman, who bathed the sore place, dabbed it dry and patched it with plaster. 'That's the lot, I think.'

'Thank Gawd for that,' Grandma said, pulling down the leg of her long pink bloomers to hide the damage, and straightening her flannelette petticoat, her skirt and her flowered overall over that. 'That's all you're getting, gels! I dunno, if I'da known I was gonna be the floor show, I'd've put on me frillies.' This attempt at cheer was for JoJo's sake, but the little girl simply frowned. The old woman shook her head, 'Never even thought about the telegraph pole. I mean, you know it's there else how would we get our electric? But you forget, don't you? I never expected it to come through me blooming ceiling!' She tried to laugh but her face contorted with misery.

Dorrie hugged her. 'It's all right, Gran. You're safe, that's the main thing.'

'I know, I know.' She gripped Dorrie's hand for strength. 'It's only bricks and mortar, easy mended, but it was a shock. One minute I'm thinking about making us some Ovaltine, next minute it's raining slates and bloody birds' nests and I'm picking glass out of me backside!'

'It could have been worse,' said Lucy, trying not to smile.

Could it? They hadn't had to be dug out, Dorrie supposed, like her mother in the war, but it had been bad enough. With the solid weight of the oak tree behind it, the pole, from some snowy forest in Norway, had gored through the garden and, in toppling a second time, had sliced through the cottage like a knife through piecrust. Wires vibrating now with elemental power, it had leaned through the top window, seeing stars, while the contents of the room whirled around on a roar of wind, dust and doilies, bird bones, books and brassieres, eider-

193

downs and dressing gowns, like a batter whisked by a monstrous beater.

Precious things had clattered and crashed to the floor. The oil-lamp was blasted off the mantelpiece, the bowl and ewer sent skittering off the wash-stand by a muscle of curtain. Pictures and mirrors beat against the wall in frenzy, smashing glass, rugs and bedspreads bucked and heaved. Dorrie and her grandmother had staggered from the room, blinded by flying debris, holding tight to each other and to their aptly named hurricane lamp as they fought to latch the chaos behind them. The mad moon, leering through the hole in the roof, had watched them go, shredding clouds with its Creamola smile.

'I mean, why, out of all the houses did it have to be mine?' The tears were forming twin puddles along the lower rims of her glasses.

'Dry your eyes, Ma,' said Lucy. 'When the wind drops we'll have a sort out. Save what we can and take photos of the damage for the insurance. Doubleday's responsible for the structural stuff. There's nothing you can do now except get your head down. Dorrie's room's all right, isn't it?'

Grandma sniffed and nodded.

'Well, she can sleep there and you can take Joe's place. Keep my feet warm. Come on, JoJo, beddybyes.'

The storm had blown itself out by the morning. The sun was shining and no more than a gentle breeze stirred the branches of the oak tree, still sprawled where it had fallen, across the heart of the village. Buds were swelling along its length, preparing to beat the ash tree nearby. The dawn chorus was more circumspect. Their nests were in ruins, their young lost in the fall or to sharp-eyed foxes and, having no babies to feed and no recognisable territory to patrol, they'd comforted themselves with worms and woodlice pecked out of the exposed root ball. Now they were too fat to sing.

The villagers came out to look, to say good-bye, armed with box Brownies. The children swarmed over the tree's bulk, bouncing astride the springiest boughs, swinging, daring each other to climb higher, shouting for Mum to watch, for Dad to catch, squealing with faked joy, for no one was happy at its passing.

Everything was out of kilter. The tree, the famous tree, Queen Victoria's Jubilee oak, had always been there, a landmark, a focus, as long as they could remember.

It was their barometer, their nature table, the first indication of the state of the morning when they drew back the curtains. They'd seen it looming from fog and screened by rain, its bare branches rimed with frost and steaming in sunshine. How were they to mark the passing days if there were no birds building nests, feeding their young, flying away, no buds unfurling, tender green, going through the palette to viridian to rust, no plumping acorns in furry caps? No gall wasps, no oak apples, no squirrels, no falling leaves?

Where would the children play? Where would

the lovers sit and dream, now that the old iron seat, braceleting the trunk, had been squashed flat? Where would the young mothers gather to compare notes, rocking their prams, where would the old people reminisce?

But, country people are ever practical: what was done was done and it couldn't stay there, blocking the lane, filling their gardens like some overnight Jack-and-the-beanstalk monstrosity. Who would clear it away if not them? The council? There must be dozens of trees down in the county. You could wait forever, and the need was urgent. Look, poor Nora Potter's roof was caved in and you couldn't get near the front of her house to get a ladder up.

All hands to the pump.

Not the men, of course, who had to go to work, reluctantly, not the children, who had to go to school, but the women, the old men, and Joe, back from the night shift, his face ashen when he thought how close his family had been to disaster.

They were already hard at it, sawing and hacking and carting the logs round to the cellar when Dorrie, in a borrowed jumper and an old pair of Lucy's overalls, stripping off the smaller branches and twigs for burning, became aware of a familiar presence behind her, arrogance oozing from his mutton-chop whiskers.

She half-turned her head, pretending not to notice him. He clearly didn't recognise her up close so she carried on chopping away at the branches. She hardly needed to delve into his mind to see which way his thoughts were heading – his aura was livid with greed – but she did anyway and found wormy oak panelling needing renewal, and beams and doors and tables and chairs and chests that he was already imagining in various stages of construction, and logs were being heaped beside his antique fireplace, too late for questions of rights to be resolved, *fait accompli* being nine-tenths of the law.

He was composing his words, assuming the role, rehearsing righteous indignation. What the hell did these peasants think they were doing, making off with his timber?

What could a mere schoolgirl do to stop him intimidating his tenants?

She raised her voice, ostensibly for Lucy, hidden in the crotch of two massive boughs, higher up, to hear. 'Another year or two and the tree would have been tapping on Grandma's front door. And yours.' The saw continued its steady rasp, creamy sawdust continued to drift down to the wet grass but Dorrie sensed her aunt had tuned to her wavelength, had noted the presence of the squire.

Her reply was punctuated with grunts of effort. 'Another year or *four* ... and it would have been coming through ... the damn roof and killing us all!'

'I bet they didn't think it would grow so big, those villagers when they planted their tree,' said Dorrie, taking up her cue. 'Oh hello,' she said, acknowledging the landlord at last. 'Have you come to help?'

'*The-e-eir* tree!' he demanded, slapping the tree

197

with a proprietary air. (A *hand*-ba-a-ag? thought Dorrie.)

Her erstwhile saviour, the younger Doubleday, grown even more handsome overnight, was tramping through the mud in glossy wellies from Mrs Stone's, next door, a saw in his capable hand. He meant to help.

'Well, yes,' she said, 'The plaque says so, doesn't it? *Planted by the people of Great Bisset in this the Glorious Jubilee Year of HM Queen Victoria...*' She was making it up, hoping her predictive powers were up to scratch. She hadn't seen the plaque for years. Doubleday's protruding eyes had narrowed to slits and he was flicking anxious glances this way and that to gauge others' reactions. Some had stopped work, leaning on axes to listen.

She carried on, freewheeling, fingers crossed. 'It's a well-known fact that the tree came from someone's front garden – a sapling?' She hazarded the guess and they all nodded encouragingly. 'Anyway, it could only've been about ten years old when they transplanted it. Had to tie it to a stake to stop it being blown over.'

'Ironic,' muttered Doubleday, casting a disapproving eye over his son who had taken the other end of Joe's two-handed saw, nodding hello to Dorrie.

'Can't 'ardly credit it,' put in Horace Batts, stretching his broad back. 'Bloody great thing that oak growed into.'

Lucy chimed in, arms and chin resting on the rough bark, looking down at them. 'They hadn't much in 1887, even less than now, but it was something they could do – plant a tree to honour their Queen. On their land.'

'*Their* land?'

'Oh yes. It's a common, the green. An ancient right of the people, for common grazing?' But his face remained steadfastly blank. 'For villagers to feed their pigs and geese and milk-cows.'

He frowned, watching his hopes of misappropriation slip away.

Dorrie added her two penn'orth. 'It dates from feudal times, doesn't it, Auntie? We learned about it in school.' That bit was true. 'Every village had a common. They generally had a big pond, didn't they, for their ducks and geese to swim on?' Enthusiastic nodding all round. It sounded plausible.

Lucy said, 'That's right. Great Bisset drained theirs to plant the tree.'

Possibly.

'Hmm,' Doubleday said, walking purposefully towards the upended seat, now a tangle of iron slats. He was going to check on the wording of the plaque. Oh. Dorrie held her breath, watching his expression. He was raising his eyebrows, pursing his lips. Lucy gave her the thumbs-up.

The same thought occurred to them both. Better make sure Joe unscrewed the plaque before Doubleday did. It wouldn't do for it to go missing. Goodness knows whether there were any papers in County Records to substantiate their claims.

As far as the villagers were concerned it was settled.

'Fetch a tidy sum, I shouldn't wonder.' Horace, Granny Batts' bachelor son was rubbing his beefy hands. 'All that timber. Get a few four-be-twos out o' that.'

Joe stopped sawing long enough to draw their attention to the cost of getting their monstrous oak tree carted away to a saw-mill. They'd need a crane to move a thing that size, he averred. It had to be all of seven feet in diameter. And where would they send it? The nearest saw-mill was out Harborough way, twenty miles or more; they'd have to pay for special transport. And for having it cut up into manageable lengths. Then they'd have to find customers, timber-yards or cabinetmakers. It would all cost time and money. Having sown the seeds of doubt he resumed his own, less ambitious sawing, nodding to John Doubleday, who pushed as Joe pulled, steadily and rhythmically. When the bough fell and the two sawyers were dragging it to where a pile was starting, the old men began their murmuring.

'Cabinetmakers want seasoned wood, not green,' a toothless old boy reminded them.

'How long, Elbert?'

'Couple o' year, or more,' he said, stroking his whiskery chin.

'Couple o' year!' exclaimed Horace, who couldn't wait that long.

'En't a lot of call for green wood, these days.' Elbert was getting into his stride. 'They used to make them timber-framed houses with green. Fresh-hewed timbers they were. Oh, they split and cracked like billy-o till the house settled down but they held up – lasted hundreds of years. Same wi' ships.'

'I know all about them old houses,' hissed Horace, lowering his voice as Doubleday picked his way back through the mud. A track was worn where everyone had had to check for themselves that the tree really had been uprooted, that it was beyond saving. 'And ships. Only they b'ain't making wooden ships no more, Elbert, nor wooden houses. Only folk who wants to buy oak nowadays will want it seasoned for *furniture*, tables and chairs and such.' He winked and jerked his head in their landlord's direction. 'And panelling. You can't have no splits in panelling.'

'Ah. Right you are, 'Orace!' They all nodded, wily now, almost catching on.

The huddle broke up, as Doubleday came within earshot.

'So that's settled, then. We'll share the logs among the folks round here and let the bulk of the wood go to the highest bidder, like. 'Course,' Horace's cunning little eyes began to gleam, 'if Mr Doubleday could use some o' the timber up at the 'all, I reckon we could see our way clear to letting him have a ton or two, cheap.'

Doubleday looked sour. 'I'll let you know,' he said curtly. 'Now then, John,' he turned to his son, who was gathering up the sticks that Dorrie had cut, 'what're we going to do about number five?'

'That's not your house?' The boy actually looked concerned and Dorrie nodded. 'Good Lord!' he exclaimed. 'Is everyone all right?'

Dorrie explained how Grandma had escaped with cuts and bruises.

'She does have somewhere to sleep for a night or two? Until we can get the repairs done?'

'Well, it depends.'

'John ... a word.' As Doubleday took his son aside, eyebrows cocked and curtains twitched. There was jiggery-pokery afoot. One thing was certain, Nora wouldn't be back in her bedroom in a 'night or two'.

'Is Mrs Potter at home?' The florid face was as impassive as ever. The boy appeared chastened and embarrassed as he carted his bundle of sticks to the bonfire.

'She's in our house, minding the kids. Hang on a tick.' Lucy clambered down from her perch. 'We'll go round the back.'

Walter nosed the Wolseley into the lane and immediately applied the brake. Another fallen tree. They were used to them now, having had to reverse, squeeze by and go all round the houses avoiding them. Luckily Eric had known all the by-ways but it had taken them ages. They'd had to stop to move branches and a fence that had blown into the road, even a tarpaulin, caught on a hawthorn and draped across their path.

But this was by far the biggest tree. The lower branches must have stuck thirty or forty feet into the air, perpendicular to the trunk which rose at an angle from the ground, supported by a trestle of thick, broken branches, and its trunk so thick they'd had to prop stepladders at intervals along its length for ease of access. It was a few moments before it dawned on Flo that this was Great Bisset's oak tree and that her mother-in-law's front garden had all but disappeared beneath it. Moreover, there was a hole in the cottage roof. Her hand flew to her mouth. The front bedroom. Dorrie!

But, far from being crushed to a pulp, Dorrie came bounding towards her, wielding a small chopper like a dirt-streaked Red Indian. On the warpath. She even smelled the part as she threw herself into Flo's arms – smoky and sweaty. Over her daughter's impossible hair Flo saw a bonfire blazing on the green and a young man tending it.

'Mummy!' There was a catch in her voice and, for a moment, Flo sensed a child's need in her tall daughter. But as she held her away to read her eyes, she saw the glow fade and a guard come down. Then there were just words, said kindly but they hurt just the same. 'You didn't have to come and get me. I said in my note I'd be back. It would have been today if I could have borrowed the money from Grandma, but...' She gestured dramatically towards the tree, on its knees. 'I couldn't leave them to it, could I?'

This was not the time for recriminations. As Dorrie gabbled out the story of how Nora had escaped being felled by the telegraph pole, even Flo had to admit that the girl's presence had been timely. Now she understood the dark circles but not the tearstains. Nor the restraint.

They had another source entirely. It wasn't the fact that the landlord was refusing to foot the repair bills to Nora's cottage. That had made her angry but it was no more than they'd expected, she said. There was something else, something in the way Dorrie looked at Flo, as though trying to uncover truths. She blinked.

Lucy was waving from among the branches and she hesitated before returning the greeting, unsure of her welcome after the seven-year rift. She worried her lip with her teeth as her sister-in-law trod carefully under and over the massive boughs, balanced along the trunk to a stepladder, came down backwards and hurried over to them. There were calluses as the brown hand shook the white one, awkward as a stranger's. The two men got out of the car and Flo prepared to introduce them.

'Lucy!' Eric grasped her shoulders, kissed her cheek. They knew each other! He let her go and his hands spread in appeal to some higher being. 'Isn't this d-d-dreadful!' Flo felt for him. Since leaving his home, his stammer had become more pronounced. Yet he didn't strike her as a shy man, quite the reverse. He'd larked about and played the fool, as well as the piano. And that was a funny thing: when he'd sung to them last night there hadn't been a hint of his affliction, just a vibrant baritone voice and perfect enunciation. She'd almost choked on her chicken when they'd told her that part of his repertoire was public speaking. But they were serious: apparently, when faced with large audiences he was perfectly fluent. 'And there was no w-w...' now he sucked air and jerked his chin, determined to communicate '...warning, that's what I c-can't understand. What a t-t-t ... what a shock for poor N-Nora!'

He stood back to let Walter embrace her sister-in-law, and that was when Flo saw that the old woman hobbling through the gardens, carrying one red-haired child and steering two more around jutting boughs and twigs and finally through a neighbour's gate, was Arthur's mother. She'd aged so, Flo hardly knew her. She didn't seem to recognise her either, barely sparing her a glance.

'Eric? Blimey, mate, what you doing here? Was you at the meeting last night? Oh on, you said, didn't you? Don't s'pose there was many turned up, not with the weather. And Wally! Oh, you're a sight for sore eyes, and all. 'Ere, I reckon I might be able to put a bit of building work your way – what d'you think?' She nodded towards the wreckage. 'Come in for a cuppa, anyhow. And I'll tell you what, Wal, I reckon if you go through to my kitchen and look in my cake tin, you might find some of that spice cake you like so much. You go on. I'll be there in a minute. Lucy, take the kids. It's time you had a break. And you, Dorrie – go along, duck. I want a word with your mum.' So she had noticed her.

When they were alone, Nora regarded Flo with steely coldness. How drawn she was, Flo thought. She must have been up half the night, what with the storm damage and all.

'Well, Flo, it don't never rain but it pours – that's what they say, innit? My Gawd, gel, your ears musta been burning as you was coming along. You been the sole topic of conversation this last hour or so. Ain't she, Mum? I say we just been talking about her, ain't we?'

Flo stiffened. It was the awful matter-of-factness of it that was so alarming. The old woman's face was stern. 'Oh yeah, my mum's here,' she said. Flo felt for the solidity of the car behind her. If the worst came to the worst she could sit inside and lock the door. Sound the hooter until someone came to her rescue. Her neck prickled as the raving continued.

'She's been finding out a few things, Mum has. See, Dorrie told us she was given a lift by this pervert.'

Her hand flew to her mouth. 'Oh Dorrie...'

'Nothing happened, she's all right,' Nora hastened to assure her. 'But Mum, being the girl's guardian angel, shoulda known, see, if Dorrie was in any sort of danger. And nobody had said nothing. Any old how, cut a long story short, it turns out she wasn't in no danger at all. He was just looking out for her. As you do, if it's your own.'

'If it's your...?' She didn't understand. Could someone have mistaken Dorrie for their child? Is that what Nora meant? Or what, in heaven's name *did* she mean?

The old woman looked so tired, labouring her point, that Flo's heart went out to her. 'His car was a Rover, Dorrie said, a dark red one.'

'A dark red...' She caught her breath as the penny dropped at last. 'Frank used to drive a Rover,' she said slowly, and Nora sighed.

'Frank Leary,' she affirmed. 'He's her dad, isn't he? And my Arthur's a bloody fool.'

Chapter Eleven

A pantomime. A lunatic game of charades. One word, four syllables, the first two meaning 'grown-up', believe it or not, the third, the same as the fourth, suggestive of mistakes and uncertainty. Put two and two together and you have her. The adulterer.

The scene is the witch's parlour, made doubly gloomy on a truly mad March day, by a giant uprooted tree, offstage, blocking out the light. Centre stage, an old woman is kneeling before a newly laid fire, pulling her cardigan tighter.

'It'll cetch in a minute.'

Flo shivered, but it was presentiment that laid its icy hand between her shoulder-blades. The accused, she thought, awaiting judgment.

Crockery clattered next door and children's voices rose and fell. Her sister-in-law was preparing lunch for everybody so that Joe could get off to bed and the little boys could have a nap. A fitting moment for Flo and Dorrie to go off somewhere quiet and 'have a little talk'. Nora had offered her front room as a confessional.

Her attitude had softened when Flo had stumbled, faint, against the car. The boy had come across to help her indoors and her mother-in-law had patted her arm and said, 'Oh Flo,' and 'Oh Dorrie.' But it hadn't been shock that had felled her.

Flo knew that Frank was Dorrie's father and it was relief that buckled her knees. It was over; the long years of pretending and lies were done with. There'd be ructions at home when Arthur was told. Wife and daughter booted out. Bag and baggage. And then what would they do? She shrivelled with foreboding but even then, part of her was thankful. Surprising, that. What was even more surprising was that Nora and Dorrie were so sure. Flo had never been that certain.

Her daughter seemed to be taking it pretty well, considering the bombshell it must have been. Past the crying stage by the time Flo had arrived, she sat pale and still now, in the armchair opposite, staring into space, her brow furrowing and then relaxing, her mouth contracting and then softening, as his had done. As if she were carrying on an internal conversation. Inclining her head, leaning forward slightly as though asking a question or listening to an answer, and nodding slowly as though things were gradually becoming clearer, beginning to make sense. So like him. The set of the eyes, the unruly hair, the cleverness, the imagination, the artistic flair, so utterly unlike Arthur. On good days she had convinced herself that Dorrie took after her. On bad days she'd known that, when he was tired, yes, there had been a slight cast in *his* left eye.

She rolled her head slowly along the top of the chair to ease her foreboding, her eyes flicking over the worn chenille of the tablecloth, to the sideboard, crowded with familiar faces, her own among them, smiling up at Arthur on their wedding day, down at baby Dorrie in the photo-grapher's studio.

How long would it be, Flo wondered, before she was cast out of that gallery of Potters? Torn to pieces and burned? Along with her cuckoo baby.

Her eyes moved on quickly, following a hideous pattern of fern fronds up the wallpaper, around a cynically *Laughing Cavalier* to the ceiling where dark patches of oil and water bore witness to at least two of last night's catastrophic events.

Nora followed her gaze and her shoulders sagged. 'Oh bli, I never seen that!' She sighed companionably. 'Times I've had that ceiling done,' as though there weren't a great chasm between them. 'It's had Jack's foot through it and all sorts. Tomato sauce, the time young Peter shook the bottle and the top come off, and soot from when the Valor stove went wrong. Never seen nothing like it. It *wouldn't* shift. Not with carbolic, nor Vim. Had to be replastered. And then old Charlie kicked the jerry over, didn't he, and we only had whatsit dripping through. Oh Gawd!' But the laughter was false, the lines rehearsed, embellished and trotted out for strangers, cover for real thoughts. The mask dropped, revealing anxiety. 'I should've got Wally to look at it while he was here.'

Wally (Councillor Walter Barrington, of the Housing Department, a useful chap to know from all accounts), had had to get back to Town for a meeting and Eric had gone with him. How on earth those two intelligent men could be

209

involved in something as shoddy as spiritualism, Flo could not imagine. But then they were a surprising couple, to say the least.

Horace Batts trundled past the window pushing his barrow of logs. He nodded to them, his fleshy face running with sweat. Nora tutted and drew the curtain across. In the gloom Flo saw her mother-in-law light the hurricane lamp and set it on the table, fussing as though she had two invalids on her hands.

At last the fire was crackling to her satisfaction and she went out, struggling to fasten the latch: the wood was warped and the door didn't fit. She always left it open, that door to the kitchen, to let the warmth from the range, and her own presence, percolate through. Flo had to get up and lean against it. Dorrie looked up.

'He said you went to school together.'

'Did he?' She supposed it was as good a way as any to lead in to the big news: Hiya, kiddo, I'm your daddy! Nora could fantasize all she liked about guardian angels and ghosts, it was quite clear to Flo what must have happened. He'd been driving along, spotted this poor little waif wandering along in the rain who'd turned out, by a fluke, to be Dorrie. He'd offered her a lift and, impulsive as ever, decided there and then to break it to her. Great sense of timing, Frank.

They'd started on the same day, at Brick Lane Infants, she and the snotty-nosed 'herbert' crying for his mum. She'd lent him her hanky, warm from her knicker leg, scraped her beetroot onto his plate at dinnertime and slept on the next rush mat when it was time for afternoon

210

rest. He'd soon got into the swing of school, soaking up knowledge like a sponge. So clever he'd been promoted, up and up, through the year-groups to the top class of the juniors where, six years later, she had eventually caught up with him, found him outstripping the teacher in maths, reading Dickens for pleasure, bored out of his mind with Tudor history, and fed up with writing prize-winning 'compositions' – *A Day At the Seaside* (he'd never been further than Hackney) and *My Favourite Pet* (a spider in a matchbox) – to keep him quiet. He'd walked her home through courts and alleyways and smog, lending her his moth-eaten old scarf to stop the yellow poison entering her lungs. He'd bought her sweets, sent her a Valentine's card and on Saturday mornings filled her up with cliff-hangers at the Rialto, enough to see them through the week. He'd be Tarzan to her Jane, or the cowboy or the sheik or the pirate and she'd be 'the girl'. He'd have to rescue her from the Indians or the desert or slavery, whatever fate-worse-than-death he devised. There was never any love-stuff; they were just together, the stars. It was understood. Other kids got bit parts if they were lucky.

Neither was to take up the place they'd won at grammar school. Flo had to learn a trade and he'd had his future mapped out for him, his mother insisted, on the docks with his uncles.

The Hubbards moved to Walthamstow when Flo was fifteen, round the corner from Aunt Polly and Uncle Wilf, partly because Alice wanted to be close to her sister, now Uncle Wilf was on his last legs, partly because the Battle of Cable Street had put the wind up her. She spent the rest of her husband's life trying to get him to go for a job at the London Rubber Company or Ever-Ready Batteries, where work was not so hit-and-miss as down the docks. But Dad never gave up his union card and continued to catch the bus for Wapping every day, until the January morning he ran for it, slipped on a patch of ice and broke his back.

Flo heard, from his mates that came to the funeral, that Frank had got in with a bad lot, the same bunch that had half-inched the tin of ham that Mum had carved up for the sandwiches. She almost choked. But everyone was at it, her mother said. She'd known a side of beef come over the dock wall. It'd been popped into a pram, quick as a wink, covered with a blanket and wheeled round to Flo's Aunt Maud's to be jointed and handed out to each of the hungry families in George Street. But Flo was not amused. She sent a message back to Frank telling him to keep his ill-gotten gains to himself. A week later she received a Valentine's card, postmarked Whitechapel, with the heart crossed through and the words *Consider yourself divorced* scrawled inside. She blinked.

Dorrie was gazing at her, a soft look on her face. 'Oh Mum.'

What? She hadn't said anything, had she? No, she was sure.

'So when did you meet up with him again?'

How calm she was. Where were the cruel words, the accusations, the stamping and spitting Dorrie of two nights ago? A blazing row would have been more appropriate, certainly no more than she deserved. To have her daughter like this, willing to listen, to understand, it ... well, it made her feel distinctly uneasy.

'Mum?' she prompted. Dorrie looked quite pretty without her glasses, even though the lazy eye didn't quite focus. Until she smiled. The brace made her look as if her teeth were all bad. And you hadn't to take any notice of the hair, of course. Flo was sure a perm would be an improvement – 'Toni' did those home perms now, but Dorrie wouldn't hear of it.

'Was it before or after you married Dad, er, your husband?' Her eyes were suddenly salt-pink and Flo realised the effort she was putting into self-control. 'Sorry.' She cuffed at her nose. 'It's no good – he *is* my dad. He brought me up and I love him, I suppose, even though he is impossible sometimes.'

''Course you do. I – I love him too,' Flo said. She thought it might be true. 'But it's a different sort of love from what I felt for Frank.'

'Frank,' Dorrie whispered.

'Didn't he tell you his name?'

'He might have.' She was being evasive.

'Dorrie?'

'Yes, he probably did but it didn't click.'

'What do you mean, it didn't click?'

'I knew there'd been a man in your life called Frank. I didn't know he was my father.'

'*How* did you know?' And Dorrie's face closed like a sea anemone prodded too sharply. Flo cleared her throat, as the little brown bear came

213

to mind, the wretched teddy that Dorrie still took to bed. It was worn and patched and Flo had had to sew an insert to strengthen a wobbly neck, and replace a lost eye with a button that didn't quite match the other. She'd known, years ago, when Dorrie had named it Frank, that it was no accident. 'How did you find out, Dorrie?' she repeated, more gently. 'Who told you?'

'Mum, I...' She seemed about to make some sort of confession, but changed her mind. 'I can't remember.' There was a pause as they both contemplated the lie, then the distraction. 'I've seen him before, Mum. He was the man who untied me when the kids left me in the park that time.'

She wasn't surprised – he used always to be spying on the girl. Watching her. He'd been convinced of his paternity, even if Flo wasn't. 'He took an interest,' she said flatly.

'Don't you see him any more?'

She shook her heard firmly, and Dorrie's eyes opened wide.

'But you're still stuck on him?'

Damn. Was she so transparent? She swallowed. Dorrie didn't need to know all the details. She was just a kid, when all was said and done, and some things were private.

Almost as though she had read her mind, Dorrie said gently, 'Look, Mum, until a couple of hours ago Arthur Potter was my dad and Grandma was my grandmother. Now it turns out I'm nothing to do with them. It would be nice to know about my real dad. What he's like.'

Flo sighed. 'You met him yesterday, didn't you? You know what he's like.'

'Yes, but I wasn't paying proper attention. I didn't know he was my dad then, did I?'

This wasn't making any sense. 'I thought he told you.'

'No, all he said was he knew you. He didn't say how well.' She blinked away a twinkle.

'I don't get it, Dorrie. How did you find out he was your dad if he didn't tell you?'

That closed look again. 'Gran,' she mumbled.

Nora? How long had *she* known? From her attitude that morning Flo somehow didn't think she was the one who had planted the name Frank in the girl's mind all those years ago. 'How did she find out?'

'Search me,' the girl shrugged. Then, 'Someone told her, I think.'

So she was the subject of village gossip now. Flo shook her head, resigned to it. She was past caring.

Dorrie was waiting and, of course, she had a right to know. What could she say? That Frank was a reptile, a smooth-talking bastard who would break your heart? That he was utterly irresistible?

'How did you meet him again?' prompted Dorrie, tucking her legs under her, settling in for a long session. But it was so hard. Flo bit her lips. Every day at the salon she talked about anything and nothing to complete strangers, under the racket of the dryers. Not about Frank, of course. That was hidden deep. It came between them and was why she had no real friends. Women always know if you're holding something back. But her daughter was her daughter and that was different.

'I don't...' she faltered, 'I...' She couldn't. 'Perhaps your dad, er, Arthur, ought to be the first to hear all this.' Though the thought of telling him, seeing his face, the hurt in his eyes, gathered in a lump in her chest. 'I owe him that.'

'You owe *me*, Mum.'

'I know, I know,' she sighed.

It began easily enough with familiar faces and places.

'Nanna Hubbard and Aunt Polly settled down in Walthamstow, widows, both of them, by the time war broke out, but they still kept up with their old friends and neighbours in the East End. They'd all meet up for a chin-wag on Sunday mornings down Brick Lane market, and there'd be parties, and all the usual weddings and funerals. But the real get-togethers were when they all went down to Kent, hopping.'

'Hopping?'

'Hop-picking. They don't do it so much now, not round our way, but when I was young there'd be lorryloads of us Londoners off down to Kent in September to pick the hops, women and kids mostly, and old men. The other men would come down at weekends, if they could, or if they were laid off. The schools'd be half-empty.'

'Oh, that sounds all right!' her daughter said pensively.

'Yeah. Yeah, it was. Though it was no holiday

camp, no mod cons at all, but that didn't matter somehow. You all slept in these corrugated iron sheds, bum-to-bum, with nothing between you and the dirt floor but a straw mattress. And you washed in a bucket and you cooked over an open fire. Wonderful.'

Dorrie was making a face.

'No, I mean it. You'd have loved it, mucking in and sharing. And the work wasn't that hard. Boring, more than anything, filling sack after sack with hops, hour after hour, week in week out. But it was out in the fresh air and you made it fun. Stories and sing-songs and that. And a bit of a knees-up of a Saturday night. Weekends there'd be a few men around to liven things up. No, it was all right.' She nodded as memories flooded her mind. ''Course in 1940, the time I'm talking about, there weren't any men around to speak of. Well, there were the dockers – they were needed for unloading the ships – but your dad and all his brothers were away fighting the war, with all the other men. It was down to the women to keep the home fires burning and, come September, it was us who had to get the hops picked. Not that we minded in the least. Oh Dorrie, you won't believe what a relief it was to get out of Town for a week or five. London in the Blitz was no picnic, I can tell you. Arthur didn't see it like that though. He sent me a letter saying I should stop at home. He might have believed in the "common people" but not that common.'

It is not that I do not trust you, dear, he'd written,

217

don't think that. I just feel bad about my lovely wife having to rough it just for a few bob extra which I am sure we can manage without.

She had made excuses for him. He was just a bit possessive and that was understandable. They'd only been married a year, when all was said and done.

Her mother curled her lip. 'Nah,' she said, 'loada flannel, gel. Don't take a blind man to see what's bothering Mr God-Almighty Arthur Potter.' It was the drink talking. 'He thinks we're scum, don't he, us 'oppers? He thinks we're bleeding riff-raff.'

That wasn't true, Flo insisted. Arthur's family weren't part of the hopping crowd but only because poor Nora spent every waking minute scrubbing floors up at the hospital, or washing people's dirty linen or bringing up her family. She simply didn't have time for holidays. But she certainly never regarded her neighbours as riff-raff. She'd have loved sitting in the back of Bert Stack's lorry (on 'temporary loan' from the builder's yard), atop the raggle-taggle pile of furniture, with her family and friends around her and a couple of large 'seedies' clasped to her bosom.

'I ain't saying a thing against Nora Potter,' said her mother. 'Salt of the earth, old Nora. But your Arthur's too big for his bleeding boots. Ain't his fault, I suppose – can't be easy having to be a father to all them brothers of his, and the girl. All the same he takes too much on hisself if you ask me. My Gawd, I won't forget your wedding in an 'urry.' Indignation flared with the

218

memory, staining her cheeks. 'What I have to drink and how much is down to me, specially if I'm paying. Who the hell did he think he was, eh, laying down the law? He's *your* husband, not mine. If you're daft enough to let him boss you around that's your look out. He ain't poking his nose in my affairs! If I was you, Flo, I'd make the most of it while he's away. You mark my words, once he gets his feet under the table, when the war's over, you can kiss goodbye to hopping.'

'So I made out the letter arrived too late and went anyway. Well, I had to do my bit. Last chance.' She grinned. 'Couldn't have the boys going without their beer, could I? The government were giving us their blessing and a full tank of petrol. So that settled it. Hopping here we come!'

Dorrie squeezed her lips together. 'And that's where you met *him* again? Frank Leary?'

She nodded.

The day had begun badly. They'd been woken by bony knuckles rapping on the door, and without waiting for an answer, a sparrow of a woman had flung it open and stood stiffly silhouetted against the day.

'Rise and shine, gels, the sun's burning yer bleeding eyes out!'

'Where's our Polly got to, then?' Her mother was blinking against the light.

'She's at the stand-pipe, Alice, 'aving a sloosh down. She asked me to give you a call. Reckons your clock's stopped.'

'Eh? Oh, it never 'as!'

'Oh May, I said you was to wind it up!' Evie, their friend from Bethnal Green, was distraught.

'I did, I did!' her daughter insisted.

'What's the time, then, Mrs Paycock?'

'Nearly seven o'clock, duck.'

'Oh, my Gawd!' said her mother. 'Come on, gels, look lively. Flo, fetch us a bucket of water. It'll 'ave to be a cat's lick this morning.'

While they wiped the sleep away with flannels and cold water and struggled into their work-clothes, while they tied their curlers into protective turbans, Mrs Paycock spread beef dripping on five doorsteps of bread, and they managed to eat them as they hurried through the hop-garden, fifteen-year-old May ahead of her mother, Evie, whose job it was, with Flo, to lug along the hopping stools and folding chairs. Aunt Polly and Mum brought up the rear with the tea-pot and a tin lunchbox containing bread and mousetrap cheese and a few hard-bakes, all they could muster in their haste.

They found a knot of their neighbours already working at the 'bins', beside a mound of hop-bines, when they arrived. Flushed with the rush, they looked around for spaces to set up their own seats.

'Afternoon, gels. What 'appened? Out on the tiles, was we?'

'You could've given us a shout.'

'Thought you was up, all the racket you was making!'

'Racket? Oh, that was Aunt Polly; something was itching her.'

'Here, slip in next to me.' Betty Craddock who lived next door to Polly stretched her friend's sack over the wooden frame. 'You're all right, he ain't been round yet.'

'The men've only just dumped this lot.'

'Give us yer sack, May.' Lou Medhurst, who lived on Evie's landing, disappeared into her hessian 'bin' and scooped some of its contents into the girl's sack.

'Oh Lou, there's no need–'

'You'd do the same for me, lovey, wouldn't you?'

Others, too, shared their spoils so that when the foreman made his rounds ten minutes later, all the hoppers appeared to have been at work for an hour.

'Morning, my lovelies, all present and correct? Some more than others, eh?' He'd got eyes in the back of his head.

Aunt Polly decided on diversion tactics. 'You got any Flit, Charlie? Some 'orrible insect's been crawling round in my bed. I've got bites in some very funny places!'

'Get you some calamine, shall I, Polly? You show me where and I'll dab it on for you!' His lewd grin had the women hooting and cackling, like a barnyard, and Flo smiled. As they settled to their work, they could hear him a few rows up. 'Morning, ladies, all present and correct?'

'He's a caution, ain't he, though?' Lou chuckled, her double chins jiggling on her flower-sprigged overall. 'Geein' all the gels up, makin' 'em work twice as 'ard to get in his good books.'

'Get in his underpants, more like – eh, Polly?' Betty, also from the 'buildings', chortled and her hands, already stained green with hop-juice, made obscene gestures.

'Gaw bli, he's a bit long in the tooth, ain't he?' Her mother elbowed Flo in the ribs, adding rudely, 'Even by your standards, Polly?'

'Beggars can't be choosers, Alice,' her sister said archly and winked. 'And you know what they say about snow on the roof.'

'Well, at least at your time of life there ain't likely to be no little accidents, eh, Polly?'

'He must have sired a fair few over the years. Bleeding World Service, he is.'

'Men like that should have it chopped off.'

'Ooh, not yet, Betty.' Lou's fingers were flying over the vines. 'We want our share before that happens, eh, Flo? You all right, duck? You look a bit dicky ter me.'

'Want to have a lend of me hat, gel? The sun in yer eyes, is it?'

'Come and sit round this side, in the shade, Flo.'

'No, no, thanks. I'm all right.'

But she wasn't. She felt out of sorts. Being late had cast the day in a new slant. She was seeing things and people, especially people, with jaded eyes. The sun was still warm, the air still sparkled, skylarks still scraped the underside of heaven but their joyous trilling teetered on hysteria. The cries of the children, romping among the rows of green bines, had become fractious and shrill, and the women, whose talk had been a balm, were grown shallow. And coarse. Even the pretty green catkins seemed past their best and the smell was stale and unwholesome, like a sleazy bar-room joke. Perhaps Arthur was right and they were a 'rough' lot. Perhaps she could do better. Or perhaps she could have done better than Arthur.

She watched May's slender green fingers darting among the stems like snakes' tongues. A few years ago that would have been her sitting there, with her hops tumbling into the sack. She'd had her life before her. Her choice of men. And she'd chosen him.

'Penny for 'em, Flo?' You weren't allowed to look glum or to have secrets.

'Worth more'n that, Aunt Polly.' If she was having doubts it was too late now and nobody's business but her own. She stood up and stretched, poking damp tendrils of hair back under the headscarf. Her sack was full. She hoisted it over her shoulder and, staggering under the weight, dived into the lacy jungle to have her pickings weighed.

Stumping down the row in her Wellington boots she realised that her sock, which had been steadily creeping down past her heel, had become altogether unbearable. She stopped to see to it, put down her sack and tried to lean against a handy post, which moved away and left her flat on her back! From this undignified position, she found herself looking up into the sky and a pole-man's startled face.

'Watch it!'

'What?'

'You nearly had me over!' he snapped.

'Sorry?'

'You leant on me stilt, you daft bitch. I could've broke me fucking neck.'

'And I could've broken my back!'

'Well, mind out, then!'

'*You* mind out!'

She was blowed if she was going to move out of the way of any foul-mouthed yobbo, even if he was young and good-looking, and she propped herself on her elbows and kicked off the troublesome footwear. Her sock was round her toes. It wasn't until he took another step, skewering the boot to the ground, that she was able to appreciate the advantage that twelve-foot-high stilts gave the wearer. He continued snipping the bines off the top wire, and letting them fall, sighing, to the ground, as though he didn't know full well what he had done.

'You're on my boot,' she said, coolly enough. But when he took not a blind bit of notice she had no choice but to try and drag it free. He wobbled and squawked and she tugged all the more.

Without warning he stepped off the boot, so suddenly that she fell back with it, soft-landing onto her sack which toppled, spilling out an hour's work onto the baked ground.

'Oh,' she wailed, struggling to her feet and hopping around on one foot, 'look what you've done, you bugger!'

Then he came sliding down the stilts, as though they were greased. He took a moment to unfasten himself from the harness and to lay the poles carefully along the path and, only then,

224

began scooping up the hops. His silence was unnerving until she noticed his shoulders heaving.

'Piss off!' she snapped. At which he erupted. Rich, full-throated, belly laughter. At her expense. She could have hit him.

'I don't need your help, Leary.' For she had recognised that laughter. Remembered nine-year-old Frank hooting at a Buster Keaton film in exactly that way. Helpless with it. 'Go on, bugger off!'

'Oh, you should have ... should have *seen* yourself! Oh, what a sight! Funniest thing in ages!' And he continued to laugh and laugh until she found she was laughing with him. It must have been funny from up there. Birds' eye view of her tugging at the boot, like a thrush at a worm, and then falling over backwards, when it was released. She smiled and began to chuckle. He was on his knees, hunting hops through tears of blind merriment and that was funny, too. She'd never been able to stay cross with Frank Leary for long.

He was staring at her, laughter slowly draining from his face. 'You should smile more often – you're a good-looking girl.' Then, 'Don't I know you from somewhere?'

He said he was down for the weekend. Normally he'd be getting in a bit of overtime, but it was so quiet down the docks these days with so few merchant ships getting through, there was hardly enough work to warrant going in weekdays, let alone Saturday. Jerry had the seas sewn up. Bleeding U-boats everywhere. Besides, what did you do of a Saturday night if

225

all the girls were down in Kent? You could go dancing with your mates, he supposed, and get yourself a reputation, but it wasn't his idea of a good time.

While he talked he picked fresh green hops from the bines he'd just brought down, scattering them over those scooped up from the path. Some pernickety measureman might have thought the dust weighed unfairly, he said, and make her start again.

He was just an old friend. Her mate from junior school. So why did they look at her that way when she told them the story of how she'd bumped into him? Was there something in her voice? In her eyes? Were her cheeks too pink, her hands too fluttery? Why didn't they rib her the way they did Aunt Polly? Where were the coarse remarks? It was a funny story. Flat on her back in the hop-vines. They could have made something of it. As she looked round the group at the bins, mouths tightened by an almost indiscernible notch, eyebrows quirked almost imperceptibly, and eyes flicked anxiously in her direction before lowering to the work again. That was the difference, wasn't it? Aunt Polly was a widow. Fair game. While Flo was a married woman with a husband away fighting for his country.

So when Ma Kendall struck up a polka on her accordion that night, and he asked her to dance, she declined. When he pulled up a chair to sit beside her and talk, she dragged old Harry Paycock up for Boomps-a-Daisy. When he asked her if he could get her a beer, she said she was all right, even though she was gasping. And when he then grabbed May, sweet and pretty May, for a slow and earnest waltz with one-two-three personal tuition, she realised she had a splitting headache and would be all the better for an early night.

She couldn't believe her feet were doing this, stepping so quickly through the grass away from the best party in ages, not giving her a chance to change her mind. Other men, husbands and sons, had come down for the weekend bringing with them a barrel of beer and a fiddler. Someone had rigged up a string bass from an orange box and a broom handle and, what with the ukelele and the accordion, the joint was jumping. And she was running away. It just didn't make sense. Well, it did if you couldn't take your eyes off a bloke and he wasn't your husband.

Mrs Paycock's hut loomed out of moonlight. She had to be quiet. There were kids asleep... And someone behind her. She turned and a torch searched her face, blinding her.

'Flo? You all right, are you?' His voice was a whisper but the concern sounded genuine.

Her heart was hammering too fast. She'd faint and really make a fool of herself. Or she could tell him to take a running jump. He knew she was married. She'd flashed the bright, new ring in front of his nose enough times this evening.

'Go away, Frank,' she said. 'Go and shine your torch in someone else's eyes.'

'Don't go in just because of me,' he pleaded. 'The party's only just got started. If you come back I'll leave you alone. Cubs' honour.'

Now that was very presumptuous of him. Fancy thinking that he had driven her away from the party! True, but what an ego. She couldn't help smiling.

'I don't know what you mean,' she said coyly.

'You do,' he said. And she knew he was deadly serious. After the briefest of pauses he said briskly, 'Look, if you go back, I'll take myself off somewhere. I've got a book to read and a torch to read it by. I can't promise to be happy as Larry but I'll try. How's that? I'll keep right out o' your way the rest of the weekend and there won't be a thing for anyone to tell your old man.'

That was what she wanted, wasn't it? Exactly what she wanted. How had he known?

'And if I don't?'

'If you go to bed now, girl, you'd best lock your door, because I tell you, I am having a very hard time of it trying to be a gent.'

'It doesn't lock,' she said in a wee small voice.

'Looks like you're going back to the party, then, don't it?'

This was not what she told Dorrie, of course. She said that she had met Frank again in the hopfields, that they'd grown fond of each other and that, on her return to London, he had become a regular visitor to the Hubbards' house. It was wrong of them, she made no bones about it, 'carrying on' while her husband was away at sea. But she was besotted with him. She'd thought he felt the same. When she discovered she was pregnant she didn't know what to do.

Arthur had been home on leave – the baby could easily have been his. Or it could have been Frank's.

'Mu-u-um!' wailed Dorrie.

Flo made a wry face. 'I know, love. I'm sorry. Frank was always convinced you were his. He begged me to leave Arthur.'

'Did he?' A terrible hope shone in her eyes.

Flo grimaced. 'Dorrie...' How could she make her understand? 'See, Frank was a bad boy. I suppose that was his attraction in a way. He was ... exciting. Unpredictable. And that's fine in a lover but he'd have made a pretty rotten husband and father.'

'You don't know that, Mum!'

Oh she did. He was clever. He was 'fly'. He would bring her things which were obviously 'knocked off': clothes and food from the States, luxuries you'd die for in time of austerity. She told him not to. She could manage without. It wasn't fair when there were people going hungry.

So he gave it to her mother. Everyone was at it, Mum insisted, squirreling away the latest bag of currants, or tin of treacle in the larder. You made do and you mended and you saved your coupons but it was plain daft to look a gift-horse in the mouth. If you didn't take it, someone else would. Did Flo suppose all them high-ups were going without, them as could pay? No, they bloody well weren't. They still had their marmalade for breakfast and their ham for tea. There were shortages to be sure but if you really wanted something it could be had, if you knew

229

where to look. And Frank knew where. He was a Godsend.

Flo wasn't sure about that. God wouldn't have much to do with a shady character like Frank. But Flo couldn't get enough of him.

The night of the bomb he'd been coming round, to 'talk things over'. Again. She'd made up her mind, at last, to write to Arthur and ask him for a divorce. When she told him the baby wasn't his he wouldn't be able to refuse. There'd be a scandal and she and Mum would have to move away but she could support herself, with Frank's help, she was sure. Mum would see to the baby while Flo cut hair, and then, after the war, when he could leave the docks, Frank and she would set up home together, a little cottage by the sea, somewhere they weren't known. He'd get a decent job and they'd all live merrily together. She was going to tell him over tea.

Dorrie's Nanna had taken herself off, with bad grace, to Aunt Polly's to leave them a clear field. She didn't approve of this, she made it clear. Not that she objected to Flo stringing him along, so long as she was discreet about it. She didn't mind drinking his booze, wearing his nylons, making use of him, she said, but for her daughter to ruin her life for a scumball like that, to throw away what she had with Arthur: respectability, security and a decent, hardworking husband... No, she couldn't go along with that at all.

She needn't have worried. He never turned up.

'So what do you think of that, Dorrie?'

'Sounds almost like he knew what you were planning, doesn't it?'

230

Chapter Twelve

It wasn't a joke, not entirely, though from her mother's arch look and short laugh it was clear that she thought it was. He couldn't have guessed what was in her mind, she said: she didn't know herself, until a few minutes before the bomb struck and, in any case, according to him, he'd been on his way. Got caught in the same air raid. Finished up in hospital.

Oh yeah? thought Dorrie cynically. If he was as awful as Nanna Hubbard painted him and had had an inkling that Mum had changed her mind, had been planning to lumber him with a wife and child, he might well have stayed away. On the other hand, clairvoyantes tended to be kept in ignorance of anything that concerned themselves.

It occurred to her that if Potter blood didn't run in her veins, Frank Leary could well be the one to thank for her psychic genes. It helped if you could blame it on someone else. Like coarse honey-blonde hair or a lazy eye.

And it would explain how he had managed to be there for her at precisely the right time the day before. It had probably come to him, out of the blue, in the middle of some dirty deal with Harry the Horse, or Reggie Kray, or, more likely, just as he'd lured half a dozen giggling women – 'Come on, gels, come and see what

I've got!' – into examining his stock of cheap nylons, outside Woolworth's. There'd have been that numbing premonition of poor Dorrie plodding wearily along the A12, hungry and penniless, the orphan of the storm; he'd have looked at his flash gold wristwatch, and realised that he might just make it if he put a wiggle on. He'd probably said, 'Gotta love yer and leave yer, gels!' and snapped his suitcase shut, nylons still fluttering from its jaws, as he flung it into the back seat of his Rover and roared off into the sunset. Except that she couldn't remember a flash gold watch and the sky had been like lead.

And that time Jenny and her brother tied her up. Maybe his turning up hadn't been the happy accident it had seemed. Why should he have been out walking at that time of night, after all? He hadn't even had a dog. Could be he'd been on his way to a gambling den or worse, and had a psychic tip-off that she was a prisoner in the park; come hotfoot to the rescue. Perhaps there'd been other times. That man over the Town Hall, for instance, could have been him, though at seven years old, all men paled to light brown beside her dark-eyed daddy. She'd taken Stephen out for a walk in his pushchair. Mum had been baking and Dorrie had been sent outside to amuse the little boy. She'd strapped him in, like Mummy did, opened the front gate, like Mummy did, pushed him across the road and walked him beside the municipal daffodils, leaving him parked by the pond, just for a moment, while she went to look at some frogs playing piggyback close to the edge. There'd been a splash and the handle was sticking out of the water, bubbles plopping, ever-decreasing circles and a dummy bobbing on the surface.

He'd appeared from nowhere, Superman in a suit and trilby, to pull the streaming pram from the water, with the toddler still strapped in. Between them they'd got Stephen's wet things off, and wrapped him in the man's jacket. It was only a short walk back to the prefabs, she wheeling the sopping pram, the man carrying Stephen, who'd stopped yelling by then. Somehow he'd known the man had sweets in his pocket. Mum had been so shocked, she'd laughed and cried all at the same time, and now she remembered, the man had given Mum a cuddle. It was only afterwards, when Stephen was tucking into a freshly made jam tart and the man had gone, that Mum had remembered to smack Dorrie, once for crossing the road and once for drowning her brother, and the little girl had thought that was probably fair enough.

Now she came to think of it, he might also have been at the Coronation party – that voice in the crowd who'd told those fibs about the Everest news being on the wireless. Frank to the rescue. A knight in slightly tarnished armour. It was possible, she thought; even bold Sir Lancelot had his darker side.

But just how bad was he? Mum said he was clever, wise beyond his years, yet he was denied the chance of furthering his education. That would make you resentful, wouldn't it? Wouldn't worms of envy gnaw away inside you? Might you not do awful things then in protest? And if you were also psychic...?

He might be very bad indeed. Yet he did good things like rescuing her. It was too difficult. She couldn't work him out. He was a rogue but he'd loved her mother; begged her to run away with him, hadn't he? And he cared about their child. If he had had a premonition that a bomb was going to fall on Mum's house, he'd have gone over there, surely, and dragged her out before the bomb landed, wouldn't he?

She had to know what manner of man her mother had loved.

Reading between the words, between the shadows in her mother's eyes, Dorrie discovered memories, like snapshots. Here, the pair of them were sitting, side by side and dreamy, on swings in the park; there, he was larking about with a millet spray down the High Street, making her squeal with laughter. Now, they were walking in the forest, holding hands; then, he was pressing her against a brick wall, her skirt round her waist, groaning. There was a closeup of an eye, golden speckles in the iris; then a study of lips compressed in deliberation. Memory had captured the flare of a nostril, a lock of hair that had curled round her finger, nuances of expression from excitement to wonder, pity to sorrow. He was roaring with laughter, whispering secrets, sulking, arguing, puffing scorn from a cigarette, sleeping, crying, kissing her. Mum had loved him so much. She couldn't have loved a complete louse.

But that was long ago. Something had turned

her love sour since then, something that she whisked to the back of her mind with a toss of her hair.

Then Grandma was knocking on the kitchen door and they were having to prise up the latch again to let her in with the tray of steaming soup, courtesy of next door.

If only she had known who he was yesterday afternoon. If only she hadn't run away. There was so much she would like to have asked him.

Lunch for the three of them was a silent meal, broken only by Grandma's slurping and the desultory scrape of metal on china. The question that occupied each mind and sapped Lucy's leek and potatoes of savour seemed, as far as Dorrie could tell, to turn around the bonds between them, and how and whether they should be severed. Mum's feelings towards Grandma were coloured by guilt, of course, but her eight-year antipathy seemed to have softened now that Wally and Eric had been introduced into the mix. And Grandma was reluctant to sit in judgment even though society might expect it of her.

Dorrie calculated that the time was right, when spooning had slowed to a standstill and older eyes were glazed and faraway. She said, in a voice pivoting nicely between naivety and longing, 'You'll still be my Grandma, won't you?'

'Oh, Dorrie.' The look that passed between the two women told of pity and regret. Perhaps a squint did have a sort of innocent appeal.

'I mean, I know you won't be *really* my grandmother, but you'll still be Stephen's, won't you? And he is my brother and I do love you.'

'Oh Dorrie,' they said again, their eyebrows crumpling.

'I mean,' she went on, thinking 'in for a penny,' 'I don't see why we have to tell Dad at all.' Their ears flattened as though she were touching nerves. Dorrie looked up from a study of her black-rimed fingernails. 'It's not as if we're suddenly going to go off and live with Frank Leary or something. Mum hasn't seen him in years and I don't think I'd like him at all, from what she says. It's a shame to upset Dad for nothing. And Stephen. Isn't it?'

That gave them food for thought. Grandma shook the salt cellar over her soup, not noticing that none came out. Mum laid down her spoon in defeat and sighed.

'That person who told you about Frank, Nora, they're bound to tell other people, aren't they? Suppose it gets back to Arthur via some busybody? I'd never forgive myself.'

'She passed over, that old woman,' Grandma said, with a straighter face than Buster Keaton. 'Quite sudden, weren't it, Dor?' who frowned and tried to look suitably sad. 'They called us in, didn't they, duck? And she said she had something special to tell us. Just us, like. Even Lucy don't know. Don't worry, Flo, Arthur won't never find out, not unless one of you tells him. He won't hear it from me, that I do know.'

'Oh. Oh Nora, that's so... Oh, thank you.' Flo put her arms round Grandma and gave her a kiss. The soft cheeks flushed with pleasure and the wrinkles round her eyes were wet as she gave Dorrie a broad wink, under cover of reaching for some bread.

But Mum's puzzled frown deepened. 'That old woman, what was her name?'

'Steggles,' said Grandma.

Mum considered Grandma's maiden name, her head on one side, her eyes half-closed, then she shook her head decisively. 'No, doesn't ring any bells. Whoever she was, though, she must have known me, or Frank, seen us together. Unless,' a thought slowed her words, 'my mother's let something slip. But I wouldn't have thought, even in her cups...'

'She never mentioned your mother.'

'Mmm. Had she lived here long?'

'Came here about the same time I did.'

'See, I'm thinking that she could have been from round our way – a nosy neighbour who'd seen him coming and going through our front door in the war and put two and two together. Couldn't quite bring herself to take it to the grave, mean old bag.'

She didn't see the air beside her shimmer with indignation.

Grandma said hastily, 'She did used to live in Walthamstow, now I come to think of it.'

'Aha!'

It would be their secret, they decided. They mopped their plates and finished the meal, quite replete.

Grandma invited them to stay for the weekend, and Dorrie begged. Could they? It did seem silly going back to school for just one day. They never did anything on Fridays anyway, specially at the end of term. It was all Drama competitions and Easter bonnet parades. John Doubleday had broken up already. There were some advantages to going to boarding school. But, as Mum pointed out, Arthur and the old ladies were expecting her back that evening and there was no way, with the telephones still not working, that she could get a message home to tell them otherwise. She would have to go but, she paused, Dorrie could stay if she wanted. Flo would phone Miss Clements in the morning and tell her, not about Dorrie's running away, of course, but about Grandma's emergency. Dorrie was staying to help, wasn't she?

'And besides, there's four sheep-hearts going to waste in the fridge and a rib of beef. Arthur won't know what to do with them. Never mind, you've got me for another hour or so. I'll get the four o'clock bus back to the station. If someone wouldn't mind seeing Dorrie onto the train Sunday morning?'

Yessss. With a bit of wangling and whining maybe she could get out of going back then. She would put her mind to it.

'Shall we go and have a look at your bedroom, then, Ma?'

They went up the stairs discussing the pros and cons of scrubbing the floor before the builders arrived that afternoon. Wally had said he'd get someone onto it straight away, if she was paying cash, and he was a man of his word, was Wally. She'd told him to send them round the back when they came. They'd be bound to have a lorry for their bricks and tiles and ladders and things. She and Flo could strip the bed and take down the curtains and she'd have them washed and dried by nightfall. It was good drying weather. They'd bring down the ornaments, the ones that had survived, and give those a soak in some soapy water. And there were some things under the bed in suitcases she didn't want strangers poking into. They were a bit heavy. Perhaps Flo...?

Dorrie was out of the front door, making herself scarce. Poor Grandma. The likelihood of the damage being repaired this afternoon was small indeed. The ornaments would be wrapped in newspaper and packed into cardboard boxes, while the suitcases, containing the more precious gifts from grateful clients, Dresden shepherdesses and chimney sweeps, Royal Doulton plates, crystal goblets, silver candlesticks, would languish in the cellar for years to come, forgotten and gritty with coal dust, while another slowly filled up under the bed.

No one else was back from dinner. The bonfire had burned low and she gave it a poke. Wood ash, fanned by the breeze, glowed pink in the sunshine, almost liquid, a nest for a phoenix. She built up a wigwam of twigs and branches, relishing the hiss and crackle and the sting of smoke in her eyes, thinking that it was a waste, all this fire, all this energy, thinking about potatoes in their jackets and wondering vaguely if she could make charcoal, for drawing. Not that she liked drawing with charcoal. It was messy and wouldn't rub out properly and you had to spray it afterwards, to fix it, otherwise your picture smeared. But it was good for smoothing the shine on a horse's hindquarters, or on a vase, or for suggesting a cloud of hair on a medieval lady. Guinevere. She was just going off into a reverie about the charcoal-burners of old and thinking that it was a funny sort of job to have, when a rusty squeal of iron on iron made her teeth fur. John Doubleday was opening the gates of his father's house to let out a pick-up truck from whose great hook there hung, like a fish, a Rover saloon car with flat tyres and a massive hole in its radiator.

Her heart lurched. He must still be there. Somehow she'd managed to forget that she'd immobilised his car and that, of course, he'd have had to impose on the Doubledays for shelter and the use of the phone. And his host was such a pompous old bore. Poor Frank. She had thoroughly spoiled his evening.

Trying to appear nonchalant, she squinted through the smoke as John loped across the green, almost as though he were running up to bowl. And then, she winced – he did – he bowled! No ball left his hand but it could have, easily. Oh dear, and she'd thought him so grown up and sophisticated. Quite nice-looking, too, in a dark and moody sort of way. The girls at school would have been pea-green. What a pity.

'Trouble with the car?' It sounded indifferent enough, she thought.

'Sorry? Oh,' he turned to watch the sick motor being hurried out of sight, 'it's not one of ours,

240

actually. Chap came by yesterday to arrange an interview with Dad. Pranged his car in the woods. Ran into a fallen tree, I gather. Interesting fellow – freelance journalist. Gathering material for an article about haunted houses.'

'Haunted houses?' she echoed in a bat-squeak.

'Not that ours is,' he hastened to assure her, 'but these old heaps generally have as many ghost stories as cobwebs and I suppose he thought it would be worth a try. Yes, he missed the main entrance in the rain and ended up in the back lane. Easily done.'

'Oh dear.' She could hardly keep a straight face. So Frank was a con-man along with everything else. 'He stayed the night, then?'

'No, no, I took him over to Sowness. I was on my way back when I met you. He had someone else to see. Someone else with a ghost. It should make a good story.'

'Fascinating.' She tried to sound enthusiastic but she was so disappointed. She'd missed him. She could have gone over there, apologised, told him that she knew she was his daughter...

'Yes, Dad was most intrigued. He asked him to call in when he collects the car. It's the smell of money. Gets him every time.'

'Money? Did the, em, journalist offer to pay him?'

'Not to my knowledge. No, I expect Dad was thinking of all that wonderful publicity. People will come flocking to Stanbury Manor if it becomes known as a stately home with its own resident ghosts. Good grief. And only seven and six on the door. A bargain.'

'I thought you said there weren't any?'

'Oh, absolutely. No such thing. But Dad's not one to let something as trivial as honesty stand in his way. If you could have seen him last night! He was positively animated. Talking about wheeling out Great-grandfather's untimely demise and cooking up spooky goings-on in the East Wing.'

'You don't like your father much, do you?'

'Does anyone?'

Good question.

He really was rather weird, this boy with his lah-di-dah accent, but then his mother was dead, poor thing, which Dorrie thought accounted for rather a lot. Her mother wouldn't have let her out to saw up a tree in clean clothes, a new sweater, and a cravat! Well, honestly! Even his Wellington boots were clean. His haircut wasn't the usual short back and sides. For a start it, too, was clean, not a trace of brilliantine and it flopped over his big brown puppy-dog eyes in quite an attractive way. If you liked that sort of thing.

There were a few things he didn't like, mostly the things she did like. Football for a start, not because it was a plebs' game or anything, he assured her. He just had none of the right ball skills. Nor did he swim. And he couldn't paint or draw for toffee; he wasn't a musician and he sang like a ferret, he said. Cricket was his passion. He spoke French passably well but only because they'd had so many holidays in Normandy. Mother had friends there. She'd died when he was twelve. He didn't go into it.

One thing in his favour was that he didn't seem to notice her brace or her squint, unlike her horrible cousin Peter, whose current nickname for her was 'Gnasher'. John made no reference to her imperfections, having been properly brought up.

He was well read. Not *Lucky Jim* or *Fahrenheit 451* but impressive novelists like Tolstoy, Pasternak, Hemingway and Steinbeck. You got time for it at public school, he apologised. She offered to lend him her *Catcher in the Rye* if he'd send it back to her when he'd finished. He was amazed that she'd never been to the theatre, never heard of Beckett. She was amazed that he'd never seen *Blackboard Jungle* or *Rebel without a Cause*. Never *heard* of James Dean!

He'd read *1984* but dismissed it as poppycock. Communism would never get a foothold in Britain, he declared. She told him, with something approaching pride, that her father was a rabid Red who spent every waking hour planning the Revolution, a bit of an exaggeration, but it sounded interesting. They had a polite discussion, then, about class and agreed that, by birth and upbringing, he was upper and she was lower but respectable. He doubted whether, even under Communism, real equality was conceivable. There would always be bright, single-minded people with drive, who would seize opportunities, who would excel in their chosen field, and get so much more out of life because they put so much more into it. Money didn't come into it, he thought. He knew some good words, did John Doubleday. 'Conceivable' was one, 'dichotomy' another. But she could tell that the turn the conversation was taking alarmed him.

Her worst fears were confirmed when he confessed to being a mathematician. His ambition, incredibly, was not to be a landowner but an accountant! Glory be, she thought, here was someone who claimed to know all about simultaneous equations!

When she discovered that he had no idea who Bill Haley was she decided they could help each other. He could explain her maths homework to her and she would initiate him in the gentle art of rock 'n' roll.

But they would have to hurry or the record shops would be shut.

Mum said if John was driving to Doddinghurst perhaps he would take her to the station as they hadn't seen the bus all day. She guessed the main road was still blocked. They could buy Dorrie's train ticket while they were at it and then Flo would feel easy in her mind about there being enough money.

They played 'Rock Around the Clock' on Grandma's wind-up gramophone and his face when he first heard it, was a picture.

'What do you think?'

'It's not Beethoven.'

'I'm glad to say.'

He was enthusiastic, she'd say that for him. But somehow his long, loose frame didn't lend itself to dance. There were altogether too many arms and legs. At first she had him jigging to the music, just to get the rhythm. This was how they had taught themselves at school one lunch-hour. Once you could really feel the beat you could proceed to the footwork. Peter had picked it up at his youth club and she'd taught it to Jenny and Pam. For once, they'd agreed, he'd taught her something useful, rather than the usual crude jokes and how to blow bubble-gum.

In no time John was hopping around like a lunatic, not at all the neat, compact dancer that Peter was, despite or because of his inch-thick crêpe soles, his 'beetle crushers'. She tried to explain to John that you hadn't to get too wild. You were supposed to do this with a partner who was meant to anticipate your moves. She demonstrated the turns and twirls and showed him how they could be controlled, so you didn't knock anybody over in a crowded ballroom or swipe them round the ear.

Grandma poked an anxious head round the door.

''Ere, you Dorrie,' she said, 'don't you forget your poor Uncle Joe, asleep next door.' But once she'd satisfied herself that the ceiling wouldn't fall down, she put down the parsnip she was peeling, picked up her skirts and joined in. Auntie Lucy brought the children in to watch, while their tea was cooking, and bounded around with Joanna. Little Richard was soon singing 'See ya later, Nannalator' which was, near enough, what was on the B side and, before long, the room was full of rockers, young and old, from this world and the next. Granny Farthing was in the thick of it and, for a ghost,

245

she was pretty lively. She had brought along her friend, Robbie. He was studying for his exams, she said and needed the outing. Let off the leash, he was the maddest of them all, flinging himself about, without regard for person or property.

'Can't you look where you're going!' Dorrie had yelled, when she tripped over, trying to avoid him as he leapt backwards through the wall, leaving one foot waggling through the mantelpiece, and Granny doing the Black Bottom all on her own.

John thought it a hoot that she should have yelled like that at the armchair, especially since she'd fallen straight into his arms. He didn't understand her pitying look at all.

Eventually, of course, Joe came down, yawning and cross. He'd put his ear-plugs in, expecting Nora to have the workmen banging about, so it wasn't noise that had woken him, but the smell of spuds boiling dry.

Lucy's strangled horror brought the session to an end. But later that evening as John was helping Dorrie sort out the function of x and y in her algebra homework, and wolfing down Grandma's veal and ham pie, 'See ya later, Nannalator' wafted through the thin walls, played on piano with lots of twirls and twiddly bits.

'He plays well, your uncle.'

'Does he?' She'd thought he was showing off.

'Mmm, they're all right, your family.'

'Salt of the earth,' she said. But he looked hurt.

'Sorry, was that patronising? I mean, they're what a family should be. You're lucky.'

'Don't I know it,' she said. He was all right, too. A bit of a twit but he couldn't help it. She could forgive him almost anything, now that simultaneous equations were no longer a mystery.

Wally's builders did eventually turn up. At seven o'clock, after John had gone back to his bleak house, after the men had finished work on the council estate and had had a couple of beers. It was too dark for them to see anything. They had a look around by lamplight, rattled tiles and shook joists and made more plaster come down. Couldn't make a start, they said, until the pole was removed. You'd need a crane.

'A crane!' croaked Grandma. 'In my front garden!'

Oh yes they'd need a crane, whoever took it down.

'Can't *you* take it down?'

Oh no. More than their job was worth to move a telegraph pole.

Whose job was it, then?

That was hard to say. It would have been the Electricity Board if there'd been just electric wires attached, but there were telephone wires, too. There were rules and regulations. Demarcation.

'Forget it,' said Grandma, 'we'll sort it out.'

And you needed to get ladders and scaffolding up to fix the tiles and do the brickwork. Couldn't do anything with that bloody great tree out the front. You'd have to have that taken away first. Sawn up and taken away. Council might do it for you but it was quicker to get it done yourself, if you could afford it. And then you needed somewhere to mix your concrete. No good mixing it round the back and having to come round the side with your buckets and wheelbarrows, or tracking mud through the house. Get the tree taken away and then you were talking. But, in the meantime, they'd nail corrugated iron sheeting across the hole in the roof to stop the rain coming in.

'And what about the hole in the wall?'

They couldn't do much about that, missus, if the pole was still stuck through the window. You needed to get on to the electric people.

Chapter Thirteen

The headlines roared *CHILD KILLER CAUGHT* but that wasn't the reason her hairdresser's heart lurched. The thick mop behind the newspaper was the same bleached brown as his daughter's, reminding her of beech leaves on the forest floor in winter, before the first frost.

'Frank?' She had to say something.

The paper was his refuge on the crowded train, and he moved it only fractionally, with a withering scowl. Then his eyes widened like a startled deer's, and the paper crumpled into his lap.

'Flo,' he murmured, as though she were unreal. 'Bloody hell.' His nostrils flared to take in oxygen. 'Sit down, sit down,' he said, coming to, quite pale as he stood up to give her his window seat.

Suddenly boneless, she sank onto the warm upholstery, and had to force herself to be light and easy. 'To what do we owe the pleasure, Frank? Not like you to be slumming it on our old branch line.'

He was going to his mother's, he said. She couldn't manage stairs these days so he'd bought her a bungalow over in Highams Park.

Bought. Just like that. He must be rolling in it. It was all right for some. There was poor Dorrie in National Health glasses, with darns in her elbows, living in a prefab, and him handing out bungalows right, left and centre.

Had he noticed her burning cheeks, her twisting hands? So what? She didn't care. She observed, sweetly, 'Of course, your car's in dock, isn't it?'

'How did you know?' Sharp suspicion narrowed his gaze.

Rush hour on the Liverpool Street to Chingford line is not the time for recriminations. Fellow travellers may look as though they're deep in their novels or the share prices or studying the scabs and sores of London's sooty backside as it slides past the window, but they're hanging on your every word, hungry as wolves for real life. And you have to raise your voice over the racket of the train. So she simply told him that she'd been up to Great Bisset to fetch Dorrie home.

She saw his expression alter, his brow clear, watched him craning his neck to scan the compartment for sight of his darling daughter, and secretly relished his disappointment.

'I left her there,' she shouted in his ear and then explained how the storm had brought down the tree on the green and damaged her mother-in-law's house, that Dorrie was staying to help with the clearing up and to keep her grandmother company.

'She all right, is she?'

'Nora?' she said wickedly. 'A bit shaken, naturally, she's an old—'

'Dorrie.'

'Yes, Dorrie's fine.' But she couldn't keep up the pretence. 'No thanks to you!' she snapped. He deserved it.

He rocked, against the movement of the train. 'What? How did you know?'

'I guessed,' she lied. 'Maroon Rover? Your description? It didn't take much working out. Poor Dorrie. She turned up at Nora's looking like a drowned rat, apparently – soaked to the skin. You abandoned her, Frank, in the worst blooming storm in living memory!'

'That wasn't my fault, Flo.'

'*You* gave her a lift,' she accused, '...to heaven knows where.' She slid a glance at the woman beside her who seemed to be stuck on a sentence at the bottom of the page. 'And then she had to get out and walk when your car hit the tree.'

He frowned, 'Hit the–? Oh, she told you that, did she?'

'I can't *believe* you'd let her go wandering off by herself! You might have known she'd get lost. She had no idea where she was, poor kid. Out in that storm in the middle of nowhere, with murderers on the loose – she was frightened out of her wits. I mean *anything* could have happened, something really awful.'

Other passengers were frankly shaking their heads and tutting. She felt better now that it was off her chest, but for some reason he was looking quite puzzled, as though she were talking in riddles.

'Something spooked her, Flo. She couldn't get away from me fast enough.'

251

'Really?' Dorrie hadn't said anything about being spooked. 'You must have said something.'

'I didn't. She had no earthly reason to run away.'

'And did you go after her? Try and explain? Oh no, not you. You were too wrapped up in your blooming car.'

'Flo, it was *me* she was running away from. I didn't want to scare her any more. And we were almost there. I don't see how she could have got lost.'

'Well, she did.'

'I'm sorry.' Of course he was. His strong face sagged with such remorse she wanted to take it in her hands and...

'Anyway,' she said briskly, 'it's all water under the bridge now.' She paused significantly, before dropping her bombshell. 'Now that she knows who you are.'

She saw it explode in his eyes; saw his pupils, the twin reflections of herself, dilate. Then his breath was hot against her ear. '*What* does she know about me?'

'Everything,' she said, backing away. He was too close.

'You told her?'

She shook her head. 'Nora told her, and I filled her in on the details.'

'Nora? How did she–'

'Oh it's a long story – I'm not going into it here.'

Hurt flickered across his face as he slapped his pockets for his cigarette case, took one without offering it to her (not that she smoked), tapped it on the silver lid and lit up. The drag to his lungs was long and introspective. When he blew it out, the smoke stung her eyes.

'So how was she – Dorrie? How did she take it?'

If he could have seen that wretched tear-stained face... 'How do you think?' she said bitterly. 'It was a dreadful shock.'

He shook his head in despair and she relented. Goodness only knew how that Steggles woman had discovered their dark secret but she had, and Dorrie knew, and it was as much Flo's fault as his. 'She seemed to have got used to the idea by the time I left.'

For a moment he hung over her, hands gripping the luggage rack, head resting on his arms. His eyes were hidden, his overcoat draped open, enclosing her. If she'd wanted she could have unbuttoned him, run her fingers over his skin, caressed him, and none of these Nosy old Parkers any the wiser. In the old days...

But this was not the old days. She coughed.

He started. 'Sorry,' he muttered, drawing away, taking another hefty drag of his cigarette. 'I dunno. Sorry,' he repeated. He looked so helpless and embarrassed. Little more than a child himself. Stephen looked like that when he'd taken something apart that he couldn't put back together again. 'I thought we'd agreed to keep it to ourselves. I...' He cleared his throat. 'I didn't think you wanted her to know.'

'I didn't. But now she does I think it's probably for the best. It's cleared up a lot of things for her.' She waited for his comment but as he simply raised his eyebrows, she went on: 'We're not, um, we thought no good would come of telling Arthur.'

He nodded understanding. 'Do you think it would help if I saw her, you know – talked to her?'

'No, Frank. Leave it now. Please.'

In the silence she studied his good cloth coat. There was a button missing and a stain on the lapel. A closer look told her that the cuffs were worn to the weave. Someone wasn't looking after him.

'How's Marion?' she said, for want of anything else to say. What did they have in common, after all, apart from Dorrie?

'Marion?' His eyes glazed as though he was trying to remember. Then he said, 'Okay.' Clearly, he didn't want to talk about her.

'And your baby?'

He pressed his lips together. 'Yeah,' he said eventually, nodding. 'Yeah.' But his eyes were so troubled she knew it was a lie.

'Frank?'

He was staring out of the window, at neglected backyards, where sooty weeds and stained mattresses grew. She knew he wasn't seeing them. Dorrie did that, switched off mid-flow. The woman beside her felt it safe to turn her page.

They had stopped at a station – Clapton. There was a movement towards the door, and suddenly he was tugging at her arm. 'Come on, Flo.'

'But I – this isn't my–'

'Please. There's a few things we've got to sort out.'

So many reasons why she shouldn't. All the lies and complications of the past – life was so much easier without this man. Bleak. Sterile. But straightforward.

She had to get home to Arthur. Get his tea. Play the good wife and mother. Be respectable, for Dorrie's sake. She'd told the girl the affair was over. It was, long ago. She couldn't. No, she definitely couldn't.

'No, Frank,' she pleaded, 'we've said it all.'

It was too late, anyhow. The last carriage door had slammed shut, the guard had blown the whistle, steam was up, pistons were in motion, wheels were squealing arthritically.

He flung open the door and jumped down onto the platform.

'Come on.'

Her high heels skittered on the concrete as she landed, strained to snapping. Her ankle twisted. She was going to fall. But there was a steadying hand under her elbow. The train began to pull away.

'What *you* looking at?' Frank yelled, yobbishly, at a woman staring at them from the window. She'd forgotten how rude he could be, what a loudmouth. What was she doing on this sordid station platform with such a man? Someone leaned out to pull the door to and the train was gone.

'Oh God, oh God, oh God!' She pressed her fingers into her skull. This was such a mistake.

'It's all right. There'll be another train soon,'

he said, not getting it.

He led her into the waiting room, empty but still smelling of people, their breath, their smoke, newsprint, peppermints. It seemed as though all her senses were heightened. Tingling. He'd always had that effect on her. She shivered violently, not with cold, but still she went to warm her hands at the feeble little fire, really to avoid having to look at him. When she felt his hand on her shoulder she shook it off.

She didn't want this. Not again. Finishing with him had been so hard. The crying jag had lasted for weeks. Arthur had made her go to the doctor's, thinking she was ill, but she hadn't taken the pills she'd been prescribed. What use were pills for a broken heart?

All because Marion was pregnant. Marion, his wife. The woman he went home to every night, after he'd been with her.

After those fictitious evening classes on a Monday night. Not that she didn't know as much about dressmaking as any City and Guilds' teacher, but Arthur wasn't to know that. While he warmed her children's bedtime milk and read them *Wind in the Willows*, she was learning the intricacies of adultery and a hundred and one new ways of making love.

Arthur had liked to show an interest. When he enquired, she told him that she was learning about stiffening and shrinkage, about openings and plackets, about stroking gathers and inserting gussets. Love had made her mad, made her tempt fate, made her tiptoe around the landmine of Arthur's wrath. In a way she wanted him to find out, and in a way it would have been disastrous. So she kept her face straight and continued taking risks.

It was a drug and they were addicts. Couldn't get enough. They made love where and when any opportunity arose, and in every possible manner. Sometimes they could take their time, slowly and languorously in summer meadows or among the leaves in the forest. But it wasn't always summer and it wasn't always easy. Then they found bliss on the back seats of cinemas, against park railings and in shop doorways. Once, when they had found themselves alone in an empty carriage, they had even made love at frenzied speed, between stations on this very line, she sitting on his lap and spreading her skirt over his nakedness.

She found herself dreaming of making love to him and would wake to find herself throbbing and wet. On those nights she was so wretched, so desperate, her restless twisting and turning would wake Arthur, who promptly assumed his rights in the matter. But he was a poor substitute and his grunts and sighs just made her angry. When he turned over with a contented sigh to sleep, she would be left high and dry and wide awake.

Frank presumably had the same sort of dreams. Else how had Marion become pregnant?

Marion had always been, for her, a shadowy figure. There was a photo in his wallet and she looked exactly how Flo had imagined her. A thin smiling ninny in expensive clothes. She was someone he went to the theatre with, or on holiday with, or had dinner with at some posh restaurant, an adornment for his arm, someone whose parents he had to be nice to. He had to consider her if they were out late, if it was her birthday or if she wanted to go shopping up Town. But she was never cause for jealousy. Like Arthur, she hadn't counted. Until now.

'Why?' he'd protested, when she'd told him she was ending it.

'Because she's having a *baby!*' she wailed, and punched him in the chest, convulsed by sobs.

'I don't get it,' he said, his own eyes filling. 'How's her baby going to make any difference to us?'

'It's *your* baby. *You* put it there, you stupid oaf. How *could* you?'

'She's my wife, Flo. If I didn't screw her now and again, she'd soon twig I was getting it somewhere else.'

She punched him again, too weak with tears to pack any weight behind it. '*I'm* your wife, *me*, in all but name. She's nothing. You've always said she was nothing. A meal-ticket, you said she was, and you go and screw her and give her your baby, you bastard!' Another wave of sobs washed over her. He reached for her and she flung away. 'No, don't touch me. I can't bear it, Frank. I'm the one should be having your babies, not her, not that boring old *cash-till!*'

'Flo, love...'

'But I'm not your love, am I? I'm just your bit on the side. Good old Flo. Good for a quickie round the corner and that's about it. No better than a common tart. Worse – at least a tart gets paid.'

'Oh Flo, *don't!* It's not true and you know it.'

He almost looked as though he meant it.

Well, of course. He could spin her any yarn he liked, twist her round his little finger, tell her he loved her, tell her he lived for the time when they'd go away together, when the children were through school, when he'd saved enough to start his own business, all the old flannel, knowing she'd lap it up hungrily. Only now it was different. Now he and Marion were having a baby of their own and he would never leave the marriage. It was suddenly very clear.

'You did it on purpose,' she accused him.

'What?'

'You screwed her on purpose. You wanted a baby.'

'No, Flo, it was an accident.'

She ignored him. 'It wasn't quite solid enough for you, was it?' she sneered. 'Your future. A little bit shaky, was it? Old man Thurley looking at you sideways, listening out for the patter of tiny feet? I bet he was like a dog with two tails when you told him, wasn't he? Gave you another little push up the ladder, did he? And Marion? Nothing like a baby to cement a marriage. Make it rock solid. Got your feet under the Thurley table now, haven't you, Frank? Eh? Good and proper. And everyone's well pleased. Except Flo. But Flo's out of your life now, Frankie-boy, so you don't have to worry about her any more.'

'He didn't live long, our Geoffrey.'

259

'Frank!' He'd always known what she was thinking. The draughty fire lost its attraction. She hadn't expected the baby to die. In her experience babies were rosy dimpled little cherubs. They might get ill but they always got better. 'Oh that's terrible. I'm sorry.' She had to ask. 'What was the matter with him?'

'Nothing.' His voice was flat. 'Nothing at all.' He took a fortifying breath. 'He was doing fine, and then one morning we woke up and f-found him dead in his cot.'

She gasped, her imagination fizzling like spit off a griddle. Had someone ... had Marion...? But she couldn't ask. Poor Frank, though. Poor, poor Frank.

'Well, afterwards, I – I went a bit crazy. I guess I thought it was my fault. Marion thought so, too.'

Her 'Why?' was too sharp. More gently, she said, 'What made her think it was your fault?'

He sighed. 'Because I was the last one to see him. I'd fed him his bottle. Marion,' he began and then shook something, some unwanted image from his head. Was she drunk then? Incapable of seeing to the baby? She'd always been fond of a drink, his wife. 'I'd put him back to sleep ... on his stomach,' he added.

'What's wrong with that? Both my babies slept on their stomachs.'

'I know, that's where I got the idea, seeing Stephen sleeping so soundly. The doctors told her there was no reason for him to die as far as they could see. No physical reason. It was as if he'd just decided to pack it in. Stop breathing.

Oh, God. Oh, it was all so bloody awful!' He slumped onto the bench, elbows on knees, large hands dangling hopelessly. He seemed to be staring at dog-ends on the floor. With an effort he raised his head, sought her eyes. 'I was looking for answers, Flo. Why I should be allowed to live, with *my* rotten record, and an innocent little kid, just because he had an overload of my frigging genes...'

She didn't pretend to understand that and when he saw her puzzlement he dropped his head onto his hand. Eventually, he looked up again.

'I ... well, I prayed, Flo. Dunno what for exactly. For him, I suppose, at first. But then,' he sighed, 'for me. Because I suddenly saw that Geoffrey was better off dead than in the land of the living with me as his dad. What a terrible thing, Flo, eh? 'Cause what could I have done for him, when all's said and done? Taught him all I knew? All the dodgy tricks? All the scams, all the double-crosses? Big deal. Just as well I hadn't had charge of young Dorrie, eh? I dunno if it was God answering my prayers or what, but it struck me then, what I was. I mean, *really* what I was. It was like looking through the wrong end of a telescope at this greedy, strutting, ridiculous little pillock. What did I think I was *doing* down here? Ducking and diving through life, kidding myself, never facing up to the truth, the fact that I was a complete and utter waste of space, a useless, loathsome piece of shite.'

He was fighting tears.

'You were bound to be depressed, Frank,

losing your baby...'

'Depressed? Jesus, Flo, you don't know the half of it.' He paused, bit his lip, and somewhat abashed, said, 'D'you know what I did? I took myself up the top of the Town Hall. Onto the roof. I was gonna top myself, I swear to God. In a way I guess part of me *did* die.'

He fished in his pocket for his handkerchief and blew his nose hard. Sat silent with it scrunched up in his fist. More than anything she wanted to put her arm round his shoulders, kiss away the sadness. But she knew it wouldn't solve anything.

He pulled at his lip, and then half-smiled to himself, a smile almost of resignation, before seeming to remember she was there.

'And then, well, something happened, something extraordinary, Flo. There I was crawling about up there among the puddles and the birdshit, blubbing like a baby, and ... and, well, the Town Hall clock struck ten o'clock – nearly knocked me blooming head off – and *I saw the frigging light*. I know it sounds daft but that is exactly what happened – dark tunnel, angels, the whole shooting match. I thought, This is it, Leary. You're done for. It's a straitjacket for you, next. Me ears were aching with the old clock chimes; it felt like all me fillings had been shaken loose but it was bleeding wonderful. Peaceful, you know? I just lay there, flat on me back and lapped it up. And when I come back down the Town Hall steps it was like I knew what I had to do.'

He sniffed. 'See, there's things about me you

don't know, Flo, things I've never told no one. Gaw, they'd have thought me a right Mary Ann, if I had. But, after that, I knew it was like a gift I had, and if I used it properly, everything would be all right. Know what I mean?'

No. But she thought she knew what must have happened to him. Billy Graham was big news. On the television, in the papers. People were being redeemed right, left and centre. It was the 'in' thing. Last year Dorrie had gone to one of the revival meetings at Wembley Stadium with Jenny. They'd been raving Christians for all of two months, despite Arthur's scorn and Stephen's ridicule.

But Frank? Cock-of-the-walk, Jack-the-lad, dodging-and-dealing Frank? He'd never go down on his knees to anyone, least of all God.

Her incredulity must have shown because he shrugged. 'I only know it made sense for me, Flo. But I couldn't do it on my own. I'd heard of these people, this sort of religious group, and I went along to their meetings a few times and, well, it was okay. I fitted in.'

He'd had more luck than Dorrie, then. She'd gone the rounds of the churches trying to find one that suited her, and failed. Apparently she knew the truth and they didn't. The arrogance of youth. Flo secretly suspected that either the demands were too great (that she renounce the sins of the flesh – make-up, films, rock 'n' roll, pretty clothes) or the boys didn't amount to much!

Unlike Dorrie, Frank had kept it up and had discovered, unsurprisingly, that the import-export business didn't tie in with his new-found ideals. Thurley's was riddled with corruption. Goods were bought cheaply from countries where men and women were treated like cattle. They lived and worked in appalling conditions, wearing themselves to sticks, losing life and limbs and sight for the sake of a few rupees or francs or pesos. The goods were sold for three or four times what Thurley paid for them and that was called honest capitalism. Tax-dodging was par for the entrepreneurial course, and smuggling, though, of course, it wasn't called that.

The new convert tried to put things right. He owed it to baby Geoffrey to deal fairly, he said, boycotting goods that were faulty or suspect, or that had blood on them. And profits went down. He improved conditions, spread the workload, employed more staff and brought in new safety measures. Costs soared. His father-in-law hit the roof and told him to mend his ways or else. And else it was.

His wife begged him, 'Please, Frank, do as Daddy asks.'

He explained that he couldn't. 'She was none too pleased,' he told Flo wryly. They'd had a blazing row in which she accused him of marrying her for her money. And he had to be honest, didn't he?

'Oh Frank,' said Flo, trying not to laugh, 'I bet she skinned you alive.'

'She threw a few things,' he admitted. 'I told her about you, too.'

'Frank!'

'Not by name. I just said that there'd been

someone else.' He frowned. 'I shouldn't have – it was petty. I wanted to hurt her and it wasn't her fault.'

She took a deep breath. 'So now, I suppose, you're out of a job?'

'No, I'm working, just not at Thurley's, thank the Lord.'

She didn't tell him that she'd tried to ring him there the previous day. Only yesterday? A lot had happened. 'What do you do?'

'A bit of this, a bit of that. Freelance stuff. But I suppose you'd still have to call me a middle man.'

'What, like before, in import-export?'

'Similar.'

'You're happier now, though?'

'Oh sure. I'm my own boss. I get out and about. I'm thirty-five, free, almost single. Life's pretty good.'

Did that include his sex-life? she found herself wondering. Damn. She didn't want to think about that, about him and some other woman. But he was a man. She couldn't expect him to live like a monk. But why was she concerning herself? It was well and truly over, they both knew that. His love-life was nothing to do with her. All the same she couldn't help being curious. She tried the subtle approach.

'You're a bit of a rover then, up and down the A12, picking up stray fourteen-year-olds?'

He snorted. 'No, that was the car before she wrecked it.'

'*She* wrecked it? I thought you drove into a tree.'

He made a sound that could have been derision, could have been a cough. What did it mean? Had Dorrie interfered with his steering in some way? Seen the tree coming up and grabbed the wheel? Before she could ask, his expression changed, to one of utmost seriousness. 'Flo, you *do* know about her?'

'What do you mean?'

'No, you don't, do you?'

'What?'

'That she's ... gifted.'

'Oh yes, they told me at the school. She's a clever girl. The highest IQ in her year. Like you at Brick Lane. Only she's going to make the most of herself. She's going to get on.'

'Yeah,' he nodded, an eyebrow cocked, 'she will if I have anything to do with it.'

'I told you on the train, Frank – you aren't going to.'

'Flo, she's my girl. I want to help her.'

'She's Arthur's,' she said firmly. 'I'm not having big upsets interfering with her studies. Or with Stephen's. He's got to have his chance, too. She knows about you – leave it at that. If she wants to get in touch that's up to her. She's old enough to make up her own mind. So I'd be glad if you wouldn't keep popping up all over the place. It was kind of you to help her out yesterday but there's an end to it, Frank.'

When the next train came in, crowded, they boarded it, stood strap-hanging and thinking their own thoughts. When she got out at Hoe Street she didn't turn and wave.

Chapter Fourteen

Grandma was convinced it was a plot and they were all in it. Doubleday, Barrington and the builders. They were all bent as nine bob notes. They wanted her out of there, so they could turn the cottage into a bijou home for some fat git as Dorrie had predicted.

'And they laid on the hurricane just for you, did they, Ma?' said Auntie Lucy.

'Wouldn't put it past them. In league with the devil, old Doubleday. You mark my words,' she said darkly, 'if we ain't careful he'll have us all out by Christmas – me, you, Battses, Stones, the whole row.'

In vain they told her that Dorrie's vision had been of thirty or forty years hence, when people wore underclothes on top, but she was adamant. A crane to move a telegraph pole? They wanted to plough up her garden with them blooming caterpillar wheels. Make it impossible to live there. Oh no. She wasn't as green as she was cabbage-looking. She would show 'em.

When he came home from work next morning, Joe found he'd been commandeered into the upstairs party. With Granny Farthing dancing attendance, he and Dorrie and Lucy pushed, while Grandma directed operations from below.

'Pull, 'Orace! Put yer back into it, mate. Come

on, Vicar, pull. 'Ere, where you off to, young John? Come over here and give us a bit of an 'and, will yer? Right, on my say so, *heave!*'

'Whoa, whoa!' yelled Joe from upstairs, hanging onto the pole for dear life, as Lucy and Dorrie were shunted backwards and forwards across the bedroom floor. 'You've got to lift the bloody thing. Lift it! Else it'll be crashing through your downstairs window, as well.'

'That's what I said, "Pull it and lift it!"'

Horace muttered some obscenity and the vicar pretended not to hear.

Between them, ignoring Grandma, they pulled and pushed until the very tip of the telegraph pole was resting on the very edge of the window sill. Then the three upstairs scampered downstairs to help the three in the garden lift the pole clear of house and tree and to lay it along the grass verge outside for disposal by the proper authorities.

Grandma gave them tea and cake as a reward. But not so much as to sap their energy which was needed for the next job: nailing boards across the joists and the window and a piece of old lino over them. If it worked for the chickens it would work for her. It would be dark in the bedroom but it would help keep the rain out. She didn't intend her damage to get past repairing.

'We know Doubleday's little game, don't we, Dorrie?' she winked. 'And you can tell your old man to put that in his pipe and smoke it.' John looked a bit sick, and she took pity on him. 'Ain't your fault, son, I know that. None of us can help what our dads are like, can we, Dor?'

The next task was to get the branches out of her garden and the three neighbouring ones. All morning they sawed and burned and hacked until the branches were logs piled on the green; until the sawdust had been collected into sacks for chicken runs and stables and rabbit hutches, or blown away on the wind, until every vegetable plot was piled with pea sticks and the decent twigs were being bound into besom brooms by Granny Batts and her working party of women. But when the trimmed trunk was lying, like a beached whale, with the five main boughs cropped as close to the bole as the villagers could get them, they were flummoxed.

The longest two-handed saw wasn't long enough for the sawyers to stand, on ladders and kitchen tables, one each side of the trunk, to cut it up into manageable lengths. They'd get so far down into the wood and have to stop, defeated by sheer size.

If they didn't split the tree no one would be able to cart it away, not the council nor the sawmill nor anyone – with a nod in the direction of Stanbury Manor. They still thought Doubleday was their best bet, despite John's assurances that his father wouldn't, indeed couldn't, pay for the wood. There had to be a way, there was always a way. A strategy, that's all that was needed.

They sawed out wedges in three places, at the foot of the tree, in the middle and where the branches grew out from the trunk: three cuts, eight feet apart. Then they drove steel spikes into the wedges with sledgehammers, one on top of the other. They tried to turn the monster so they could attack it from another side, but neither horses nor tractors could shift it. One of its limbs, thick as a man's waist, had embedded itself in the soft ground.

The work went on all day and the next, between the showers. The last of the spikes was driven home by torchlight. People were sick of the sound of sawing and hammering and the smell of timber. It had taken long enough. They were tired, their backs ached and the sky was like lead. They might not get another clear day at it. Finish it now. The vicar wasn't the only one with better things to do of a Sunday.

But still it wouldn't crack. The spikes were puny Lilliputian pins, swallowed up in great Gulliver's girth.

'A few sticks of dynamite'll do the trick,' said the vicar, who had been a chaplain in the war and ached for a little violence in his life. Hettie didn't sell dynamite. 'No, nor gunpowder,' she said in response to Grandma's query. Nora had had the last of her stocks to unblock her chimney.

'Well, you ain't leaving it stuck outside my front gate,' said Grandma. 'How's anyone supposed to get a lorry through to mend my roof?'

'Why don't we just burn it?' said Joe, ignoring the few half-hearted protests. 'I'm fed up with looking at it. It was a beauty when it was growing but now it's just an eyesore. The sooner it's gone the sooner we can dig a pond, or something.'

'*You* can dig a pond,' muttered Lucy. 'There's

a few things I've got to do in the house. My kids have forgotten who I am.'

'You can't burn 'er,' said Horace, almost tearfully, seeing his beer money going up in smoke.

'Well, you can't leave it to rot,' said Joe.

'Sleep on it,' suggested Lucy who, on her husband's first night off for a week, had a splitting headache, and was trying not to sound too irritable. 'We can always dig a hole and bury it,' she said more brightly. 'Perhaps we can borrow a digger from somewhere, or a pneumatic drill or something.'

As Dorrie lay in the tin bath that night, with water up to her chin, it came to her what that something might be.

'*Go on, duck,*' urged Granny Farthing, materialising in her usual seat by the fire. '*Anyone who can punch holes in car radiators can split logs.*'

'Logs!' she cried, hunting for the flannel to cover her decency. Spirits had no regard for a person's modesty. At least Grandma stayed out in the kitchen. 'Have you seen the size of it!'

'*Otherwise what's the point, Dor? Strikes me you been put in the right place at the right time. There ain't many with a gift like you've got, gel.*'

'Me and Captain Marvel,' she said with some bitterness.

'*And you'd be doing Nora a big favour.*'

'But I'm whacked, Gran. I can't even raise the energy to get out of the bath.'

'*There's no rush, mate; you ain't got them fingernails clean yet. And it ain't your energy you'll*'

271

be using. You're a channel, duck. They'll *give you all the energy you'll need. Nora!'* she yelled. *'Any more hot water?'*

The call came back to leave the girl alone. Whatever Granny was suggesting could wait for another day. Dorrie deserved a nice soak, undisturbed.

'I thought you wanted rid of that tree!'

'I do. But one more day ain't gonna make a hell of a difference.'

'It has to be tonight, Nora.'

Dutifully, wearily, Dorrie brushed her nails again. Because it was Saturday there had been a few more lumberjacks, so she had attempted to put the garden to rights, now that the branches were disposed of, raking up twigs and other debris, forking up compacted earth, making good, tying up, pruning, replanting, with Grandma rapping the window every so often in various stages of panic. 'Not that, Dorrie, that's me rudbeckia!... Watch where you're digging – there's bulbs!... Saw that broken branch off the pear tree, Dorrie. And that next one to it. Don't want them poking no one's eyes out... Be careful of that berberis! Put some gloves on, duck.'

She ached in every muscle and sinew. Now all she wanted was to lie down and sleep.

'What if someone sees me, Granny? Or hears what's going on? It's not something you can do quietly. They'll be out at the first sound of wood splintering. And how'm I going to explain how I did it? God, they'll wire me up and boil me down and bottle it – "Essence of Pansy Potter".'

But her anxieties were wasted on Granny

272

Farthing, whose reading matter had not included *Beano* or *Dandy*. She said, *'Not if you wait till everyone's asleep. They're all so tired, bless 'em, they won't even hear the thunder.'*

'Thunder?'

'Joe reckons there's another storm on the way. Don't know as how he can tell from all them bits of paper and them fronts and icy-bars but he's generally right about storms. Between you, me and the gate-post, it all has to do with Lucy's headaches.'

'But there will be thunder?' This crazy idea might actually work.

'Me roof!' they heard Grandma exclaim. Next came the sound of buckets and pots clashing and clanking and the door to the stairs slamming against the kitchen wall as Grandma stumped up to her bedroom to check on her weatherproofing, armed with sundry receptacles for leaks. Another storm would be the big test. 'It never rains but it pours,' they heard her complaining under her breath. She paused at the top of the stairs and clumped all the way down again, bucket handles squealing.

'Got to empty the bath first, Dorrie. Out you get, duck.'

The water dripped into Dorrie's room, not Grandma's, and it was only then that they remembered the missing slate. They made a hole with a screwdriver where the ceiling bulged, and left it plink, plinking into the slop pail while they went downstairs again to listen to the Saturday-night play by candlelight. The wireless ran off a huge glass battery that you had to keep topping up with distilled water. Primitive but it out-smarted power failures.

Lord of the Flies was enthralling but Dorrie found herself dozing.

'...I say boys are the worst,' Grandma seemed to be repeating. 'Little monkeys. I should know, with six of the buggers.' Dorrie smiled and closed her eyes again.

Silence woke her at the close of transmission, or it might have been her bright and breezy Great-grandmother reporting that everyone in the cottages was fast asleep, apart from Lucy who was up with the baby, rubbing his sore gums with rose jelly. She could have given him healing, but rose jelly tasted nicer. The young mother wished her niece luck, via the old ghost. Said why hadn't they thought of this before and saved her aching back?

Dorrie yawned, her eyelids too heavy to open. The voices of the old women came from the bottom of a well, nothing to do with her.

'Dorrie! 'Ere y'are, duck. Put this on.'

A smell of plastic. Grandma's Pacamac. She didn't understand. Was it raining? Why was she going out in the middle of the night? Why didn't they let her sleep? For answer a peal of thunder rippled across a few miles of sky. She remembered her mission and, groaning, fed her feet obediently into Wellington boots.

'Ready?'

She nodded. 'Are they ready – the Other Side?' Not that they were lie-abeds over there. Some slept, like Granny Farthing, but only out of habit.

'Whenever you are,' said the ancient shade.

She took a deep breath. She was bombed out, not in the least bit energetic or passionate. This was a waste of time.

Grandma opened the door to let her out. 'Best take the 'urricane lamp,' she whispered. 'Black as Newker's knocker out 'ere.'

Good idea. A person had to be able to see where she was directing her so-called power. Guesswork wouldn't do. Holding the lantern high into the slanting rain, she stepped onto the gravel path. It crunched. 'Ssshh,' she told it. Mustn't wake anyone up. Ye gods she was nervous. Her stomach was in knots. She trod carefully on the squelching grass, thinking how she'd aerated it that afternoon, all for nothing. Picked her way over the flattened privet hedge rather than use the squeaky front gate. Country-folk were especially alert to squeaky front gates.

And there loomed the tree, a giant slug, slick and grainy and well over seven feet in diameter. But the mass of branching wood made it, at this end, a huge bulk that raised the trunk off the ground at least another four feet. Even if she stood on tiptoe, she couldn't possibly reach the sawn wedge the men had made on top and she wasn't about to go climbing ladders in the dark and the rain. She'd break her neck. She'd just have to do the best she could from ground level.

Lightning flickered over the rough bark and picked out the silvery end of a metal spike just above her head. A weak spot. She'd aim for that. Water splashed over her fingers and up her sleeve to her armpit as she raised the hurricane

275

lamp to it. Ugh. This wasn't fair! Why her? Her grumbles were interrupted by an earsplitting crack of thunder. Mustering all her spiritual strength, Dorrie released a whoosh of power that sent her flying, slithering on her plastic mac through the mud. With a splintering and cracking to match the thunder, the branching stumps fell away and the severed trunk pounded into the ground, sending tremors through her bones.

Trembling, she struggled to her feet, discovering that her wellies had scooped up vast quantities of surface water and mud. Swearing resignedly under her breath, she went to examine her handiwork. It was difficult without the lamp, which had broken in her fall, but she could feel the jagged fissure against her palm. The tree had definitely split in two.

She blew a drip of rain off her nose. It was a bit awesome, that. She supposed Moses must have felt the same when he divided the waters of the Red Sea. Blimey, he must have thought, did I do that? Well, she'd made a start. As another peal of thunder rolled away she squelched on, hunched against the driving rain that tried to hammer her, like a tent peg, into the grass. She leaned against the wind, bracing herself for the next flash of lightning, that wriggled, without warning, down the sky towards her and almost simultaneous thunder which tore at her eardrums. Almost immediately, by focusing her own destructive powers, she cracked timber a second time, cleaving the trunk in two. The halves converged at the top, closing the wedge, gaped wider at the bottom, and held, a few inches above ground, like rough-cut beads threaded on a string. There was a clang of metal on metal as the spikes fell out.

Now the storm was right overhead. Lightning and thunder neck and neck. As she severed the roots from the trunk she couldn't tell which crack was electrical storm and which the splinter of wood. The roots splashed into the muddy hole from which they had come, and the monstrous log fell with a thud that sent vibrations through the soles of her wellies. She just had time to register the fact that the green had to be riddled with rabbit burrows to make that hollow sound when the log, which hadn't stopped moving, rolled with a skewed action right across her foot. It stopped when it had crushed the bones.

Nobody heard the scream that was lost in the wind and rain and thunder. Only Lucy, at the window, saw her fall, saw her writhing on the grass, saw the two mammoth logs splitting from end to end as Dorrie ran her pain up into the heart of the tree, striking back, along the grain, with all the energy left to her.

In seconds Lucy had roused Joe from his one night of sleep in a week. They both ran down in their pyjamas to fetch her in, to bring her to Nora who, with towels waiting, cursed the tree, the storm, the Other Side and their bright ideas, and wept when Joe, with wet and trembling fingers, cut away the Wellington boot and she saw the mess that had been made of Dorrie's toes.

Through veils of red pain Dorrie heard her railing, 'This is *your* fault!' at Granny Farthing, who was wringing her hands and crying ghostly tears. She hadn't foreseen this at all, she wailed. It was because there were no blood ties, because Dorrie wasn't her own.

'What's that?'

Dorrie stifled a moan. The question flew into silence and stayed there, hovering. Auntie Lucy had a towel wrapped round her head and had slipped on Grandma's dressing gown. She was attempting to compose her mind for healing. Nevertheless her question continued to flutter around the room, like a trapped bird, between the five of them, as she absently tied the dressing-gown cord.

The old women glared at each other, pulling the strings of their mouths tight, too. Luckily a child's fretful cry distracted its mother fully and Joe had to be given instructions about heating a bottle and rubbing sore gums with rose jelly before departing.

Grandma took the opportunity to pick up a sopping heap of clothes from the floor and trudge out with them to the kitchen sink. Meanwhile the indiscreet ghost was about to do the sensible thing and disappear when Lucy said sharply, 'Where do you think you're going, Granny? I need you here.' She seemed to have forgotten the question of Dorrie's blood ties, at least for the time being.

As the air calmed and the storm dissipated, Lucy talked quietly, asking them all to think of love energy, to think pink.

How, when pain filled her, dark and angry. Throbbing poisonous pain. When every nerve, fibre and cell screamed with it. When fists drummed, when teeth ground to locking and her body was rigid with it.

'Leave it, Dorrie, let it go. It's only the body. Let your spirit free. Rise above it. You can do it if anyone can. Look at the candle, love. Concentrate on the flame, the burning and flickering.'

No. She wanted to attend to her bleeding, splintered toes.

'The flame, Dorrie.'

Why should she? It was just a very ordinary candle flame. The black and glowing wick, the blue transparency of heat, the sooty smoke curling from a paintbrush flame, dipped in sunshine, its soft limpid tongue licking the air.

'And breathe deeply and slowly in, and out. With me, Dorrie, i-i-in and out. Feel the air in your nostrils, how cool it is, and ou-u-ut, how warm. Cool, and warm.'

As her aunt's voice went murmuring on, Dorrie became aware of hands passing over her, over her head, her body, and down to her feet. Her foot, her mashed toes... Quickly she looked back at the candle. A change of focus and she saw the ghost-image of light around the flame, as skilled fingers moved over and around, up and down, without actually touching any part of her. Cool ... and warm. Ghostly fingers.

'Think of a pink balloon, Dorrie, a beautiful pink balloon. Think of filling it, breathing in energy and love; breathing out pink. Gently breathing out. The balloon fills easily, effort-

279

lessly. Love is filling your lungs; pink is filling the air. Pinker and pinker. You are bathed in pink light, Dorrie. Come and look. You are healing in lovely translucent pink.'

She went, looked down from the darkness, and saw the settee with her there, propped up with cushions, staring at a candle, and floating in a shiny pink bubble. The old ladies were basking in its gentle heat and Auntie Lucy moved in and out of the rosy haze as she tended to the crushed foot, drawing off the negative aura, like red smoke, wafting it away into the outer darkness, and bathing the wound gently with cool healing light.

And she glimpsed, far away, in a corner of her mind, a lonely man with his head in his hands, unable to help this time.

In the morning she was woken by voices in the lane, voices slow with awe and discovery.

'My word, 'Orace, I never see the like o' that, not in all my born days.'

'Jest goes to show, don't it? Wonder o' nature, that be. 'Twere they metal spikes, I'll be bound, conducting the old lightning jest where us needed her most.'

'And never a trace o' scorching or burning.'

'Nope.'

'They spikes must 'ave been spot on, 'Orace.'

'Yep.'

'Well, I'll be blessed.' The vicar. 'God moves in a mysterious way His wonders to perform.'

'Near as good a job as bleddy saw-mill, begging your pardon, Reverend.'

280

'Indeed, indeed, Mr Batts. Praise be.'

''Ow'd it manage that, then, 'Orace? That slicing in 'alf?'

'Stands to reason, George, 'tis on the grain.'

'Oh arr...'

Somewhere a cock crowed and Randy Rooster IV, in Grandma's coop, felt moved to answer. Pretty soon all the cockerels in the kingdom were straining their throats to keep Dorrie from her slumbers.

An hour later the clangour of church bells woke her again. Sunday morning and no one was allowed to lie in, not even if they'd been up all night performing miracles. Dorrie moaned. Grandma must have decided to leave her there, rather than get her upstairs to the leaky bedroom. She ached all over from the settee. Somehow she had shuffled down so that her head butted one Rexined arm while her legs were draped over the other. Her calves were imprinted with two red rows of brass studs and her feet were cold.

Her feet...

Remembering, she swung her legs round to look. Put both feet on the floor and sucked pain sharply through her teeth. They still hurt, those smashed toes on her left foot. Still hurt. Like when you pressed a bruise. They were smeared and clotted with dried blood, but they did seem, when you compared them, to be less swollen. It wasn't just wishful thinking, was it? She tried wriggling them and winced, proving that the nerves at least were still working.

She needed to go out the back.

Gingerly she tried putting her weight on the foot. Not too bad if she walked on her heel. Her gabardine was on the back of the door and she put it on. Shoes, next. Her school shoes were under the sideboard but she could only get one on. The Wellingtons were unwearable, wet and muddy, inside and out, and bloody, and cut about with a Stanley knife. Barefoot she'd be bound to get dirt in the wound and it would fester and her toes would drop off. Like the Pobble. Unless...

She wound a small towel from last night round her toes. String was what she needed now. In the sideboard drawer. Grandma had given Dorrie lengths of it the day before, to use in the garden. Quietly, so as not to disturb Sunday sleepers, she pulled it open and discovered an old woman's hoarded treasures. Christmas cards. Balloons. Used stamps. Candle ends. Pencil stubs. Old ration books. Rent books. A box of buttons. And a hundred bits of string, parcel lengths, white, brown, straw-coloured, with red and black sealing wax still attached, all knotted together and wound into a prickly ball. Having tied up her foot, she tried to shut the drawer. It stuck. She jiggled it. One side went in, not the other. She pulled it out, straightened it, jiggled again. Something was caught. Paper or cardboard. Flattening her hand, she managed to hold onto it with two fingers and tease it out.

It was a photograph, in a paper cover. Rank upon rank of smug faces. Hand-knits and shiny suits and the open portals of a Nissen hut behind. The Church of the Holy Spirit,

Sowness. There was Grandma in the front, with all the leading lights and Joanna on her knees. There was Lucy beside her, holding one baby, pregnant with another. Quite a recent photo then. There were Hettie Fitzell and Granny Batts, Mabel Hooper, Walter and Eric, the whole gang. Even Uncle Joe was there, under duress, Dorrie suspected, from his sullen expression. Apart from the Torrances and possibly Eric there didn't seem to be anyone under forty. She ran her finger along the rows, and stopped. A teenaged boy gazed out at her, with hard eyes, a slick smile and the beginnings of facial hair. Just one, in all that crowd, and she didn't like the look of him at all.

She really needed to go. She put the photograph in her pocket to study at leisure and closed the drawer smoothly, took an umbrella to lean on and limped through the house.

'Just thinking of bringing your breakfast out to you!' teased Grandma, up, dressed and watching critically from the top of the steps as Dorrie hobbled back across the yard. There was a deeply satisfying smell of bacon frying from the open back door. And tomatoes. 'Thought you'd took up residence.' Then, 'Oh, bli, Hopalong Cassidy ain't in it. How's it feel?'

'Better than last night.'

'I can't see you cetching no train home today, duck.' Her sniff and grimly wagging head, as she came down to help her granddaughter up the steps, were meant to convey regret but she spoiled the effect with a huge, conspiratorial wink. 'We best tell your mum something fell on your foot, eh – a brick or something. Mister Stone'll do the honours, I'm sure,' she said, disappearing round the fence into Next-door's yard.

It was all arranged. PC Stone would pass the message on, when he went on duty at nine. 'And you can come to meeting with me tonight!'

Dorrie wrinkled her nose. 'Oh, Grandma, do I have to?'

The old face fell into wrinkles of dismay. 'No, 'course you don't, duck, not if you don't want. I just thought...'

'I'd rather not, if you don't mind. I'm not really a church-goer.'

She thought again of the photograph of the Church of the Holy Spirit, of the congregation of stuffy spiritualists celebrating some anniversary or other. They were all frumps and fuddy-duddies, without a hormone between them. Probably never even heard of rock 'n' roll or James Dean. Not her sort at all. And that was the trouble, that's what had kept her in the lavatory for twenty minutes. Because in the most important way they *were* her sort. They'd understand her and make her ever so welcome, and youth would pass her by.

'Grandma, who's this?'

She produced the photo from her pocket and pointed to the boy with the downy upper lip.

Grandma squinted over the top of her spectacles. 'Oh Gawd, where d'you find that? Oh, look at the baby. He couldn't sit still, Richard, could he?' She looked again. 'Which one, duck? Oh, him. That's that Derek Wilson over-the-school. Your little playmate.'

'They wouldn't give you tuppence for her. Not if she's dippy.'

Oh yes, she knew him now. As slimy a teenager as he was a child. Well, let's hope it did him some good, she thought, going to church. And, unaccountably, shivered.

'Yeah,' said Grandma indifferently, 'he come along to meetings for a while. Told me he was at a crossroads or some-such. Looking for guidance.'

'Did he find it?'

'Perhaps he did. He went off to training college, far as I know, to be a teacher like his Ma. Hope it stays fine for him. Can't say as I ever took to the boy. Oh, he was all right on the outside, I suppose, but I dunno, you can't help wondering what sort of person would bully a little girl like he did.'

'*And* go to church.'

'Oh, you get all sorts, Dorrie, for all sorts of reasons.'

'Not many youngsters, though.'

'No,' she agreed, understanding at last, 'not many youngsters. But I can't get out of it tonight, lovey, I'm afraid. I let them down Wednesday, didn't I? Lucy said she'd give us a lift on the bike. So long as you don't mind being left on your own? Joe's off tonight – volunteered to mind the kids. He's like you – he ain't no churchgoer, neither. If you want anything just give him a shout.'

She was bored. Lonely, too. Rain did little *mummy-daddy* drumrolls on the window, making her homesick. There was no one to talk to, as John had gone home after tea to watch the last episode of *Little Red Monkey* which was going to be really exciting and she was having to miss it, no television, a wireless you couldn't even tune to Radio Luxembourg and nothing to read but sloppy Ethel M. Dell. She put 'Rock Around the Clock' on the gramophone, but very quietly because the children were asleep next-door, and it wasn't the same at all. Uncle Joe had the Palm Court Orchestra on. Brahms or something deadly. So she read Auntie Lucy's *Picturegoer* for the umpteenth time, did a stupid crossword about film stars and fell asleep on the settee.

It rained all day Monday and Grandma had the hump because she couldn't put her washing out. On Tuesday morning it was still raining and Dorrie was minding her three small cousins. The floor was littered with children and toys and old weather maps, on the back of which were drawings of cats and dogs and birds and houses and mummies and daddies and grannies and anything else the little brats demanded.

The telephone rang. It was the Exchange to tell them that the lines were mended and that there was a call from London.

'Hello, Mum! Oh, I'm so pleased to hear you. Oh hang on a minute...' She hooked a crayon out of little Jack's mouth, wiped his snotty nose with her handkerchief and put him back in the playpen, whereupon he set up an earsplitting howl. 'Sorry about the racket,' she yelled into the receiver. 'Can you hear me? Auntie Lucy's just popped to Fitzell's. I said (Richard, give Jack the motor car, dear. I know it's yours. Just for a minute, so I can hear)... Hello, Mum? What? Oh that's better, he stopped. My foot? Oh, fine, thanks. I mean, it's not too– What? *What!* Oh Mum! Oh, that's awful. Yes, yes, don't worry. 'Course I will, straightaway. Soon as Lucy gets back. Bye.'

Dorrie fitted the receiver back on its cradle, and wound a curl of hair round her finger, absently watching Jack pulling the wheel off Richard's toy car. JoJo was peacefully drawing, quite oblivious to three-year-old Richard's roar of protest as he tried, ferociously, to tug his car through the playpen bars, much to little Jack's disgust. Forcing herself to action, Dorrie began picking up the drawings and patting them into some sort of order. When Grandma burst in, thinking someone was being murdered, Dorrie was most surprised. She hadn't heard a thing.

Her mother had told her to take the earliest train home as there had been an accident and Aunt Polly was in hospital.

Chapter Fifteen

For want of a nail, a floorboard at the Lord Clyde had come loose. Aunt Polly had tripped and smashed headlong through the doorway of the men's washroom, onto the tiled floor, tipping over her bucket of soapy water which had been propping open the door. The landlord found her two hours later, concussed and bleeding. She was soaked to freezing and her foot was still twisted in the hole.

When they got her to hospital they found that she'd broken her hip, her wrist, a couple of ribs and a number of teeth. From the pain she was in when she came round, they guessed there were internal injuries, too, but all she was worried about was her invalid sister, left all alone at home. She gave them her niece's name and place of work and only then accepted the pain-killers.

They found Flo in the middle of a perm.

'Not your week, is it, Flo?' said Betsy, witheringly, and turned her back to begin teasing tittle-tattle out of her lady's bouffant.

'I'll make up the time, Bet, I will. Promise.'

She fetched Arthur from the picket line at Cunningham-Bayliss and together they half-walked, half-carried a protesting Nanna Hubbard round the corner to the prefab and tucked her into Stephen's bed. He would have to sleep on the settee for the time being, and no arguments. It wasn't right, a young boy sharing a room with his grandmother. Come to that it wasn't right for a young boy to share with his fourteen-year-old sister, as Mum took the opportunity to point out. Something would have to be done. Then Arthur went back to his vigil, she put a chicken casserole into a slow oven and caught the bus to the hospital.

For want of a cause – leaving the works' dispute aside – Dad spent most of Monday night writing a letter to the brewers demanding compensation for Aunt Polly. Although, as Nanna Hubbard observed when she popped her head round the door to see whether Flo was back and what the chances were of something to eat, her sister had had no witnesses, no union to back her and no evidence. (Ten to one that loose floorboard had been hammered down already.) Polly wouldn't get the sweepings off the floor, they'd see. Arthur would stand a better chance of writing to Gilbey's and getting compensation for Nanna Hubbard being the way she was. It was their gin had rotted her liver!

Many would have been tempted to throw in the towel at this juncture, or to wrap it round their mother-in-law's neck, but Arthur was in militant mood. When Flo arrived home, tight-faced, just after seven, Nanna and Stephen were watching the unmoving television screen, with its 'Normal service will be resumed as soon as possible' potter's wheel logo, and Dad was on his third draft of a letter to the union solicitor. Letters to Watneys, the Housing Department and, for good measure, to Gilbey's too, were stamped and waiting on the mantelpiece for Mum to post.

Arthur had a thought. Dorrie had been allowed to sulk long enough. They'd get her home in time for visiting next day; that way, she could sit with Nanna Hubbard, who couldn't be left alone at night, and he could go with Flo up the hospital and tell Polly what he'd done on her behalf. Cheer her up. Stephen shouldn't have to play nursemaid; in any case he had Cubs on Tuesday night. The phone lines must be repaired by now. Perhaps Flo could pop up to the phone box and check? She could drop the letters in the postbox on the way. After tea, though, eh? His stomach was beginning to think his throat was cut.

By the time Dorrie got to see Aunt Polly on Wednesday the old woman was past all cheering up. Her leg was raised in some sort of pulley, her wrist was in plaster, her chest was strapped tight, her mouth was all swollen and every movement made her gasp. But it was her spirit that had suffered the worst bruising. She had begged them not to take her to Raynes Green Hospital. Anywhere but there. Raynes had been built as a workhouse back in Queen Victoria's time. The only way you came out was in a box.

'Everyone knows that,' she croaked, a slow tear sliding across her nose. And the look in her eyes was one that Dorrie hadn't seen in all the years she'd known her – a wide-eyed look, almost of surprise. In fact, it was fear.

When pneumonia set in Dorrie telephoned Aunt Lucy, who said that she'd certainly help to relieve the old lady's pain, if drugs were of no use but, she hastened to add, Dorrie should be aware that when it was a person's allotted time it was wrong to attempt to delay their passing. Perhaps the real healing that was needed was to bring peace and tranquillity to an atmosphere of fear and anxiety. Dorrie could do that.

'Me?'

'Yes, you. You've got to start somewhere – why not with someone you know and love?'

'But I'm not–' She was about to protest that she wasn't a healer when Lucy interrupted.

'You're a channel, Dorrie – remember that. You never know what you can do until you try. I'll be on hand if you get stuck. Better still, get onto Viv.'

'Viv?'

'The very same. Give her a call.'

'Phone her? But she can't talk.'

'No, ninny! Good grief, Dorrie, you are being dense.' There was an impatient click of the tongue before she explained, more gently, 'Tele-pathy, duckie – what you're good at.' Before she put the phone down she remembered to ask about Dorrie's foot.

'Foot?' She'd forgotten all about it. Mum had noticed her limping, when she'd arrived home, and had made her take off her sock so she could exclaim over the black and blue toes.

'Dorrie! My God, girl, you could have been crippled for life. I don't know – I can't trust you out of my sight.' And so she'd gone on, off at the

291

deep end. 'Fancy dropping a brick on your foot! I never heard of anything so... 'Course, you weren't wearing your glasses, were you? Oh, why can't you be more careful, Dorrie! That toenail's going to come off, you mark my words. Just when peep-toes are coming in again. Oh, *very* smart you're going to look.' Et cetera, et cetera, the woman-to-woman intimacy they'd found at Great Bisset ousted by the frustrations of motherhood. 'Where are your glasses? We'd better get them mended. A squint doesn't just straighten itself out, I know that much.'

But it did and, with Lucy sending healing over the airwaves for her toes, Dorrie was soon back in the swim of things, helping to win the challenge cup for her class and setting up a school record for the quarter-mile free-style. As she leapt around the tennis court and hared up the athletics track she hadn't time to consider how close she had come to crutches, but it was one of the things she contemplated when she was quiet. The other was the amazing reach of her Cousin Viv's psychic powers.

Her seven years of life had had no impact on the wizened little body she inhabited. She still saw the world through blind eyes, tasted it, touched it, smelled it with embryonic senses, heard it with ears that muffled every sound. Nevertheless, deep inside her brain a few essential nerves wriggled still, keeping her heart beating, her organs functioning, her juices flowing. And nourishing her spirit, which was alive and kicking and living in Newcastle, with a *pied-à-terre* in heaven.

Her psychic voice was squeakier than ever, never having known the restraints of vocal cords. Her quaint way with words, ideas rather, that hit you between the eyes, that left you feeling a bit breathless, took some getting used to. You had to keep reminding yourself that she had never spoken aloud, that spiritual communication was more direct than speech, ignoring social niceties and linguistic conventions, that she was much, much older than her years.

'Your elderly aunt is expected over there. Her time is soon. It is you must prepare her, Dorrie-cousin. Must make her peaceful about the crossing.'

'Yeah, okay,' she gulped. 'So what do I do?'

'Yourself first. You must contemplate your own death.'

'Mine?'

'When you know the transition from the Earth plane back to the subtle levels you can lead others through.'

Help! This was grown-up stuff and she wasn't ready. She was only fourteen.

'It is not frightful, Dorrie-cousin. I, Viv, have been there and back a hundred times.'

'Yes, but you–'

'Yes, but I expect death. My poor nothing body cries out for death. But a mind who splits wood should not be fearful. Who heals from a broken foot.'

Dorrie blushed. This cousin of hers knew just how to make you feel humble and guilty and altogether rotten.

293

'Seek protection now,' the voice in her head went on.

'What?'

'A channel must put herself into spiritual hands so no harm comes.'

So Dorrie prayed as Viv taught her, to the Great Spirit. She even read the Bible, the bit about putting on the armour of God. It made sense. As a further safety measure she asked Granny Farthing to remain on red alert.

And then, while Nanna Hubbard snored like a tractor in the next bed, and her guardian angels watched over her, Dorrie began to breathe deeply, remembering her aunt's voice... I-i-in and out, breathing in love, breathing out ... what colour? Gold. Bathed in the gold of a setting sun, slowly, slowly she lost touch with her limbs, as her blood turned to sludge in her veins, as her body cooled, as the wisp that her breath had become ceased to matter. As she spiralled down through her small life. The time for death had come.

And gone.

A stitch in time. Nothing at all.

Nothing but peace. Contentment spreading warm through her veins. Oozing out through her pores. Peace floating her quietly from her bones, from her muscles, from her skin, out of the body and away. No questions. Let it come. Let it begin. Now.

Upwards like a seed's shoots through the dark earth. Feeling the pull. Stretching up with long fingers, swimming up with a wiggle, with a tadpole's tail to a promise of delight.

Breaking through into dazzle.

Light. Crystalline air and light and she was part of it. Every molecule of her fizzing, turning through the bright spectrum. Off at a run now over springy ground, faster, faster, wind in her hair, skin singing, muscles and bones and sinews rejoicing in activity. Leaping and spinning with plenty of breath left to sing at the top of her voice. Singing, wildly singing. Shouting. For the sheer bubbling joy of it.

The light taking shape, *presences,* running and springing beside her, catching her up and whirling her into dance, sharing her light and love and joy. Delicious. So *so good.*

Afterwards she was sure she'd walked on a path sparkling with quartz, bordered by tiny sweet-smelling flowers and herbs and lichen-covered rocks warmed by sun. She knew it was a mountain path, though she had never climbed a mountain. There were sounds of insects and birdsong, the trickle of water, the soft crunch of firm soles on the path. Otherwise an exquisite silence, an idea of heaven that she might have imagined. As she continued along the path she knew that she was coming back, being led gently down into her body by her cousin, the go-between spirit. And she thanked them all for letting her visit.

She took to going up to the hospital after school, sitting with her aunt before any other visitors arrived. Polly was having trouble breathing now and didn't always feel like talking. She wasn't always awake, even, but Dorrie spoke to her as though she were. She sowed a few seeds in the weary old mind, about places and people, schoolfriends, Polly's girlhood, about working in the Penny Bazaar and joining the Federation of Women Workers, about meeting Wilf who worked on the docks, about the wedding, about their neighbours. She watched the seeds germinate, put out roots and flower. Then she simply garnered what she had seen in the eye of the old woman's mind.

'It's the Dockers' Day Out. Remember? All the neighbours excited? You're all off for a charabanc ride to Southend, Aunt Polly. Such a blue sky and the fields sprinkled with poppies. You've never seen anything so lovely. Look – there's a windmill, the sails hardly turning. You're leaning out the window to catch the breeze. Gawd, what a pong! What's that? Slurry?

'Just when you're beginning to think you'll never get there, you turn a corner and there's a silver thread over the smoking chimney pots. The sea! You can see it, you can smell it.

'On the beach now in your deckchair, toes playing idly with the smooth, warm pebbles, and here comes Wilf, a knotted hanky on his head, trousers rolled up to his knees, barefooted, coming down the steps with a dripping ice-cream cornet...'

Aunt Polly was licking her lips. 'Rossi's,' she rasped, her eyes closed in pleasure, her skinny throat moving as she swallowed. The bruises were fading now and the swelling around her jaw had gone down. But talking was no easier. She was very weak and punctuated her words with shallow breaths. 'Oh Gawd – they knew how to make ice cream in them days. Secret recipe, they reckoned. Sweet and clean and milky...'

'A real treat, eh, Auntie? Oh, you needed an ice cream, it was so hot, that day, with just a slight breeze off the sea...'

''Cause it ain't real sea at Southend, even though they got the pier. It's an estuary, innit? River Blackwater. That's why it's so muddy.'

Dorrie got the picture. 'You go for a paddle and the mud's squishing up between your toes, soft and gloopy...'

'Soft and *smelly*,' corrected Aunt Polly, nose wrinkling, seeing a little green crab scuttling out of the seaweed. There's a faint smile pulling at the corners of her mouth.

'What? Where are you now? Oh, the bus. The roofless doubledecker. Giddyup horse. Plenty of room on top. And there you are pushing Uncle Wilf up the stairs, but he's had one too many and he keeps sitting on your head, squashing your lovely hat with the feathers.'

The dry old voice commented, 'Job to get him out of the pub, that day. He was ill on the way home. Oh, he was in a bad way. They had to stop the coach!' And she laughed a gravelly laugh.

'They were good times, Aunt Polly.'

'Yeah. Sometimes.'

'And it'll be good again – better – over there. You'll have your health and strength and you won't have to scrub floors any more and you'll meet up with all your old friends and have a high old time.'

'Will I, Dorrie?'

''Course you will, Aunt Poll.'

Uncle Wilf, a young man by choice, in an ill-fitting suit, cloth cap and handlebar moustache, had been shuffling his feet over by the drugs trolley and he made his entrance now, so dramatically on cue that poor Aunt Poll clutched at her heart. But she laughed as he made his cavalier bow, flourishing a huge hat of ostrich plumes, the sort pearly queens wore. ''Ere y'are, gel. You always looked a proper treat in it. Here it is, and none the worse for being sat on.'

'Good as new,' agreed her aunt, marvelling.

'And this time next week you'll be wearing it, they tell me. How about that then? Eh? There's a turn-up, eh?'

Aunt Polly blinked, hardly knowing whether to laugh or cry.

'Dorrie'll tell you. Ain't nuffink to be scared of. I'll be there to help you acrost. And your Ma and Pop, they'll be there, an' all. An' you and me, we'll go in together, arm in arm, like in the old days...'

The old lady was entranced. Down in the deep dark caverns of her eyes, hope glittered. She listened to them all, spirits of friends, neighbours, family, who came up add their two penn'orth around this time and what they told her added up.

'Poor old gel, she's talking to herself,' said Dad, when he saw how she was smiling and nodding.

'Hallucinating,' agreed Mum. 'It'll be the drugs.'

When she died on St George's Day, she looked as though she were a child asleep on her birthday eve, a smudge of colour in her bony cheeks, her sunken mouth curved in a smile of sweet anticipation.

The strike ended a week later, when Cunningham-Bayliss agreed to union demands, and Dad was cock-of-the-walk. Oh yes, he crowed over tea, the men had all slapped him on the back, told him he'd won through and saved the day and well done, Arthur.

Ah, he said, leaning back in his chair, rosy and replete, it was good to be back doing a man's job. He'd had enough of sitting on his backside, what with funerals and sorting through dead people's effects. What a time he'd had of it, he told his mates, the neighbours, anyone that would listen.

Dorrie cringed as he sat the insurance man down to tell him.

Tight as arseholes, Aunt Polly's employers. Mrs Hubbard, being the deceased's sister and not a true dependant, wasn't entitled to any compensation. In any case, they reckoned she'd slipped on her soap. Would you credit it? Denied all liability, lying bastards! If she hadn't died, poor old cow, he'd have taken them to court, sued the buggers. That was the last time he'd drink in any of their establishments. Come the Revolution, eh, brother? The insurance man smiled wanly, not really understanding.

More to the point, he'd discovered that the house he'd thought would come to them, as

Polly's only surviving relatives, had never actually belonged to her. When Flo's Uncle Wilf had died and her aunt had moved down the street, it wasn't because she'd wanted a smaller backyard, or because of the noisy neighbours, or because she couldn't abear to live there without her Wilf, or for any of the tinpot reasons she'd put about. It was because she hadn't been able to keep up the mortgage repayments. Silly bitch had never let on. All the while they'd been thinking she was a property-owning capitalist she'd been paying rent just like them. They'd got sod-all for her sticks of furniture. And two hundred quid from the Pru wasn't even going to cover the cost of the funeral. Bloody hell, she'd been paying in all her life, shilling a week. Was the insurance man sure that was all there was? Would he like another cup of tea? No, Arthur was glad to get back to work. His Flo was fed up with strike pay and he was fed up with living on tick. Enough was enough.

In fact, thought Dorrie, ruling a double line under her algebra homework, they'd managed very well. Mum had dipped into her imagination to make a little go a long way, but stuffed cheek of pig with roasted vegetables didn't sound nearly as heart-rending as marrow-bone broth.

The following evening, he came home in a foul mood. They'd pulled a fast one, he fumed, taken him for a mug. Buggers.

Tom Ruddock was coming up for retirement so you might have forgiven 'the powers that be', as Dad insisted on calling them, for thinking that a quiet office job would have suited the old man. But he hated it.

'They've taken away me manhood,' he'd complained, with tears in his eyes. 'That's what they've done, Arthur. Skilled craftsman I was and they've turned me into a glorified tea-boy, that's what! It ain't good enough.'

It wasn't, but there was little Dad could do. The management had agreed to his demands, they insisted. Bent over backwards to 'absorb the men back into the workforce' as he'd stipulated. Oh well, they'd said, inclining their smarmy fat heads (shysters!) he should have said, written it into the demands, that the men were to have their old jobs back at their old rates of pay.

Of the two remaining toolcutters, Terry Graham was given a menial job in Packing, like it or lump it, and Paul Wicks was made full-time Safety Officer.

'One in the eye for yours truly!' he griped. 'That was mine, by rights, and they knew it, cynical bastards!' He was the one who'd brought the new government regulations to their attention, wasn't he? Oh, they'd played him for a sucker all right, screwed him good and proper. The men were all looking at him sideways... He shook his head in misery.

And they'd made no concessions at all regarding the new machine. It was there to stay. And there'd be more, you could bet your life, more machines taking over from the workers, making money for capitalist swine. To add insult to injury, they'd now brought in so-called 'experts', whose job it was to sit on their arses all day, with a clipboard on their knee, and watch you work. Their 'findings' were supposed to make you more efficient. Streamlining, they called it. Flaming bloody nerve, more like! These were top-grade, skilled men. Talk about teaching your granny to suck eggs! No, it was more sinister than that, 'cause they were rate-fixers, these work-study wallahs, anyone could see that. And what they called a fair rate was always lower, wasn't it? Never higher– Gaw, that'd be the day! No, they'd got 'em by the short and curlies. Lower rates or questions of over-manning, he'd seen it happen. Everyone looking over their shoulder, trying to spot where the chop was coming next and working like stink to make sure it wasn't them.

Management were loving it, wagging their fat chops, rubbing their greasy palms and spouting clichés.

'Can't stand in the way of progress, lads. Productivity's the name of the game. Our hands are tied.'

You felt like ramming their maxims down their throats, clitch by clitch by rotten clitch.

Peter had seen the writing on the wall and gone back to school.

Dorrie was impressed. Her cousin had always maintained that school was for sissies and swots like her. Far better to leave on his fifteenth birthday and learn a trade like Uncle Arthur, like his dad; do a man's job that paid, so he could bung his mum a few quid now and again and keep himself in fags and crêpe soles.

But when he came over to have his hair cut for Aunt Polly's funeral, he told them he'd changed his mind. If technology was going to be the devil at his heels, he thought perhaps he ought to get on top of it, rather than the other way round. He thanked Arthur for all he'd done in getting him the apprenticeship but he was going back to the County High on the first day of the summer term, to finish the year and to take his O levels. So would Auntie Flo be a doll and knit him one of those new chunky sweaters, in black, to match his school uniform?

And when she cut his hair, could she leave off the DA and the Brylcreem this time? Tony Curtis was old hat. Now the girls were going for James Dean.

Arthur sighed and rolled his eyes, but it wasn't so much teenage fads that were getting him down as the fact that Management had got away with it again.

The prefab was bursting at the seams but it was the following February before the Council caught up with them. Dorrie had just celebrated her fifteenth birthday with a trip to the Granada to hear Count Basie on stage. There was no way she was going to invite her friends home to another party, not after the fiasco at Christmas.

Arthur and Flo had refused to go out. Not if there were going to be boys around. Dad had spent the night grumbling about being shut in the kitchen, and Mum kept coming in, on Dad's orders, with more food and requests to turn the music down. Stephen thought it was wildly funny to dash in and switch on the lights, hooting at the hasty removal of male hands from female breasts. What with Nanna Hubbard creeping about, it was a nightmare.

'Don't mind me, just passing through – when you gotta go, you gotta go,' and on the way back, managing to trip over sprawling legs and bump into the Dansette, scratching the record. 'No, you carry on, I'll be all right. Just gotta get me breath.'

They were all kicked out at ten, anyway, so that Stephen, who was suddenly very sleepy, could bed down on the couch.

Never again.

And then, one day, out of the snow, came a seedy-looking man from the Housing Department, to poke around and tick things off his list. He informed them that Stephen was ten years old ... ('Fancy,' said Mum, with a touch of acid. 'Doesn't time fly?') ... and Dorrie was fifteen, too old to be sharing a room with her brother.

'Oh, but–' said Mum.

Dad quelled her with a look.

Prefabs had never been intended as permanent accommodation. Ten years was their expected life-span. Would they like to look at some new three-bedroomed houses over on the Highams Park Estate?

Three-bedroomed?

One for the parents, one for the boy, one for the girl.

What about Nanna Hubbard?

The man looked puzzled, lowered his voice and his glasses and said that he'd assumed they'd be putting her into a home, where she could be properly looked after. Intense relief flooded Mum's face. Nanna was doubly incontinent now and Mum was worn out with running around after her and trying to put in a full day's work at Bettina's.

'Oh no,' said Dad loudly. 'I'm not having my dependents put out to pasture. The old girl stays with us.'

At which Nanna Hubbard's ears pricked up. 'I ain't a dependent. I pay for my keep,' she insisted.

The housing man affirmed that indeed she wasn't a dependent: she had a state pension and Grandpop's insurance. If she lived with them in a room of her own it would be assumed that she was a lodger and paying rent. That constituted a misuse of council property.

'How come?'

'Clause seventeen, under the *Tenants may not* section – conduct private business from council premises.'

'Ridiculous,' said Dad.

'That's as may be,' said the man from the Housing, 'but if your mother-in-law is found to be occupying her own room, for rent, you will be evicted. There is, however, nothing to stop you having your mother-in-law stay as a guest, sharing with your daughter, for example, or sleeping on the Put-U-Up.'

'I ain't sleeping on no Put-U-Up.'

'And nothing to stop her helping out with

household expenses, of her own volition, of course.'

A crafty gleam stole into Nanna's rheumy eye. 'Volition' meant that she didn't have to if she didn't want to.

A craftier gleam crept into Dad's. There was always the threat of the Home.

Three bedrooms it was, then, and Nanna Hubbard to continue sharing with Dorrie. Neither was thrilled at the prospect.

'I ain't never gonna manage them stairs, Flo,' the old woman whined. 'It suits me here, on the level. Why can't we stop here?'

'You won't need to manage the stairs. I'll bring your meals up to you.'

'I ain't gonna be castrated up there, Flo.'

'Eh?'

'Out of sight, out of mind. A prisoner in me own bed.'

'Incarcerated, Mum.'

'Well, I ain't. I want to see what's going on. And what about the telly? I gotta come down and see the telly. 'Ere, 'ow about I sleep on the Put-U-Up?'

'You said you didn't want to.'

'Never mind what I said. The Put-U-Up can stay put up and that can be my room, that back room.'

'You can't have a room of your own, Mum. You heard the man.'

'Oh, he ain't to know. How's he gonna know?'

'You'd have to go up for the bathroom and toilet and you can't manage the stairs, Mum. I won't be there to help you – I'll be at work.'

'I can wash in the kitchen and I can have a jerry by the bed.'

Flo's face betrayed her dismay.

'Oh, if I'm too much trouble...' The old woman's lip trembled. 'One thing about Polly, she never complained. Heart of gold, my Poll.'

'Polly didn't have a telly, Mum. You were happy to stop upstairs. And you didn't need your sheets changing all the time.' It was at the front of her mind and it just slipped out.

'I can't 'elp it.' Tears began to roll down the withered cheeks. 'I'm an old woman.'

'You *can* help it, Mum. If you can make it into the front room in time for *Take Your Pick* you can make it to the toilet without messing the bed. You do it on purpose and I don't know why.' Now *she* was sniffing back tears.

'I don't.'

'Oh, come off it! I've watched you, Mum, squeezing it out, going red in the face like a baby messing its nappy. You must really hate me, to make all this work for me.'

'I want Po-o-olly,' wailed Nanna Hubbard.

'Don't we all.'

'She would never say such cruel things to me.'

'She would if you'd messed *her* sheets.'

'Oh Polly, why did you have to leave me? You was the best sister anyone could have.'

Mum sighed. 'Oh don't cry, Mum. I'm sorry – I'm just tired, what with the packing and Betsy at work and everything. Come on, dry your eyes. Dorrie'll help, won't you, love? It'll be best for everyone if you're in the same bedroom as her, Mum. She seems to know when you want to go.

We'll manage, I'm sure.'

As it turned out, they didn't have to manage for long.

They moved into Ainsley Crescent in May and let Nanna Hubbard have her own way – the back room, the Put-U-Up and Mum running around after her, emptying her slops and changing her bedding, before setting out for 'Snips', a rather select salon with up-to-date equipment and pink fluffy monogrammed towels, a brisk walk across the River Ching and up Hale End Road.

Her new employer was Charles, who had been trained by Raymond, Mr Teasy-Weasy, himself. Dad said he was a poofter and Mum said so what? He was kind and considerate and all the customers adored him.

Three weeks after they'd moved in, Stephen, the first to arrive home from school, found Nanna Hubbard lying dead at the bottom of the stairs. She was fully dressed, her head was at a sickening angle and she was stinking of gin. By the time Dorrie breezed home on her bicycle, her spirit was sitting on the top stair, gazing with academic interest at the wreckage below.

'Oh, Nanna,' breathed Dorrie, 'what a way to go.'

'*Never felt a thing, Dor. And didn't I always say them stairs'd be the death of me?*'

Stephen was in the kitchen, peeing thankfully into the kitchen sink. Dorrie had found him waiting for her in the road, hopping from one foot to the other, not being able to bring himself to step over the body to go upstairs.

'Not the stairs, Nanna, the gin!'

They found the empty bottle propped carefully on her pillow in lieu of a note. No further explanation was necessary.

But: 'Where did she get it from? Why did she? How?' Stephen bombarded Dorrie with questions.

How had she managed to climb the stairs?

'She crawled, Stephen. Like a baby, on all fours. And when she got to the top she turned and threw herself down.'

Why was self-evident. She couldn't face getting old without Aunt Polly.

As for the gin... The man in the off-licence round the corner was so sorry. He had no idea that the lady was ill or he wouldn't have sold it to her.

'You bloody liar,' said Dad. 'She could hardly walk, poor old Nan, and yellow as a flaming canary. You could see she was on her last legs.'

On the contrary, said the man, taking the insult on the chin, she had seemed such a bright little body, telling him all about the house-warming.

'House-warming?'

'She was really looking forward to it. A real old-fashioned knees-up, she said it would be, with all her family and all ... and...' His words dribbled away as the grieving relatives wagged their heads in denial. But he could see they were upset, he said. Why didn't they let him do the beer for the wake? He could give them a very reasonable discount.

'How reasonable?' said Dad.

Chapter Sixteen

Dobb's Weir was a great swimming place. It was on the River Lea, past the sink and sludge of Tottenham, past the cranes and the dirty barges, past Ponders End, the drab marshes and the football fields, out where the grass was a tenderer green, unsullied with soot – Broxbourne. You could get there by train or bike or bus. Or you could get there by car, easy-peasy, if you had one – which they did now – a second-hand Ford Popular. Black.

The money had come as a surprise. A real windfall. Mum had been sorting through Nanna Hubbard's things for suitable bits to make into a rag rug before taking the rest round to the old people's home when, tied into an orange Paisley headscarf, she'd found Grandpop's medals for surviving the first war, a silver fob-watch and chain with his father's name engraved on the back, his spectacles and, in a leather-covered box lined with velvet, a man's wedding ring, a pair of gold cufflinks and a matching tie-pin. In a brass tobacco tin with *King George V* impressed on the lid there was a sunburst brooch, set with small diamonds, Aunt Polly's gold bracelet, another – a simple gold band to fit a baby's wrist – a 1920s-style rope of pearls and crystals, and her mother's engagement ring that had grown too small to wear.

'Bloody hell!' Dad had said when Mum set the cache before him. 'That's worth a few bob, that lot. You'd best see what you can get for them.'

No question of keeping them. No questions, full stop. Like, would they be Dorrie's little teeth that had dented that baby bracelet? How and where had a docker acquired pearls and diamonds? No curiosity. No imagination. No sense of romance.

A man called Mickey Tonks had given her two hundred and seventeen pounds ten for the lot. She gave Dad the two hundred, and it was enough to buy the car and to pay for driving lessons. On the afternoon he passed the test he took them all out for a spin to Dobbs Weir: Peter, who'd just finished his A levels and was at a loose end, squeezed into the back with Dorrie and Stephen. They bowled along between flowery verges singing 'She'll be coming round the mountain' and 'You'll never go to heaven', at the tops of their voices.

As they shed their work-clothes and stood gleaming in their bright summer skins, Mum sat hugging her dress round her knees, staring at the rushing water. It had become too big for its banks, she told them dreamily, too full of itself, too wild and fast, so they'd had to take it down a peg or two. Build a weir. Contain it. Society doesn't like things it can't control.

Or people, eh Mum? thought Dorrie, sensing that her mother's whimsy was inspired by a certain mutual acquaintance, who would put two fingers up for law and order. With a start she realised that this had been one of *their* haunts.

He'd brought her here, probably to this very spot. Here they had done 'it' and their cries had been borne away on the plash of water. No wonder Flo was moody.

And still the torrent dashed over the dam, constantly surprised at the drop into the abyss of deep water, dark and cool, for which Dorrie was now nerving herself. Mum might prefer her men and her rivers untamed, but this pool was bliss for hot and sweaty people who'd had to trudge miles across the field, it seemed, from where they'd left the car, lugging bags of egg sandwiches and cake and lemonade and methylated spirits and stoves and kettles and blankets to sit on and swimming costumes and towels.

She plunged in and, after the shock, swam underwater, loving the bubbles in her ears, the freedom to twist and curl and stretch and unwind, touching bottom and feeling the squish of mud between her toes, the weed against her legs, the current sucking at her hair and fingers, and then, as she surfaced, gasping, she shook her head in the summer warmth, marvelling at the warm perfume of meadow flowers, at the colours shimmering in the water, reflecting sky and clouds and trees and reedy banks, at the magical iridescence of dragonflies, at birdsong filtering through the roar of falling water. Perfect.

Swimming in the baths, with its vaulting echoes and stale odours was good enough for mere mortals. Nymphs and gods sported in the open. Even Dad looked right, pared down to his trunks, his hairy girth streaming water, his eyelashes glued with it. He only needed a trident and maybe a big fish or two. He was so pleased to have passed the test first time, to have been able to give them this treat, he couldn't stop smiling. Beside him, Peter was interestingly nipple-naked, more satyr than sprite, with his hair sticking up in horns and the devil in his eyes. Stephen was not godlike. He would never be anything other than a scrawny schoolboy.

Mum had never learned to swim so she stayed on the bank with her knitting, dreaming of Frank. She hadn't told Dorrie about meeting him to discuss the disposal of the jewellery, but then she hadn't needed to. She'd come home so bubbling and excited that anyone with half an eye would have guessed that the money was only part of it. Anyone except Arthur. Dorrie was disappointed: Frank was supposed to be history. How weak her mother was.

But naturally she had been curious, so while Flo told a Frank-less tale about a trip to a jeweller's, Dorrie had gently probed her mind.

Somehow he'd found out about Alice Hubbard's death; probably seen it in the *Announcements* column of the local paper. He'd sent Flo a card with his condolences and his address, setting her heart a-flutter. She hadn't put it on the mantelpiece with the others, and she hadn't thrown it away. For three weeks it had lain in her bottom drawer, among her underwear, and she took it out at least once a day, to stroke the narrow black ribbon, to trace the bold, free hand, the *Yours, Frank,* to read between the lines.

So now she knew where he lived. It was near the station – Belvedere Gardens – within walking distance of the salon. Impossible, almost, to go round to the baker's for a sandwich without passing it. Without having a wander down there, just out of curiosity; without walking past the bungalow, the one with masses of wisteria hanging over the entire front of the house and lupins in the garden. Except when the Rover was parked outside.

Not one house in this neck of desirable suburbia had been built with cars in mind. Not a garage, not a driveway, in E17, E10, E11 or in E4. Back in the dark ages, at the turn of the century, when working-class terraces and middle-class halls adjoining semis were thrown up along the Liverpool Street to Chingford railway line, it was confidently expected that the inhabitants would use the train to get about. Or the tram *in extremis.* Why else would they come here to live? No one foresaw that in the course of time, a downwardly mobile chap named Frank Leary would come here to live, bringing his Rover behind him. And where was he to put said vehicle when he was home from work. Why, in the road, of course. A red Stop signal to Flo. Proceed no further.

Or a red rag to a bull.

Seeing it there that Saturday morning had helped her to a decision. She hurried home, emptied her bag of the weekend's butchery and bakery and greengrocery and put in the orange paisley scarf and its contents, and this time, instead of walking backwards and forwards a dozen times past the house, she summoned her courage and went and knocked on the door. His face, when he opened it, was a picture.

Flo, on witnessing her beloved's astonishment and delight, was moved by a corresponding rush of love and desire. And Dorrie, the intruder, was alarmed to find her own heart beating with excitement, *her* palms damp and delicious pulsings going on where all should be secret and still. Gosh, she thought, withdrawing in confusion. She'd never experienced anything like this before. This was X-certificate stuff, for which, at sixteen, she was now qualified. But fancy! Her own mother! At her age!

Maybe she'd just better ask her outright. Get the censored version.

So she told her a lie, that she had seen the Rover in Hale End Road, and Frank getting out to post a letter. Flo owned up then. Yes, he lived close by. She hadn't known that when they moved here, she hastened to assure her. It was a nuisance but she was sure they could both be sensible about it.

Had Flo seen him, was her next question and, with a show of great reluctance, her mother admitted that she had.

You see, she told Dorrie, it was all very well Arthur telling her to go and sell the stuff, but she didn't like to go to just any old jeweller. She had a feeling that some of the pieces weren't strictly kosher. Diamonds and pearls – on a docker's pay? Grandpop was always coming home with stuff that had fallen off the back of a

315

merchant ship. He'd once turned up with a five-foot-long elephant's tusk. (What had become of that, Flo wondered now. Probably at the bottom of the Thames if Nanna Hubbard had had anything to do with it.) Now Frank would know, if anyone did, of 'fences' and suchlike shady characters who wouldn't ask too many questions. He might even go with her to talk to them. Dorrie had to understand that it was only as a last resort that Flo had turned to Frank for help.

Yeah, yeah, her daughter thought.

He'd invited her in, though she'd arrived smack in the middle of their dinner. His mother was there, of course, Widow Leary. A garrulous old biddy, Irish as they come, with a permanent cigarette on, sometimes two. As a result her skin was the colour and texture of cold porridge, her white hair, swept back in a tidy knot, was smoked yellow as haddock, as was her ceiling, and a tarry film dulled every surface. Flo hadn't seen her since her schooldays but the old woman remembered her.

'Ah surely, Florence Hubbard as was, Frank's little playmate. Always said you'd be a looker when you grew up. Aren't you the one to blame when I sent him for a loaf and he came home with the crust only? He'd've had me believe that was how they'd sold it to him till I tanned his hide and then it turns out you were starving and he'd had to pick out the crumbs for yez.' Frank winked hugely. Flo didn't remember anything of this. 'Well, well, let's hope you're as hungry today. It's only tripe and onions but there's plenty.'

Mum had to say that she'd eaten already. The sickly-sweet smell was enough to turn your stomach, she told Dorrie. What with that and the stink of fags, ancient and modern, she could hardly breathe. Quickly she told him why she'd come and tipped the spoils onto the tablecloth. Mother and son exchanged glances and spooned more of the disgusting mess into their mouths.

Frank chewed more slowly, turning the medals with an appreciative smoke-stained forefinger. 'What d'you reckon, Ma?' he said. 'Mickey Tonks?'

The old woman bunched her mouth and nodded. 'If he's still in the land of the living. It's been a while since I've set eyes on that one.'

'No, he ain't dead, I know for a fact.'

The widow frowned what could have been a warning at her son and said quickly, 'I think we'd have heard.' Flo caught a flick of eyes in her direction. Clearly there was something she shouldn't know about.

He didn't have much to do with that crowd, he explained, since he'd got in with the church. He'd lost touch.

'The church?' Dorrie was taken aback. This didn't sound like her roaring boy of a father.

'Didn't I tell you? He's a reformed character. He actually asked me if I'd like to go with him to a service.'

'Gosh. You're not going, are you?'

'Dor-*rie!* What do you take me for? I'm a respectable married woman. I don't frequent such places.' But her grin faded as Dorrie frowned, all too aware of how Mum felt about Frank, what he did to her insides. 'Don't you trust me, love? I told you I only went round there to get Nanna's things valued. I've said I'm stopping with your Dad, and I shall.'

Dorrie gave her a quizzical look.

'I'm not leaving him, Dorrie.'

Dorrie raised her eyebrows.

'I wouldn't dream of it, not while you and Stephen both need me at home.'

'So you won't see him again?'

'Well, it might be difficult, living so close.'

'Mum...'

'All right – not if I see him first. How's that?'

Unconvincing.

Dorrie walked out to the middle of the weir, preparing to dive into the deepest place. Water gushed round her ankles and over the lip of the fall. Dad and Stephen were larking about near the bank, swimming through each other's legs, tipping each other over, splashing and yelling.

He was treading water midstream and staring at her. Just staring. It was quite off-putting. He was Peter, after all. A cousin. Family. He shouldn't be looking at her like that, even if she was sixteen and curving this way and that. She glared at him, rudely. 'Seen enough?' she asked pointedly, at which he seemed to come to, pushed a hand through his spiky hair and thrashed his legs to take himself under.

She flipped into the water. Down into the cold rush of darkness and even as she was forcing herself up again she sensed there was something wrong. The sound as she hit the surface was of zigzag clamour. Yellow shrieks and brown shouting. People running along the banks where there had been nobody before. Dad was standing waist-high in the shallows, and Stephen was there, too. Safe. So that was all right. Where was Peter? On the bank – there – retching into the grass, with Mum beside him, white as a sheet, her arm round his shoulders.

It was a girl, a small girl in a pink dress, five or six years old, whose body must have come rushing down the river, over the weir, swirled into the reeds and stayed there, with paper bags and frogs for company. Her face was washed clean of tears, her eyes and bruise-blue lips were clamped shut in water-bloated skin. Her lightly etched brows were unreadable. Neither horror nor fear had registered.

Dad pulled her dress down to hide her nakedness. But they'd all seen. Something terrible had been done to her, worse than drowning. And Dorrie knew. She could see the man in the bed, see his smoothly smiling face, hear him speaking to the child beside him. 'Look, I have a surprise for you.' And her wonder turning to revulsion as he pulled back the bedclothes.

Then, with a ripple, the sound closed in as water filled her ears and nose and mouth. She couldn't breathe, but it didn't matter.

Hands grabbed her, yanked her out of it. Up. Up. Suddenly she was coughing, dragging in air, fighting to get out of the river. She tried to help them as they hoisted her onto the bank but her limbs were boneless. Fancy fainting!

Stephen wanted to talk about the dead child all the way home in the car. About the stretcher they'd laid her on, the red blanket they'd pulled over her face, about the ambulance, about the police roping off the area. Why would they do that? What clues would they hope to find when they'd taken the body away? Why did she need an ambulance if she was dead already? Did Dad think she'd fallen in? Had they missed her from home? Were they out looking for her? Who had done it? Was it someone she knew? Until Mum screamed at him to shut up, shut up and Dad had to pull over because she was so upset.

'I've had enough, Arthur!' she sobbed into his shoulder. 'Enough death! Mum and Aunt Polly, and Dorrie nearly drowning, and that poor little girl. It's all so savage and cruel. Oh God, I hate men!'

Peter held Dorrie's hand in a painful bone-white grip. Who was supporting whom here? 'God,' he said, over and over. He smelled of sick.

Still wrapped in the picnic rug, Dorrie shivered in the heat, hardly daring to breathe. The car windows were wide open to give her air. She shouldn't be doing this. She shouldn't be here, in the car, with this soup of secrets in her head. She had to hold still or it would spill over. His face. His name. Her ears buzzed with it. She even knew where he lived, having travelled with the little girl, whose name was Penny, all the way from the infant school gates, in his car, in his spanking new Triumph Herald, through the busy streets to the new police flats overlooking the Plain. It had occurred to him to drown her in Connaught Waters, but that was too near home, so he'd gagged her, packed her in the boot and driven through the forest to Waltham Abbey and thence to Broxbourne.

Sleep, that night, was out of the question. Suffocating heat slunk through the open windows and breathed foul air into her nostrils. Her blanket lay in a sweaty heap on the floor and the sheet was about to go the same way. She missed having Stephen in the room. His quiet breathing sometimes soothed her when she was wakeful.

That man was sleeping. How could he do that? How could he put that little girl out of his mind and calmly sleep? He ought to be tortured with remorse, beside himself, writhing, knuckling his fleshy mouth, tearing his thin hair, blubbering to God to forgive him. He'd killed a little girl, done terrible things. But there he was, sleeping, his brow smooth and untroubled, dreaming dreams of his dead mother.

She couldn't leave it alone. Over and over, the oily *'Look, I have a surprise for you,'* slipped into her mind. The bare arm throwing back the blankets. The child's incomprehension. What was it? An animal? A hairless live thing, warm to the touch, jerking.

Dorrie eyes blinked open on a heartbeat. *Penny wasn't the first.* And if Dorrie didn't tell the police what she knew, he'd do it again. Soon, maybe tomorrow, another child would have to go through that. But if she told, if she made them believe her, they'd all know about her gift.

Call her a witch.

She could do with talking to Grandma or Auntie Lucy, but they were still on holiday, some cottage in Devon that wasn't on the phone.

Uncle Jack? She just had to whistle, he'd said. But what could he do from Newcastle?

Viv? No. It was too dreadful a thing to talk to a little girl about. She was only seven, despite her years.

Who, then?

Dad was still up, watching the commercials. Her eye, too, was drawn to the Chandleresque figure in a raincoat and trilby, standing under a street-lamp to light his cigarette. Her mouth pinched with disgust and her nostrils flared. She hated that one. It always reminded of that other man in a raincoat, hurrying through the war-torn streets of London in the blackout. People running, this way and that, for shelter – wardens yelling *'Get under cover!'* Sirens wailing, blood chilling, enemy aircraft bearing down. Her mother, her silly pregnant mother, was about to be bombed. He *had* known. He *had*. Of that Dorrie was certain. What wasn't clear at all, what mattered more than anything, was whether, in her vision, he was heading towards the house or away from it. She rather suspected the latter. Skunk.

'You're never alone with a Strand' wittered the voice-over, preaching to the converted: the room was wreathed in smoke and the ashtray at his side was overflowing. Poor Dad. He'd been trying to give up; down to two a day. Then this had to happen.

'Not asleep yet, Dorrie?'

'I can't, Dad. It's hot and...' She shook her head, unable to put her fear into words.

'I know, love. You can't stop thinking about it, same as me. Whyn't you have a couple of aspirin, eh? Tell you what – boil up some milk while you're out there. A cup of Ovaltine'll do the trick.'

'Do you want one?' Why else would he have suggested it?'

'Go on then,' as though she were twisting his arm.

She went through to the kitchen. She could still hear the telly.

'Murraymint, Murraymint, too-good-to-hurry-mint.'

She could read him like a book. Poor old Dad, how he'd hate it if he knew how transparent he was. 'Play your cards close to your chest' and 'Never let your right hand know what your left is doing' were his favourite maxims and he chuckled to himself to think how he was deceiving the world. Strangers saw a hail-fellow-well-met who drew them out, who got to know their strengths and weaknesses, everything there was to know about them, without giving anything of himself away. A negotiator. A manipulator. And proud of it.

Few friends could get past the shape-shifting shell; jovial and serious, by turn, they only ever saw themselves reflected; he took his colour from them. Except his political colour, which was strong and Marxist and true. 'From each

323

according to his abilities, to each according to his need.' No dissembling there. It was the creed he lived by.

After the strike he'd redoubled his efforts on the men's behalf, fighting tooth and nail over every fall in piecework rates, every man laid off. He had some small victories but, inexorably, he had to give ground: automation was a fact of life, productivity was king. Bastards! But someone had to stand up for the men. They expected it, relied on him. His job was clear-cut and defined. No question.

At home he had trouble adjusting, never being comfortable about exposing his soft underside. They all knew about them, knew that he took refuge in tough poses but they didn't dare tell him or take advantage.

Saturdays you'd find him down the High Street with the local commies, handing out leaflets while one of them harangued the Saturday shoppers. He wasn't averse to doing a bit of tub-thumping himself. So embarrassing when you were out with your friends buying nylons and make-up and trying to chat up the bloke on the record stall.

Usually it was about the rotten job the government were doing. He'd crowed like a cockerel over Suez and cried real tears (of laughter) as Eden dug his own grave. 'What a cunning little plot,' he chortled. 'You get Israel to attack Egypt, and then you sneak in with France and occupy the canal zone on the pretext of separating the combatants. Nice one, Anthony. Except you forgot to tell Uncle Sam what you were up to, and didn't he tan your hide?'

He hated the Americans – 'our masters', he called them – and rubbished their every move. Mostly he hated their bomb which was aimed at Russia, and Russia's bomb which was aimed at the US. He hated Britain for being piggy-in-the-middle and doing nothing about it.

'You don't *really* think whitewash and brown paper are gonna save you, do you?' he harangued anyone that would listen. 'Have you *seen* the pictures of Hiroshima? You'll be blown away in the first wave – that's if you're lucky. 'Cause no matter how long you stay in your nuclear shelter, girls, you're going to die of radiation sickness. And it ain't a pretty sight. What's that, lady? I'm frightening your kids? I should bloody well hope I am frightening them. I'm frightening meself. Good God, woman, it'll be the end of the flaming world.'

'He really believes it, doesn't he?' Jenny had insisted on stopping to listen.

'Well, of course. So do I.'

When Jenny realised you got to wear a groovy little black and white badge if you joined the campaign and that you could go to CND meetings and talk to serious and personable young men she became an enthusiastic Ban-the-Bomber.

When a Protest March was mooted, to Aldermaston and back, over the Easter weekend, she nagged her doting mum for a duffle coat. A long weekend away from prying eyes, sleeping rough with young and healthy political animals, her cup runneth over. She was a bit taken aback when she found out that Mum and Dad Potter, Stephen and Peter were also going, and thought that perhaps she would walk with the Woodford branch, who were a cut above the Walthamstow mob. In looks, anyway.

Dorrie was very impressed by her family standing up for their convictions, despite the rain and the discomfort of their makeshift shelters. Television cameras followed their progress and the few times she saw Jenny was when they were looking for people to interview. By then the new duffle coat was muddy and there were grass stains up the back. A boy Dorrie had never seen before, with crisp curly hair and bee-stung lips held a dripping mac over her head as she spoke into the microphone. Even so, her mascara had run and her hair hung lankly down. She really looked as though she were suffering for the cause. Dorrie wasn't near enough to hear what she was saying, but it looked very earnest and intelligent. When she got back and saw the film on television, the gallant campaigner was moaning about her blisters and her lack of sleep. She certainly looked very tired. That was before the camera panned down to her mud-spattered feet. She was wearing what had been her best shoes; dinky little pointy toes and lavatory heels. Giggling for her audience, she flapped the loose sole and turned her pretty ankle to show how the heel had worn down by at least half an inch.

'Didn't you tell your friend to take some sensible shoes?' said Dad accusingly, when he saw the report.

'She had a pair of lace-ups in her rucksack,' Dorrie said crossly. 'I don't know what she was playing at.' Though she did.

Dorrie had enjoyed the march better than any family holiday they'd ever had. The roughing it, the making the best of things, the laughing in the face of adversity, or authority, or whatever. Just laughing. It had been great. When they'd got to Aldermaston, they'd all shouted slogans through the wire, including Mum, and waved their banner: *Walthamstow says Ban the Bomb* in red appliqué, on a yellow silk background, with a black and white skull and crossbones neatly embroidered by Mum. United in a common cause.

Dorrie loved them all: Dad who seemed really relaxed and happy, for once, and was even seen to give Mum a hug in public; even Peter, who wasn't so bad, after all. Sometimes he even talked sense. When they got back to Trafalgar Square and Dorrie was jostled by a mounted policeman, pushed over by the horse's backside, Dad and he both flew to her rescue, calling the policeman a 'fascist bastard' and worse: a combination of farmyard terms that Dorrie had never heard before. Even the policeman looked shocked and the horse reared. That might have been because Peter tried to draw a CND symbol on its bum with his biro.

The milk rose up the saucepan with a hiss and she poured it over the malted grains. Angry voices on the soundtrack and the orchestra

327

crashing around, indicated a struggle, working up in a crescendo. Then silence. Gunshots and a scream. It must be near the end.

He was glued to it when she came back; took his Ovaltine almost without looking up. 'I need to talk to you, Dad,' she said, 'when this is finished.'

'Uhuh,' and he slurped up a mouthful of the hot liquid, swallowed and smacked his lips. Then he belched. Mum had hinted that she might leave him when Stephen had finished school. She could see why she might want to.

While she waited she picked up an envelope and sketched him, slumped in the armchair in his bulging singlet and braces, his jowls heavy with five o'clock shadow, a sheen of perspiration catching the light from the standard lamp through his black, thinning hair. He was old, she realised, in his forties, a lot older than Mum. And Frank.

At last the hero locked lips with the heroine and the credits rolled up. Then he switched off and watched the little white dot fade to nothing before turning to her.

'About today was it, Dorrie?'

'Mmm.'

'Terrible thing,' he commiserated. He had brown Ovaltine stains at the corners of his mouth and cigarette ash on his vest.

'Dad I – I know who did it.'

'Eh?'

'I can see him. He's got this smooth, thin sort of face and high round cheeks and lips that curl. And he's got straight dark brown hair, combed straight back, thick eyebrows and slippery eyes. I know his name, Dad. I know where he lives. The make of his car. And I keep seeing him, Dad, with that little girl, Penny.'

'Dorrie, Dorrie...' He shook his head, patted her hand. 'It's all right, sweetheart, it's just a dream you've had.'

'No, it's not,' she said indignantly. 'I'm psychic. Like Grandma, like Auntie Lucy and Uncle Jack. I'm psychic and I can see this man.'

'No, Dor,' he said kindly, this man who thought he was her father. 'You're an ordinary kid who's had a rotten day. You've been asleep and you've woken up from a nightmare.'

'Ask Grandma, then. She'll tell you.'

'I'm sure she will. When you gonna learn, Dorrie? Grandma's round the twist.'

'Dad, Grandma's a medium. No end of people will tell you, reliable people. And Lucy's a healer. She healed me when I crushed my foot. It runs in the family.' Ignoring, for the sake of argument, the fact that she was not related to him.

'*Crushed* your foot? You mean that time you dropped a brick on it?' She waved it aside and he went on, 'That cleared up by itself, Dorrie. Don't exaggerate. The only thing that runs in this family is an overactive imagination. Okay, I'll accept that Ma's pretty convincing but Dorrie, love, there's no such thing as ghosts and extra sensory whatnot. It's a proven fact.'

'And Uncle Jack?'

'Oh come on. He's a clever chap. He'd never–'

'He writes a column in a newspaper up North,

answering people's questions about their dead relations. And he helps the police track down criminals.'

'Does he? I thought they had dogs to do that!' He laughed heartily at the joke.

'Dad, it's true.'

'If you say so, sweetheart.'

'Dad.' She was near to tears. 'Please believe me. I know who this man is, this murderer. We've got to tell the police before he attacks some other little kid.'

'Dorrie, I'm not taking you to the police so you can tell them you've been seeing things. They'll have me inside for wasting police time and you in the nut-house.'

'So how do I know the little girl's name is Penny?'

'You don't. Nobody knows who she is. You've had a bad dream.'

'*No*, Dad.' Tiredly, as she cast around for inspiration, it came to her. She licked lips that were suddenly dry. 'Dad, I *am* psychic, you've got to believe me. I can do things – channel psychic energy. Watch.'

A neat hole in the screen was what she was aiming for. She never meant it to explode like that – with a *whoomph!* that shook things off shelves and rattled pictures, with sparks crackling and fizzling along wires and glass and valves and television intestines and bits of walnut veneer flying everywhere, and flames and fumes and soot blackening ceiling and walls and silk-handworked cushions. White-faced and open-mouthed they stared at the flare-up in the corner until with great presence of mind, Dad pulled the plug from its socket, and then ripped up the hearthrug to beat down the flames.

When it was safely smothered he turned his attention to Dorrie and, with all the force of his despair, slapped her face for a second time. Then he stomped up the stairs. The word of explanation he'd offered Mum as he pushed by her and Stephen, rooted, by now, in the doorway, was 'Overload.'

The next morning when the *Daily Mirror* named the dead child as little Penny Marshall, aged six, and pictured her smiling brightly for the school cameraman, with a milk tooth missing, he recollected that one of the policemen at the scene, at Dobb's Weir, had let slip the fact that the victim matched the description of a child reported missing the day before. That's when Dorrie must have heard the name. See, he said kindly, as though forgiving her some misdemeanour, these things could always be explained if you tried hard enough. Or explained away, thought Dorrie bitterly.

Chapter Seventeen

'I see they haven't caught that bleeding pervert yet, then, Flo?' The adjective, so beautifully articulated, was a sore thumb among the cut-glass vowels.

'She doesn't like to talk about it, dear.' Charles inclined his head in Flo's direction, wrinkling his pretty nose. He must have caught the whites of her eyes rolling despair in the next mirror.

'Oh, rats. What an utterly insensitive bitch I am – I didn't think. Sorry, darling!' But after a respectable pause: 'He won't get far, don't worry. The police are hot on the scent. They'll catch him soon, I'm sure, and then we can all sleep at nights.'

Flo forced a smile. It was kindly meant but she was sick of it. Lips, mindful of her feelings, mouthing words so that she wouldn't hear, eyes following her, studying her, watching for her unguarded sigh or frown or groan, and making *moues* of condolence when she met them in the mirror. Business had trebled in the last fortnight. She was famous. They were all greedy for it, tongues hanging out to discuss the crime in particular and child-killers in general. It was a dirty scab they needed to pick at.

'It's your children I feel so sorry for.' The client's face, suffused with high living and the salon's heat, rose above the hairdresser's pale green overall like a rosy dawn. 'The damage to their young minds. They're not likely to forget a thing like that in a hurry. That's one thing they never consider, do they, these bastards? The effect it's going to have on the poor creatures who come upon the body.'

Flo's lady joined in more earthy tones. 'Animal, that's what he is. I hope they string him up.'

Gently but firmly, Flo pushed the woman's head down so that she could snip a hairline between the rolls of fat.

'I know what I'd like to do to the swine,' came the voice of gentility, 'and hanging comes way down the list. By the way, just a fraction more off the fringe, don't you think, sweetie? I don't want to look like a bleeding sheepdog.'

Strangled gurgles squeezed past the double chins. Flo let her up a couple of notches. 'Some of the mums was saying they didn't see how it could be that bloke James Halliday. He's backward, that's all. Likes to hang around the kiddies 'cos he's got the same mental age as them. Wouldn't hurt a fly, they reckon.'

Charles looked into the mirror, raised an eyebrow at himself. '*I* wouldn't hurt a fly,' he simpered, working his scissors. 'But I'd have that bugger's nuts off soon as look at him.'

'Oh don't! Oh Charles, the idea! Oh, I know I shouldn't laugh.'

'Well, it makes my blood boil, dear. Now, if we shorten the fringe we'll lose the line. Trust me, dear. We'll just tease this up a bit here ... as the actress said to the bishop.' He bent to his work, backcombing and feathering, leaned away, head aslant, to assess the result. He flapped his hand. 'And the police! Brains in their size twelves, duckie! I mean, why tell the world an arrest is imminent? That's sensible, isn't it, dear? Did they think the murderer was going to sit on his bum and wait for the Black Maria?'

'Marvellous, isn't it? Our wonderful boys in blue! Oh, yes, that's lovely, Charles. Oh, you are a clever boy. Isn't he a clever boy, Flo?' The woman paused to light a cigarette and to pick tobacco off her tongue with bright red pincers. 'To be fair, they do say he's not very bright.'

'You don't have to be bright to get the better of the Hertfordshire constabulary, dear, just determined.'

'Or have a mother who can spot which way the wind is blowing.'

'Penny short of a shilling if you ask me, dear, hanging round the school gates every day.'

Up bobbed Flo's lady. '*Always* there, they reckon. Seemed to think he was gonna play with the kiddies – a grown man of thirty!'

'Oh, how truly awful.'

'Mad as arseholes, if you'd pardon my French, ladies.'

Genteel titters and ribald hoots and Flo ran the clippers over quivering flesh. Charles was their pet, their delight.

He picked up a hand mirror for the back view and pouted critically at their reflections. 'Well,' he said, 'they know who they're looking for now, that's something, I suppose. Did you see him on the telly last night, dear? That photo? Those were killer's eyes, if ever I saw them.'

Flo wasn't so sure. Radio Rentals were being very sniffy about replacing the telly so she'd had to glean her information from the rusty snap they'd printed in the *Mirror* the other day, with the headline HAVE YOU SEEN THIS MAN?

James Halliday, sitting in shirt-sleeves on a kitchen chair beside his mobile home, looked a roly-poly innocent, his smile that of a simple soul, showing more interest in his bag of chips than in his mum holding the camera.

Father and daughter were still hardly speaking to each other, a fortnight after their row. If she'd had anyone to run to that night, Dorrie would have been off again, sure as eggs, and who would have blamed her? It was getting to be a habit with Arthur, this flying off the handle. And it was always Dorrie who got the brunt of it. What was the matter with the man? All right, so he'd had a day of it, that day, but they all had. Finding that little girl had been horrible. Vile. They'd all been upset. And he was so good with the kids after- wards. A real dad, saying just the right things. She'd been proud of him.

And then he had to go and wallop Dorrie. Pity they didn't have a cat. He could have kicked that when the telly blew up. It had been the last straw, more than he could take. But it wasn't her fault, when all was said and done.

Short fuses seemed to have been the order of the night. When Flo had gone up, after washing the walls down and putting the cushion covers and the rug in to soak, he was wide awake, fidgeting and farting and wanting her to comfort him. She'd squeezed over to the very edge of the bed and pretended to fall asleep immediately, breathing deeply, ignoring the sighing and the rubbing, the fumbling for her hand to be placed on his hardening penis, ignoring the prodding.

'What?' she'd snapped eventually.

'You're a hard woman, Flo.'

'Me?' she said. 'You're the one who hit our daughter. For nothing.'

'You don't understand.'

'No, I flaming don't.'

He'd huffed and humped over into his own space, his resentment twitching across the divide like sharp little arrows. Any other time she might have taken pity on him, if only to get some sleep, but tonight, after all she'd been through, she reckoned he could whistle. And snore eventually. She didn't dare poke him to get him to turn over – he might have got the wrong idea – so she'd taken her pillow downstairs and left him to it.

For a week there'd been a pall of misery over the house, despite the sunshine flickering on the newly plastered walls and the warm breeze wafting the nets. It was shock, of course. They were all grieving for that small life cruelly taken.

It couldn't have happened at a worse time. How the kids were expected to concentrate on their exams with all that at the front of their minds...

She'd find Stephen sitting at the dining table staring blankly at his books. Once when he was

out of the room she'd taken the opportunity to
dust and his rough book had fallen open at a
page defaced with obscene cartoons of violence
– daggers dripping blood, gross hands tight
around skinny necks, lightning doodled absently
into the eye-socket of a skull, mouths screaming
words culled from lavatory walls.

'Oh Stephen...'

She'd had to say something, tell him that, of
course, he would feel like this, that she would
have been worried if he hadn't tried to express
his horror in some way, get it out of his system,
that she understood.

He'd turned concerned eyes upon her. 'Are we
going to get a new television then, Mum?
Duncan Morrison reckons they do good ones at
Visionhire.'

So much for damage. Children were more
resilient than you gave them credit for.

Arthur was the one ... as unbearable as a sulky
child, slopping and slumping and making a
great show of being unable to eat, unable to
read, unable to sit in the same room with anyone
for long. He was getting on her nerves. When
eventually she lost patience and asked him if she
could help, if there was anything she could get
him, he sighed and rolled his eyes. She supposed
she was to take that to mean that he was
suffering. She shrugged and went back to her
sewing: a sweet little bolero to go with Dorrie's
new dress. She'd been lucky to get that remnant.
It would keep the chill off on summer nights.

She felt him staring at her, knew he'd wanted
more. She put down her work.

'I don't suppose it's occurred to you,' he said when he had her attention. 'If anything's upsetting *you* you don't make any secret of it. You let everyone know, screaming and crying and carrying on.'

She couldn't think of any occasion when she'd actually screamed. She'd felt like it, mind. Often.

He went on. 'A man has to exercise self-control. We can't cry. That's not to say I don't feel things just the same as you. More so, if the truth be told. Anyone with a ounce of sensitivity would have realised that.'

A scream would have expressed her feelings nicely. Instead she picked up her sewing again. That's what all this was then, this petulance – manly self-control!

'But there you are, what can you expect?' Off he went, having made his point, pompously tutting.

If it hadn't been so irritating it would have been funny, specially since Dorrie had begun referring to the strong, silent head of the household as the 'prima donna'. After Stephen's desperate plea it occurred to Flo that Arthur's self-pity might have more to do with the fact that he was missing Wimbledon fortnight than with murders and batterings.

It was a relief that Dorrie's sense of humour had returned. Her black dog had been the most worrying. During those first few days she'd bitten her lips to bleeding, and woken every morning with a scowl already in place, after so little sleep. Flo would find her still working or writing letters in the early hours of the morning.

She'd looked truly dreadful, thin and pale with her eyes glittering on dark saucers. The morning she'd read in the paper that they were about to make an arrest she'd gone dish-white.

'No,' she'd moaned. 'He's not the one! They've got the wrong man, Mum,' she'd insisted, her eyes glistening like peeled grapes. 'It's too easy, picking on old Whatsisname.' She checked the paper. 'James Halliday.'

'He is the local nutter,' Stephen had said, reasonably. 'I'd have gone for him.'

'Too obvious,' his sister had argued, between the sips of sweet tea that Flo was feeding her, 'and too easy. I mean, if you think about it, it can't possibly have been him.' She pushed the cup away, stronger now. 'Thanks, Mum. See, no one saw them, for a start. Mrs Marshall reckons she was only a couple of minutes late and Penny was already gone. Vanished.'

'So was he,' said Stephen, displaying, Flo thought, a depressing knowledge of events. 'That's how the cops twigged it was him. He was always hanging round outside the school, wasn't he? And that day he wasn't. Well, no one remembers seeing him. He'd been and gone, with Penny, who was first out. Whippet-quick.'

'That's what I'm saying – old thingy, Halliday, is a slow-witted, bumbling sort of bloke. Everyone says. So how's he supposed to have whisked her away? Specially if they all knew him? How's he meant to've got her to go with him without any of those busybody mums either seeing him or giving him what for? And then he's got to get her to Broxbourne or wherever he chucked her in the river. He can't drive so he'd have had to've used public transport, and someone, surely, would have noticed a lively, chatty little girl, from all accounts, in the company of a slightly dippy man. Unless ... unless she was dead by then.'

'He's still got to get her body there, Dor, and I don't know how, unless he put her in a suitcase or draped a coat... No, you're right – he can't have. Not *and* be back home for tea with his mum for seven o'clock.'

Arthur had been listening to them, his eyes cold, his lips twisted into a sneer. 'Animal cunning,' he'd muttered.

But Dorrie didn't hear him. She was deep in thought, a frown steeling her eyes. And then she'd gasped and looked up as though someone had walked over her grave. Not waiting to finish her Shredded Wheat she'd grabbed her satchel and rushed out.

Flo and Stephen had exchanged glances. They all wanted the police to get the right man but Dorrie seemed so agitated, it was as if she knew something they didn't.

By teatime she seemed calmer, though Flo could have served up wallpaper and paste for all the notice she took of the meal. She hardly said a word to anyone that night, just did her revision and went to bed.

Then they waited. Nobody except Dorrie knew what they were waiting for. The arrest, Flo presumed. The suspenders were killing, Stephen said. But when, one morning, a letter arrived for Dorrie, it was clear from her sharp intake of joy, that this was what had kept her on hot bricks all week. It was remarkable how an almost visible load seemed to fall from her shoulders as her eyes devoured the handwritten pages. When she looked up at last, after refolding the letter and carefully replacing it in the envelope, her cheeks were flushed pink.

She wouldn't say who it was from. Stephen had made a crack about a lover-boy and she'd gone for him hammer and tongs, warning him to keep his snoopy nose out of her business or she'd flatten it. Then she'd pounded up the stairs to her room.

'Oi, oi, oi!' Arthur had been roused to shout after her. 'That's no way to carry on, young lady!' And he'd muttered, ineffectually, about bits of girls throwing their weight around, so Flo was obliged to remain downstairs, holding tight to her own curiosity, and smoothing ruffled feathers with fresh cups of tea.

But all the same, love-letters... Flo found herself sighing. Perhaps it was from that good-looking boy, John Doubleday. So well-spoken and such nice manners. The fact that he was heir to half Great Bisset was neither here nor there. It would be wonderful, of course, if Dorrie married for love *and* money. That would be great – the ideal combination.

Oh God, the girl *must* make a better job of it than her stupid mother had done...

But she was only sixteen. It was far too soon to be thinking about marriage. Sixteen and a half.

Dorrie's cup overflowed. English Literature O

level had been a doddle – she'd known they'd ask that question about the supernatural in *A Christmas Carol*. Art Still Life, two mackerel on a plate, had been a joy, and Maths had been easy-peasy. Only French had been *formidable*, said with grimaces and two hands around her throat. She was noisy and silly and everyone was quite convinced it was love. When Flo had left for work this morning, Dorrie was up and trying to drown the vacuum cleaner with 'The Rock Island Line'. Flo had drawn the girl's attention to the hiss and thump of Arthur, also getting up steam in the bathroom, suggesting she leave the singing until her father had gone off to his soap-box in the High Street, but as she closed the front gate the bedroom window was flung wide and the voices of vacuum cleaner and daughter rose on the morning air. 'Don't You Rock Me, Daddio' followed her down the street. Stephen had already made good his escape, from both singing and Hoovering. He was off to celebrate the end of his third-form exams with a trip to the Science Museum.

Saturday wasn't the best day to be in work, sweltering over Alma Cogan kiss curls, when the rest of the world was out in the sun. The salon was packed to the gunnels with wash-and-sets that would spend the rest of the day gently restrained by chiffon scarves until the unveiling around seven-thirty, when skirts would crackle and waists would whittle in time for the Assembly Hall dance or the sixth-form hop.

Even Dorrie had taken to threading fuse wire

through her hems and, only yesterday, Flo had woken to the drip, drip, drip of three full-skirted cotton waist slips that Dorrie had soaked in starch and left hanging over the bath. Only it wasn't starch, Flo discovered when she came to iron them – it was some sort of sugar solution. Several ounces of Tate & Lyle had burned to caramel at the touch of her iron and had taken forever to clean off. And when Arthur had run his Friday-night bath he found it grainy with dried-on sugar and a column of ants, stranded on the rim, regarding him and their drowned comrades-in-arms with some dismay. Even after he'd swilled them down the plughole and changed the water he swore that he emerged stickier than when he went in. Dorrie's name was mud.

And all for the sake of fashion. The idea, apparently, was to look as much like a lamp-shade as possible and, to this end, you pulled in your waist and stuck out your skirts. Flo's soft leather belt was ruined. If she'd known Dorrie was going to make those two extra holes she'd never have let her borrow it. She wore her shoes flat these days, and her hair up in a pony tail: probably the best she could do with it, failing a perm. Flo had to admit that it didn't look too bad, with those wiry curls framing her face. It wasn't *her* idea of chic but you couldn't tell the youngsters anything. Not Dorrie anyway.

She was growing up. Sixteen and a half and off to some coffee bar tonight with Peter, to see one of those skiffle groups. Goodness knows what the kids saw in them. How could you call it music when it was all washboards and orange boxes? Still, it would do her good to get out, even if it was only with her cousin.

'Flo... How're you fixed, my lovely?' The words were whispered in her ear and the hope that had never quite gone out, flared through her veins. But her nostrils were already identifying the man by his scent, and it wasn't the smoke and soap of Frank but *Tweed* by Lenthéric. Charles's plucked and prettified reflection appeared over her shoulder. His flat voice continued to slide over her. 'I've been stood over there, dear, drinking my milk-and-a-dash and watching you unpinning this irresistible creature...' He flashed his perfect smile at Flo's fat lady, who melted with delight. 'And I had a whim, dear. You know my whims, don't you, duckie? My little creative flashes?' She had to smile. Every word leaked innuendo. 'I knew I'd do something very silly if you didn't let me comb her out.' He half-closed his eyes like a cat, making up to her. 'Would you, Flo? Oh go on, you have all the fun!' Gently he nudged her away from the mirror's centre and began removing bobby-pins from the coils of stiff hair, his half-moons twinkling, his eyes flicking backwards and forwards, from glass to reality.

Turning his head he muttered, 'Your daughter's outside with a crisis, dear.' Arthur might refer to the man as a 'pansy' but he was the kindest employer Flo had known.

Dorrie was standing there with a suitcase and a swollen lip. 'I'm not stopping in the house with *him* a minute longer! I hate him – he's vile!'

'Dorrie! Oh love,' she said as she took the girl's face in her hands, wincing vicariously as she examined the split flesh, 'and you were so happy,' as if that made it worse. It didn't, of course – it was as bad as it could possibly be. For them all. She had to ask, 'What's he done?' even though she could see. He'd hit her again. Tears of anger stung her eyes. How dare he – she wasn't even his!

She needed to hear the whole story but not as a spectacle in pale green overalls, wringing her hands on the pavement in front of *Snips'* plate-glass window. In spite of Charles's diversionary tactics, intense interest followed them across the road to the station café where a corner table at last afforded them some privacy. They ordered tea and a milk-shake with a straw.

'He slapped me and I tripped and fell against the chest of drawers and my brace somehow got busted.' For the first time, Flo realised that Dorrie's teeth were not metal-plated.

'What the hell's the matter with him?'

'He just doesn't like me, Mum.'

'I'm sure that's not true. You were such friends.'

'Not any more.'

Dorrie described how she'd left the Hoover running in Stephen's room, as you do when it suddenly occurs to you that you might not have a pair of matching stockings to wear that evening, so Arthur hadn't heard her entering her own room intent on rummaging through her bottom drawer.

'He was sitting on my bed, Mum, reading my letters.'

'What!'

'I mean letters are private, aren't they? He had no right...'

'Oh Dorrie, I'm sorry.'

'So I told him...' She paused to tongue her injury reflectively.

'You *told* him?' Flo was sceptical.

'Well, I shouted a bit.'

'You ranted and raved.'

'Well, he shouldn't have.'

'No.'

'He said a girl shouldn't speak to her father like that and—'

'Oh Dorrie.' She had an idea what was coming.

'I told him he wasn't my father.'

Flo felt sick, as though she'd been punched under the ribs. Dorrie sucked carefully on her milk-shake and watched her warily.

'Mum?'

Flo drew in a long, shuddering breath. Her head was buzzing. What were they going to do? What *were* they going to do?

Dorrie whispered, 'Sorry, Mum.'

Flo swallowed. Wished her head would stop this confounded buzzing so she could think. Cleared her throat instead. 'And that's when he knocked you across the room?'

'Mmm.'

'And then what?'

'Well, then nothing really. He called me a evil little bitch and stormed out and I started packing.'

'Where were you going to go?'

'Grandma's,' as though she wondered how Flo could even ask. Flo raised quizzical eyebrows and was gratified to see a flicker of doubt appear in her daughter's eyes. 'I – came to ask you for the fare.'

'He's *her* son.'

'But she loves me like her own. She said.'

'Does she? Dorrie, he's her eldest, her first and favourite. She won't want you coming between them.'

Dorrie's jaw jutted. 'She'll take me in,' she said stoutly.

'And where do you see me ending up, now that you've told my husband that I've been unfaithful to him?'

Her daughter's eyes opened very wide. Their focus was straight and true – the cast seemed to have gone completely. 'With Frank,' she said. She seemed very sure.

'Really? I doubt it, Dorrie. He's not given me the slightest hint that he's still interested.'

In fact she'd not seen him for months, not to speak to, and then he'd been very arm's length. Well, so had she, for that matter. His mother had been in to have her hair done, and had chattered about everything under the sun except her son. Her reticence on that subject was remarkable, as though she were under orders to say nothing. She had let slip that he was away.

'On business?' Flo had probed.

The old woman had looked flustered; played for time in her handbag, trawling for fags. Flo had waited while she lit up and only then did Mrs Leary feel able to nod, adding mysteriously, through her veil of smoke, 'If you can call it that.' She glanced around the salon for flapping ears. 'High jinks and shenanigans, from what I hear.'

She wouldn't be drawn and Flo didn't like to appear too interested. It sounded like other women. It really did sound like it.

'Anyway,' she said now to Dorrie, 'where does poor Stephen fit into all this? As the guilty party I've a feeling they'd make me give him up. I...' A dry sob surprised them both. 'I don't think I could bear that.'

'Oh Mum.' Realisation brimmed and slid down her cheek. 'I'm sorry.'

'Do you think you might feel sorry enough to go back home and tell Arthur that you'd made it all up out of spite?'

'That's what he thinks anyway,' Dorrie croaked through quivering lips.

'Don't cry, you're making your lip bleed.' Gave her a handkerchief to dab with. 'Didn't you mention Frank then?'

She shook her head quickly, and her pony tail hardly moved, so certain was she. Perhaps all was not lost.

'Come with me, Mum. I don't want another clip round the ear.'

'No,' agreed Flo, thinking hard. 'I'll tell you what – we'll phone Lucy and see if they can have you for a day or two while your dad cools down. Maybe she'll meet you at Doddingworth. I think you'd be best off out of it, don't you? And then I'll go home at the usual time and sort things out. Don't worry, I can handle him.'

348

'Mum, would you do me a big favour and call in at Peter's for me? Tell him I'll go to the coffee bar another time.'

'What did your last slave die of?' Then she thought about it. 'I'll pop into Visionhire while I'm round there. Make a down payment. That'll cheer your dad up.'

Chapter Eighteen

He wept. At first he wept. He was so sorry. He couldn't think why he let her get under his skin. Just ... she'd changed. The things she said. It was that school, giving her big ideas. She scared him, the way she spoke to him – as if she had no respect. No respect. And they used to get on so well. He knew he shouldn't hit her, but she goaded him. She did.

When Flo suggested that perhaps he shouldn't have read her letters he bristled. Said that he'd had to. It was his duty. You had to keep an eye on what your kids were up to. Boy-mad they were, she and her friends. Standing on the corner with that Jenny and Angela – he'd seen them. Laughing. All that smutty talk. It wasn't right. If that's where their high IQs led them then he was glad he was a simple chap. Look at the nasty suggestion she'd come up with... No. He couldn't bring himself to tell her. Filthy suggestion.

Flo said nothing. She knew she simply had to wait.

'What happens to them at that age, I don't know. She made out I had no right going through her things, Flo. I said, a father has every right. And she says, Flo, she says, how did I know I was her father? How did I know you hadn't been seeing someone else in the war while I was away serving king and country. I mean, what a dreadful thing to–' His brown eyes glazed. 'That's when I hit her, Flo. You would have, an' all, if you'd been here. What a thing to say when I've only ever wanted the best for her. Ungrateful little...' His mouth quivered briefly and then he was strong.

'Anyway, just as well I did cast me eye over some of her letters.' He held up a sheet of deckle-edged paper and shook his head over its contents. 'My Gawd, I never thought a daughter of mine... She's only been writing to some idiot at boarding school, Flo. John someone. You know anything about this? Well, he might be capitalist scum but I feel sorry for him. He's in a right stew. Moony ain't the word for it. I mean, there's all the old flannel – he needs her, longs for her, can't sleep, can't eat, can't work and the A levels are just around the corner. Et cetera. Now this is the bit. Listen to this, Flo. *There is only one way to ease this pain, Dorrie. I must see you, hold you, take you with me to the stars. It'll be so wonderful.* Dirty little toe-rag. Now tell me I didn't do right. It's a father's job to protect his kids.'

Flo couldn't trust herself to speak.

'I don't think they've done anything yet. And they won't neither. Not if I have anything to do with it.'

'What are you going to do?'

'Write to his headmaster, that's what. I'm not having no chinless wonder messing about with my little girl.'

And then he felt in his pocket and produced,

with a flourish, the letter that had arrived last week, the source of Dorrie's happiness. Now then. What did Flo make of *this?*

'No,' she said. 'I don't want to, Arthur. It's not right.'

'Read it.'

So she took it from him. 'Who's it from? There's no address.'

'It's postmarked Newcastle-upon-Tyne. Who do you know up there, eh? Go on – have a think.'

'No one. Well only your brother, Jack.'

'It looks like his writing, an' all. But you read it and see what you make of it. Go on. It's a real cloak and dagger stuff.'

Dear Dorrie,

As you see, it worked. What a team, eh? The quick were quick and the dead were pretty nifty, as my old granny says to tell you. A formidable network, if I may say so. An excellent idea. And do congratulate the elderly sisters. (No names, no evidence.) Your vision arrived here intact, we think, with a bit of added invective from the lady with the gin bottle. It's rather like that game they play at parties – Chinese whispers – except that this has far more serious consequences. We were all appalled to learn the details of the little girl's kidnap and murder, and thought the elderly lady's language quite appropriate. So sorry that you had to see it all so explicitly. It must have been a terrible shock then and a terrible burden for you now. But don't worry that it was too upsetting for my child and her friend. Spirits are old in the ways of the world and unlikely

352

to be shocked at anything man sees fit to do to man or child, or beast, for that matter.

I passed on your vision to friendly policemen at this end, claiming it as my own, as you suggested. It wasn't difficult to track the man down, given all that information. He is not the one they suspect, as you say. That one is innocent. We all agree that the poor bloke should not have to go to gaol and suffer all that torment. His 'escape' is in hand, and he and his mother will remain hidden for the duration. The real murderer is one of their own – at the hub of the Vice Squad in London, would you believe? How we are going to persuade him to give himself up, I don't know. 'Nil desperandum' as they told me at school. A concerted effort from all and sundry, especially sundry, should do the trick. Have no fear, he will be brought to justice, and in this life, too. I am assured by those in the know. Meanwhile you have done all you can.

Love from us all. X X X

'Well,' Arthur demanded, as she tried again to make sense of it, 'what's their game, eh? What are they playing at?'

'I think it means they're trying to catch the murderer.'

'Yes, dear,' he said patiently and just a touch sarcastically, 'I got that much. Come back Jennings, the Boy Detective, all is forgiven. But who are "they"? That's what I want to know. Jack's "old granny" is *my* old granny and she's been dead for twenty years or more. And "two elderly sisters", one with a liking for gin? Tell me that's not your mum and Aunt Polly. We're

353

talking ghosts here, Flo. Spiritualism and all that crap. Dorrie *said* Jack was a clairvoyant. Told me the other night. Did you ever hear of anything so wet? A grown man... Still, I suppose it's having that poor scrap of a daughter. It's enough to send anyone round the twist.'

Sadly he raised his eyes to heaven and shook his head in pity. She watched, as though from a long way off, as his face darkened.

''Course you know what we've got here, Flo? With "friendly policemen" and whatnot? There's a ring of them. It's a flaming conspiracy. A ouijee board conspiracy.' He waggled his head at his own cleverness. 'But it ain't funny,' as though she were the one who had smiled. 'They're trying to divert the course of justice, Flo. It wouldn't surprise me if Ma ain't got her finger in it somewhere along the line, and my dear little sister. They're all tarred with the same brush.'

Flo realised, of course, that belief in any religion other than Communism was 'wet', according to her husband, but, because he knew them so well, he'd always allowed his family their idiosyncrasies with an indulgent smile, recognising the comfort it gave them. She'd often thought that it was a pity his tolerance and understanding didn't extend to the rest of the world. This was the first time he had ever shown the slightest hint of disloyalty towards his family and it alarmed her.

Because he was so wrong. They'd been down to Great Bisset twice since the oak tree blew down and been welcomed with open arms. You got a feeling about houses and the people who lived there. You could walk into one and shiver, knowing instinctively that the people were cold and distant, and that the handshake they gave you was grudging, the kiss perfunctory. Nora's home was always warm and spicy, from the cakes she baked, the logs she put on the fire, the freshly laundered linen, all for her visitors. You could tell, at the first sip, that even the tea was brewed with love. There never was a kinder, more ingenuous person than Arthur's mother. Except Lucy perhaps, though she did have her head screwed on a bit tighter. She would never get mixed up in anything illegal; neither of them would. They couldn't have a darker side.

True, she'd had her doubts years ago when they'd walked in on Nora's séance but she knew now that Arthur's mother would have had nothing to do with anything wicked. It had actually helped, seeing *Blithe Spirit*, last year, as Walter Barrington had suggested. It had made her see that spiritualism was all quite harmless: a bit mothballs and mould really. Fusty and fuddy-duddy. Wishful thinking for lonely and directionless people. What was the name of the medium in that film? Madame Arcarti? Dorrie had fallen off her seat, laughing. She couldn't be mixed up in anything so daft. She wasn't even a Potter.

And yet. Here was Jack's letter implying that it was all Dorrie's idea, this – whatever it was – sabotage?

'You think Dorrie's tied up in it, do you, Arthur?'

''Course she is. All this talk of visions – she's in it up to her pretty little neck. When I think...' and he nibbled a hangnail as he did so; spat it out as he reached a decision. 'I'll tell you something now, Flo, that'll make your hair stand on end. It was her busted the telly that night. Put the 'fluence on it, she did, just by looking at it. She told me she was one of these 'ere psychics, Flo, and I believed her.'

'What!' she gasped. Perhaps Arthur was the one round the twist.

'She's bloody dangerous, Flo.'

Dangerous? Dorrie? She wasn't. Well, not often.

And the more she thought about it, Flo couldn't deny that certain images were flooding her brain just then, of broken windows, smashed pictures, cupboard doors hanging off their hinges. Of books being burned through with what looked like a red hot poker, of a heavy pile of 78s being picked up and flung against the wall, of bedside lamps that exploded and pipes that burst. She was always very apologetic. 'Sorry, Mum, it was an accident!' or 'Sorry, Mum, I lost my rag.'

What Arthur was suggesting was possible. Dorrie could be violent, if only at certain times of the month. She could well have 'busted the telly' in a fit of rage. But Dorrie didn't have 'fluence. She wasn't even a Potter. Of that there was no doubt now. If there ever had been.

Another June. 1941. A Friday, and Flo was picking her way home from *Bettina's*, past the smouldering ruins of the previous night's raid. They'd thought the Blitz was over when Hitler turned his attention on the Soviet Union but he'd surprised them all. Flo and Alice had been readjusting nicely to unbroken nights when the warning siren had wailed through the stuffy blackout.

'Not again!'

'Likes to keep us on our toes, does Jerry,' her mother had said, filling the bulges in her shoes with bunions. They'd grabbed their jackets and torches and spent the rest of the night in the Anderson shelter, wide awake to the steady racket of warplanes and anti-aircraft fire and the spasmodic crump, crump, crump of bombs falling, so close the earth shook and the spiders fell out of their webs. It had been two weeks since the last raid and they'd got out of the way of sleeping through the din. Besides, it was far too hot. Despite the carrots and cabbages on the roof, protecting the corrugated iron from the worst of the sun, the shelter was like an oven. They'd come up for air at about four, after the last of the Luftwaffe had rumbled, empty-bellied, home to Hitler. Exhausted, they could only stare at the sunrise, violent with pinks, reds and oranges, echoing the fires of the night, and streaked with black and purple smoke that the sun made beautiful. A grey pall lay over the rooftops across the backyards. When they hurried round the block to see what had happened they found that great swathes of streets between Farnan Avenue and Spruce Hills Road were laid waste. Fire engines were putting out the last of the flames and people were crawling over the ruins like maggots over meat. Flo and her mother, two roads away, had been lucky.

Like every other able-bodied person, Flo'd picked herself up and gone to work. Forest Road itself seemed to have escaped a direct hit, though it was closed to all traffic, except prams and handcarts and emergency vehicles, being strewn with bricks and rubble and heaped with salvaged furniture, beside which sat rescue victims, dazed and dirty, waiting for ambulances. Manhole covers were up and maintenance men were turning off water supplies and capping gas pipes. It had taken her twenty minutes longer than usual to reach the salon.

A few customers failed to keep their appointments and those that did turn up were shocked and silent, as washed out as she was. A new hairdo was the last thing on their minds.

It had been a long day and she was looking forward to her tea and a lie down.

Without the houses, it was possible to see how steep Walthamstow was as it ran down to Chingford. People were scrabbling and slipping up and down the slope from Forest Road, lifting prams and small children over obstacles, avoiding jagged edges and water spouts, determined to keep going no matter what. The shopping still had to be brought home, letters had to be posted, people in hospital had to be visited.

She stopped to watch as half-naked men toiled in the afternoon sun, to hoist a full barrel of beer from a cellar. A cool dankness of hops arose from the hole, mingling with the smell of sweat. Two men heaved on ropes and others strained from below, a reversal of normal procedure. The pub had been flattened; its sign, The Wood-cutter's Arms, scorched and split by an alcoholic explosion, lay in the gutter like many a drunk before it, while the publican was attempting to salvage what he could. At last with a grunt the barrel arrived at the pavement edge and was rolled clattering up the sloping tailboard of a waiting dray. The horses were nervous, blinkered or no. They could smell the destruc-tion, the blood and dust and smoke and fumes, and they pawed the ground anxiously. She didn't fancy a kick from one of those mighty hoofs and was about to cross the road when she heard someone calling her name, looked down the hill and saw him waving. Frank. He was helping a pregnant woman over some steps that sprang up out of the rubble and went nowhere. She waved back. It was ages since she'd seen him: at Lou Medhurst's daughter's wedding, back in March. No, tell a lie, he'd brought her over that bolt of knocked-off gingham cloth. She'd refused it; sent him away with a flea in his ear. But discovered he'd come back and poked it through their front-room window. That was two months ago, since when every kid in the street had had new summer shirts and dresses and no clothing coupons, and blue and white check curtains now fluttered at many a kitchen win-dow.

He'd heard about last night's bombing, he said

when the woman was safely delivered to the main road, from a mate who lived over this way, so he'd hopped on his bike and come as soon as his shift finished, to see if she was all right. He'd had a long natter with her mum, who'd put his mind at rest about their safety. He'd helped her out with a few tins of peaches, washed up on the dock, a leg of lamb and a bottle of stout. Couldn't get any more in his saddle bag.

She raised her eyes to heaven. He was incorrigible. What *was* she going to do with him?

Was that an offer? he grinned. What about taking him for a picnic? Alice had filled a Thermos and made a few sandwiches – Tartex and tomatoes. Pretty foul but they'd keep the wolf from the door.

How could she resist such cheek? His eyes were alight with anticipation, his fingers twitching with it. He was gorgeous. Not film-star gorgeous, not like Arthur: his nose was lumpy and his eyebrows almost met in the middle – criminal tendencies, a sure sign, her mother had informed her darkly. And his hair was all anyhow, bleached on top by the sun and dark with sweat underneath. He could look nice when he made the effort, but right now wasn't one of those times. His boots were cracked and dusty and his trousers streaked with dirt. She guessed he'd been working in his singlet, like a navvy, but the shirt he'd put on over his nakedness was mapped with salt from the ride through the East End in seventy-five degrees of heat. He smelled physical and musky and in need of a bath. She wanted to kiss him.

Instead she hitched her skirts to stop them catching in the wheel, perched high on the saddle and let him ride away with her down the hill, her hands on his broad shoulders moving up and down to his feet on the pedals, her hair flying. They dismounted to go uphill and he wheeled the bike along the kerb. They walked apart, still strangers, to forestall wagging tongues. But they talked.

They told each other funny things that had happened at work, changing voices to suit the players. His comments were hilarious, his roar of laughter startling. Arthur didn't like the way she told stories. 'Get to the point,' he'd say testily, panicking her, robbing the tale of its punchline and the telling of any pleasure. Frank listened to her, whether she was relating an anecdote or making a serious comment on the way the war was going. He considered what she'd said before agreeing or disagreeing, unlike Arthur who would interrupt and override with his sensible, well-informed, political arguments gleaned from some dry as dust newspaper like the *Daily Worker*. A woman with an opinion? Bound to be stupid.

They spoke of things that interested them, novels and films, mutual friends and each other. Agreed that they couldn't wait for late September and the hopping fields.

In Knighton Woods the rhododendrons were out. Vivid reds and pinks and creamy-white, glowed through the trees like bright dresses. Planted when the land was part of a huge estate, they were left now to bloom for the delight of dogwalkers and scruffy boys up to no good and clandestine lovers, also up to no good. He picked a spray of crimson flowers and fastened it behind her ear. His touch excited her. She felt exotic and strange.

They propped the bike against a tree and sat down for their picnic beside the shady pond, munching the bread and marge and meat substitute and trying to find it tasty. It was peaceful listening to the whistles and warbles in the trees, though neither knew one bird from another. Well, Flo thought she knew a black-bird's song, though it sounded eerie over water, and Frank recognised a robin when it hopped down for some crumbs and that was good enough. The others were a bonus, he said, sent by kindly Queen Titania to flit among the leafy branches and sing for their delectation and delight. She leaned back on her elbows and closed her eyes, utterly content. Childhood fantasies were still satisfying. Frank stroked her eyelids and whispered that she would fall in love with the first creature she saw when she opened her eyes. Then he held her head still so that when she opened her eyes it was a squirrel she saw, sitting bolt upright, watching her.

She smiled, serene in the knowledge that they both knew who she really loved.

Suddenly the air was alive and shimmering and they were slapping their arms, legs, necks.

'Ow, Christ! Vicious little buggers!'

In a moment they had stuffed the picnic back into the saddlebag and left fairyland in favour of a gnat-free zone.

They found it, far from the beaten brack, a patch of sunny emerald grass set in a thick ring of rhododendron. They laid the bike down and themselves beside it. If they were quiet, no one would know they were there.

Loving every bit of it, every touch of his lips and fingers, loving the look of him, the bones of his face, the smell of his open-air skin, the crispness of his honey hair, loving his laughing eyes and the magic she saw in them, loving his body, honed hard and smooth and brown and demanding, loving his voice, murmuring against her ear, loving his thoughtfulness, the time he took, loving his love, she came and it was different. It was complete. There was a richness and roundness in her womb that she'd never felt before.

Afterwards, on the way home she told him about it.

'You're pregnant, then,' he said in delight. 'You're having my baby, Flo. You'll have to marry me now.'

He was so naïve.

The next day, after a good night's sleep, she wasn't so sure. She didn't want to be pregnant. Perhaps she wasn't. Perhaps she'd fooled herself about that feeling. She felt no different at all now. Just guilty. What she was doing was wrong. Taking risks. She gave herself a stern talking to, one of many. She was married to Arthur, a decent hard-working man with a trade, and prospects after the war. This wasn't any way to behave, just because she was lonely. She had to be strong. He trusted her. She'd give up seeing

Frank. It would hurt but she wasn't doing herself any good.

When Arthur came home on leave a fortnight later, he was attentive and handsome and she knew that she didn't want to lose him, couldn't bring herself to hurt him.

A week after that, Arthur was back fighting the War of the Atlantic, and when Frank invited her to see *Citizen Kane* at the Gaumont, she had the strength to refuse. By then she knew she was pregnant, one way or another. Now she'd have to stick with Arthur. She couldn't have an illegitimate child; wreck her life. She didn't go hopping that year.

Luckily *Citizen Kane* won Orson Welles an Oscar, and it was still doing the rounds on a dark October night when Frank asked her out again. Not that either of them saw much of the film. A month later the bomb dropped and he dropped out of her life.

Of course, Dorrie was Frank's child, conceived under a rhododendron bush. She was nothing to do with Jack or Lucy or Nora or even Arthur's dead grandmother. Psychic blood didn't run in her veins.

Unless *he*... No, no. She almost had to smile at the notion that Frank might be clairvoyant. Good Lord, what an idea.

But perhaps you didn't have to inherit it. Perhaps it was an accident of birth. Or pre-birth. Perhaps it was all that talk of fairies, in the woods. Or, more likely, it was being buried alive when Flo was four months gone. Because although Dorrie wasn't, couldn't be psychic – there was no denying it, she had her moments.

Like when she'd scrawled *Frank* in crayon on Arthur's sailor hat: Flo had never forgotten that. As if she'd known then who her real dad was. It had to have been coincidence.

Then there were those terrible dreams. All kids have dreams but Dorrie's were so vivid, they really upset her. And everybody else. All about volcanoes erupting and trains crashing and the rivers fizzing and killing the fish.

'But Mummy,' she'd wailed, tears streaming down her little face, her lazy eye turning in, 'it's really real. There's fireworks coming out of the mountain and the people is being deaded.' Not that they bothered her for long, those nightmares. Other, more pleasant dreams would come along and she'd wake up with a smile on her face, burbling about weddings and princesses and...

They couldn't be, could they? Portentous?

Princess Elizabeth did get married that year. But the papers had been full of it for ages. That's what it was, of course. Dorrie had seen the pictures.

And she'd stopped having them. Or she'd stopped telling Flo about them. Unlike Stephen. He'd come down to breakfast most mornings, his head fell of nonsense, machines mostly, robots and space ships. Arthur reckoned he was inspired but she knew it was all the fault of that *Eagle* comic.

She was clever at predicting things, though, old Dorrie. Little things, like 'Take your umbrella, Mum, it's going to rain,' and not a cloud in the sky. And once or twice she'd told them the winner of the Miss World competition, and Wimbledon, but she might just have had good judgement. They should have put money on it. She did seem to have a knack of predicting world events. Uncanny.

She'd always hated Arthur's hero, Joseph Stalin.

'How can you admire him, Dad?' she'd said, when Arthur was extolling Uncle Joe's virtues. 'He's done terrible things, killed millions.'

'Lies!' Arthur had screamed, banging the table, and Dorrie had buttoned her lip, thinking she was in for another clout.

But she'd been right. Hadn't old Khrushchev denounced him only last year? She'd been right about Suez, too. Somehow she'd known Nasser was going to nationalise the canal and that Eden would be exposed in a stupid plot with France and Israel to keep the canal open. She'd known, too, that America would take it badly, that Britain would have to withdraw, unconditionally, at the United Nations' say so, to prevent a world crisis.

And that thing about the Hungarian uprising: 'You're wrong, Dad,' she'd told him. 'The Russians won't let them get away with it. They'll invade and there'll be a terrible massacre, just you wait and see. What will you do then, when your friends the Commies are seen to be bullies and mass murderers?'

They'd thought it was just talk, just smart-aleck, grammar school cleverness.

'Oh Arthur,' Flo whispered now, as memories sprang up like chiffon scarves in a drawer, memories that went right back to Dorrie's infancy, memories that Flo had wrapped in reason, popped into a dark recess of her mind and shut away. The talking to herself, the switching off and staring, the tantrums. They'd thought when she was little that she was brain-damaged. And lately, that bad temper – had she really cracked that window with her fist, pulled that cupboard door off its hinges? She wasn't that strong, surely? And the coincidences were amazing.

Only yesterday he'd been laying down the law about her going to the coffee bar this weekend, really getting into his stride. She was too young. He knew some of the lads that frequented 'those places' and he didn't want a daughter of his associating with that sort of riff-raff.

'Peter's going.'

'What's good for the gander isn't always good for the goose and besides, you're getting too pally with that boy. He's your cousin, after all.'

'Sorry?'

'*You* know.'

'No, I don't. Tell me, Dad, what's his being my cousin got to do with anything?' She was goading him. Being nasty.

'Don't give me your cheek, madam,' he'd said.

And she'd just said, 'Oh b–!' and all his precious papers had been blown off the table, floating and fluttering as though a mischievous little breeze were playing with them. The doors and windows were all open, of course; it was so hot. And *still*. Flo would have sworn that there'd been no draught. No curtains had moved nor doors banged.

Poor Arthur had been so flustered by the time everything was picked up and sorted he'd said, 'Oh, do as you like!'

The more she thought about it, the more persuaded she was that Dorrie might very well have extraordinary powers, that she could indeed have blasted a hole in the television.

He noticed, at last, that she was beginning to shake.

'Oh Gawd, sit down, sit down. Take it easy, old girl.' He bustled about fixing cushions at her back, fetching a chair for her feet. Then came the soft soap. 'I didn't mean to upset you, love. It's probably not nearly as bad as I say. Could be I'm quite wrong.' Though the way he said it made it clear that he was never wrong. 'Can I get you something? A drink? Where is she all this time anyway? On the corner, I expect, cracking jokes with her mates while we're left to imagine the worst. Gaw bli, I'll give her "visions" when I get my hands on her!'

Chapter Nineteen

'He wants locking up.' Grandma took one look at Dorrie's split lip and her faded eyes skinned with tears. She looked utterly weary, Dorrie thought, as she puzzled over her son's violence. 'I don't know what's come over him. He never used to be like this.'

'It's me, Grandma.' She'd had time to think about it on the train. 'I rub him up the wrong way.' She didn't say 'frighten' but that had also occurred to her.

'Don't make excuses for him, Dorrie. All right, so you say things you oughtn't, but that's part of growing up and it don't give him the right...' She didn't trust herself to finish the sentence. She and Lucy exchanged bitter glances and, as she ushered her daughter and granddaughter into the parlour that was bathed in the afternoon sun, her lips, worn thin with life, were twitching to a mental scolding.

Tea was drunk in bleak silence as they watched Dorrie struggling to sip through the swelling.

'Tch!' tutted Lucy eventually. 'I can't sit and watch this. Come here, Trouble,' as though she were talking to one of her own. Dorrie put down her cup and submitted thankfully to Lucy's laying on of hands. Warmth spread from her fingers and a tingling began that was finally too ticklish to bear. She pressed her lips together

369

and found that the swelling had gone down and the raw wound closed. It still hurt to smile but it was better. At least she could talk properly and there was a lot of news to catch up on: aunts, uncles, cousins, new jobs, new houses, new loves.

'I thought you'd have the Hallidays here,' she said, looking round and finding no telltale signs of visitors, shoes under the sideboard, jackets on the back of the door.

'No.' Lucy was stern.

'She wouldn't let me,' Grandma complained.

'You're getting on, Ma. He'd've been too much for you.' While Grandma's lips gathered in pleated petulance, Lucy went on to explain that the village would have been agog. Strangers? Who? How? What? Specially one so drawn to children. Seeing him all smiling and soppy at the school gates, they'd have put two and two together in next to no time.

Far easier for them to blend in with the trippers at Sowness. They'd rented them a nice beach hut right on the sands, with bunk beds and cooking facilities and from there they could paddle and sunbathe to their hearts' content.

Mrs Halliday had thought it best not to tell James why he was there. It would have upset him terribly if he'd thought that a child had been hurt. And as for the police suspecting *him,* he wouldn't have understood at all.

They were on their holidays as far as he was concerned. He'd only been for day trips before, by train to Southend and Maldon and a charabanc outing to Brighton. Never before had he ridden pillion on a motorbike with his arms round a pretty lady, and Mother in the sidecar, all roaring madly up the coast to goodness knows where. Never before had he woken in a bed not his own, with the sea in his ears and the gulls mewling. It was like his reading book. *Look at John. John can swim. Nip is a dog. See Nip dig. John and Nip play in the sand.* But it was real sand, real sea and every day he could watch the slap and seethe of their eternal conflict. It was all very exciting. He was growing a beard and, with his new sunglasses, the salty tan and his smart peaked cap with its anchor badge, he looked like a real fisherman. *He* said so, the nice man who brought them fish and chips and pies and sandwiches and doughnuts and cups of tea and ice cream, who took him for walks along the beach while Mother had her nap.

'Who's that then?' Dorrie enquired.

'They take it in turns, people from the meeting hall.'

'They're taking an awful risk, aren't they, harbouring a wanted man?'

Both women nodded, their expressions reflecting the seriousness of the matter. Dorrie realised that this was probably the first time either of them had ever knowingly broken the law, and it was all her doing. It had been her idea to whisk James Halliday out of harm's way. She couldn't bear the thought of his being arrested for a crime he hadn't committed and having to spend time in gaol with other prisoners who regarded 'nonces' as fair sport.

'I'm sorry,' she said.

371

'Don't be daft. It's a good cause and we're all glad to help, ain't we, Luce? You couldn't possibly have managed it on your own.'

'And the confession? How's that going?'

'All right, I think,' said Lucy. 'I know it's keeping them all very busy over on the Other Side. We haven't seen Granny Farthing for days.'

'Do you think it'll work?'

'I don't know, Dorrie. It should, the amount of organisation that's gone into it.'

'But...?' she prompted.

'But he's not normal, is he? I mean, most people would cave in at the first taste of what little Viv's dishing up but there's no knowing how he'll react. He's mad to start with and powerful, too. That's the danger.'

'She's a case though, ain't she, old Viv?' said Grandma fondly.

'She's a holy terror, Grandma. I'd hate to have her mucking about with my subconscious.'

'Grief!' Grimacing at the thought, her aunt picked up a newspaper to fan herself. 'Anyway they've got another session planned for tonight. We'll just have to wait and see how it goes.' She blew over her lower lip to cool her face. 'Is it just me or is it like a bakehouse in here?'

'Just thought I'd whip up a cake,' Grandma explained. 'Ginger – Dorrie's favourite.'

'Mother!' Lucy remonstrated. 'You haven't lit the range? Today of all days...' Sighing and tutting she unbuttoned her collar, and announced that she was going to sit outside until Joe came home with the children. It was too hot indoors. When Flo had phoned they'd been about to take a picnic to the buttercup field. Auntie Mabel had gone with them. (Mabel Hooper from the farm, that was.) She loved Lucy's brood and took every opportunity to spoil them. She was providing the food. Joe had immediately offered to fetch Dorrie from the station – Mabel's chatter drove him to distraction – but it was so seldom the kids saw their dad, with the unsocial hours he kept, that Lucy had insisted she be the one to go.

'I'm sorry,' Dorrie said again. 'I seem to be messing up everyone's lives.'

'For goodness sake, girl. I'm delighted to see you. Delighted to have a break from the kids if the truth be told. Now take off your shoes, bring your chair and we'll get our knees brown while we have the chance.'

In Great Bisset you sat in the front garden to sunbathe, among the flowers. The backyard was all washing lines and chickens and vegetables, with a whiff of Jeyes from the WC and the 'bombie' and bonfire smoke, so why would you sit out there on the cobbles? You couldn't peep through your eyelashes at people going by in the lane, you couldn't listen to the boys playing cricket on the green, you couldn't hear the ducks on the pond and watch the church on the hill for the moment when the bride and groom came out for their photos. You couldn't pass the time of day with the Doubledays, leaning over the gate to compliment Grandma on her roses.

'I see you have visitors!' the Lord of the Manor bellowed down the length of the path. 'To what do we owe this pleasure?' John, looking tall and gorgeous with a flop of dark hair falling over his sunglasses, raised a hand in laconic greeting.

Dorrie nearly fell off her chair in her haste to sit up and pull down her skirt, sure she'd been showing more than was decent. She didn't want to give John the slightest encouragement. Not after that letter. Her mouth was dry. Had she actually been asleep? Snoring?

'Oh, hello,' she dithered, adjusting her gipsy blouse to cover her bra strap. Oh God. How long had he been back? She'd only sent her *Dear John* letter three days before. He might not have received it. How bloody embarrassing. What if he were reading things into her presence in Great Bisset? He was so vain, he might just think she'd come for his benefit.

'Just finished your GECs, ain't you, Dorrie?'

'GCEs, Grandma,' she mumbled. GEC was the electrical company. For the first time Dorrie was aware of comparing her grandmother's comfortable speech with Mr Doubleday's precise diction.

'Come to clear the cobwebs out your 'ead, ain't you, duck?'

'John's in the same boat. Sat the last of his A levels last week. And now we can do no more. Just sit tight and hope for the best, eh, what?'

She dared to glance at John, who raised his eyes to heaven. What was that look? Despair – about the exams? Or was it about the home truths she'd been forced to tell him. How she couldn't believe he'd really meant all those things. How she thought she understood how a lonely, motherless boy, shut away in that school, with the exams on top of him, could let his imagination get the better of him. How he might persuade himself that he was in love. Be prompted to write steamy letters. How she valued his friendship but was not ready for anything deeper. She thought she'd been kind. Let him down gently, when she could have laughed in his face. But if he hadn't even received it...

'Now, Mrs Potter, the reason I called. I was rather hoping you'd been reconsidering my proposal.'
'Eh?'
'When we had the roof mended last year, I'm sure we broached the subject. Mmm? A little something we said you could do for me in return?'
Grandma was playing dumb.
'Ghosts, dear lady, ghosts.'
'Didn't think you believed in 'em.'
'Good Lord, does anyone with a grain of sense? All illusion, isn't it?' Grandma didn't flinch. 'Though there was someone – journalist chappie – a year or two back. Came to give the house the once-over. Seemed to think the place was haunted, eh, what?' He sniggered in a superior sort of way. 'Never got back to me, now I come to think of it – damned inconsiderate – *and* I missed the article in the *Telegraph*. You didn't see it, did you? No, probably not. Actually he's the one gave me the idea. Paying guests, what do you think? You know the sort of thing *"Stay overnight in a haunted manor house –*

experience of a lifetime." Could be quite a respectable sideline, what?'

Grandma shrugged. Why was he asking her?

'It occurred to me that you would know all about these things, Mrs P, being in the field, as it were. You'd know all the wheezes.'

'Wheezes?'

'Oh, you know – ectoplasm, disembodied voices, spirit writing, that sort of thing, nothing too expensive. I rather wondered, if you were free, whether you'd have time this afternoon?'

'What, *now?*'

'Four-thirtyish?' He glanced at his watch. 'Say ten, twenty minutes? I've invited a few friends. Perhaps you would care to join us for tea and give us the benefit of your expertise?'

'Oh. Oh no, I...' She searched for an excuse. 'I've got Dorrie here.'

'Bring her, too. Be company for the boy. What about you, Mrs Torrance? Perhaps you would grace us with your charming presence.'

But Lucy declined ungraciously, muttering that she was expecting the family home at any minute.

'Pity, pity. Perhaps another time? Well, then, Mrs P, *à bientôt.*'

Lucy managed to keep the lid on her scorn until the landlord had swaggered out of earshot and then, as Dorrie sashayed up the path, hand on hip, in exaggerated mimicry, she let rip. 'Incredible! *À bientôt!* Who the hell does he think he is?'

Grandma raised wet eyes to heaven. 'Oh my Gawd,' she sniffed, wiping away a tear of laughter. 'You got any idea what he's after? Eggdoplasm? What's that? For stopping eggs going off? Put some in a bucket, shall I, instead of isinglass?'

Lucy wasn't laughing. 'He thinks you're a fake, Ma, and he wants to know the tricks of the trade so he can charge money for scaring people out of their wits.'

'Should be interesting,' said Dorrie, fastening a sandal. In more ways than one, she thought. That lingering lost spaniel look John had given her as he'd turned to go had convinced her that firmness and plain speech were needed. He was clearly harbouring some wild sort of hope. 'I bet you wish you were coming, don't you, Auntie?'

'Well, I would if Joe were home, but only to keep an eye on you two. To be honest, it gives me the creeps, that house.'

'Me an' all,' admitted Grandma. 'Still, we'll gird our loins, eh, Dorrie – put on our spiritual armour?'

'Sorry?'

'Think positive,' explained Lucy, 'but you do, anyway. Don't worry, I'll be with you in spirit.'

'I'll just run an iron over me party frock,' said Grandma.

Washed and tidy and flustered by the rush, Dorrie and her grandmother arrived, arm-in-arm at the ornamental gates, where John was waiting for them.

'Hi there!' His grin was too eager, oh dear, and his aura a smouldering red. On a hot day like today, she thought. He was polite enough though, taking Grandma's other arm to help her over the ruts. 'It's murder up here in the dark. Guaranteed to break your ankles.' He went on to explain that hardcore and gravel came a long way down the list of his father's priorities. The roof wanted mending, the guttering replacing, the walls repointing, not to mention all the interior stuff, plumbing, redecorating and so on. They'd sold everything that was saleable, all the old four-posters and Chinese vases. They hadn't even been able to afford to have the oak tree sawn into useful lengths. It was being stored at the mill. Transport and storage cost a fortune. They had until the end of the year to pay their bills, then they forfeited the wood.

'But it still belongs to the villagers, doesn't it?'

Hence the urgent need for at least one other source of cash.

'At least he won't have to pay your school bills any more. Won't that help?'

'Drop in the ocean, old thing.'

'But what about university?'

He gazed at her long and hard and his cheeks stained an unwholesome pink. Oh no you don't, she thought, shielding her eyes as if from the sun, remembering the purple prose of his letter and realising that this glimpse of his 'soul's passion' was an attempt to make her feel guilty. Somehow, he was trying to tell her, his future depended on her.

'University is looking less and less likely,' he was forced to explain. 'He wants me here, managing the business, as it were. He was telling me about his plans, last night. All the spare cash is going into this new venture.'

'What about...?' She cleared her throat. It was suddenly quite hard to speak. 'Has he thought about selling off some of his land to the council or a building contractor?' as though it had just occurred to her. Grandma gave her a poke. 'Well,' she said, to them both, 'it's doing him no good and people are crying out for houses.'

'It's Green Belt, Dorrie,' he said gently. 'All round Great Bisset. He'd have built on it himself if the law allowed it.'

'What, even here?' She swept her arm to encompass the lawns and the paddock, the orchard and the woods, the area she had envisioned as streets of houses. 'His own grounds? They're his to do with as he likes, aren't they?'

'Oh, he'd never agree. Good Lord.'

'He'd still have the house and a bit of garden.'

'And what an outlook – a council estate! No, it's not a runner, old girl.' And then, as they helped the dumpy old woman over a particularly hazardous pothole he said, 'But something'll have to be done before someone breaks their neck. Not everyone's as hale and hearty as you, Mrs Potter.'

She should be, thought Dorrie, with a psychic healer living next door, sorting out her digestive problems and her rheumatism as they arose. But she was getting old.

It suddenly struck Dorrie that one day, Grandma too would die. As with Nanna and Aunt Polly, there would be an absence where she had been. Her hair, at seventy, was white now, bleached by the sun and a touch of Reckitt's blue in the final rinse that made her tan, from gardening and front-gate gossip, a startling contrast. And her memory was going. She'd told Dorrie the same story about Hettie Fitzell's chronic bronchitis twice since she'd arrived, with the same observation about sixty fags a day and how Lucy had refused to lay hands on the village shopkeeper until she stopped smoking.

Dorrie was aware, as the old woman paused to admire a rose, to sniff its fragrance, with her hand on her chest and relief in her eyes, that it was a pretext. She needed a rest. The long walk was tiring. It must be horrible to be old, she thought, to see your skin wrinkling, your hands gnarling, feel your joints stiffening. At least flowers weren't aware of their bloom withering, didn't know that their dance with the wind would soon be over.

Nanna Hubbard had always looked sickly, even before she'd been taken ill. Dorrie had called them her 'thin' and 'fat' grandmothers and thought of them almost as town and country opposites. But they'd both had the same sooty London roots, both been widowed, both been dirt-poor. Both had brought up families on their own. Both had lived through the two world wars. And both had taken up with 'spirits' of one sort of another. Nanna Hubbard's had killed her. The elderly were vulnerable. Brittle. A fall could kill them. Grandma must be cherished.

She was breathless as they mounted the sweep of steps at the entrance to the house, and distinctly apprehensive.

'What exactly does he want from me, your dad?' she said.

'Nothing dreadful, don't worry. Just ideas about setting up this haunted house thing. Any tips you might have about sound effects and mechanical devices.'

'Eh?'

'Grandma doesn't know what you're talking about, John. She's a genuine medium. I've told you.'

'Oh right,' he said, but he didn't understand. She'd tried a few times to explain about their psychic connections but it seemed as if things that couldn't be explained by numbers or formulae were not worthy of his attention. He was clever but a bit of a twit, all the same.

The main doors were thrown open to the heat-wave but the entrance hall struck cold and the visitors' bare arms prickled with gooseflesh.

'Parky, innit?' Grandma remarked and Dorrie shivered agreement. It wasn't merely the dankness of an unlit stairwell, or the uncarpeted stone that rang to their footsteps. There wasn't a draught and it wasn't the chill that comes from damp. It was Auntie Lucy's 'creeps' and it settled on every surface like a miasma. The high ceilings were bleak with it, the oak-panelled walls were dark with it, the great mirrors were spotty with it, the furniture was wormy with it. And so many things were dead with it: bears and zebras lying skinned on the floor, stags severed from their bodies, high on the walls, fish stuffed and mounted in glass cases, birds in bell-jars, rows and rows of matching butterflies, pinned for display, not to mention the portraits of the dead that lined the walls.

'Face like a wet weekend at Brighton,' was Grandma's considered opinion of one lugubrious Edwardian they passed in the corridor.

'Great-grandfather,' muttered John. Grandma tutted and patted his hand in sympathy. Then gave him a look of real concern. She might have been struck by the family likeness. John, too, was looking like a wet weekend, his mouth pinched around some inner grief, his eyes small in a suffusion of swollen tear ducts. He had just tried to put his arm round Dorrie, with a whispered 'Did you get my letter?' and her cold shoulder had, she felt, told him all he needed to know.

Grimly silent, he ushered them into a small drawing room, where a pair of winged armchairs harboured a Dr and Mrs Bussage. He was a small man, with pebbled lenses and a liking for Madeira wine, it seemed, and she wore pencilled-in eyebrows, a pageboy haircut, a pinstripe jacket and skirt over a fabulous body, and a secret smile which she flashed at Doubleday whenever she thought no one was looking. A second woman, Mrs Emberley-Smythe who, Grandma whispered, ran the stables in Stanbury, was plump and pinkly powdered and probably in her forties. She was hovering beside a plate of egg sandwiches at the central table. Grandma spotted Ralph Doubleday silhouetted against the window, with Mr Emberley-Smythe, who owned the stables. She made a beeline for him.

'Glad I weren't born with a silver spoon in me mouth,' she announced. 'I'm sorry for you, mate,' causing the two men to slop their tea and John to groan. Dorrie glared at him and he turned his back, to direct his anguish at one of the many rectangles of pristine wallpaper from which a mirror or a picture, perhaps, had been recently removed to be sold. How rude he was. How childish and petty and boorish.

'I say, steady on!' said Dr Bussage. For a moment Dorrie thought she had spoken aloud but realised the remark was addressed to Grandma.

'What makes you say that?' Doubleday actually seemed amused.

'You can feel the misery coming out the walls,' she declared. 'Can't you, Dor?'

And Dorrie had to admit that you could.

It had gone from bad to worse, as Grandma told Auntie Lucy, who had been standing at the window watching for them. Granny Farthing was already sitting waiting for them in her favourite armchair by the fireplace. The cat with the bus-ticket ears sat on the arm, its white socks tucked neatly out of sight.

Grandma made straight for the kitchen and flicked on the light switch, but Lucy wasn't interested in tea. She wanted all the gory details. *Now.* Grandma hovered in the doorway, slightly flummoxed by the break in routine, but was persuaded to come back in, sit down opposite her ghostly mother and tell all.

Her voice took on an exaggerated upper-crustiness as she parodied their host. "'You dewn't mean to say the ewld place re-ahly is 'aunted?" he says. What could I say? I knew he was poking fun and all his cronies was laughing up their sleeves. Septics, every one. I knew we was the entertainment, me and Dor. "Come and have tea and cakes," he'd said to them. "Floor show laid on. I'll get old Ma Potter over and you can watch the lower classes making prats o' theirselves."

'Dorrie looks at me and I look at Dor, and it's like she's reading my mind and me hers. I can almost 'ear her saying, "Go on, Grandma. Let's show 'em." She'd 'ad words with John, she tells me, but I never knew that at the time. So I says, "Well, Mr Doubleday, there's one way to find out." Because that's what he wanted all along, weren't it, Dor? A free reading. They'd been watching that film, that *Blithe Spirit*, you could tell. I mean, there was this round table, all ready. You only had to take off the cloth and the tray and the plate of egg sandwiches. Well, they had the maid do that – Fifi, they called her. Young John acted like he was quite taken with her, but that was only to do Dorrie in the eye, I realise that now. So guess how many chairs there was? Eight exactly, for me and Dorrie, Lord Muck, Dr and Mrs Bussage and the Emberley-Smythes and John. So wasn't that lucky? I said to Dorrie, didn't I? I said, "Hold onto your hat, gel, this is gonna be a bumpy ride!"'

'I had my fingers crossed for you,' said Lucy.

'Yeah, so did we. And toes, an' all. 'Cause it

was Dorrie's first time doing a séance, wasn't it, duck?'

'Absolutely. Gosh, Auntie, I was petrified. A sneer on every face except John's. All those dark spirits waiting in the woodword and he just sat there looking wet.' She licked her lips that had gone dry again at the memory.

'Oh, poor John. What's he done?'

'It's a long story.'

'Any old how,' said Grandma, 'we rolled up our sleeves, didn't we, Dor? Got them all sat down and holding hands, and I was just thinking we might've bit off more'n we could chew when up pops your Granny Farthing, cat and all! Gawd, I was never so glad to see anyone in all my born days.'

'Well, I thought you could do with a bit of moral support,' said Lucy.

'Good job we come round when we did, eh, Puss?' said the old ghost. *'I was just gonna give you an update on old Whatsisface down in Chingford, and then I was off again, but when Lucy said you was over the Doubleday place I thought, "Come on, cat, let's go and have a bit of fun." And we had a smashing time didn't we, gels? Pulled out all the stops.'*

'They go their money's worth.'

'You charged them?' cried Lucy.

'Be truthful, it never entered my head, Luce, only *she* starts sniggering – Mrs Emberley-Smythe: "Cross your palm with silver, do we, Mrs Potter?" Turned out it was just her little joke.'

'So what happened?'

'Oh, all sorts. The old table was bumping

around, pictures, what was left of 'em, was falling off the walls, doors and windows banging; we had screams, real blood-curdlers, and groans and clanking of chains – a bit of a chestnut but it goes down well. Couldn't see much, that was the only thing. They pulled the curtains but it wasn't really dark enough. Bright sunshine outside wasn't it? They'd've had a better show later on, I expect. But that pong of sulphur was a stroke of genius, Mum.'

'*What pong of sulphur?*'

'I thought you...'

'*No.*'

'Oh.' And, 'Oh my Gawd,' as realisation spilled across her face. 'It was them blooming egg sandwiches!' she exclaimed.

Granny Farthing said, '*Oh Nora! Oh, poor Mrs Emberley-Smythe!*' and clapped a bony hand over her mouth. A chuffing noise came from her nostrils and her shoulders began to shake. Her face became a contour map of mirth as her eyes disappeared into folds of ancient wrinkles.

Grandma snorted and began to giggle. Dorrie caught it too, and then Lucy, and soon all four of them were hooting with laughter and mopping their eyes. The cat scooted off to more saintly climes.

'Any old how,' Grandma managed to wheeze eventually, 'we dug up a few family skellingtons between us.'

'Many, were there?'

'Dozens, Auntie.'

'There was that pretty chambermaid, wasn't there, Dorrie? Crying and hollering, she was.

Course, she was up the duff, poor little thing, on account of old Sir Roger, and she was gonna let on to the then Lady Muck, Doubleday's great-grandma – only Sir Roger gets to her first with his blunderbuss. Makes a right mess of her nice starched apron. And he buried her in the cellar, see, under the kitchen. They think it's the drains for years. And then there's old Henry Double-day, a mean old git from the sound of it. Nearly eighty when the family decides they can't wait no longer for him to part with his money. They pull straws, don't they, as to who's gonna do the dirty deed, and the Honourable Hugo gets the short one. Smothered the old boy, in his bed. He's next to go – hanged hisself in the stairwell. Oh, there was loads of 'em, Luce. The number of eldest sons winding up dead of broken necks off balconies, and drownings in the river would make your hair curl. And it was all hushed up and got round.'

'What did the Emberley-Smythes make of it all, I wonder? And the good doctor?'

'The good doctor was out for the count. But the others was goggle-eyed, Luce. As for Mrs Bussage – poor Phoebe – she was took bad, wasn't she, Dorrie? Had to go and lay down. And Ralph Doubleday was *so* concerned, so we stopped then. Don't want no one having heart attacks over a few ghosts.'

'So you're not quite such a joke now, eh, Ma?'

'I dunno, Luce. He looked a bit put out, did old Ralph. I mean, it was a show up, weren't it, in front of his mates and all? I bet they'll think twice before they buy a used car off him, eh?

What a pedigree! Twisters and thugs and murderers, the lot of 'em.'

'They weren't all bad, Grandma. What about his granddad?'

'Yeah, George was all right. Oh Luce, you shoulda seen old Ralphie jump when he reconnized the old man's voice. Dorrie got him off to a T. And some of the things he talked about, like a wooden horse he'd made for him, and times they'd gone fishing and that, you could tell they was ringing bells. But you know what it's like. Afterwards when they think about it, they convince themselves it was all a con, a set-up.'

'John looked a bit sick,' Dorrie recalled. 'Hardly said a word as he was seeing us out.' She sighed. 'Looks like it's the end of a beautiful friendship, doesn't it? I dunno, why do they always have to get serious?'

'*He'll get over it, sooner than you think,*' said Granny Farthing. '*We've stirred up a right 'ornets' nest over there, between us, and they'll be buzzing around tonight. Won't be much ardour left to cool, I shouldn't think, by morning. They're gonna have the pants scared off of them, him and his dad.*'

'But they did want a haunting,' Dorrie reminded her, tongue in cheek, 'and this way he won't have to spend a penny on gadgets.'

'*There's hauntings and hauntings, Dorrie,*' observed Granny Farthing darkly. '*Which reminds me, I shouldn't be here. I'll have to love you and leave you, girls. Lucy, perhaps you'll do the honours? Tell 'em what I told you. Maybe I'll have better news for you tomorrow. Where's that cat?*'

Here, puss, puss, puss! Gawd, is that the time? Viv'll kill me.'

And she was off.

'Right, how about that cup of tea now, Ma? No, you sit still, you look whacked.' Up from the table Lucy sniffed the air and made a face. 'Oh Ma, whatever've you put on the range now? Not another dead mouse? I've told you to check the coal.' They could all smell it now, a sour, vaguely familiar sort of smell. Dorrie had almost identified it.

Sighing and tutting Lucy ducked out into the kitchen. 'What the...? Oh Ma! You've only left the iron on, you silly!'

'No, no, I remember switching it off before...'

'Well, you must have switched it on again when you came in.' Quickly she flicked up the tiny light switch. It was bright enough to see the kitchen table and the iron, with smoke curling round its base, burning its way through layers of sheet and army blanket to the scrubbed wood beneath. Lucy grabbed a teatowel and lifted the appliance onto its trivet, away from the damage, and tugged the connecting plug from its socket. The other end of the lead dangled from the overhead light, beneath which stood a sturdy kitchen chair.

'And I've told you not to go climbing about on chairs,' she scolded. 'That's the whole point of having me next door, so you can knock.'

'We was in a hurry, Luce, and I just had this frock to do.'

A snort and 'Where's the blooming lightbulb?'

'On the mantelpiece.' Grandma scurried across the room to find it and hand it, like a naughty child, to her daughter.

The tall woman reached up to unplug the iron lead from the light socket and replace the bulb.

'Switch!' she ordered.

Dorrie switched. She felt as guilty as her grandmother. She should have checked that everything was in order before they left, but it would have been role reversal. Grandma was the capable adult. If she chose to climb about on chairs because she was too short to reach the light-bulb she must have known what she was doing.

It wasn't the first time. As Lucy held up the ruined blanket, past iron-shaped accidents were evident. The table was slightly scorched but there were darker brands nearby.

'Oh Ma, what are we going to do with you?' Now that the emergency was over Lucy could allow herself to be kinder.

'Time I was put down, innit, Luce?' She was looking pale and lost.

'Cup of tea?' Dorrie volunteered. They were surprised: Dorrie was the guest. But the great black kettle was simmering, as always, on the hob and Dorrie had only to fill the pot, assemble the pretty bone-china cups and saucers, and adjust, with difficulty, to the idea that her grandmother was fallible.

Chapter Twenty

Down   in darkest North Chingford, in his cosy bachelor flat overlooking the golf course, Detective Inspector Gerald Webb, the murderer of six-year-old Penny Marshall, was discovering that a child molester's lot was not a happy one.

They were waging a two-pronged attack on him, Lucy reported through a mouthful of ginger cake, bombarding him with dreams and apparitions. She stirred her second cup of tea and took another slice from the tin that Dorrie had fetched from the pantry. She wasn't daft, Grandma. She knew that as soon as the sweet spice burst upon their palates, order would be restored to her household. Lucy had already admitted that the incident with the iron could have happened to anyone. She'd done it herself, in fact. Electric irons were a menace. You had to be careful. And Grandma was a dab hand with cakes, that no one could deny.

Dorrie wetted her finger and dabbed up her last crumbs as her aunt delivered Granny Farthing's news.

Cousin Viv had delved into the murderer's head and dug up any number of nasty secrets and desires, dating back to babyhood when his mother, in indulging her own sexual whims and fantasies, had set the ball rolling, as it were. By the time the cherubic Cubmaster had got hold of

Gerald, there wasn't really much left to corrupt.

Simply by cutting and pasting scenes from Webb's life, a creative spirit with a penchant for puzzles and cryptic clues had put together such an unnatural and horrific mix of images that the murderer would lurch from his dreams with staring eyes and self-pitying whimpers, and then, finding himself awake, would immediately long for sleep again. But Viv's nightmares were nothing compared to the rest of the night's entertainment.

The sound of trickling water would presage a ghastly vision of the child. It wasn't her, of course. No one would dream of subjecting poor little Penny to further torment. Her spirit was far away, healing nicely on sunny lawns with loving grandparents and fluffy kittens. But he wasn't to know that.

The door handle would turn and in she would trail, weeping and dripping water and slimy weed. She would fix him with a pale blue stare and point an accusing finger in the traditional way. 'Murderer!' she would lisp. 'You killed me to satisfy your twisted desires. You must give yourself up. Confess! Confess!' Other childish apparitions would join her then, whingeing and wailing – a terrible din, according to Granny Farthing, a mother's worst nightmare, a roomful of screaming kids. Grown men would quail. Finally the studio portrait of Webb's dear old mother would crash to the floor. For it was her death three years before that had precipitated the first murder. Before that he had never felt the need to kill, merely to ravish.

At the sound of tinkling glass the spectres would vanish but it would be some while before he dared to move, to unravel himself from his ball of blankets. The picture would be back on the wall and, in his head, a desperate licking of wounds. Jesus. Get your breath, mate. Breathe. Come on, Gerry, get a grip. It was only a dream, that's all it was, even if it did give you the screaming abdabs. Phew. Jesus. That's better, deep breaths. Get up now, out of bed. Come on, come on. Do something, take your mind off it. Jesus, she had a lot to answer for, that little slut. Six years old she was and flaunting her sexuality like that. Begging for it. Making him do those terrible things. So he'd had to kill her. Put an end to it. And now she was preying on his mind. And all those other brats. Getting into his dreams. Jesus, he'd never had dreams like that before, as though it were really happening. And night after night of it. A hefty slug of whisky at bedtime was no help at all. He'd just bomb out quicker and still have the dreams. Look at his hands. Shaking. Little tart, she'd deserved everything she'd got.

They were even making comments at the station, saying he was looking pale, overdoing it, that his unparalleled clear-up rate wasn't worth it, that he should maybe see a doctor. They were jealous, of course, and it wasn't a doctor he needed. Only one thing helped the screaming abdabs.

That had been the latest bulletin from Granny Farthing and it wasn't at all what Dorrie had hoped to hear.

'What've they got planned for tonight?'

'More of the same, I imagine.'

'But it's not working.'

Lucy puffed her lips with regret. 'It doesn't look like it.'

It had worked with Scrooge. Dickens had only to rattle Jacob Marley's chains and send the miser on trips to his Past, Present and Future Christmases to reform him. But Scrooge had had a conscience. Gerald Webb was a psychopath, and their aim was not so much to teach the man the error of his ways as to bully him into giving himself up and confessing to murder. Dorrie had thought – they'd all thought – that it would only be a matter of time.

What more could they do? 'If we're not careful,' she said, 'he'll kill someone else.'

She could see it so clearly. Another child, a little older, a boy this time, his hand tucked into Webb's, so trusting. She squeezed her eyes tight to drive out the vision, picked up a pencil to occupy her nervous fingers. Grandma had been doing a crossword. She, too, liked puzzles.

'You'd think,' said Lucy, 'that with all our resources, we'd soon have him licked.'

'We're psychics not psychiatricks,' said Grandma. 'We don't know how horrible minds like his work.'

Dorrie tapped her toe on the floor for inspiration and doodled with the pencil on Grandma's newspaper. Lucy chewed her lip.

'Still, there's more ways of killing a cat,' the old woman continued, 'than by stuffing it full of cream.'

'Mmm?' Dorrie barely glanced up as her grandmother turned the paper round.

'Look what you're doing, duck. There's your answer.'

'Eh?'

'Your drawrin', gel. Who is it? Go on, whose face is that?'

Lucy leaned over to study the tiny sketch and exclaimed at the likeness. 'He even *looks* like a rat.'

Dorrie wasn't aware that she'd been drawing anything in particular, but, of course, it was a face. *His* face. His smooth brow and sneering mouth, his heavy-lidded eyes, the cowlick of greasy hair. DI Gerald Webb. But it was hardly surprising. She'd had his image at the front of her brain since it happened, as they all had. It was how they'd been able to centre on him with their visualisations.

'Now,' Grandma tipped her head, as though adjusting the seasoning in a stew, 'supposing you was to do another one like that, only bigger, and give it a title, like *Gerald Webb, Child-killer* and send it to him. What do you think he'd make of that?'

It was an idea. It would show him that someone knew or had made a lucky guess.

Grandma's face was strained with thought. 'You could draw a lot of pictures, telling the story, like one of them comic strips.' She wetted a thumb, turned the pages of the newspaper until she came to the right one and stabbed *The Flutters* and then *Garth* with a gnarled finger. 'There y'are,' she said. 'Starting with him waiting outside the school and her coming out the gates, then they're driving off in the car, arriving at his flat... Get the idea? Right up to the time he drops her in the drink, poor little mite. You could even put balloons coming out of their mouths with the things they said. That way he'd think someone's been looking right over his shoulder.'

'It's horrible, Ma.'

'What he's done is horrible, Luce.'

'No, I mean for poor Dorrie to have to draw.'

'How'd you feel about it, Dor? Could you manage it?'

'I ... I suppose so. But I don't think...'

'Gawd, I wished I could draw. *I'd* do it.'

She took a breath. There was a flaw in the old woman's plan somewhere: drawing was no good. She prayed for clarity. 'Grandma, you could. Anyone who knew the case, knew how Penny was injured, knew the way child molesters work, would know exactly what had gone on. They wouldn't have to've been there or read the murderer's mind or anything. Anyone could draw a cartoon, stick-men, anything – they wouldn't have to be good at drawing. They'd just have to show what happened and he'd get the message. I don't know what message exactly. Knowing him he'd probably think it was a bad joke. That someone was having a laugh at his expense. He'd probably think it was one of his mates on the force. Some people have a twisted sense of humour.'

'But you could put in details that nobody else would know, like – I dunno – ornaments, pictures on the wall.'

'Any mate of his who'd visited the flat would know about them.'

'But you'd draw their likenesses. Him and the little girl. I mean that there,' she stabbed again at the newspaper, 'that's him to a T.'

'It wouldn't make any difference, Grandma, if it was a flipping oil painting. Good, bad or indifferent, a drawing's no good. You can put what you like in a picture. I could draw him in bed with a chimpanzee, if I wanted. And he knows that. He'll take no notice. Drawings aren't real. They don't *prove* anything, not like a photo.'

'No, but it wouldn't half put the wind up him if he thought someone was onto him.'

Would it?

'Enough to send him toddling down to the police station, Ma, to write out his confession?' Her aunt wagged her head. No, thought Dorrie, it wasn't likely. 'I mean,' Lucy continued, 'he's a copper. He's going to say, "So where's your proof, clever dick?" He knows that if we had a scrap of real evidence we'd be down the police station ourselves, not wasting time drawing pretty pictures.'

She was right. All the same, it would do no harm to let him know that someone had connected him with the murder.

She would have a go.

Lucy fetched Joe's mapping pens and indian ink, and a child's sketchpad, just begun. Primitive, Alfred Wallis pictures. Fantastic streets of houses like Wobbly columns of bricks. Figures

397

floating sideways up to their front doors, cars crawling like flies. Innocence. She flipped the page and stared at the white expanse. The older women discreetly withdrew. *Saturday Night Theatre* was just starting.

She couldn't do it. The pen and ink cartoons that Grandma had suggested were impossible, almost profane. You couldn't make light of death. Like Nash, commissioned to record life in the trenches, she found her pen-strokes building up, fleshing out the solid shapes, needing to linger on the tragedy, to make the actors real, three-dimensional beings. This was fact, had happened. By the third attempt her hanky, a tight ball in her left hand, was sodden and blackened from mopping stray tears that dropped onto the paper and swirled with ink. She leaned back in the chair and took a recovery breath.

Take your time, Dorrie-cousin. Whenever you're ready.

She put the lid on the bottle and selected a B pencil for shading.

What did he really look like, in profile? There was the slope of his forehead, the sheen of his skin, his nose with a slight bump, his mouth with the full, slack lower lip, his receding chin. She closed her eyes.

Right now he must be getting ready for bed, pouring himself a stiff toddy, swallowing aspirin. She could see him, tousled and weary after a week of disturbed nights, turning back the covers, longing for sleep and fearing it, too. He must be getting used to the pattern of the night, the dreams, the materialisations. She knew what Viv's plan was. Like the Chinese water-torture, the constant drip, drip, drip of repetition would erode his resistance. Eventually he would crack.

Possibly.

But what if, just for once, Robbie, Granny's protégé from the North, who was in charge of lighting and special effects, what if he chilled the June air so that, as DI Webb lay quaking in his bed, marsh mists stole in through the open windows of the second-storey flat? What if they layered dankly among the tall reeds that were, by now, rustling beside the wardrobe? Somewhere, off-stage, that noise would begin, the noise he dreaded, of trickling water – a brook running over stones.

Go on, Dorrie-cousin, go on.

See, Webb stuffs his fingers in his ears to block out the familiar watery chuckling, and watches in horror as the doorknob begins to turn.

'No!'

He leaps from his bed and falls upon the handle to hold it tight, to shoulder the door and keep it shut, already aware of silt and stones squishing disgustingly between his bare toes, of water lapping round his ankles. Something moves, caught in his wild eye. A troop of little grey frogs is hopping along the chest of drawers where lily pads grow instead of doilies. Powerful wings beat overhead and a smell of stagnant mud rises from the shallows. And as the mirror mists on a pale protagonist wrestling with a door, the words *Confess, murderer!* are etched upon it in Nanna Hubbard's clear and cursive hand.

'Nanna Hubbard?'

'We're all doin' our bit, Dorrie.'

'What about them little frogs, Dorrie, dear?' Aunt Polly's voice joined her sister's in the ether. *'I thought they'd be a nice touch.'*

Despite his sobbing efforts, his knuckles gleaming bone-white, the handle twists inexorably against his slick grasp and the door flies open on a river in flood. He is hurled against the back wall with a force that knocks the framed Queen's Award for Bravery to the floor and the breath from his body. He hears it go bubbling past his ears as the undertow catches him, turning him over and over, in Blind Man's Buff confusion, so that when he claws upwards to the surface he hits the floor where the bed-legs are and there is no escape. Then he does a really stupid thing – he gasps for air to scream. And the water that fills his mouth and sears his nostrils turns to fire in his drowning lungs. As it had in hers. His brain boils. His arms thrash uselessly. He tries to pull his legs in, push his feet away, but he can't. His large body hangs heavy beneath him, covered in bubbles, like a pox, as the pores breathe their last. And then, floating into his quiet aquarium, with blue lips and weed in her hair, comes the luminescent figure of his young victim. Her open eyes glide towards him. Her lips move. *Confess,* she hisses.

When he dares to wake, minutes or hours later, clutching the blankets tight about his head and shuddering with shock, the flood has gone, the river has reverted to tile-effect lino and goatskin rug. Only a smell lingers, of stale fear. And the bed is wet.

There. It was done. The pad was full, the story told. Not quite what Grandma had in mind, perhaps. The inside tip of her middle finger was pencil-concave and sore. Absently she massaged the stiffness. In her ear there was a crunch of gravel, in the corner of her eye, a flurry of movement. Her grandmother started from sleep as a tall figure loomed in the open doorway. 'Room for one more inside, Gran?'

Peter.

He'd hitched a ride, he said. Auntie Flo had given him Dorrie's regrets, told him she'd gone to Gran's for a day or two to recover from the exams and he'd thought, great idea! A weekend in the country would set him up nicely. He hadn't fancied the skiffle group anyway and he knew they'd both be delighted to see him! 'So here I am. You don't mind, do you, Gran?' giving the old woman a peck on the cheek. 'I'll kip down on the sofa – unless Dorrie wants to share!' turning to her with a mad grin. 'Wotcha!' He brushed her face with his lips. 'What's that? Homework?'

Startled, she stuffed the sketchbook under the newspaper, feigning modesty, but he persisted: 'Come on, let's have a butcher's.' In seconds it became a physical struggle, good-humoured on his part, as he tried to prise her hands from the paper.

''Ere, 'ere, 'ere, pack it in, Pete!' cried Grandma. 'Let her be. You ain't too old to feel

401

the back of my hand, you know.'

He ignored her. 'Dirty pictures, Dorrie?' and set about her with tickling fingers. At the moment Grandma cuffed him, Dorrie stood up, swung round and struck him on the shoulder, her eyes blazing.

'Ow!' he cried, ducking to avoid worse, his arms up to protect his head. 'All right, all right. Feign lights!' Then, spotting the cake tin, he prised off the lid and proceeded to help himself to a wodge of ginger cake. 'Any tea going, Gran?' he mumbled, spitting crumbs. 'I'm parched.'

She was actually glad to see him, they both were. Grandma had always had a soft spot for her grandson and Dorrie was beginning to realise that he wasn't entirely repugnant. Kissing cousins, in fact, could be quite as useful as older brothers. He could always be relied on to bring a gang of mates to parties and school fêtes and concerts and things. Jenny had actually been out with his friends, Ian Worsley and Kevin Bright, though she said Kevin was a groper and Ian couldn't kiss for toffee. Angela had a crush on Peter but was too shy to do anything about it and, in spite of Dorrie's throwing them together at every opportunity, he didn't seem at all interested in pale and pretty Angela. Personally, Dorrie couldn't see what her friend saw in him. He wasn't bad-looking, she supposed, specially in the jumper her mother had knitted for him, but then, who wouldn't look sexy in a big black chunky-knit sweater? No, not sexy! Good grief. Peter didn't come close to her idea of sexy, no matter what Dad thought. Whatever had put that word into her head? John, now, with his knitting-pattern looks, was a dish, as Jenny would say, not up to Rock Hudson standards but passable. Definitely passable. Pity he was such a drip.

Peter was more your swarthy Welsh miner type, Stanley Baker in *How Green Was My Valley*. Dark and satanic in a Potter sort of way. (Peter Potter – what a name!) Though he was tall. That was always a bonus in an escort when you were tall yourself. Jenny and Angela were five and a half footers, too. The Three Musketeers. All for Anyone-Over-Five-Foot-Ten. Dorrie had actually been out with Mickey Dawlings, another of Peter's friends. Once. Nice boy but he'd only come up to her earlobe. Embarrassing or what!

Unfortunately her cousin had the personality of a Neanderthal. No manners. Look at him now, tucking into Grandma's cake without a by-your-leave. The beatings Uncle Mick had given him had achieved nothing but bitter contempt for the bully and all that he held dear. Now he seemed to take a perverse delight in being rude, thinking nothing of sitting in the only empty seat on the bus while you tottered over on your high heels every time the bus moved off. At a pinch he'd stand up for an old lady if she looked frail enough – he liked old ladies – but not for you. If you scowled hard enough he might offer a knee. Take it or leave it, woman. As for opening doors or saying that you looked nice – forget it. He was more likely to wrinkle his nose and beat away the fumes of your exclusive *White Fire* (seventeen and six for a teeny, tiny sample bottle), going 'Phwoah! What's that terrible pong?'

His dad didn't come after him with a stick any more. Not since Peter had wrenched it out of his hand that time and broken it across his knee. 'Come on, Dad,' he'd dared him, dancing around their tiny living room, fists bunched and ready, 'if you want a fight, I'll give you one,' but Uncle Mick had slammed out of the room in disgust. Auntie Joan had had to plead with her husband not to throw Peter out: she'd miss what he was giving her from his work in the market, setting up the greengrocer's stall before school and working there on Saturdays. So they'd let him stay but he and his father had hardly spoken since.

These days, Peter seemed to divide his spare time, what little there was of it, between the snooker hall, the gym, and their house in Highams Park. He was always round, bringing his homework, too, if he hadn't done it already in the school library. He and Dad would argue politics and worry about the bomb and South Africa. Sometimes they'd all troop down to CND meetings at the Standard pub, in the room over the bar. More often Dad and he went on their own. Then they could drink and swear and put the world to rights as only men can.

What was it Dad had feared with his 'he's your cousin' business? Some sort of incest? If he only knew... Apart from Stephen, who didn't count, Peter was the one boy she could talk to without having to worry whether her hair was tidy and her seams were straight or whether what she was saying made absolute sense. But romance? Good grief, forget it!

Grandma went to make more tea and he trailed after her, dwarfing her. She heard the murmur of their voices in the kitchen. Young and vital, old and creaky.

Him: How was she keeping in this hot weather? Tired, was she? Why didn't she let him go and fetch the water? And did she really need the stove lit, just for a pot of tea?

Her: Everything all right at home between the three of them, was it? Mick not throwing his weight around?

Him: Was she still doing the rounds, speaking at meetings? Shouldn't she be thinking of knocking it on the head, taking it easy?

Her: How had the exams been, them A-levels? When would they tell him how he'd done? Well, at least he had his job on the stall, eh? He'd let her know, wouldn't he, if ever he was strapped for cash?

Asking questions, answering. Sounding out. Listening hard for the sub-story, the subtle unsaid. Was that a quaver in her voice? Was she still on top of things? Was he in trouble? Too big for his boots? Scared about the future? Was *she?*

Dorrie knew that this wasn't the first time Peter had visited his grandmother on his own, but it hadn't occurred to her before that his bonds with Grandma were as strong, as enduring, as Dorrie's. Maybe more so. Peter didn't have parents who loved him. Grandma was his lifeline. There were so many who loved her, had claims on her, better claims than Dorrie's. All the little Torrances next door, Brian and Barbara and Jean. Not to mention Uncle Percy's hordes and Uncle Siddy's crowd. And Cousin Viv. Yes, what about *that* special relationship? Did Grandma love them all the same?

'What's this – Thumbelina all over again?'

Peter was leaning over her shoulder staring at a drawing of little grey frogs. Shit, it was the sketchpad, open. She was drawing again, on the back of an Alfred Wallis. How had that happened?

She kept her cool. 'Thumbelina?'

'Don't you remember, when we were kids? Some street party or something? No, it was here, at Gran's. You had a...' he searched his memory '...a picture book with frogs in it. Thumbelina. Everyone kept reading it to you. I scribbled all over it. I was so jealous of you getting all the attention. They gave me a good hiding for that.'

'Serves you right,' Grandma said. 'You was a little demon in them days. But she was no angel, Miss Butter-wouldn't-melt. She give you a nasty bite.'

Dorrie didn't remember any of this. Peter held out his hand. There, in the cushion of the big brown thumb, six teeth-marks, two above, four below. Very similar to those on the little gold bracelet that Nanna Hubbard had left. Had she been a biter, then?

'I didn't.'

'You did. Scarred me for life, woman.'

'Sorry.'

'Trophies of war,' he grinned. She had the impression that he was rather proud of them.

'I must have hated you.'

'I was a bit of a toe-rag.'

'Ain't changed much,' said Grandma caustically.

They laughed. And then he picked up the sketchbook and examined the frogs more closely. Intensely. She could just remember drawing them. 'Why did you put them on top of a flipping chest of drawers? What you call that? Surreal, is it? What else have you got?'

Before she could stop him he'd flipped over and back to the picture of the mirror and the words *'Confess, murderer!'* written in the mist. Just visible through the cleared letters was a reflection: Webb in his pyjamas and struggling with a door. It was cleverly done, if she said so herself. He turned to another. Webb's body covered in tiny bubbles. And another and another.

Slowly he handed her back the pad. His hand was unsteady. Now there wasn't a hint of humour in his face. 'Who is that, Dorrie?'

'It's a man called Webb. A policeman. I – I...' She bit her lips. 'He's the one that murdered Penny Marshall, not James Halliday. Don't ask me how I know.'

A flicker of pain as he hesitated. He had actually gone very pale. 'Dorrie, I... Do you have any more?'

She had forgotten what the next one was. She peeped. A man's bare feet with mud oozing between the toes, water spreading over stones from under a closed door. She let him see it, sure that he'd make neither head nor tail of it, and watched, fascinated, as he slumped into the chair beside her and stared at the study of the accusing child. Then back and forth, silently flipping the pages. Sweat beaded his forehead as he buried it in his hands.

'Dorrie.' He looked up and there were dark shadows in his eyes. His tongue slid over dry lips. 'I've been having this dream, over and over, about that bloke – Penny Marshall's killer. That's *him*. I mean, you've got him off to a T.' He shook his head, mystified, and drew a deep shuddering breath. 'The dream starts with him standing at his bedroom door trying to hold back a flood that eventually drowns him. And there's frogs and a mirror that gets steamed up and those very words. I ... You've picked my brains, woman.'

Chapter Twenty-One

'You're having me on,' he scoffed weakly. Poor Peter. He wanted so much for it to have been some sort of a joke. Dorrie was halfway to squeezing his hand when she stopped herself.

'It's a fact,' Grandma assured him. 'Mind-reading's the least of it. She ain't just a pretty face, your Dorrie.' Dorrie frowned. Since when was she his? What sticky mixture was Grandma stirring now? The old woman turned to her, head cocked. If you didn't know that the glint in her once-brown eyes was sharp as a freshly honed kitchen knife you'd have thought of innocent puppies. No hint of frailty now or feebleness of mind. 'Funny, though, you not knowing it was Peter's dream you was drawing.'

'Mmm. Great minds think alike, eh, Pete?'

'Oh hell, this is beyond me.' He scratched his head and tried to work it out. 'It was a dream, a recurring dream.' His hands hovered over the drawings, now detached from the pad and laid out on the table before him. 'And this bloke Webb – I mean, I've never even heard of him before. And you've known from the start it was him?' She nodded. 'Why the hell didn't you say so?'

She gave him a pitying look. 'Think about it.'

'But you're sure it's not Halliday?'

'Quite sure. And so were you to have dreamt all that.'

He paused, trying to formulate the right question, 'How could it ... how could you have known? Every poxy detail?'

'Things sometimes pop into my head. They can be world-shattering events or Mum wondering what to give us for tea ... or you dreaming.'

He shook his head, at a complete loss. 'But why me? I'm not the one who... I mean, it should've been *him* having the dream.'

Grandma stiffened, her mouth twitching impatiently. Dorrie said carefully, 'I think it probably was. Tonight.'

'Bloody hell!'

And the medium's eyes danced with secrets. 'And it would've been a bit more than a dream,' she said provocatively.

'How much more?'

He had a right to know. She said, 'To all intents and purposes, he – his spirit – experienced drowning while he slept.'

'No more'n he deserves,' said Grandma.

'What, *real* water?'

'No, of course not, but real enough.'

'Blimey.' He retreated into his chair, his eyes darting from one to the other. 'So what you're saying is, you're like a couple of witches? You lay spells on people?'

'No, that's *not* what I'm saying!' Dorrie spat, and was immediately sorry. It was just so annoying the way people always linked clairvoyantes with the black arts. 'It's not magic, Pete,' she said more kindly. 'Nothing to do with devils or demons or anything. Not a spell. Gosh, if I could charm him into making a confession that would be something, wouldn't it?'

Chin on fists he scowled suspicion at her. It was all very well Grandma extolling Dorrie's skills, but she respected the minds of those close to her and didn't probe, except when there was no help for it. A mind should be a place of safety, for private feelings and prejudices. If you say one thing and think another, or reserve comment, there's only you to know, unless your barricades are breached, your private thoughts invaded, your secrets known and your lies exposed. Then you face humiliation and contempt and, depending on the sort of animal you are, you bare your teeth and attack, or you turn tail and run. Of course, if you're Grandma, you have nothing to hide, particularly from a favourite grandchild. If you're Auntie Lucy you have learned to erect strong barriers. But if you're a kissing cousin...

Gently she tried to explain about the Other Side and the spiritual help she received from those who had passed over, and he snorted derisively.

'You were quite prepared to believe in devils,' blurted Dorrie, almost in tears, 'why not ghosts?'

'Astral entities,' corrected Grandma, airing her knowledge, insensible to sideways looks. 'Don't get me wrong, duck, they ain't lah-di-dah, not our lot. They're the likes of you and me – my old mum and a few other old dears on your grandad's side, Dorrie's gran and Auntie Polly. And there's Robbie, of course, one of your Auntie Susan's little patients that passed over,' she explained, ignoring Peter's tuts and rolling eyes. 'Not so little now though. He's come a long way. Oh, he was a poor little thing, break your heart. Something wrong with his bones, there was. Mind, he had no chance.' She glanced quickly over her shoulder for eavesdroppers and, with a mimer's exaggeration and a gossip's relish, mouthed, 'His old man was a drunk – gone now – a right dark spirit. Mum's on the game... And they both bashed him about, ill as he was.' Then, with the juicy bits out of the way, she reverted to normality. 'So your great-grandmother took him under her wing when he passed on. Don't think you ever met your Great-granny Farthing, did you – my mum? No, 'course, she'd've been long gone, time you come along. Any old how, she and him, they been keeping an eye on Dorrie. You an' all, if you did but know it! And they let her know straight off who the bastard was done little Penny in. She knew the bloke they wanted to pin it on wasn't nothing to do with it. Wouldn't surprise me if it wasn't Granny give you your dream.'

'You forgot Viv. Grandma.'

'*Viv?* Uncle Jack's Viv? You're joking, aren't you?' Peter asked.

'Her spirit is free. Pete. That's how Jack and Susan communicate with her. Through the spirit.'

'She's all about, is Viv. Head of operations.'

'Head of...?'

'Got them all organised, ain't she, Dorrie? And they've really been giving him a rotten time. Terrible dreams and them spectral visitations.

Any ordinary bloke would've turned hisself in, first off. But he's stubborn, see, on account of he's a pervert. That's right, innit, Dorrie?'

His shoulders sagged. 'I'm trying, Dorrie,' he said, massaging his aching brain. 'Believe me, I'm trying.' He sighed and cast around for help. The knobbed and fretworked wireless cabinet was still burbling quietly on the fireside cupboard. 'What you're saying is half the Potters are on a different wavelength from the rest of us.'

'Not all the time.' It was a good metaphor. 'But we can tune in to a different station.'

Grandma said, briskly, 'You can learn, if you want.' She seemed to be trying to persuade her grandson to do just that. 'If you can't beat 'em, join 'em. Susan had to. What with Jack and then young Viv being the way she is. They reckon we've all got the makings of psychics in us, don't they? Even you, mate.'

'No fear. Leave me out of it.'

'Oh yeah, you'd be surprised. 'Course, late starters ain't never as good – it's like learning the piano. But you're younger than me and your Aunt Lucy was. We never come to it till late, did we, not till after we'd had our first, em... Till we'd lost our, em...' She cleared her throat and, for some reason, blushed to the roots or her curly white hair. 'Till we got married,' she managed at last. 'Have another bit of cake, Peter.'

Gosh, marvelled Dorrie. Fancy that. Of course 'virginity' was the word Grandma had been unable to get her tongue round. She didn't dare look at Peter but she felt the air move as his ears pricked up. Was it the same for boys? she wondered. Would that act be as significant for him as it had been for, gosh, Grandma and Aunt Lucy? And Auntie Susan, presumably. If the genes ran true. He might have done it already. At eighteen, he well might have. Gosh.

Grandma had recovered her dignity and was describing her own shortcomings. She could communicate with the Other Side but she couldn't do the mindreading or the precognition or the healing, not properly, though she sometimes gave Lucy a hand. But Dorrie was their pride and joy, a virtuoso.

Without a word he took up the sketchbook and turned to the unfinished picture of the frogs. Nodded.

'What were you going to do with this? And the others?'

Oh. Slowly she raised her eyes, met her grandmother's, licked her lips. Drawings were not proof, not like photos, to be sure, but you can't take photos of dreams.

Grandma suggested that he finish her crossword: 'Take your mind off it, duck,' while Dorrie finished the frogs. She was off to get her beauty sleep, she declared, with a vain attempt at humour. Sunday was a busy day in her calendar.

'She's looking tired,' Peter whispered as soon as she'd gone.

'She's had an exhausting day,' she said. They both had. But she carried on smoothing the soft graphite with her finger and flicking her eraser over it to give the effect of light on water, reluctant to finish. It was strange to be so emotionally down, so utterly miserable, and yet so full of creative fizz. She knew that if she went to bed now the drawings would flicker through her mind, over and over like a silent movie. She'd never get to sleep.

Screwing the cap back on his pen, Peter yawned. 'That's me done.'

'Finished the crossword?'

He shook his head. 'Brain's given up. Too much to think about tonight.'

'Poor old Pete.'

He inhaled and slowly let out the breath. 'You going straight up?'

'Well...'

'Only I thought I'd stretch my legs for a bit. Just up the road and back.'

A small voice twittered in her head like a sleepy, slightly anxious bird. But a walk was what she needed to calm her down and she owed him her company, at least. He must be bursting with questions.

They went the back way so as not to disturb their grandmother, tiptoed across the cobbled yard to the entry beside Lucy and Joe's and emerged where the gardens fronted the green. The night was warm and scented with honeysuckle and stock and Dorrie stopped to smooth the exquisite sweetness of it into her bare arms, a balm to heal the spirit.

'Cold?'

'No, no,' she smiled, pleased that he was at least sensitive to her needs. Grandma's revelation about psychic awakenings had had a strangely disturbing effect. One might almost describe it as titillating. Scales seemed to be falling from her view of dear old dependable Peter. He certainly wasn't as pretty as John Doubleday, but she thought he might be growing on her. When he regarded her with those deepset black eyes, she felt a sort of lurch inside; whenever he smiled and those creases appeared, like long dimples, in his cheeks, she felt like touching them.

They found themselves drawn, through swishing silver grass, to where the moon admired its three-quarter profile in the starry depths of the pond. It floated there, eyeing them leerily, from its barricade of pale reeds. A frog croaked and she shivered.

'You *are* cold. Do you want my shirt?'

'Good God, no!' His attention was making her feel quite peculiar, almost self-conscious. 'Stop worrying about me. I'm just not very fond of frogs at the moment, or ponds.'

The whites of his eyes gleamed in the moonlight. 'Sorry,' as though it were his fault. 'Didn't think. Come on.'

He took her hand and led her smartly and silently past the church and up the lane where Hooper's neat hedges kept the fields in trim.

'You might have told me you were psychic,' he said, when they were striding towards Doddingworth at a rate of knots. At least, he was striding, she was running and skipping to keep up. 'I thought we were mates.'

'Do you tell *me* everything?' Did he have to go so fast?

'Looks like I don't have to.' She tried to let go but his hand held hers in a vice. 'All these years and it turns out you've been reading my mind!' He sounded angry.

'Peter, Peter,' she puffed, at last. 'For goodness sake, where are we going? Slow down!'

He stopped, then, in the middle of the road and took her by the shoulders. His fingers dug into her sunburn and she winced. She couldn't see his face, just his silhouette against the stars.

'It's true, is it? You read minds?'

'I can, but I don't often. It's prying.'

'Well, pry a little, woman. What am I thinking?' He gave her a shake.

'Peter...' His intensity frightened her. She'd never known him like this before. Not with her.

'Go on,' he taunted, 'see if you're right.'

'No.' She turned her face away. 'Let go of me!' She tried to twist out of his grasp.

'Look at me.'

She wouldn't. 'Don't bully me, Peter. I don't want to know what you're thinking. It would only spoil things. I don't want that.'

'Too late, sweetheart – it's spoiled already.' As tears sprang to her eyes, as she shook her head in denial, he caught her chin, forced her face in line with his. 'Tell me,' he growled.

Very quietly she said, 'Stop it, Peter.' His glittering eyes challenged her to their depths. She saw confusion. She saw... 'Please,' she begged.

And as suddenly as he'd rounded on her released her, swung away as though he couldn't bear the sight of her.

'Fuck,' she heard him say.

In despair and disgust she turned and blundered back towards the village, her eyes swimming with tears. She knew this was how he'd react. That's why she'd never told him.

She heard him coming, metal segs striking gravel as he ran.

'Dorrie. Dorrie, wait.' He caught her up. 'Don't, oh don't cry.' He put an arm round her shoulders.

'I'm not,' she lied, twisting free and sniffing. Blast the boy.

His arm dropped limply by his side. 'I ... oh God, I hate having to apologise to you.'

'Why?' She turned her head away to wipe her eyes.

'You don't know?'

She sucked her teeth. 'If I knew I wouldn't need to ask, would I?'

'All right, all right.'

'Well?' she said shortly, not giving an inch.

'Because I'd have to say, "Sorry, Dorrie" and it sounds so corny.'

A dry laugh caught in her throat.

'Dorrie, please, look at me.'

'What?' giving him a stony stare.

'If you can read minds you know what.'

'What?' she repeated. 'You're gonna have to tell me, Pete, I'm not going to make it easy for you.'

'You know.'

'I don't.'

His face, in the darkness, was invisible, apart from silver flickers of night in his eyes, and on his smooth young lips when he licked them. In contrast his mind was a blaze of light, a bright stage in a dark theatre. But she remained silent, staring blankly at the action. She would not, *would not*, see whatever it was he was so shy of telling her.

'Oh come on, Dorrie, help me out.'

For answer she raised an eyebrow and pursed her lips tight, too tight for speech.

He sighed. 'I'm sorry I upset you. I don't want to spoil things between us either. I think we're pretty good ... well, I hope we're, em, friends.' He took in a big breath of night air and out came the words in a rush: 'I'd rather be your friend, knowing you can read my mind, than not be friends at all.'

Knowing you can read my mind... That was saying something, she thought. That was saying, *'Knowing you'll discover my secrets, that you'll probe all my weaknesses, it's okay, I'll let you.'*

That was saying a hell of a lot. He must trust her. He must be quite fond of her. Maybe. It was nice of him, anyway.

'Oh come here, dope,' she said, and reached up to kiss him on the cheek.

Someone, he or she, or both, gasped with joy or relief, or simply because the breath was squashed out of them when he opened his arms and crushed her against him. Alarmed, she stiffened, and then, as his mouth, warm and insistent, moved over her own, all the separate, slightly worrying emotions that Dorrie had been feeling towards her cousin, fused into mouths and teeth and tongues. Gosh. That's what it was all about then. She'd been wanting to do this all along. With him. Who was reading whose mind here?

She closed her eyes and, just out of curiosity, allowed herself to dip into his thoughts.

And was washed away on a tidal wave. It took her breath away. It was delight, it was laughter, it was crazy, it was wonderful. Who'd've thought it? That he had all this locked up inside him? Only a fraction had showed in his glistening eyes. The rest, the intense feeling, the passion, had been buried deep and tight, as it grew and grew.

'Oh, Dorrie.' His groan was muffled but it alerted her to what was happening in the physical world. His lips were hot on her neck and his fingers were inside her bra, stroking and gently kneading her nipple. Gosh. She decided he couldn't possibly know the effect that it was having on her, that it was like an electric charge crackling through her insides, switching on incredible stirrings and throbbings in all sorts of unmentionable places, so unmentionable she was blushing with shame. Or something. Now she couldn't breathe at all. But she didn't dare tell him. He might have stopped.

She was finding it increasingly hard to keep her balance, to stay upright, in fact. Not only were her knees turning to mush, instinct and gravity were pulling her down to the grass verge...

She loved the smell of him, the scrunch of his wiry hair in her fingers, his teeth nibbling her ear. She loved the pressure of his thighs and that hard insistence in his trousers. The weight of him on top of her. She loved it all. But this was getting serious.

Gently she disengaged herself. 'Peter...'

Like a sleeper he surfaced, blinking into reality. His teeth gleamed. He was grinning.

'You read my mind.'

'Didn't need to,' she said, through bruised lips. 'It was pretty obvious. I'm not ready for that. Not yet. Sorry.'

He swallowed. 'Yeah, you're right. Come on, then.' He helped her up and brushed grass seed off her skirt, lingering over her bottom. He seemed to like it. Before she could protest he had pulled her to him again and their teeth were clashing. She was awfully glad Arthur had broken her brace. There was something to thank him for after all, though what she'd have done tonight with a split lip she didn't know.

Little by little she steered him homewards.

'I don't know what my dad's going to say,' she said. 'Kissing cousins shouldn't, according to him.'

'Sod that,' he said dismissively, and kissed her again. She left it at that. It wasn't her secret to tell, after all.

'What are the clues?' They were head-to-head over the crossword, reluctant to part, even for sleep.

'Eleven across *"Passes on without a struggle"*, two words, five and four letters.'

'"Passes on?" Gosh.' She was reminded of the ghosts of Stanbury Manor, whose passing was going to have to be assisted, sooner or later, but it wasn't something to worry Peter with, not on top of everything else. 'Well,' she said, "passes on" is hands, isn't it? That's the first word, HANDS. What? Hands over? Hands down?'

'HANDS DOWN,' he decided. It was all to do with inheritance.

'Well, that's appropriate,' she said, removing one of his from under her blouse so that he could write it in with swift, slanting left-handed letters.

'So what's one down then? *"He's just up and looking less tired,"* seven letters, first letter F, fifth letter H, last letter R.'

'Just up?' she laughed. 'That's appropriate, too.'

'Mmm,' he murmured. There followed a short interval as he traced her eyes with his finger. 'I've always loved your eyes, specially the wonky one.'

'Oh God, is it wonky now?'

'Slightly.'

'It's because I'm tired.'

He kissed her closed eyelid and said, apropos of nothing, 'FRESHER! That's it. Just up ... at university. And looking less tired – it has to be FRESHER.'

She yawned. 'Oh God, but I'm not. I'm going to have to go to bed.'

'I'll just fill that one in.'

'Where's your pen?'

Sighing, he picked it up and dropped it again as though it were alive. A navy blot soaked into the paper. 'It moved!' he marvelled.

She giggled, 'It's only Viv. She loves puzzles. Go on, let her do it.'

'No fear!'

'Chicken.'

The magic word. Now he had to prove himself. As he plucked at the pen, his mouth muscled tight, and fell slackly open again as the empty squares were filled with small, neat letters: FRESHER. Then the pen, with Peter's hand attached, completed the five other missing words at lightning speed and moved to the busy margin of the paper. Among worked-out anagrams and Dorrie's sinister doodles, a message appeared.

Hello, Peter-cousin. Welcome to you and a big thanks for the dream. We had fun. Not so the detective who is now primed for confession, I am sure. The drawings will clinch, surely. Goodnight to you and to Dorrie-not-cousin, also. Love from Viv.

'What does she mean, Dorrie-not-cousin?'

'Typing error,' she said, too tired to go into long explanations.

His eyes narrowed. 'Dor-*rie!*'

'What?' She couldn't meet the reproachful look.

'I don't pretend to understand how she does all this,' he flicked at the paper, 'when she's so ... helpless physically, but one thing's quite clear from the way she writes – that little kid's a stickler. Meticulous. She doesn't make mistakes. If she says you're not her cousin, there has to be a reason for it.'

She gazed at him adoringly. He improved minute by minute. Even if he couldn't read minds (and wouldn't it save a lot of trouble if he could?) his judgement of people was red hot. Better than hers. She gave in and smiled.

'She's a little stirrer.'

'So? What? Are you adopted or something?'

'Illegitimate.' It was the first time she'd said it aloud. There were a few first times tonight. It was a harsh and ugly word, like bastard. It made her eyes sting. 'I'm not Arthur Potter's daughter, so we're not related, you and me.'

He took her hands. 'I thought there was something,' he said, leading her to the sofa, where she could snuggle more comfortably into his shoulder and tell him about her mother's affair with an unnamed docker in the war.

'Dad doesn't know.'

'I didn't think he did. Not with the ear-wigging he gave me, warning me off. He spotted I was keen on you a month or two back.'

'Well, I didn't.'

'No. For a clairvoyante you're pretty dim,' he teased. 'Anyway he got quite shirty, your old man. Told me if I had any ideas about you to forget them. Intermarriage isn't good for the genes, apparently.'

She said firmly, 'I'm not thinking about marriage, Peter, not for a long, long time.'

'Me neither,' he said, without a trace of hesitation. 'Places to go, things to do. But your dad was quite clear. Much as he liked me, he said, he wasn't having you and me spawning two-headed freaks.'

'Freaks, maybe. The Potters are a weird bunch.'

'Look who's talking!'

'Imagine if our kids had something awful like the Habsburg jaw.'

'Habsburg? Isn't that the boxer, lives in Eddison Road? If any of our kids looked like him I'd kill them.'

She hit him. 'The Habsburg dynasty, dope. Ruled Central Europe for centuries. Interbred madly and finished up with chins like open drawers.' She demonstrated, pushing her lower jaw forward as far as she could. 'One of them couldn't chew solids because his teeth didn't meet, and *his* son was born with his jaw dislocated so badly there was a hole under his left ear. Velázquez had to paint his portrait showing his right profile, which is unusual, because the left side was so awful. *Things* kept appearing in this hole.'

'Ugh!' There was a pause as his stomach settled, then, 'Dorrie, you didn't tell your dad this tale, by any chance?'

'Yep. It's probably my fault he gave you what for. But I wasn't to know you'd seduce me, was I?'

'*Seduce* you? Chance'd be a fine thing.'

'Anyway, you didn't let Dad put you off. That was nice.'

'No, well, I talked to Gran about it. She said we were made for each other. Not *quite* sure what she meant by that, but we seem to have her blessing, whatever we decide to do. I take it she knows that Uncle Arthur's not your dad?'

She nodded. 'And she's not my Grandma, either. That's the worst thing about this. I wish,

425

I really wish she was.'

'That can be arranged,' he grinned. 'One day,' he added hastily, seeing her begin to frown. 'If we're still together. Come to think of it, I wouldn't be surprised if it hadn't already occurred to her. Get us together and she could still be your granny. By marriage.'

They froze as the ceiling creaked above their heads. It could have been the house cooling after the heat of the day or it could have been an old lady climbing into bed after listening through the floor to a conversation that concerned her intimately. Throwing their arms around each other they stifled their giggles in various warm and receptive hollows and crevices.

Chapter Twenty-Two

What had woken her? The breeze fluttering the curtain? A grey finger of light scratching at the cracks in the ceiling? Erotic images winging their way from the mind of the sleeper downstairs?

She stretched, smug as a cream-fed cat. Allowed his dream to waft around her like gauze about some coy Botticelli nude. Closed her eyes and saw herself as his subconscious invented her, pearly and voluptuous, her nipples tender pink, her hair golden. Slipping into that rosy image like a hand into a glove, she felt her skin begin to tingle, her pulses to quicken. In the dim confines of the room she kissed her smooth inner arm, substituting her lips for his, moved her fingers to her breast where, in his dream, his tongue was flicking, and then down to where he was stroking between her legs, finding it wet. She gasped. Would he do that? And that? In his dreams? Her breath was coming quickly, she was groaning, *'Oh Peter, oh no, oh yes!'* when the cottage was shaken by fists pounding on the front door and she shot out of bed.

'Mrs P! Mrs P!'

Dorrie was halfway down the stairs when she heard Peter working back the bolts and growling, 'Bloody good mind to punch your poxy teeth down your throat. No bloody sense... Bloody Sunday morning, people a-bloody-sleep... Gonna give my gran a poxy heart-attack!'

It was Doubleday in a frenzy, a moth-eaten overcoat slung over his pyjamas, leather mules on his feet and his wisp of gingery hair sticking up anyhow as he attempted to elbow his way into the house. He looked to Dorrie as if he'd had a fright or a rough night or both, but Peter didn't care who he was or what his humour, he was not going to let the man within spitting distance of their grandmother. If the landowner wanted a fight he could have one, he said, giving him a backward shove, and another. It was startling to see him so aggressive but not so surprising knowing the rudeness of his awaken-ing.

'Peter, Peter!' Grandma called from the stairs. She was having to take them slowly. The 'screws' always gave her gyp first thing in the morning. The banister creaked as she leaned all her weight on it and Dorrie felt a stab of fear. If she fell, if she died, there'd be no saving her. Her face was strangely naked without her wire-framed glasses and her dressing gown hung loose, cords trailing. She only had to put a foot wrong...

'Don't rush, Grandma,' Dorrie said, glad when the old woman reached ground level. 'Here, let's make you decent.' There was a comb on the shelf over the range and Dorrie ran it through the flattened curls until they fluffed out in a cloud of white. Between them they found her glasses and fastened her dressing gown. It was five past four.

'I'll put the kettle on,' Dorrie whispered. 'You go and give him what for.'

The stove had been banked up overnight and she riddled it to make the ashes fall through, then levered off the hob and poked in sticks of kindling and some small coal. Not too much or it would put out the tiny glow. Even over her racket she could hear Doubleday's raised voice. Grandma wasn't saying much. Even Peter had lost his tongue. Gently she opened the damper. Only when the flames began to roar did she shovel on more coal and replace the heavy cast-iron lid. That done she filled the kettle and set it on the stove. By then she knew the worst of it.

Ghosts had rattled around all night – bones, sabres, chains or anything else they could lay their hands on to ensure that Doubleday didn't get a wink of sleep. Heavy footsteps had clumped along the landing, water or some other more viscous liquid (Doubleday hadn't felt inclined to investigate too closely) had dripped rhythmically and incessantly in the next bedroom, and spectres had come and gone, at will, through his room, in and out of the walls, up and down through the floorboards and ceiling. It was like Piccadilly Circus, he said. It occurred to him that, of course, the master bedroom would attract the most attention and when there seemed to be a lull in the traffic, he'd crept out of bed and scurried downstairs looking for peace and quiet, but there, slowly turning on a creaking rope in the stairwell, he found the Hon Hugo and, by the time he reached the kitchen, the chambermaid was

429

there, wringing her hands and sobbing fit to bust, with a bullet-hole in her apron. Few had died quietly, it seemed. Moaning and shrieking and lamentations had continued all night and he had spent the last couple of hours curled up with his horse in the stable. And it was all Mrs P's fault. She had to do something!

'You said you wanted haunting,' she said reasonably.

'I wanted it to *appear* that way, woman. Controllable by switches and pulleys. I didn't ask for ... didn't *dream,* there'd be this infestation! You've got to get rid of them!' he stormed, banging his fist on the table.

'Steady on,' said the old woman. 'These walls are thin in case you hadn't noticed.'

He lowered his voice a decibel or two. It had to be done now, this minute. What did she expect him to do – camp out in the stables? A fine thing when a man couldn't call his home his own, when every room was occupied by some blood-splattered spectre moaning and complaining.

Unnoticed by the bullyragger, Peter caught Dorrie's eye as she stood in the doorway waiting for the kettle to boil. One quizzical brow rose like a raven's wing and he circled his forefinger at his temple. *Was Doubleday round the bend?*

She explained, 'Mr Doubleday got Grandma and me to hold a séance yesterday afternoon over at the Manor.'

'It was a bit of fun, child. Nobody seriously believed that we'd be visited by a ... by a plague of ... of...' He was lost for words.

'*Fun?* But we understood you wanted to raise

430

the family ghosts in order to attract visitors. Apparently,' she said for Peter's benefit, 'some people will pay good money to spend a night in a haunted manor house and be scared witless.'

'And now you've changed your mind?' Peter addressed the landlord.

'Well, quite. The sooner your grandmother gets over there and sorts it out, the better.'

'Oh,' said Grandma, from her high horse. 'Really? Well, I don't know as I can. Not on me own.'

Doubleday went a shade paler. 'You do perform exorcisms?'

'Friendly persuasion, I call it. See, your average ghost, he don't want all that bell, book and candle stuff, just straightening out about a few things. Most likely he don't even know he's dead, poor soul, on account of he's been done in. His spirit was shot out of his body without a by-your-leave and he ain't got no idea what's going on. Like he's a fly caught behind a curtain. The window's open but all he knows is he's trapped. He can't get a word of sense out of no one round him and he's in such a tiz he can't hear them on the Other Side trying to tell him to come over. You gotta go careful. It's a shock for a ghost, being told he's been dead two hundred years and he'd be best off out of it. If he gets the wind up and goes buzzing off half-cocked, there ain't no knowing where he might finish up. Don't want him burning in hell, poor devil. Now you got dozens of the buggers over there, a bleeding football team. One at a time I'd be all day and no dinner hour. Any case it

431

wouldn't be safe, not on me own. No, Mr Doubleday, I'm gonna need reinforcements, mate. That ain't gonna be easy, of a Sunday. Busy day, Sunday.'

'But...' His cry of dismay was almost heart-rending. Here was a man who wasn't used to having his demands denied.

Dorrie stopped wrestling with an image of flies in football boots and asked, 'How many others would you need, Grandma?'

'Oh, I dunno, two or three. I know you're strong, Dor, but you ain't never done one of these before. Might take a couple of goes to get the hang of it. Luce'll help out, I'm sure,' – try and keep her away, thought Dorrie – 'but the others'll have to be brought in from Sowness and Lowestoft and Diss – all over.'

'Sounds as if it might cost you a bit, squire,' said Peter, 'to make it worth their while. What do you think, Gran, a tenner each plus expenses?'

'Sunday rates,' agreed Grandma, wetting her lips and trying to keep a straight face. 'That's if you want it done today, of course.'

'Oh yes, yes, soon as you can.'

'Problem is, these light evenings. Best really in the dark.' She was cruel. The poor man's face was getting longer and longer at the prospect of having to wait until nine or ten o'clock that night. 'You ain't got no blackout left over from the war, I don't suppose?'

'No-oo,' came the dismal reply. Then he brightened. 'But the lounge has shutters.'

'Well, I'll see what I can do. Maybe we can

arrange something for this morning.'

His relief was audible. 'But I don't know if I can afford–'

'Perhaps we can come to an arrangement,' said Dorrie brightly. 'Mutually beneficial. An idea I've had – I've already mentioned it to John.'

'Have you?' he said faintly.

'He didn't say?'

'No,' he said shortly, paused, then revealed with a curl of the lip that John, his 'snivelling son', had bolted at the first sight of spectral appearance and hadn't been seen since.

Dorrie thought that sounded rather sensible, actually. In thrillers and chillers her antennae twanged whenever people insisted they'd 'be all right' alone in a house when a murderer was on the prowl, knowing they were doomed. And when they actually heard noises on the stairs in the middle of the night, why on earth did they get up to investigate? 'Don't open the door!' she would whimper, peeping through her fingers but, of course, they always did, and deserved all they got.

'So you were in the house by yourself last night?' she observed.

Doubleday grunted.

Was that a yes? There were the servants, of course, but old Jeeves or Jenkins or whatever his name was, lived in a cottage in the grounds, according to John, and Cook, she of the egg sandwiches, and Fifi, the French maid, lived in the village. Then there was Phoebe Bussage, of course. Making hay while her husband slept off the Madeira.

433

'Right then, I think we've got the picture. Don't worry, Mr Doubleday,' said Peter, manoeuvring the man through the door, 'we won't let you suffer too long. Now I, for one, need some sleep. We have a busy day ahead of us. Cheerio.'

As Dorrie backed the door closed, she could hardly contain her laughter. Grandma said, 'Ooh my good Gawd!' and Peter swore.

After a cup of tea they went back to bed but Dorrie slept only fitfully. There was too much to think about.

There was Peter. There was the clearing at the Doubledays. Gosh. This was growing up fast. And even as she was telling herself that she must stop saying 'Gosh', she found herself staring at the waking face of Gerald Webb, his mouth in rictus, as if on a scream...

...Of anger, of red, roaring anger. He refused to be afraid, to feel any namby-pamby cowardly emotion. Anger was safe.

Another bloody dream. Where had it come from? And why? Jesus. He mustn't think about drowning. Even as the word entered his thoughts he was bucking with terror. No, oh God, not the screaming abdabs. He would drive himself mad. He would. Because that was the thing, wasn't it? He'd brought it on himself. Must have. All that stuff must have been in his head. Where else do dreams come from? All that stupid guilt: no need for it, no need at all. He was a policeman. It was his job to crush evil. All that rot about confession. Confess to what? Doing his duty? Pathetic how the mind can play tricks. Laughable.

How would he feel when he saw the pictures she'd drawn of that very dream: the frogs, the water, the mirror, the little girl? Would he dare to be afraid then? Would he be so afraid that he would want to make it all stop? By confessing? Would he? Or would his twisted mind manage to explain the drawings away, too?

It was almost nine when they told Lucy, and then Grandma got to grips with contacting her friends. They could hear her through the party wall, above the background of the wireless and the occasional squeals of children. She was still wary of the telephone and tended to hold it at arm's length, which was just as well for the person at the other end who would otherwise have been deafened. Well, it was a long way from here to there. You had to shout. Dorrie and Peter gave up any pretence of reading the Sunday papers.

'*That you, Eric? Oh Wally ... Eric there, is he? Well, get him up, mate – this is an emergency.*' There was a pause as she waited. Then, at top volume, the situation was explained and Eric co-opted for the project. '*What about who? Gladys? I doubt it. She's got her daughter coming over today, and the new baby. Who else? Who? Name rings a bell. Don't think I know him, do I? Oh that's why then, if he subs for me, stands to reason I ain't never met him. So this bloke, do you think he'd help out? You sure? Put Wally on, again, dear, will you?*'

'*What do you think, Wal? Only, if we got this bloke we wouldn't need to ask Glad. So how soon can he get here, your friend? Sooner the better, really – old*

435

Doubleday's tearing his hair out. Yeah, right. So that's me and Luce, young Dorrie and Eric and this pal o' yourn, that should be plenty. Eh? Yeah, come up to see me, she did, all on her own. Oh yeah, she's a big girl now.'

Peter nudged Dorrie.

'And Peter, my grandson.'

She nudged him back.

'Try keeping him away ... Eh? Oh yeah, love's young dream.'

They sprang apart as though she could see them. But there were no spy-holes in the wallpaper. Had they been so obvious this morning over breakfast? Touching, looking, trying not to grin like Cheshire cats? Probably. Cheeky old woman, though, discussing their love-life with all and sundry.

'Well, that's just it, Wally, it don't look like we're doing no good at all. No. No, she's drawn some pictures though – thinks they might change his mind. Eh? Pictures of a dream she's sent him, Wally. Bit of a shock, yeah. Like we're showing him we know. Hope so. Yeah, we'll have to wait and see. So you'll tell Eric eleven? And fetch your friend over? Right. Bye, then, dear.'

Dorrie slid a look of dismay at Peter and they both inhaled deeply. Mention of Webb had made them forget to breathe. The papers were still speculating about the whereabouts of James Halliday, nicknamed 'The Fiend'. There had been unsubstantiated sightings as far afield as Minehead and Stirling. Somebody had even seen him boarding the ferry at Dover. And while he was free, of course, every child was in danger.

436

There were pages packed with articles about men who preyed on children, unsolved murders, about how child-killers should be punished, what the parents of the victims thought about it all. Those were the headlines: *Hanging's too good for him*. Dorrie nibbled her thumbnail. The predator was psyching himself up for another kill. And soon.

At eleven o'clock, as church bells gave up on lie-abeds, four mediums and Peter, who had insisted on coming too, were waiting on the steps of Stanbury Manor for Ralph Doubleday to stop scurrying here, there and everywhere, like a coot, and let them into his haunted house.

'How far does he have to come, your friend?'

'Sowness,' said Grandma, shortly.

Eric was anxious. 'Walter went off s-s-straight after b-b-breakfast ... to, em, to take over the, em, b-b-business m-m-matter. I c-c-can't think what's happened.'

'Don't worry,' said Lucy, rubbing his arm to take the stutter away. 'I'm sure they won't be long, and if the worst comes to the worst we'll have to do what we can, just the four of us. We'll manage. We've got Granny Farthing and Robbie to do the honours from their side and Viv as go-between. As long as there's someone manning the defences we should be all right.'

'And someone to make the tea,' said Grandma, nodding happily as the butler joined them, looking somewhat apprehensive. He'd always felt a sadness in the kitchen, he admitted, despite Cook's bustle and laughter, and wasn't too surprised to learn that that was where the chambermaid had met her fate. Unlike Cook, he was a sensitive soul, and if a perturbèd spirit was abroad, so to speak (he actually said 'perturbèd'. but it was wasted on Grandma), he would rather not be handling the best china when it happened. Grandma assured him that the kitchen would be the first to be cleared and, with that thought in mind, suggested that they'd better go in. Perhaps a quick prayer wouldn't come amiss.

Doubleday waited by the front door, nervously rattling his keys, an older, wiser man than the arrogant host of yesterday. He hadn't been back, he said, since he'd vacated the premises at first light. Some kind person had provided him with clothes and a shave, and presumably a meal, to boot. Good old Jenkins, thought Dorrie. Or Phoebe Bussage.

Inside, the house was like a tomb; not a sound, not a peep from the ghosts. They must have worn themselves out. But the chill of the vestibule clung to the visitors as they made their way to the lounge, and Eric wriggled as though an icicle had been dropped inside his crisp white shirt collar. Lucy shivered and raised her eyes to heaven and Peter rolled down his shirtsleeves.

The lounge was on the first floor, the room from which Doubleday had spotted Dorrie trespassing two years earlier. The stale warmth struck them as they entered, unpleasant as an ash-tray. There was a great barren fireplace with crossed swords above it and a tapestry fire-screen depicting a gory battle-scene, across from which a gigantic black oak chiffonier stretched almost the length of the wall. At one end, like a brooding black toad, sat a two-foot-high Buddha, and at the other, as a counter-weight, an ornamental clock, all pillars and turrets and curlicues, stopped at seven twenty-five. Dorrie searched for a deep meaning to this arrangement while the shutters were being closed, but could find none. A grand piano, scuffed with neglect and out of tune, as Eric quickly discovered, straddled one corner. He gave them a few bars of 'The Deadwood Stage' and gave up. The room wasn't in the mood.

'Think positive,' whispered Auntie Lucy, smiling bravely as she joined her niece and nephew on one of two matching chesterfields, opposite Grandma, in baby-blue Courtelle, and Eric, sharp in knife-crease flannels, blazer and cravat. He took care with his clothes. He was a 'bachelor gay' according to Grandma. Dorrie had always thought that meant that he chose to live alone rather than marry. Yet he lived with Walter. That must almost be as bad as having a wife. 'Nancy-boy' had flitted across Peter's mind, but she was sure he was wrong. Charles, Mum's boss, was a nancy-boy, according to Dad. He wore drainpipes, curled his hair and plucked his eyebrows, a real show-off, but the kindest man on earth, Mum said. Meaning that Dad wasn't.

She hoped Mum hadn't got into trouble last night, for giving her the fare to Grandma's. She didn't actually want to go back home tonight. Or ever. Suppose Mum hadn't talked him round? She usually did, but just suppose? What would Dad do when he found out that she and Peter were more than just friends? What if Dad hit her again? She couldn't *keep* running away. If Mum had married Frank – if Frank had been her father from the start – they would all have been happy. For Mum's sake and hers he'd have gone straight. He'd have helped Mum to understand about clairvoyancy, and life would have been so different for their gifted daughter. But then she wouldn't have known Grandma.

And then there was Detective Inspector Gerry Webb. What if he didn't confess? She swallowed. Positive thinking, Auntie Lucy had said. Some hopes.

It felt like sitting in a waiting room at the dentist's or somewhere equally sterile and nasty, without the option of a six-months-old copy of *Reader's Digest* to take up the tedium. There was a coffee table between the two ranks of visitors, the latest thing from America, wildly out of keeping with the rest of the room, but there was nothing on it to read, just a carafe of water and a few glasses on a tray. Two standard lamps were switched on, but they only seemed to add to the gloom.

'*Who's died?*' said Granny Farthing tactlessly, materialising on the arm of Grandma's chesterfield and gazing round with undisguised distaste. '*It's like a bleeding funeral parlour in here, all these long faces. And the furniture don't help. Anyone want a pear drop?*'

'Shove up,' said Dorrie. Peter obliged and looked around for someone to fill the gap but

440

Robbie already had. There was no need, of course, and he flowed into the overstuffed arm without any obvious discomfort. He was all grown up and everything he'd ever wanted to be: fit, early twenties, in the prime of life, with a knobby pear-drop in his cheek. He wouldn't grow any older now. They made a handsome couple, he and Viv, for she, too, was with them in spirit, resting a proprietary hand on Robbie's broad shoulder. She was blonde, eighteen or nineteen years old and with Auntie Susan's delicate prettiness. So different from the crippled shell she'd vacated in Newcastle. Would it come right for Dorrie, too, in the afterlife, and for Mum and Frank? Perhaps there was a right person for Dad too. Someone who liked being bullied. Would it all be sorted out?

'*Cheer up, Dorrie not-cousin-yet,*' grinned Viv. '*Developments are happening.*' A truism? A conundrum? Meaning what? That Viv knew something she didn't. Unaccountably she began to feel more cheerful.

'Coming along nicely,' she replied, smiling for the first time since entering the room. Peter squeezed her hand gratefully. 'How about you?'

'*Ditto,*' she said smugly, and Robbie looked up at the girl with a smile of complete devotion.

'Dorrie,' said Peter anxiously, 'who are you talking to?'

'Viv.' She squeezed his hand back. 'Don't worry. Tell you later.' His Adam's apple slid bravely up and down his throat.

'Let's get on with it then,' said Grandma. 'Now Ralph, there ain't no need for you to stop

441

in here if it worries you. In fact, you'd be best off on sentry duty. Don't want no one barging in, do we? Got enough distractions to be going on with.'

For some reason they were all looking at Dorrie.

'What?' she demanded.

'You ready, duck?' but that wasn't it. Was it about Peter? She cast around for clues, but barriers were up and her probes were deflected. Of course, they'd all armed themselves against takeover by dark entities. She thought she'd better do the same.

It was heartbreaking to see the phantoms, victims of violence, beating an obsessive path to madness, over and over the same baffling ground, like caged animals, indifferent to anyone else, alive or dead.

The only way to get them to notice you was to tune yourself to their wavelength. Even so the little chambermaid was in such a state of agitation, rubbing ineffectually at her blood-stained pinny with her hanky, and worrying about the dreadful things Her Ladyship would say, it was some minutes before she realised that Grandma and Eric were trying to make themselves heard over her wailing. She had forgotten the reason for her predicament and was quite taken aback when Grandma reminded her about her 'interesting' condition. Then she threw her apron over her head and refused to be comforted.

She'd lose her job and whatever would become of her? And if His Lordship wouldn't provide for his bastard then she'd threaten to tell Her Ladyship. Little by little her sobs subsided as she realised what had happened, that His Lordship had shot her and that she had been a ghost for seventy years. Eric explained that the baby's spirit had already departed and was flourishing on the Other Side. What really won her over, however, was the thought of getting out of her dirty clothes and putting on a clean apron.

'One down, sixteen to go,' said Grandma, opening her eyes. 'Oh bli, Peter, you all right, mate?'

He was white and shivering. '*W-What* was th-that?' he stammered.

'What?' they all asked.

'That t-terrible feeling of c-c-cold?'

'Tch,' tutted Grandma. 'Sorry, son, I should've warned you – it's as they go over to the Other Side. It disturbs the atmosphere, see. Even if there's a roaring fire, all the heat goes out of the room. What you need is a nice cup of tea to warm you up.'

As Dorrie and Lucy rubbed his arms to get his circulation moving, she summoned the landlord from his post on the landing. 'You can tell Jenkins he can put the kettle on now.'

'Is it done?'

'Her in the kitchen's done. There's a few more besides. You'd better tell your man to knock up a few sandwiches for later, unless you want us all fainting away for lack of nourishment. And Ralph,' she beckoned him down to her level, so she could whisper, 'not egg, eh? They ain't conducive.'

The next to be approached was the grumpy old man, Henry Doubleday, who knew precisely why they wanted to be rid of him, he declared, and he had no intention of going: they could be quite clear about that. The only way they'd get their hands on his nest egg was over his dead body.

Grandma sat him down and explained, gently, that that was, in fact, what had happened. His murderers, his own family, were all dead and gone and it was too late to do a thing about it. He listened but he wasn't convinced.

'It's a trick,' he snarled. *'You just want to find out where it is. But I shan't tell you, I shan't.'* And he clammed up, stubborn as only old people and children can be. They assured him they had no interest in any personal fortune, that it was still there, wherever he'd hidden it, and could stay there for another hundred years for all they cared.

'Come with me,' said the beautiful Viv, and not even an old miser could resist her charms. Off they toddled, hand-in-hand, and where she took him, through the closed door, was to see the Hon Hugo, dangling at the end of his rope.

'Hugo,' the old man sobbed. *'Dear boy! Why? Why?'*

Viv broke it to him that Hugo, his favourite grandson, had in fact, been the instrument of his death, and he remembered then, how he had woken that night, unable to get his breath, found a pillow over his face and strong hands pressing down.

'As you see,' said Viv, *'the dishonourable deed lay*

so *heavily upon his conscience that he preferred finally to die than bear it. Nobody even suspected that a fortune resided in this very house. The liquid assets in the bank very soon ran dry, all stocks and bonds were swiftly converted and spent, and today, the Doubleday family is down to selling its heirlooms.'*

The old man groaned. *'I was goin' to tell him, stupid boy, I had it planned. They would have been my dyin' words, to him alone, and he would have been eternally grateful. Too late now, too late. Me own damned stupid fault.'*

'It is possible you shall meet and mend on the Other Side.'

'Is it? Shall we? Hrrm. And this Other Side, m'dear, will you be there? Dashed trim little filly, if I might say so,' and, having recovered a little of his *joie de vivre,* he patted her bottom in a decidedly old-fashioned way. Robbie, deeming it high time he had a hand in this, took the old boy by the arm and, gently but firmly, led him out onto the astral plane.

'Now then, Dorrie,' said Grandma, refreshed by tea, 'how about it?' Ready to have a go? You can do the dishonourable Hugo if you want.'

It wasn't her fault, they assured her, but whose if not hers? You couldn't blame Walter. He'd swallowed his breakfast and set off for Sowness straight after, according to Eric. If traffic had delayed him, if the beach hut was all locked up when he arrived with just a few salty towels flapping on the line and a bucket of shells on the step, it wasn't his fault, either. The beach would have been bristling with deckchairs. He was bound to have had trouble finding them.

You might have blamed Doubleday for not being there to prevent the intruder barging in at the critical moment though, in the circumstances, deserting his post was perfectly understandable. That, also, was down to her.

It was easy to get Hugo to accept his death. The rope was still round his neck. What he couldn't face was an afterlife. His guilt was such, he felt, that he should go on hanging and suffering for all eternity. Hell's retribution, no matter how painful, amounted to being let off the hook. They told him, then, that his grandfather was waiting for him on the Other Side, so sorry about his suicide, ready to forgive and forget. In fact, as Dorrie told him, the old miser blamed himself. If he had made his intentions clearer, sooner, if he had told the boy where his secret wealth was hidden, Hugo would not have resorted to such extreme measures. Depressed as he was, the Hon raised a spark of curiosity. Always supposing there had been such a hoard, and it wasn't simply a ploy to get him out of the house, where was it? There, Dorrie was unable to enlighten him and he, again, hung his head.

'In the library.'

'How do you know that, Grandma?'

'It's where we found him, prowling up and down, guarding them books with his life. Sad, innit? On his poor old feet for a hundred years... I wondered why he chose to be there rather than in his bed where he belonged.'

Which was when Doubleday, with his ear to

the door, must have taken off.

Hugo was determined to be miserable. Dorrie tried all sorts. His feelings of guilt did him credit, she said. Pity others didn't have the same regrets, mentioning no names. But a hundred years was punishment enough, and perhaps he should now be thinking of his progeny and how they felt. A man hanging in the stairwell was not the most decorative of home furnishings, after all. And, if it made him happy, she was sure the Other Side would have no objections to his bringing his rope with him.

He was, she felt, almost persuaded, when a man burst into the room, apologising for not having arrived earlier.

Too late he saw Dorrie's jaw drop, heard her squeak of dismay. Too late he grasped the situation and put out a spiritual hand to grab the rope as it whisked by.

'Oops!' murmured Auntie Lucy, as the Hon Hugo vanished into thin air, and Frank Leary was left clutching at straws.

Chapter Twenty-Three

'Sorry, Dorrie,' groaned the latecomer. And it did sound corny.

Her mother would have been proud of her. 'S'okay,' she thought she may have said, bravely, witlessly, even though something awful was happening. She blinked hard but jagged splinters of light crazed her vision.

Peter, beside her, slopped water into a glass, one-handed, the other being gripped fast by hers. But she couldn't drink. Her head was like lead, more than her neck could support.

'...between her knees.' Lucy's voice was muffled by a heavy beating of wings. Iron hands tipped her forward. 'And can someone open a window?'

'...bit of light on the subject.' Grandma said, through a funnel. 'It won't make no difference now – the damage is done.'

Shutters banged and the carpet bloomed round her feet, queasy greens and browns. She should sit up, look at him in the light, but not yet. Her eyelids fell shut again. She heard the drag of a window on its sash. Another. Felt a movement of air. Breathed.

'Takes you that way when you're interrupted. You shouldn't *never* butt in on a medium in a trance. You of all people should know that.' Someone was getting at someone.

'Are you all right?' His voice was shockingly close; heavy fingers were stroking her hair and her nerve endings winced. She shook him off with a grunt of annoyance, and forced her eyelids apart. He was perched on the coffee table, his face contorted with regret. 'I could kick myself,' he said, 'barging in like that. I didn't think. Can you forgive me?'

'Ain't her you should be asking. Poor old Hugo's the one's gone whizzing off like a party balloon. Gawd knows where he'll finish up.'

Wordlessly he dropped his head, in hangdog mortification. Over his tender bald spot she caught Grandma's heavy wink. What was that supposed to mean? Let him suffer? Did it refer to his dramatic posture? Or was it simply to cheer her up?

'But I am, very sorry,' he repeated, gazing into her eyes now as though they were the only people in the room.

'You two know each other, do you?' demanded Grandma in surprise.

He nodded, absorbed in her. Remembering his manners he said, 'I, um, I gave Dorrie a lift once.'

And? she urged mentally.

But he wasn't going to tell them. Someone had to, surely?

With difficulty, she raised her head with its cargo of rocks, heard blood draining from her ears. Behind him, her grandmother's face shrivelled with suspicion. Her granny-ghost sat beside her like a small smug spider, waiting. *She* knew. It was she who nodded curtly. Begin.

Dorrie inhaled deeply. 'He's...' Her voice came out all wibbly-wobbly. She cleared her throat and the words spoke themselves. 'He's Frank Leary.'

'The medium,' Lucy spelled out, for her mother's benefit. She and Eric had both appeared on the same platform with him, she said; given psychic readings in adjoining curtained cubicles.

Grandma turned down her mouth, shook her head. The significance of the name was lost on her. And just then, glimmerings of memory peeked through the clouds, and she gasped. Granny Farthing frowned a warning and pressed a crooked finger to her lips. It wasn't their place to tell.

Grandma's hand flew to her mouth. 'Oh blimey! I knew I'd heard the name somewhere,' she said, miserable with self-reproach. 'But I never thought! When Eric said he had a mate who could help us, I never twigged it was *him*. Oh Dorrie, I wouldn't've had this happen for the world. It's all my fault.'

'What is? What's happened?' said Lucy, realising at last that there was more to all this than a bungled exorcism.

Eric, too, was looking perplexed and awfully afraid that he'd done something wrong. 'I don't quite follow. Frank's d-d-done scores of c-c-clearings. Best m-m-man for the job.'

'That's as may be. All the same he's–'

'*Nora!*' Mother-to-daughter menace. Grandma held her tongue.

'Is somebody going to tell me what's going

450

on?' Lucy demanded. Ma? Granny? Frank?'

'Oh Lord.' The sigh that fanned Dorrie's hot cheeks wavered slightly. 'This *is* a bloody mess. Your mother's going to have my guts for garters. She told me to keep away from you.'

'But you didn't, did you?' Dorrie said tiredly. 'You knew if you stuck around here long enough, our paths would cross.'

'No, sweetheart,' he said, so firmly she had to believe him, spreading his fingers for emphasis. 'I've done my damnedest to keep out of your way. I only ever come up here when I know you're safely in school, and generally it's subbing for your gran which is why we've never met. Just so happens I was on me holidays at Sowness, and Eric asked me if I'd keep an eye on Hallid– on our mutual friend.' He turned for Eric's nod of confirmation. 'Wish I'd gone to Cornwall now. But I'm sorry I mucked up your exorcism.'

'My first,' she pouted childishly. 'He was on the brink. And you made me lose him.' Her mouth contorted without warning and a tear dribbled down her nose.

'Dorrie!' Peter was all concern. 'What's the matter? Oh, don't cry. Please don't.'

'No, leave her,' said Lucy. 'Tears are healing.'

'She's not ill, is she?'

'She's had a plateful, poor kid. Falling out with her dad, for one.' Dorrie's throat squeezed on the memory, ached with it and turned it into one sob, then another. 'And old Gerry Webb and all that.' Worry and fear bubbled up, diluted with tears. 'And late nights, I gather,' Lucy

451

added archly. Was nothing hidden from these clairvoyantes? Or had Auntie been watching from her window again with a fretful child? Either way, neither way, she didn't care any more.

There's nothing so freeing as a good howl or so loud and ugly and blotchy and embarrassing to others. The shades hastily, discreetly, took their leave. Time they checked on Webb, they muttered. The men shifted uncomfortably, feeling they were somehow responsible.

Sod them, thought Dorrie, her emotions in shreds. His turning up like that wasn't fair; it was the last blooming straw. Surely there were settings more conducive to sensitive father-daughter reunions than ghost-infested stately homes, and an audience of nosy relations? What was Fate playing at?

There was her aunt, the healer, saying, 'It's all right, honey. Let it out,' and patting her heaving shoulders as though burping an infant, and there were Frank and Peter vying with each other as to whose handkerchief she would accept, the pristine, monogrammed and crisply ironed one or her erstwhile cousin's rather grubby offering, and somehow she saw the funny side, somehow her smile muscles twitched. Pointedly, she took the grubby one and blew her nose on it hard.

Peter was encouraged, as the gulping tears subsided, to ask, 'Will somebody *please* tell me what's going on. Who *is* this chap – apart from being Frank Leary?'

Eyes that had been averted were now focused.

On her. It was her story.

She drew in a long, shuddering breath and had a final sniff. What a wet, snivelling thing she was. What a show up, in front of everyone. 'Could I have that drink of water now, please?' she asked in a small voice. Peter passed her the glass and she drank gratefully. It tasted foul: dusty and warm, but it helped.

At last she said, 'This is my dad, Pete. What I told you last night? This is him. Frank Leary.'

'What!' Lucy rounded on her. 'Dorrie ... what are you saying?'

'Mum and Frank were ... were lovers, Auntie, and they had me.'

'You mean, Arthur's not ... not...?'

It was like tacking up notices on a board for all to see. 'He was away. In the war. Mum was lonely. She and Frank were old friends. They were at school together.'

'Well!' She seemed quite shaken. 'That's a bombshell! Oh, poor Dorrie. I...' But realising she had no healing words to offer, she turned on her mother. 'Did you know about this, Ma?'

Grandma nodded reluctantly. There were tears in her eyes. 'Coupla years ago. The Other Side thought it was time we knew the truth. I promised Flo I wouldn't say nothing, Luce.' It was an apology. 'Not to Arthur nor no one.'

Her daughter snorted. 'Not like you to keep your trap shut, Ma.' As the implications sank slowly in, disgust wrinkled her freckled nose. 'I can't believe it. *Flo?*' She shook her head. 'She's the last person... And while Arthur was fighting the war. Just married and she was carrying on

453

with this charmer? Oh, lovely. Oh, that's really nice. What a bloody little whore!'

'Oi!' flashed Frank, his fists bunching. 'Leave it out, will you? That's her daughter sitting there!'

'Pity you didn't think about her before you bedded her mother.'

'Luce! That's enough,' said Grandma sharply.

Peter, with his arm round her to cushion the spasms of trembling, murmured, 'It's all right, it's all right,' when it wasn't and it would never be.

'Well, at least Dorrie knows. Poor Arthur's being played for a mug, bringing up someone else's child. Doesn't anyone consider him in all this?'

'Wouldn't do him no good, knowing, not now, and don't you go telling him, Luce.'

'As if I ... God, Ma, what do you take me for? Poor Arthur, it'd destroy him.'

'Oh, I know,' mourned her mother. 'Oh, what a thing to happen, eh? I knew I should've asked Gladys, visitors or no. Oh Gawd, I could murder another cup of tea. Where's Doubleday when you want him?'

Not at his post, evidently. So off she went in search of the kitchen and other amenities, leaving her daughter to fume.

Frank studied his nails, and rubbed his chin, and shuffled his feet. Got up to examine the ornaments, those that were left and the dingy pictures on the wall, while everyone else examined him.

He was patently not what he seemed. Those

grey flannels, that open-necked shirt, those sandals were sheep's clothing. This was a libertine, despite the wind-tanned skin and unruly hair. Look at the gleam in his eye, the generous mouth. Typical of loose morals and lechery.

'Feeling better?' he enquired as he passed behind the chesterfield.

'A bit,' Dorrie allowed, and hastily fought back a reassuring smile. No concessions, she told herself firmly.

Peter observed, 'If I'd been Auntie Flo I wouldn't have had any doubts at all; about who Dorrie's dad was.'

'Eh?'

'Well, you look like you're related.'

'What!' she hooted, too loudly and rudely. 'Oh no, we don't!'

Her father's eyes glazed with hurt and his nostrils flared. He clamped his mouth shut and swung away, ostensibly, this time, to look out of the window.

'Dorrie!' Peter chided her in a whisper.

She shrugged nastily, blushing nevertheless. Why did he bring out the child in her? The spoiled brat? Why did she want to hurt him? She didn't hate him.

But if he thought she was going to be a pushover, like Mum, he could think again! He'd have to work a bit harder than that! He was a stranger, sixteen years a stranger, who'd deserted her mother and left Dorrie to Arthur's care. He would have to earn the right to a relationship.

Besides, she thought petulantly, everyone said

she looked like her mother.

There might a small likeness in the jaw, perhaps, and the set of the eyes. In fact, he wasn't bad-looking considering his age; a bit scrawny, a sort of ageing James Dean, with that colouring – her own colouring – and the slight cast in the amber eye.

And he had her crazy, misbehaving hair, though not for much longer, by the look of it.

And, of course, they had their clairvoyance in common. For two years she had suspected it might be so. Now it was confirmed. He was a medium and she couldn't be cross with him for that, for knowing what she knew, for feeling how she felt.

What else might she have inherited? Bad temper? Varicose veins? She didn't have them yet but he might. Through others' minds, she had seen, more or less, who she was, but many of the whys and hows and what made her tick, those that weren't explained by her mother's genes, had always been a mystery.

Perhaps Frank Leary had the answers.

He turned from the window and met her gaze. Nodded slowly. *If it'll help,* he was saying, *go ahead and probe.*

Before, in the transport caff, he'd fended off her telepathic probe; now the doors of his mind swung open at a touch.

Here, trumpets jazzed and the joint was jumping; there, a string quartet played Schubert. Here was the homely bustle of the East End; there, tall beeches silently raised vaulting forest arches in prayer. Here was roaring laughter, roisterous friends, wine, women and a knees-up; there were books, hundreds of them, on all subjects, piled high, open and annotated, earmarked and laid aside. Frank dipped into projects as he dipped into people, as they took his fancy or for journalistic research and, when his interest waned, he moved on. Life was too short to specialise.

So here was the ducking and diving docker, with an eye on the main chance, and a bright and breezy, free and easy way with him that Flo's staid and steady sailor boy could never hope to match. Frank had never been to sea. He had none of Arthur's love of ship-shape discipline and spit-and-polish attention to detail. Frank wrote his newspaper articles with too many words and flashes of last-minute inspiration. His talks at spiritualist meetings were off-the-cuff and very moving. He'd probably wooed Mum the same way, she thought – instinctively and with flair.

She came away bemused, unsure what to make of him or of herself. She didn't recognise that easygoing affability, those dilettante enthusiasms, that flash-in-the-pan brilliance in herself. Perhaps it was too soon to know. Or too late. She was afraid she might be staid and steady like Arthur, who never took risks, never said 'What the hell...'

She was alone at the coffee table. Eric and Frank were over by the window, too animated to be discussing the landscape or the weather, but she wasn't interested in eavesdropping. Peter and their aunt were across the room by the piano. Lucy was running her hands over the keyboard, an inch or two away from the notes, as though she were healing the wretched thing. Surely not?

Grandma returned, hard on the heels of the butler, who opened a small door in the wall and produced plates of sandwiches and cakes and an ornamental pot of tea with a magician's flourish. Peter was asking why, if they were clairvoyantes, they hadn't been able to foresee Dorrie's father turning up like this.

Frank seemed to find that funny and Lucy gave a short, almost mirthless laugh. 'You can't predict your own future, only other people's. And then only sometimes.' She pressed a few keys experimentally and, even to Dorrie's untrained ear, there was an improvement.

'But you can foresee what'll happen with Gerald Webb, can't you? How long before the police catch up with him?'

'No idea,' she said, adding, 'It's because we're all involved, you see, Pete.'

'You've really no idea? Gaw blimey. All these poxy dreams and visitations and you haven't a clue whether they're going to work or not?'

'Nope.'

'And sending him Dorrie's drawings?' Peter asked.

'Shot in the dark,' admitted Lucy, running her thumb up the white notes. The trill had an ominous sound and she shut the lid with a bang and a reverberation of piano wires.

'That's better,' said Grandma, and Eric, who

had been drifting that way, cracking his fingers in anticipation, changed his mind and resumed his seat, but whether the old woman had been referring to the piano, the refreshments or people's tempers, it was hard to say. 'Now,' she urged, 'come and have a bite to eat, everyone, do. Salmon and cucumber – quite fresh – I opened the tin myself. Lucy, you be mother, will you, duck? And then I reckon we'd best get on with this blooming clearing.'

'Can I just say something?' asked Frank, pulling up a chair. 'This game you're playing with Webb's mind... do you have the slightest idea how dangerous it is?'

What right had he to poke his nose in? Dorrie stared at him frostily. The others simply ignored him. Talked over him or carried on munching their sandwiches and sipping their tea. Then she understood. The others hadn't heard him. He was in her head, mind to mind.

'When Eric asked me to keep Halliday out of harm's way,' he was thinking, 'I thought it was just until the police were persuaded that they'd made a mistake. Call me naïve, but it didn't occur to me you were working on *Webb*. I know I'm a scallywag and you're not going to take a blind bit of notice of what I say, but Dorrie ... the thing about a psychopath is he's unpredictable. Trigger-happy. If you go on driving him into a corner with your dreams and your drawings, he might just make a great leap of rationalisation and kill again.'

It was what she feared most.

'Some find solace in drink. Webb takes com-

459

fort in sex, in abusing children. D'you know, I interviewed a child molester once for an article. He was in prison, waiting to be hanged – and do you know what he told me? He said he loved children. Loved them so much he couldn't bring himself to hurt them.'

'But...'

'*Listen!* So he killed them. That way they wouldn't feel the pain when he did what he had to do to them.'

'What!'

Peter turned to her. 'Sorry? D'you say something, Dorrie?'

'Pass me a sandwich, Pete.'

'Webb probably doesn't think he's done anything to be ashamed of. Like the chap I spoke to, he probably thinks the law is unjust.' He shook his head. 'A madman like that isn't going to be too concerned about pictures and dreams.' He breathed a heavy sigh. 'Oh God, you're such an innocent. You all are – your grandmother, your aunt, your pretty little cousin from the North... How can you predict which way he's going to jump?'

'We can't. But if he does "jump" the wrong way, we'll know, straightaway.'

'Will you?'

'Granny and Viv and Robbie are down there now, keeping an eye on him. And I seem to have a sense of what he's up to.'

'But suppose you don't make it there in time? The spirits can't do much to stop him if he picks up some kid.'

'Uncle Jack, Viv's dad – he's psychic, too – has

some police friends on standby. They'll get through to Chingford police on the radio. They'll have to move on him then, if only out of curiosity. They'll catch him red-handed.'

'My God, girl, do you know how dodgy that sounds?'

'So what do you suggest?'

'I think we ought to get back pretty sharpish. Today.'

'We?'

'We. You'll accept a lift this time, won't you? Shouldn't take us long to polish this lot off.'

Two pots of tea and a round of Lemon Barley later they were still at it. Grandma was dozing. Bulk-clearance was too much for her, even spreading the load between them. Lucy had taken over from her mother to partner Eric, and Frank and Dorrie, to her surprise, seemed to work together well. Far from having nothing in common, she discovered that, psychically, they were on precisely the same wave-length, anticipating each other's moves, having the same instinctual regard for the lost souls, the same light, almost playful approach that charmed the most reluctant spirit across the Great Divide.

Peter had wandered off, bored with the company of entranced mediums and violent fluctuations in temperature.

It was almost three o'clock and there was one more ghost to lay. She didn't say much, just mooched around the servants' quarters upstairs and dripped blood through the bedroom ceiling. A governess, she'd slashed her own wrists. A private matter, she declared, tight-lipped and stern. Nothing to do with them. It was tricky. Unless she told them the reason for her despair they had no leverage, no way of persuading her that things could be better. Viv was the one to crack these cases – she could get into a spirit's mind – but it was her shift at the stake-out, Webb-watching.

Was it for love? they tried.

Least said soonest mended. In other words, mind your own business.

It was then. An illicit love-affair – or un-requited love? Love of a pupil? Of another servant? Of the master – the mistress? They didn't dare ask for fear of rousing her wrath. She was a formidable lady.

And then the door opened soundlessly and Peter slid into the room, on careful tiptoe, his mind jangling with excitement, and they both came back to earth with a bang.

'Sshh!' hissed Lucy, who had been sitting quietly, waiting for them to finish.

'Oh shit!' said Peter when he saw Dorrie's eyes rolling. 'You didn't lose him, did you?'

'Her,' said Frank, with difficulty, fingertips at his temples. 'It's all right, she's just gone back to her room.'

'Sorry,' he said, with a black scowl. 'I tried not to disturb you.'

'It was your mind thumping about,' said Dorrie, squinting at him through flashing lights. 'Like a flaming herd of elephants. What's the matter?' Then she gasped, 'Not...' Tried to stand up and failed. 'Not Gerald Webb?'

'No, no. And don't kid me you're that sensitive a flower, Dorrie Potter. It wasn't my mind you heard. It's Doubleday wrecking the library, hunting for treasure!'

Grandma was stirring. 'No peace for the wicked,' she yawned.

Jarring sounds of destruction led them down the stairs and along the corridor. At the library doors they stood, aghast. The room was destroyed. Sunbeams mingled with dust, played over books, broken spines, fractured wood. Shelves had been cleared with a swipe of impatience, their contents flung carelessly out of the way. In pursuit of 'real' wealth, the bookshelves had been rocked, tipped and sent crashing across tables and chairs. Weakened by worm, the wood splintered and crumbled, releasing an ancient aroma that blended pleasantly with lavender wax and the attar of yellowing pages and printer's ink.

Doubleday and his son, who had returned and who could hardly spare a glance under his dusty lashes for Dorrie, were now hard at work with crowbar and axe, prising panels from the wall. Just as well they had the oak tree on standby, she thought.

Grandma had to raise her voice over the racket, 'Right, we'll be off then, Ralph. Thank Jenkins for the tea and that. You'll be getting our bill in the morning.'

The labourers nodded, but it wasn't likely that they'd heard a word.

'So we'll leave you to it, then.'

'No, Grandma, there's another ghost upstairs,

463

the one that drips blood into John's bedroom. We didn't quite–'

'The lady that looks like Florence Nightingale? Keeps herself to herself? We'll leave her for another time, I think. You never know, she might still come in handy for that Haunted House idea of his.'

'But what about the money?'

'Money, duck?'

'The hidden hoard.'

'Old Henry didn't believe in hoarding money, Dor. Where d'you get that idea? His was all in the bank like Viv said, or tied up in business, earning interest. What he was guarding down here in the library was his collection of first editions. Priceless, the old man said they was – *undamaged.*' The qualification was made with a nod in the direction of the heap that had once been the Literature Section. Bent, battered and torn books languished among the debris. 'Don't know what they'd fetch now, of course.'

'But he said they were hidden – that he didn't want anyone getting their hands on them.'

'Where're we hiding Halliday, Dorrie?' said Lucy.

'At Sowness,' she answered, baffled by the question.

'In a crowd,' said her aunt. 'And Henry Doubleday decided that the best place to hide rare books was in the library.'

Eric picked up a book that had just skidded out to them in the corridor. He tapped the spine and said, clearly and almost without stuttering, as though he were inspired or preaching, 'Catalogue number! The first editions were probably sprinkled among the thousands of other books and you could only find them quickly by referring to some sort of code in the catalogue number. I dunno, those that ended in -01 or something. That's what he would have told Hugo on his deathbed, so the boy could pick them out and sell them as the need arose.'

'Very clever. But we're not going to tell the Doubledays, are we?' said Lucy.

'Aren't we?' said Dorrie, heading back into the chaos. 'I think perhaps John ought to know.'

'Dorrie...'

'He wants to go to university, Auntie.'

'Where do you think he's been all night?'

'Dunno. Staying with friends?'

'Staying at Brand End with Fifi, the maid.'

'Oh wow!' muttered Peter. 'That's education, if you like.'

'Well, maybe he slept on her couch. You don't know.'

'I do, Dorrie, Granny told me.'

'The apple don't fall far from the tree, Dor. What's good for Ralph and Mrs Bussage...'

'Hmm,' she swallowed. It was a blow, but not a body blow, and not entirely unexpected. 'Even so,' she said magnanimously, 'keeping it to ourselves when we could be helping them out of a hole ... it's not fair.'

'Nor's a baboon's behind, duck.'

Quite. And people with so little regard for books...

'No, Dor,' said Grandma, 'your friend John'll climb out of this hole without our help.' She paused. 'He might need Wally's though. Takes a bit of knowhow, turning an estate into streets of dez rezzies. I have mentioned it to Wally and he says it had already occurred to him. Nice, modern houses with fitted kitchens and inside lavvies, and bathrooms with hot and cold running water. I told him to put my name down for one.'

Chapter Twenty-Four

It was a mistake. The train would have been quicker. A red-hot Sunday afternoon on the A12 and the lemmings were on the road, their one thought: to be home by teatime. Tearful kids tangled damply on the back seat of the car in front; the man behind, sunsore and livid, leaned on his horn. The sun beat down on the metal-skinned snake of traffic and cooked it, from the inside out.

They moved. Stopped. Moved again. At least Frank wasn't apologising now. He'd retreated into chainsmoking silence. Peter, next to him, was working himself up into a lather. If that poxy driver hooted them one more time...

Dorrie was trying not to think about Detective Inspector Webb coming off shift in an hour, pleasantly tired after Operation Gadfly. It was one of his favourite pastimes, queer-bashing. First you bait them, then you hook them; you reel them in and then two or three of you knock the buggers into kingdom come. He was down at the nick now, writing up his report. Covered himself in glory, hadn't he? The old man slapping him on the back like that, didn't happen every day. 'Good work, Gerry,' he'd said. 'Be surprised if there isn't a promotion in this for you.' His very words.

And the cells were heaving. All sorts there

were, from your ordinary, everyday bike-saddle sniffers to your raving queens. Even old Charlie Nicholls. Bit of luck that, catching him *in flagrante*. The looks on their faces – oh dear! Regular vicar's tea-party they were having! Six of them at it, turn and turn about. Well, it'd be a long time before he lifted another shirt, or finger-waved a woman's hair, come to that. You'd expect an artist to take more care of his hands, not leave them where a copper could stamp on them.

Yes, it had been a good day, and not over yet. The night shift had the pubs to do. Always good for a laugh, the pubs. He'd been very tempted to put in a spot of overtime. But, sad to say, he'd had to get back...

What for? Dorrie agonised. What was he planning to do, this damaged man? Sticky with dirt and the stink of public lavatories, he'd want a bath, surely? Or maybe he'd pour himself a long, cold drink. No, more likely a short, the way he'd be feeling – a straight whisky, to sting his throat, to punch the life back into him. But she was guessing. She didn't know at all what he was going to do and it worried her.

He'd be tired, that much was certain. After a week of disturbed nights his body would be desperate for sleep. His wits, his sanity (huh!) would be crying out for dark oblivion. But, of course, he wouldn't dare to lie down, or close his eyes, perchance to dream... So he'd do what? Have a wash, at least. Cook himself a snack. Beans on toast, scrambled egg, something quick. He'd have had his proper dinner in the staff canteen. And then? Switch the telly on? What would it be by the time he finished work? *Songs of Praise?* Not quite his style, perhaps. A book, then? Or the papers? Would he get down to writing some letters? Oh, please, someone, what *did* child molesters *do* in their spare time?

Go out hunting for little children.

With a sudden growl, Frank flicked his fag away and the car swung out, across the white line. What was he doing! Arthur's Highway Code was most insistent: you never overtake on a hill. What if they met something coming the other way? What if you died? What then? What about Gerald Webb?

What about little Paul Chambers?

There, she even knew his name. They had to get back in one piece. They had to save that boy.

Frank was driving blind, bent on suicide. Solid traffic all the way up, as far as you could see. No breaks. No bolt-holes. Hooters sounding, lights flashing. People shouting. 'Crazy bastard!' out of their windows as he changed down, charged on, overtaking, overtaking. Oh God, oh God, oh God.

A mirage shimmered up ahead. Became a tanker looming on the hilltop, growing bigger, filling their window, nightmare horn blaring.

'*Frank!*' she screamed, shutting her eyes as they swerved, preparing for the end.

Nothing happened. No crash. No Granny Farthing coming to meet her.

Peter was laughing his socks off.

'Yesss!' Frank hissed fiercely.

By some miracle they were back in their own

lane and about to crest the hill. Dorrie spun round and saw the tail-back stretching down the hill and miles beyond, stuck behind a charabanc with an overheated engine. Its passengers were making use of the unscheduled stop to stretch their legs and have picnics on the verge. The tanker was rumbling down the empty side of the road, the driver, no doubt, sweating buckets and wondering how on earth the driver of the Rover had known that the road ahead of the charabanc was clear.

Peter was full of admiration. Overdoing it, Dorrie thought. It was only second sight, after all.

'Comes in handy, sometimes,' Frank admitted. He caught her eye in the mirror. *'Don't worry, sweetheart,'* he told her telepathically. *'We'll be there in time.'*

'I thought you couldn't see ahead if you were personally involved.'

'Well, strictly speaking, Pete, that wasn't seeing ahead. That, just now, was more your inspired guess. It had to be either an accident holding us up or a breakdown, and up that long hill, in this heat, it was a fair bet that someone's rad would boil dry. If it had been a car they'd have pushed it off the road, out of the way, or over the hill and coasted down. The real give-away was all those blokes peeing in the hedge across the road, and the old girl setting up the picnic table – they looked like they knew the coach wasn't going anywhere.'

'Elementary, my dear Watson,' said Peter.

'You could still have been wrong and then

where would we have been?' Her heart was still racing. He'd given her a fright.

'Strawberry jam, sweetheart,' said Frank happily. Then more seriously, 'No – it was instinct. Something like that, anyway. I just had to go for it. You know how it is, Dorrie, when you know what cards people are holding, or you know the answers in quiz shows on the box.'

'You can predict the questions, too,' she sighed.

'Can you?' Peter was impressed. But she didn't want him to be. *She* wanted to be impressed by *him*.

'Bet you're wondering,' said Frank, 'if these weirdos are so flipping clever, why aren't they millionaires?'

'Uhuh.'

'When I was a kid, my old mum used to get me to call out eight numbers between one and, I dunno what it was in those days, fifty or something, and she'd fill them in on the Littlewoods coupon. Never did any good. I didn't even know what she wanted the numbers for. One day she must have put me in the picture. Told me if we picked the right teams for a no score draw we'd be millionaires. Well, that was different. I gave her her eight winning numbers and was on pins for her to collect her millions. I think she got thirty-seven pounds ten. Something ridiculous. Everyone in the country must have had the same winning line that week.'

'So what happened next time?'

'There wasn't a next time. Never did it again, not for big money. Spotted the ball once, in the local rag, when we were going through a rough patch, but it never felt right. To be honest, what it was, they sent me a warning. A dream. Oh God, it was awful. There was my old mum, all got up like some old tart: false eyelashes, and a hat like a wedding cake. Dripping with jewels. Blimey. And the most God-awful parasitic men swarming over her, pawing her. And their one idea, of course, was to fleece her. She was drinking like a fish and, in the end, killed her-self. That's a terrible thing, dreaming about your own mother's death.'

'They don't like you using the gift for your own ends. Granny Farthing gave me a right telling-off when I won an evening out with Richard Todd.'

'You never told me. When was this?'

'I was ten or eleven at the time, Peter. Dad wouldn't let me go.

'Oh shame,' said Frank, with a twinkle. 'Though you can see his point. Poor old Richard Todd, the perfect gent. Couldn't've stood the pace!'

They seemed to find that funny, her mother's lover and her own.

Peter couldn't stop giggling. 'Dinner at the Ritz,' he chortled, 'all black ties and posh frocks and this cross-eyed kid with her glasses and buck teeth. Oh,' he gasped, ignoring the thump she gave him, 'you were an 'orrible child.'

'Me?' she squealed. 'You were the one with the snotty nose and the dirty neck. And scabby knees. And yesterday's dinner down your front. Ugh!'

'But I washed up well.'

'You were fond of each other, I take it,' nodded Frank encouragingly.

'No. He made my life a misery. He really didn't like me at all.'

'I was *very* fond of you.'

'Funny way of showing it. You were always tripping me up or pulling my hair.'

'Blimey, you were playing with fire there, mate,' said Frank.

'What d'you mean?'

'This is a girl who can puncture a Goodyear tyre at twenty paces.'

'Fra-ank!'

But he took no notice of her pleading in the mirror. As the Essex countryside zipped by he entertained his passenger with a sorry tale of pickings up and lettings down and desperate measures with radiators. Peter turned to stare at her and she blushed. What was he seeing? A freak?

He wasn't laughing now. 'Shazaam,' he said flatly. The magic word that turned a wholesome American girl into Mary Marvel, the girl wonder of the comics. She bit her lips, ashamed in an odd sort of way. It wasn't like that. She was ordinary. It had been a desperate act, the last resort of a girl who'd thought she was about to be raped.

'She seems none the worse for it,' he said, meaning the car.

'Pulling well,' agreed Frank.

Man-talk. Safe, down to earth, and leaving her flat, like the damn tyres. She leaned her face on the partly opened window and let her hair whip in the wind. It was true; the car was magnificent, gliding along on air, round bends, over hills, past fields and churches and cottages and, if it hadn't been for what awaited them in Chingford, she might have enjoyed the journey. Part of her harked back, with sentimental longing, to the homely chugging of the Potter family car and the raucous singsongs that made long journeys shorter. That part of her life was over now. Childhood... She took a deep breath to smother self-pity. What shall it profit a girl if she shall gain a new father and a boyfriend, and lose the love of the man who had brought her up?

'That's what I do now, anyway,' Frank was saying. Somehow this had followed on from talk about the car. 'I write stories and flog 'em to the newspapers. It keeps the wolf from the door. I must say it helps when you can see what's going to be news. You can be one step ahead.'

'That's cheating,' said Dorrie, in return for his disloyalty.

He lowered his head to frame her in the mirror. She saw his eyes pucker with excuses and he waggled his head from side to side, working the cork from the bottle. 'Yeah,' the admission came out finally, 'but it's not as if you're leaking secrets or anything. You have to have hard evidence for that – documents. This is more drawing attention to disasters waiting to happen. If you can point to the loose screws in the system you can sometimes avert a crisis. More often you can't. More often you know they won't take a blind bit of notice, and the accidents will happen and the people will die, kids'll be buried under slag heaps, the US will go piling into wars they can't win, in spite of anything you might say. "Oh, it's just Leary off on his hobby horse again." When the worst happens you remind them you told them so. "So you did," they'll say, "so you did. But that's yesterday's news."' He shrugged. 'You can only do your best, I suppose.'

They'd just passed Chelmsford when, with her third eye, Dorrie saw the Triumph Herald drawing up outside the flats in Low Hall Gardens.

'He's back!' she breathed.

'He's early, then,' said Peter, looking at his watch. 'Thought you said he finished at five.'

'Just putting the car away,' Frank affirmed. 'There's garages across from the flats.'

'You can see him, too?'

'Only in your mind, honey.'

'What's he doing now?' asked Peter.

'Locking the garage door,' they said together.

'Oh no,' said Dorrie, 'Oh God.'

'What?'

'He's not going indoors. He's crossing the road.' She swallowed. 'He's going for a walk.'

'Stay with him, love, stay with him. I'll tell Peter what's happening. Don't worry, we're nearly there. Forty minutes, flat out.'

'Hurry, Frank.'

Hungry, roaring hungry. Must have, must have... Not food. Only one thing for the screaming abdabs. One thing. Sex. Your kind of sex. The violent, violating kind. Afterwards you'll be calm. Able to

475

sleep. No more dreams. How you were after the Marshall child. Cleansed. Peaceful. Until the dreams started. Never had dreams before, not like that, churning you up…

'Down Bury Road … past the golf club, skirting the parked cars … turning off the road, across the grass … jumping the ditch now,' reported Frank.

Good time for kids, Sunday after dinner. Mum and Dad getting a bit of shuteye, a bit of nooky, send the kids out to play. 'Don't go far! Be home for tea! Here's a bob to get yourself some sweets.' On the streets, on the loose, larking about. For the taking, mate. For the taking.

'He's walking fast across the Plain, holding his hat in his hand. His jacket's slung over his arm, collar undone, tie loose.'

Slow down, take your time. Everything comes to those who wait. Plenty of time, take it easy, Gerry. Don't draw attention. Ordinary chap out for a stroll, enjoying the sunshine, the fresh air. Sunday afternoon before tea, before … oh Jesus.

'He's shaking, got the knee trembles. What's the matter with him?'

No, don't sit down. You're doing all right. What you got to feel guilty about, eh? No need for it, mate. You were doing your job, that's all. Pull yourself together. You're not drowning. You're walking along, taking in the scenery, enjoying the fresh air, listening to the dicky birds.

'He's calmed down. Stopped to watch some blokes flying model aeroplanes.'

All right now? A dream, that's all it was, Gerry. Can't hurt you. Can't get you out here. Be all right soon. Nearly there. Can't you hear him? He's calling out to you.

'Oh God, there are kids. Their eyes are on the planes, the ones in the air, wheeling and diving, like graceless birds. One little kid has noticed the model planes on the ground. He's gone over to one, tracing its ribs through the webbing. All sorts there are – Spitfires, Heinkels, Mosquitoes. The owner's gonna let the kid have a go. He's showing him how to ready it for take-off. One-handed, on his shoulder, like a huge fat dart, pointing up. Webb's looking across, feigning interest in the plane but his eyes are on the boy. Paul, they call him, his friends. Stringy little kid, eight or nine years old, dark hair, bright eyes, athletic type. The bloke pulls a string and the engine roars. For a tiny engine it roars. Sounds like an angry bee. The boy's holding on for dear life, smoke pouring past his ear. Now they're launching it. Back and ... into the air! All eyes on the plane. Except Webb's. His haven't left the boy. Now he's stroking a dog, a spaniel; he's passing the time of day with its owner, complaining about the racket. The dog-walker goes off and Webb parks himself on rising ground to watch.'

His technique would have been fascinating if it hadn't been so sinister. By passing the occasional comment, asking questions, relating his own (fictitious) wartime experiences in the RAF, he made himself part of the group. When the children had had enough of the whine and buzz of planes and wandered off towards the lake he stayed put. It was a good ten minutes before he got up to continue his walk, heading off in a different direction altogether. He knew the forest like the back of his hand and, once under cover of the trees, was able to skirt the plain, cross the bridleway further up and make his way back, along forest paths, to Connaught Waters where he found the children messing about at the water's edge, throwing stones at the ducks and paddling. They greeted him like a longlost friend.

By taking short-cuts and chances Frank managed to avoid the worst of the hold-ups and they were already on the outskirts of Walthamstow when the hunter separated his quarry from the pack. It was a simple device. Promises of ice cream. He'd need some help to carry them. What about young Paul?

The Waterworks crossroads was clogged. The lights were on the blink again and a lone policeman was directing traffic from a box in the middle.

'Damn and blast!' Frank almost ran into the back of a bus. They all lurched forward, bounced back. A lorry pitched in behind them, its nose to their bumper. There was no room to move. He drummed his fingers on the steering wheel and they waited expectantly. What would he do?'

Paul was trotting to keep up with Webb, ice cream on his mind. Webb could hardly keep his hands off the boy, but there were families picnicking up by the Royal Forest Hotel. Queues of people waiting for the bus. He had to be careful.

Frank reversed an inch, drove forward two,

back, forward, back, heaving the huge steering wheel this way and that, puffing with exertion as the car gradually turned. When the bus eventually moved, ever so slightly, he was ready. With a mighty thrust of acceleration he swung the wheel, scraped past the corner of the bus, did a U-turn out of the traffic, back the way they'd come.

Dorrie shook her head, speechless. They'd never make it in time, no matter where they went, or how fast.

Webb had hold of Paul's hand now, to cross the busy main road. He wouldn't let go until they were in the flat. 'Just have to pop home,' he was saying, 'to get some money. What sort of lolly do you want? Glo-joy? Spearmint or Banana?'

They raced to the nearest turn-off, tore up towards Chigwell, swung left, flew along this main road, swerved and skidded into that side road, that shady lane, that leafy grove, roared down another main road, and another and were at last, at last, speeding down Rangers Road to Chingford Plain.

'Look out!' yelled Peter, as a small figure shot across the road in front of them.

'Shit!' Brakes screeched and tyres squealed and Dorrie bashed into the back of Frank's seat, giving herself another fat lip. Peter came off worst with a sprained wrist. He'd put out a hand to brace himself against a crash. But they hadn't crashed and no one was seriously hurt.

When they got out of the car some woman from the bus-stop had hold of Paul's arm and was giving him what-for. 'Don't you realise, you silly little boy, you could have been killed? Didn't your mother ever tell you to look before you cross the road? Now say you're sorry to these people for giving them such a fright.'

When he started crying, she gave him a toffee and took him back across the plain to Connaught Waters where his friends were anxiously waiting for their ice creams. The kind woman gave them all toffees and hurried back for her bus.

'What happened?' asked Peter, nursing his arm.

'Amazing,' Dorrie lisped through her thick lip. 'Just amazing.'

Webb and the boy had gone through the door to the flats and up the stairs to the third floor and there, hanging by the neck, and slowly turning in the stairwell, was the Honourable Hugo Doubleday. The detective had had to let go of Paul's hand to clutch at his own neck.

'No, no!' he had gibbered, his eyes on stalks. 'Not that, not me! Don't hang me! Not me! It was her, the dirty... Six years old and a slag, a right little slag, can you believe it? She made me ... she was so vile... Jesus! Utterly...' He made a growling, vomiting sound as he collapsed in a heap by his front door, grovelling before the apparition. 'Depraved?' he went on. 'You don't know the half of it, mate, the things she made me do, the filthy little whore. You wouldn't believe. I had to wash her clean then. She was oozing vile, stinking wickedness, covered in it, all the shit you can imagine.'

The neighbours came out, heard his ravings and phoned for the police, but by that time Paul Chambers had scarpered, lickety-split down the stairs and out in front of their car. He hadn't seen the ghost at all.

Arthur was in his singlet, weeding the front garden when the car drew up.

He slid her an uninterested glance and then gave his full attention, seemingly, to a dandelion that had dared to put up leaves among his geraniums. Much more important. 'What do *you* want?' he growled.

'I've come home.'

'Come *home!*' he exploded, unable to keep up the studied pretence. 'You dare...' sitting back on his heels for a better look at her, 'you dare to come waltzing in here like nothing has happened and tell me you've come *home!* Think yourself lucky, my girl. Think yourself bloody lucky you still *have* a home. If it was up to me you'd be out on your ear. But your mother pleaded for you, *pleaded* – and after the disgusting things you said about her, too.'

'You told her, of course.'

'Of course. We were so worried.'

'Worried? Why? You knew where I was.'

'With your crackpot grandmother. Yes, exactly. Of course we were worried. All this nonsense about ghosts and visions.'

'Oh, come off it, Dad. If you were so worried you'd have come after me. You don't give a toss, not really. It's all a big act. What fathers are supposed to do.'

'Less of your–'

'Less of my lip?' she sneered. 'Not possible, I'm afraid.'

His face closed and he lurched to his feet, weighing his trowel in his hand. He seemed about to say something and changed his mind.

'Oh that's right,' she sniped at his retreating back. 'Walk away. Never mind that we have things to talk about. Never mind about trying to understand me.'

'Dorrie!' Peter was at the gate, gesturing upwards with his eyebrows. She, too, looked up to see her mother, at the bedroom window, eyes popping at the sight of the Rover, parked discreetly beyond the hedge.

'Peter?' said Arthur, retracing his steps. 'What are you doing here?'

'I was at Grandma's, too.'

'Oh? Oh, I see.' But puzzlement clouded his eye. He knew he was missing a connection somehow, somewhere. He jerked his chin. 'And who's that out there, in the car?'

'Oh, that's Frank, one of Gran's friends. He was coming back this way so he gave us a lift.'

'One of the ouijee board crowd, eh? Peter, ask him in, will you? Dorrie wants me to understand her – perhaps this geezer can shed a bit of light on the subject. Dorrie, get your mother down here. I think she'll find this interesting.'

Chapter Twenty-Five

He was in her hallway, in her house, his raucous laughter curling up her stairs. How though? And why was Arthur being so hearty, in that unbearable, cheeky chappie way he had with visitors? If he could hear himself... If she could only make out what they were saying. What was he *doing* here? Really, this was awful. A nightmare.

'Come on, Mum.'

'Dorrie, I can't. I *can't!* Tell them I'm not well. Dorrie, I'm shaking.' She sat down heavily on the bed. 'Oh, look at me!' The face in the dressing-table mirror stared back at her with naked eyes. Oh God, she looked a sight. Not a scrap of makeup, a faded old sundress, and her *hair!* She turned her head, poked hopelessly at a limp strand. It looked no better.

'You look lovely,' said Dorrie, with her swollen lip. Poor Dorrie. She'd say anything, of course, so pale and anxious. It must have taken guts for her to come home and face Arthur. Peter must have persuaded her. He was a good boy. Flo would have to go down; Dorrie needed her. God, they needed each other.

But why was Frank here? How?

'He was at Great Bisset, Mum.' Dorrie anticipated the question in that way she had. 'Don't worry, we're not going to drop you in it. Trust

483

me. Look – just pretend you don't know him.'

'Pretend?' she whispered hoarsely. When every nerve, every fibre was on alert, twanging alarm. Her teeth were chattering. Pretend? When all she wanted to do was fling herself into his arms? Was that it? Had he come for her? Now? Was this showdown time? He might have warned her. She wasn't ready. Look at her. With a shaking hand she picked up her mascara. Blonde lashes made her look even more like a scared rabbit. 'Let me just–'

'Oh Mum, you don't need it.'

'Warpaint, Dorrie. This is Armageddon.'

Arthur had them out in the garden, as though they were ordinary Sunday visitors and, though all three must have been wanting to curl up in their shells and tuck their horns away, was steering them round the flower-beds, pointing out a well-behaved and formal Peace, a tightly laced Nelly Moser and a row of neat and polite marigolds, before coming to his pride and joy, his neat-as-a-pin shed, with its tools hung trimly, primly, its matching jars of nails and screws and washers graded and filed and labelled like summer jam. Frank would be impressed but not, she thought, intimidated.

Peter, who'd seen it all before, heard the back door and broke away from the guided tour, to give her a kiss of greeting and a whispered, 'Chin up, Auntie Flo!' Was he in on it, too? Was Arthur the only one, the proverbial last to know? Apart from Stephen, up in his room, making a wireless, dwarfed by a huge pair of headphones,

484

deaf to the world, the real world. And thank God for that.

'Mum,' said Dorrie stagily, 'this is Frank Leary. He's a friend of Grandma's. Very kindly gave us a lift home.'

He squeezed her hand hard and she almost fainted. 'Mrs Potter,' he said, and her heart bounced into her throat. She couldn't do it, she wasn't even going to be able to speak. 'Lovely garden you have,' he prompted, a slight widening of the eyes telling her to play along.

'Oh,' she squeaked, utterly confounded. Arthur was frowning some sort of warning. What did *he* think was happening, she wondered. She cleared her throat to come down an octave. What had he said? Something about the garden. 'Oh, that's all Arthur's handiwork,' she gushed. She was about to ask him what he'd been doing at Nora's, then thought perhaps she wouldn't and was left gawping like a fish.

'Is there anything to drink, Mum? I'm dying of thirst.'

'Oh, of course.' And thank you, dearest girl, for providing your poor mother with a means of escape! They gave her their orders for squash and tea and she bolted for a few sane minutes, to the kitchen.

But it made no more sense as she filled the kettle, searched the cupboards for ... what? A reason. Try as she might she couldn't find one. He hadn't come to take her away. That wasn't it. Lemon squash might be.

Serving them she dropped a spoon, and the cup of tea she handed to Frank jiggled violently

485

in its saucer, but apart from that she thought she coped pretty well. Her face was burning and the pulse in her neck was throbbing for all to see, but Arthur was too busy to notice, cross-questioning the three travellers about his mother's health and the traffic conditions and other trivialities. What was it all about?

When she'd fetched the cake tin and dithered about bringing a chair to join them on the lawn, it seemed that Arthur had put all the niceties back on the shelves marked 'Visitors, for the use of', and was bracing himself for something nasty. His eyes had narrowed. His folded arms were not a shield so much as a battering ram. He was in confrontational mode, as though they were Management, trying to get one over on him. Signals seemed to be passing between Frank and the youngsters. Eyes flickered, and she had a definite feeling that this had all been planned somehow, cooked up between them. Peter and Dorrie, she noticed, were sitting aw-fully close together on the grass. Was that what was making Arthur bristle?

She said casually, 'So what did you get up to at Grandma's?' and it was the key to Pandora's box.

The words came tumbling out ... terrible words like 'séance' and 'ghosts' and 'exorcism', laced with jokes about Nora's offensive landlord and his sycophantic guests, wound about with talk of great-grandmothers and disabled cousins and murdered chambermaids and men hanging in stairwells. They were all chipping in, even Peter, who apparently wasn't a psychic, not like

Dorrie, whose gift they should treasure, and Frank, who was a medium of renown and a telepath.

'What!'

Thankfully Flo's convulsive jerk was matched by Arthur's. His plate went flying in the air as he stood up.

'All right,' he cried, 'the joke's gone far enough. I don't know what you've been up to, Dorrie, but trying to cover it up with lies, and getting Peter to help you, it won't wash, it won't wash at all. What, d'you think I was born yesterday?'

Then Dorrie, very quietly, told him to sit down and he was so surprised, he did so.

'Think of an object, Dad. Anything at all that I can't possibly know about.'

At first he declared that he wasn't in the mood for party tricks, that he couldn't think of anything. From the way he was glaring it was pretty clear that any thoughts he might have had were distracted by Peter stroking Dorrie's palm with his finger. But he wouldn't say anything, not in front of strangers.

'Go on, Dad,' she urged. 'Think of an object.'

Gritting his teeth, Arthur screwed up his eyes and thought.

'Your hammer,' said Dorrie. 'You left it down by the back fence where you were nailing up strings to train the sweetpeas.'

He gasped. 'How did you do that?'

'Saw it. Third eye. Think of something else.'

A bicycle bell that he'd cleaned just that morning and made to work. It was lying on the workbench in the shed, waiting to be fixed to Dorrie's bike.

'Thanks, Dad,' she said.

Next was the Russian Sputnik, complete with hammer and sickle, orbiting the earth and after that, a manual called *Health and Safety At Work* in his locker at Cunningham-Bayliss.

Peter said, 'What am I thinking, Dorrie?' and it must have been pretty near the knuckle because she hit him. There had certainly been developments in their relationship over the weekend. Looked like Arthur was right to be suspicious.

She stole a sideways glance at Frank: if he was also gifted with second sight he might be able to tell what she was thinking. And, in utter confusion, she buried her face in the rose bush, beside her. He had winked at her!

'Well, one thing's certain,' said Arthur, 'they left me behind the door when they were handing out third eyes, more's the pity. Dear oh dear, what wouldn't I give to be able to see what Management's gonna come up with at next Wednesday's meeting. If I knew they'd agree a higher rate for piecework...'

First, second and third eyes glazed over with boredom.

Gradually the tension lifted. It wasn't so hard to accept, after all. Arthur even began joshing the girl about going on the stage, but the withering look she gave him put paid to any such notion. And Flo caught Frank shaking his head in despair at her husband's crassness.

It was round about this time that she noticed

Arthur's double-take. From Dorrie to Frank and back again. Flo chewed her lip. Could he see it? To her it was obvious. That look they both had, sort of far away and out of focus, to do more with lazy eyes than third eyes; the way the chins jutted, the fingers spread, the shoulders shrugged. Arthur's mouth pinched. Perhaps he thought all psychics had these features in common. How long before he noticed the springy, light-brown hair, the amber-speckled irises, the thick Irish lashes? He must be nearly there. They'd hear more than the tinkling of teaspoons as the scales fell from his eyes.

Then Dorrie told them about Detective Inspector Gerald Webb and that diverted his attention for the moment. He wagged his head in astonishment. Dorrie had been seeing this man in her head ever since they'd found Penny Marshall's body in the weir! It was him, *he*, not the man the police suspected, who had raped the little girl and killed her.

'Oh Dorrie,' groaned Flo. All that horror and her daughter had kept it to herself. Hadn't felt able to confide in her. That *hurt*. She'd tried to tell Arthur and it had ended in tears and a busted television. Flo was sure she would have helped; that's what mothers were best at. She'd have … what? Honestly? Told her not to be silly? That she was under a lot of strain and she must expect her imagination to play tricks? Would that have helped, really?

How they'd let her down. But it was a lot to ask. She and Arthur had both read Jack's letter again and again, but it took a great leap of faith to take in all that supernatural stuff. All that about giving the man bad dreams and forcing him, eventually, to a confession...

'You couldn't work a similar number on old man Cunningham, could you, love?' said Arthur.

Carefully she laid her bike beside the Rover. The mended bell tinged softly against the pavement. She bent to remove the headlamp and, by its light, re-read the number on the wall. Eighty-nine? No. The nine swung when she touched it. Turned out to be a six missing a screw in its tail. Arthur couldn't have lived with it, nor the gate that squealed a protest as she opened it. But this was the home of a man who wasn't a martyr to order, forever straightening pictures and cushions, tidying papers. Frank's front hedge was cheerfully ragged, wisteria drooped in great perfumed swags from the eaves over darkened windows and doors, and the garden was chaotic with bloom, weeds and all. Buttercups and daisies in the lawn. Their own front garden was dissected into neat beds and planted with set squares of white alyssum and blue lobelia and red geraniums. You'd think 'Union Jack', if you didn't know him better.

What should she do? Tap on the window? It might be Mrs Leary's bedroom. She didn't want to give anyone a fright at ten past one in the morning. So she rang the bell and winced as chimes ding-donged merrily, at top volume, down the hall.

He was as nice as you'd expect anyone to be who'd been jolted from a heavy sleep in the middle of the night.

'Jesus Christ, Dorrie!' he said, trying to get her into focus.

'Who is it, Frank?' A voice permeated the stale smell of smoke, but not from the front bedroom, whence a tortoise was emerging and turning slowly back into a wrinkled old woman in curlers. There was someone in the back bedroom. A young woman.

She darted to his mind, but found barriers already in place, and her probes glancing off an impregnable can of worms. He was so quick. He must have read the intention in her eyes as he'd opened the door.

'Damsel in distress,' he shouted over his shoulder, then to his mother, 'It's all right, Ma, go back to bed. Aren't you?' he said to her.

'Aren't I what?' she answered rudely.

'In distress.'

Not just me, she thought. Poor Mum.

'If you can, Dorrie,' she'd pleaded. 'I need to know.' Well, here was her answer. Other women. He was still at it, her mum's fancy man. Even now, even today, he had another woman in his bed!

'Oh, come in, come in. Just a tick, I'll get something.' He dodged into the bedroom and pulled a dressing gown off the back of the door, murmured inaudible nothings to his doxy before telling her, too, to go back to sleep, as he shut it.

'Come through to the kitchen,' he said and for a few steps she followed him. Stopped at the door.

No. Not now. She'd seen all that was necessary and she hadn't the heart for it now. She turned, fled back up the passage, mumbling, 'Mistake. Sorry to have troubled you.' She'd have to tell Mum that they didn't need him, either of them.

'Dor-*rie!*' His voice held a note of warning and, as she scowled at him she felt him brush across her mind. And what he saw there broke him up. A surprising roar of Adam's apple-bobbing laughter. As if she'd just put in a sixpence for the Laughing Policeman on Southend pier. It was impossible not to smile. When at last he could speak, 'O-oh dear,' he gasped. 'Oh, Dorrie, you've got it all wrong, sweetheart. She's not my... Good God, that's Sister Monica Dixon. She was singing at the service tonight.'

Hearing her name, a sturdy black woman appeared in the doorway, wearing some sort of African robe and a beatific grin. 'We're putting her up,' he managed to say through his slap and titter mirth and, in answer to Dorrie's unspoken question, 'Ma's got us on the couch in the living room.' He caught Dorrie's startled look. '*Me*, I mean, she's got *me* on the couch. Against my will, let me tell you.' And his wink was Sister Monica's cue to start shaking *her* sugar-fat sides, and the laugh, that came from somewhere deep, was rich and infectious.

A puff of smoke and old Mrs Leary was out again to see what all the commotion was. Soon she, too, was cackling and coughing at Dorrie's mistake. The widow knew who she was. She sucked strength from her glowing cigarette and smokily said, 'Soon as I set eyes on yez, I could tell, darlin'. You're Florence Hubbard's girl, aren't you?' A sudden alarm enlivened the rheumy eyes. 'It's not her you've come about, is it? She's not been taken bad? She was so much brighter when I saw her last, in the butcher's – Tuesday, was it? And after the terrible time she's been having of it. And you, too, darlin', you must have–'

'No, no, Ma. It's something else entirely.'

The old woman relaxed. 'You're the spit of her, the spit. It's the bones, is it not, Frank? Don't you think she's like her mammy? Same little face, same pretty mouth...' (The swelling had gone down, with Mum's cold compress. She was a healer, in her own way. And she'd sorted Peter's wrist. Or someone had. It might have been holding her hand that had done it. Now *there* was a thought.) 'Your hair's different, o' course,' the old woman was saying, 'like your da's, I expect, and you're that much taller.'

And there was Frank Leary standing beside her with the self-same wayward hair, same colour, same curl, and his mother hadn't even noticed. Perhaps Dad hadn't either ... Arthur. Perhaps they'd been too subtle for him. What else would it take?

'Now then,' continued the woman who was Dorrie's real grandmother, 'I'll trust Frank to make you a corned-beef sandwich and a mug of tea, and I'll leave you in peace to talk over whatever it is that's troublin' you so late into the night. Something that couldn't wait till morning, it must be. But keep the noise down, Frank, will you? The holy sister would like a clear head for the morning, I don't doubt.' And with that she wheezed off to bed.

Sister Monica took her leave, and they heard the bedsprings groan as she prayed the Great Spirit her soul to keep.

'So here you are, Dorrie,' he said, suddenly serious now they were alone.

'I couldn't sleep,' she said.

His eyebrows went up a notch. 'Oh yeah?'

What did he think, that she came haring round here, in the middle of the night, on her bike, just to tell him that?

Nor could Mum, she might have said, recalling how she'd come upon Flo in the kitchen, just now, her eyes hollow bowls of blue, her thoughts swirling as madly as the Disprin in her glass. But Mum's burning question would have to wait. He could lie to Dorrie just as he'd lied to her mother down the years. If it *was* a lie. There was only one sure way to find out the truth, and to read his mind she was going to have to catch him offguard. So instead she asked a question to which she knew the answer.

'I'm going to have to go to the police, aren't I?'

He spread his fingers, and gave his *comme ci, comme ça* Gallic shrug.

'He's safe for the moment but, I dunno – when, *if* he recovers his sanity, you might have to think again. They might say that a confession made while the balance of his mind was disturbed doesn't hold water. Then they'll have to let him go. Unless they can come up with proof. Evidence of some sort. Blood, hair,

494

buttons torn off, you know.'

She shook her head. 'He sent the sheets to the laundry, cleaned out the boot of his car.'

His gasp was audible. 'He put her in the boot? After he'd hurt her? While she was still alive?'

'Mmm. He wasn't as tender-hearted as the child molester *you* interviewed.'

'Bastard!'

She compressed her lips, pulled out the envelope from her duffel bag. 'I've done a few more drawings,' she said. 'I know they're not proof, not like photographs, but since he's in police custody, they might be prepared to investigate.'

'You sure you want me to look?'

Nice, she thought. Bit different from Arthur's heavy-handed assumption that what was hers was his to pry into. Tonight, especially, after Frank and Peter had gone, and Stephen had come downstairs for his boiled egg and an even more censored version of the day's events, Arthur had insisted on breathing down her neck.

How did it work? Did she have to focus her mind on an event and draw what she saw, or did she just put pencil to paper and let the spirits do the work? Was that what intuition was, really? What was the difference between intuition and inspiration? Why was she drawing this? Why him? – jabbing at a face and leaving an oily fingerprint. He'd just put his garden shears to bed with a drop of Duckham's.

Did she choose which bits to draw? Decide what was important? Who made the choice, her or the spirits? Did she make any of it up?

'Dad! Get off, will you? This is important.'

When Stephen added his eggy breath to the mix, she'd had to take her stuff upstairs and use the dressing table to work on and, of course, then Uncle Jack had called in, with his two penn'orth of hints and wrinkles that he'd picked up from his friendly policemen.

'It's not so much *what* Webb did, as where and when and who might have seen him – things they can check,' she told Frank, 'to "establish my credibility as well as helping to convict him,"' quoting Uncle Jack.

She pushed a drawing towards him. 'This is outside the school. That's him in his car.'

'Bloody hell, you *are* good. This is Penny exactly. She was one of the first out of school then. And I didn't realise she had plaits. They always show that school photo of her with a pony tail.'

'That day she had plaits. And pretty tartan ribbons.'

'And these are the kids that came out the same time she did. That little girl...'

'Margaret something. Penny called her Margaret.'

'She might remember Penny talking to Webb. And these women...'

'I don't know their names, or rather Penny didn't. They were all "Auntie" or someone's mummy. But that's what they were wearing and that's what they looked like, near enough.'

'Ah, girl, they're brilliant. If the police can

track them down they might remember the car at least – his red and white Triumph Herald. It's fairly distinctive.'

Another picture. Inside the car.

'I've detailed the dials on the dashboard. They can check mileage and stuff.'

'It really was full, that petrol tank?' he said, tapping the gauge as though it might alter.

'Yup.'

'And look, the milometer's been put back to nought.' He twitched with excitement. 'Dorrie ... he'd just filled up!'

'There *was* a smell of petrol.'

'There's a garage close to the school.' Then Frank's face fell. 'But they probably won't remember him from three, four weeks ago.'

She sighed. 'I should have gone to the police when it first happened.

'Why didn't you?' A bald question and it took her breath away.

I don't...' she faltered, her face contorting for the truth. At last she said, 'I tried. I rehearsed it a hundred times, going into the police station, up to the desk, telling them that I was psychic, that I'd had a vision about the murder, that the murderer was a respected member of their force. I even got as far as the front steps one day. But I – I couldn't go up them. I just stood, rooted to the pavement, imagining the – the sneers and the laughter. I've had to keep it a secret all my life, Frank. Nobody had to know. Mum and Dad dinned that into me from an early age. Conform. Behave. It was more than naughtiness. Peter was naughty and got belted for it. What I had, what I did was shameful, lunatic. People wouldn't understand. Even Grandma and Granny Farthing told me to keep quiet about it. When it came to it I couldn't own up to it.'

'Couldn't you have told your mother?'

'No. I was frightened she wouldn't – love me, I suppose. When I was little it used to frighten her when I did anything out of the ordinary. She'd hit me. Like Dad did when I tried telling him about the murder.'

'This parenting business is bloody hard,' muttered Frank, shaking his head.

'There was no one around at the time to ask, except Uncle Jack, and when he said that there was a way, that the spirits would help, well, I just stopped worrying about going to the police. I suppose I should have been braver.'

'Maybe. But things tend to pan out as they're meant to.' She waited, but he wouldn't say it, that if she'd gone to the police then they wouldn't have met today. He could even have said he was pleased they were getting to know each other. Why the reserve? Would she have to make all the running?

'Will you come with me?' she asked.

'Now?'

'Well, when you're ready.'

'Okay.' He didn't move, ergo, he wasn't ready. She swallowed her disappointment.

'Uncle Jack reckons Gerald Webb might have billed the police for the petrol. It was his own car but he used it on police business. Someone there should have a record of the transaction.'

'On the ball, your uncle – I'd like to meet him.'

'He wants to meet you, too.'

'If only to break my jaw for sleeping with his brother's wife!'

'Em, I don't think so. Not through the mirror, anyhow.'

'Eh?'

'Uncle Jack's the one wrote the letter Dad was on about. Viv's dad? He's clairvoyant, too. A mirror-man.'

He nodded absently and rubbed his bristly chin anyway, following another train of thought. 'They'll have to ask Webb where he was that day, just out of curiosity, if nothing else – check his alibi. I mean it was right out of his way, wasn't it?'

'He always went out of his way.'

'Yeah, you don't shit on your own doorstep.'

She didn't flinch. 'Once they get going they might even check where he was at the time of the other murders.'

'How many were there?'

'Three. Margaret Davey in Islington, Alan Brett in Tottenham Hale and Patrick Griffiths in Harold Wood.'

'Patrick Griffiths? That was ages ago. I thought they'd got someone for that.'

'They did, Frank. Poor man's in Broadmoor.'

He was staring hard at the picture of the car's interior. 'Did he clean the inside of the car, too?'

'Thoroughly – he's a policeman. There'll be no fingerprints, if that's what you're thinking, even though she was into everything, knobs, levers, glove compartment. I mean, she was an inquisitive child. She'd never been in a car before. That was his attraction – his line – Mummy couldn't get there to pick her up and had sent him to fetch her, knowing she'd like a ride in his car. Wait though...' She stared at the paper windscreen, seeing the road ahead, what was coming up. Flicked back to the speedometer which was reading forty-four miles an hour, too fast for humpy-backed bridges. Going over it, she lurched in the kitchen chair and he put out a hand to save her.

'All right?'

'Mmm – Oh Frank, she was happy then. Giggling over the bridges. She had to hold on tight.' Her breath caught on the thought. 'That's it, Frank – *she gripped the seat!* And he missed them, the prints under the seat. I'm sure he missed them.'

'Yesss! Thank You, God.' He grabbed her, plonked a kiss on her cheek and drew away quickly, embarrassed.

'Gosh,' she said, touching the place his lips had touched and wondering. About the embarrassment, not the evidence. She thought she understood. This was a man who'd had to watch his daughter grow up from a distance. He didn't want to intrude or presume, or make difficulties for any of them, didn't want to upset what he saw as their happy life together. That was true love, to want another's happiness, even if it meant sacrificing your own. Flo had craved respectability above all and she couldn't get it from him.

On the other hand – and Dorrie found that

now she didn't want to believe it – *he might be a spineless creature in a raincoat, scurrying down a war-torn street to escape his responsibilities.*

He sighed as he got up. 'Do you really want a corned-beef sandwich?' She made a face. 'A drink? Cocoa, Ovaltine?' She shook her head firmly. So he pushed up his sleeves and sat down facing her with his hands behind his head. There, nicely displayed, was the silvery centipede scar Mum had traced with her doubts. How he had come by it was crucial. If he was to be believed, he'd been caught in the same air raid that had buried her mother, half a mile down the road. His story was that he'd spent the next few weeks in hospital, with amnesia and a broken arm. This was the story her mother wanted verified. A lot depended on it.

As she stared, the smoke from the Learys' combined cigarettes layered the air, grew denser, more acrid, making her eyes smart, making her choke. The green and cream painted dresser shivered with a tinkling of crockery and glassware and the strip light dimmed, brightened momentarily and then went out. The window lit up with criss-cross tape across the panes and the potted geranium on the sill danced defiantly as the walls shook.

'Oh my God!' Without thinking she reached for his hand.

'Go on, go on!' he urged the bus but the conductor was adamant. Everybody off. There was a shelter on the corner. Best get down there, mate, if you knew what was good for you.

501

He'd leapt off the bus and kept on running, his shoes striking sparks from the frosty cobbles, echoing around the dark shops of the main road. He'd reached the High Street when the hum became a growl, when the crump, crump told him that there were bombs landing behind him. He was gasping for breath, his flat feet pounding, jarring his bones, but he couldn't stop, couldn't think. The vision had been so clear: a direct hit and Flo would be gone. He had to get her out before that happened! At Bell Corner the roar of the warplanes insisted he look up into their thundering metal bellies. 'Bastards,' he wept. 'Murdering, sodding bastards!' He had to reach her. What was the use of second sight if you couldn't act on it?

The noise was infernal, bombs dropping right and left. And still he kept going, weaving his way down the middle of the street, through smoke and red-hot bits of shrapnel that hurtled past his ears and buildings that collapsed in his wake. Until the most almighty explosion sent him sprawling. Deafened and dazed he tried to shake some sense back into his head. Told himself to get up. Flo needed him. But he could only flounder. The cobbles were slippery with frost. And water. A mains must have busted. Wait a mo. Gather your wits. Try again.

Something hard and wet slapped him in the back of the neck. And something else skidded off his shoulder. Slap, slap. Wet and cold and stinking – of fish? Of course, it had been the fishmonger's across the road that had copped it. On all fours now and his foot slipped again. Small dead eyes gleamed up at him. Hopeless cod eyes. His stomach gave a sickening lurch of fear. Perhaps he'd never reach her.

Clairvoyants couldn't envision their own future. Flo had been alone in the house, waiting for him to come and have his tea. When the bomb fell he hadn't been there.

No. It couldn't be like that! He would get her out in time; he had to. He tried again to get to his feet, but they slithered on wet scales and he was flat again. It was raining fish from a fiery sky, herring and sprats and skate and ice and parsley and bits of wooden crate and tiles and enamel trays and a brick that caught him on the back of the head and put him out of the race.

In hospital they told him that Mrs Hubbard's house was flattened, a direct hit, just as it had been in his dream. So there was nothing to hope for. She and the child were dead. Passed over. There was only one way now that they could be together. That was when his arm had got broken, when he'd thrown himself off the hospital balcony. They'd had to put him in a padded cell, he was raving so. It was February before they'd let him out. And then, when he realised his mistake, it was all too late. Dorrie had been born, Arthur had been informed that he was a father and so, with discretion being the better part of valour, Frank Leary made himself scarce, dropped into the void.

Somewhere along the line he'd withdrawn his hand from hers to light a cigarette. Now he was wistfully rubbing the scar, which was a fishbone, not a centipede, Dorrie decided. A fishbone for a fishy story. Fishier even than the one he'd told Mum, which had, of course, been the sanitised version, leaving out the clairvoyancy and his own heroism, leaving out the fact that he'd tried to commit suicide when he'd thought she was dead. Yes, a fishbone was more fitting for the unfleshed truth, when all was said and done. Though nothing had been, of course. Not yet. Not until she got back home and relayed all this to Mum, who was waiting up.

'Are you really a reformed character?' she asked coyly, her head on one side.

He laughed his surprising roar of a laugh. 'What a question!'

'Mum says you are. She says you invited her to church.'

'Hardly church. The meeting hall in Walthamstow. It's my local. I had some crazy idea that if she saw me in action it might make her think better of me.'

'Did it?'

'She wouldn't come.'

'Perhaps she'll come with me.'

'You?'

'It's my local, too, or it will be, now that Mum and Dad know what I am. And *I* want to see you in action.'

'Oh.' His lips parted. 'Oh,' he breathed again, 'that's, that's great.' He looked away into the future, and back. 'Yes, I'd like, that,' then shook his head helplessly. 'God knows where all this is going to lead,' he muttered. 'Some almighty bust-up – I can see it coming. Well no, I can't, and that's the tricky bit.' He drew on his cigarette, and watched the smoke spread over the yellow ceiling. 'Ah well,' he sighed, *'Que sera sera*, as they say. I just hope we don't have to hurt too many people. And in answer to your question, well, maybe I've grown up a bit. It happens when you accept what you are. And I've stopped fighting it – my *gift*.' His voice was gently scathing. 'Let's say I'm trying to let God do the driving, Dorrie. You lumbered me with this second sight, I've told Him. *You* deal with it.'

Yes. That was the right answer.

'She loves you,' she said, as a reward.

'I know.' He sighed again. 'One fine day ... as they sing in the opera.' He sounded very Irish.

'I think she was hoping it would be today.'

He looked at her sharply. 'Was she?'

'She couldn't imagine why else you would come to our house.'

He was nodding, puffing slowly on his cigarette, his eyes guarded slits. He was miles away. Or maybe just a short step in the dark. Would he jump into his Rover and go charging round there, Lancelot on his steed? Wake the street with his knocking? Would Mum lean out of her window? Dorrie could just imagine it.

'Frank, go away, it's the middle of the night!'

'Get your glad rags on, gel. I've waited long enough!'

And in the time it took her cuckolded husband to stagger downstairs, pulling on his braces, gathering his wits, would his wife have thrown herself into her lover's arms and gone riding away? Leaving her children to Arthur's tender mercies?

Oh no, she wouldn't! She'd better not. But what then? Frank was hardly likely to bundle the two of them into the Rover as well. Was he?

'Let's see what else you've got there.' His voice pierced her dream; brought her crashing back to earth.

'What?' she demanded almost irritably.

'Your pictures,' he prompted. After all, that was why she'd come, wasn't it?

He passed over the arrival at the flat, with little Penny asking for her mummy. He passed over the one of the child sitting on Webb's lap. It looked so innocent, until you saw that his hand was about to creep under the skirt. That had been the most difficult picture to draw. Sickening. She'd kept adding unnecessary touches to the clock on the wall, the cactus on the sideboard, the curtain tie, anything rather than get to grips with what was going on in the armchair.

And then came the bedroom scene. Frank shifted in his chair to study it more closely, propping up his forehead with his fingers. There was nothing to see, only the Bravery Award and the photo of his mother, the wallpaper, the figurine lampstand. She had hidden the bodies with a sheet. Only the heads showed, Webb's slimy smile, his arm raising the cover, the child's look of incomprehension.

Something dropped onto the paper. A tear.

Keeping a hand over his eyes, he raked his dressing-gown pocket for a handkerchief and, when he blew his nose, she saw that his eyes were bleared pink.

'Oh Dorrie,' he groaned. 'I'm sorry.' Not corny at all. 'What they've put you through, poor kid.

Seeing what that bastard did for kicks. I tell you, girl, if the law don't get him, I surely will.' He shook his head, and his jaw knotted with disgust. 'You've still got those other pictures, have you – the drowning ones?'

She nodded.

'Hang on to them – we may need to jog his memory.' He was about to push the papers back to her when something caught his eye.

'Just a–' He looked closer. 'Dorrie, she's only wearing one ribbon.'

'I know, and I can't think where she lost the other one. It could be important. I mean, if it turned up in his flat that would be something, wouldn't it?'

'Wouldn't it just! Could it have been sucked up in the Hoover?'

'Doesn't have one – only a carpet sweeper. But he did have a thorough go round afterwards. Didn't find a hair ribbon.'

'And he changed the bed, you say?'

'Mmm – and looked underneath.'

She got up to see the picture from his angle, leaned over his shoulder, breathed in the smell of him, smoke and soap, and a mysterious something else that seemed so familiar and so dear. Chemistry? They were probably the same blood group, too.

She stared at the picture, the small head on the pillow, the naked plait. 'Help me look for it,' she said.

For answer he gently brushed her mind, added his prayer to hers and, together, they scoured the room. Under the carpet, under the wardrobe

... they kept coming back to the bed, the divan bed, latest style. No iron bedstead for him, with springs, bars at the bedhead and bars at the foot. A sprung mattress on a low, free-standing base. And a screw-on headboard.

'I know where it is.' The words almost floated out of their heads, wrote themselves on the picture.

'She struggled so, poor kid,' he said, 'the ribbon came off.'

They could both see it, bright red and green tartan, still in its bow, squashed down between the headboard and the mattress.

He smiled up at her and she hugged him to her. 'Great minds...' she said.

Back home, in bed, Arthur jerked awake. He'd made the final connection.

The publishers hope that this book has given you enjoyable reading. Large Print Books are especially designed to be as easy to see and hold as possible. If you wish a complete list of our books please ask at your local library or write directly to:

Magna Large Print Books
Magna House, Long Preston,
Skipton, North Yorkshire.
BD23 4ND

This Large Print Book for the partially sighted, who cannot read normal print, is published under the auspices of

THE ULVERSCROFT FOUNDATION

(1)	21	41	61	81	101	121	141	161	181
2	22	42	62	82	102	122	142	162	182
3	23	43	63	83	103	123	143	163	(183)
4	24	44	64	84	104	124	144	164	184
5	25	45	65	(85)	105	125	145	165	185
6	26	46	66	86	106	126	146	166	186
7	27	47	67	87	107	127	147	167	187
8	28	48	68	88	108	128	148	168	188
9	29	49	69	89	109	129	149	169	189
(10)	30	50	70	90	110	130	150	170	190
11	31	51	71	91	111	131	151	171	191
12	32	52	72	92	112	132	152	172	192
13	33	53	73	93	113	133	153	173	193
14	34	(54)	74	94	114	134	154	174	194
15	(35)	55	75	95	115	135	155	175	195
16	36	56	76	96	116	136	156	176	196
17	37	57	77	97	117	137	157	177	197
18	38	58	78	98	118	138	158	178	198
19	39	59	79	99	119	139	159	179	199
20	40	60	80	100	120	140	160	180	200

201	211	221	231	241	251	261	271	281	291
202	212	222	232	242	252	262	272	282	292
203	213	223	233	243	253	263	273	283	293
204	214	224	234	244	254	264	274	284	294
205	215	225	235	245	255	265	275	285	295
206	216	226	236	246	256	266	276	286	296
207	217	227	237	247	257	267	277	287	297
208	218	228	238	248	258	268	278	288	298
209	219	229	239	249	259	269	279	289	299
210	220	230	240	250	260	270	280	290	300

301	310	319	328	337	346
302	311	320	329	338	347
303	312	321	330	339	348
304	313	322	331	340	349
305	314	323	332	341	350
306	315	324	333	342	
307	316	325	334	343	
308	317	326	335	344	
309	318	327	336	345	